MW01491511

Dandelion Is
Dead

Dandelion Is
Dead

Rosie Storey

Berkley
New York

BERKLEY
An imprint of Penguin Random House LLC
1745 Broadway, New York, NY 10019
penguinrandomhouse.com

Book design by Alison Cnockaert

Library of Congress Cataloging-in-Publication Data

Names: Storey, Rosie, author.
Title: Dandelion is dead / Rosie Storey.
Description: New York: Berkley, 2026.
Identifiers: LCCN 2025005901 (print) | LCCN 2025005902 (ebook) |
ISBN 9780593954348 (hardcover) | ISBN 9780593954355 (ebook)
Subjects: LCGFT: Novels
Classification: LCC PR6119.T6854 D36 2026 (print) |
LCC PR6119.T6854 (ebook) | DDC 823/.92—dc23/eng/20250422
LC record available at https://lccn.loc.gov/2025005901
LC ebook record available at https://lccn.loc.gov/2025005902

Printed in the United States of America
1st Printing

The authorized representative in the EU for product safety and compliance is
Penguin Random House Ireland, Morrison Chambers, 32 Nassau Street,
Dublin D02 YH68, Ireland, https://eu-contact.penguin.ie.

Mango, this one's for you

Certain moments the whole earth seemed a grave. Other times, more hopefully, a garden.

—Lorrie Moore, A Gate at the Stairs

Dandelion Is
Dead

Part One:
The Lie

April–May 2025

1

Saturday, 5th April

Poppy

"Hey, lovely lady," the man in the car called through his window. For a minute, maybe longer, he'd been crawling next to Poppy as she walked home.

Perhaps, if it had been dark, or if she hadn't been on a road with such fancy houses and coiffed front gardens, Poppy would have presumed she was about to get abducted. Bundled into a boot and kept forever in a cellar on a dirty mattress, listening to a dripping tap. But it was two in the afternoon, and the houses on either side of the street probably had studies where mummies were in meetings talking about content, or wellness. And above them, four bedrooms where children called Arlo and Margot dreamed sweetly every night.

Besides, Poppy was naturally fearful—she'd been born a shade dweller, sprouting in the shadow of her raucous sister. She'd grown in the gaps where Dandelion was lacking, and where Dandelion flourished, Poppy had stayed, quite happily, small. But now she was sisterless and she needed to be braver. So she stopped walking and turned to the car.

Everything about the man in the driver's seat was gray and

middling, including his suit, which had a subtle sheen. Poppy stepped off the curb and was about to say *Hello*, or something totally normal, but as she bent down—she saw his open fly.

Poppy dropped her phone and it smashed on the tarmac. She looked down at her phone, then she glanced at the man's penis, then up at a small teddy bear that was hanging from the rearview mirror. The teddy had its tongue out and was holding a faded heart with pink stitching that spelled *HUGME!* The two words forced together, conjoined into one.

If Dandelion had been there, she would have lurched her whole body through the open window and ripped the man's head off—Poppy could see her sister doing it—blood gushing up and out of him like a flock of birds in flight. Dandelion would have pointed and gargled a throatful of ridicule. Dandelion would have screamed, scratched, spat. Set his car alight.

Next to Poppy's face, the man was muttering. He maybe said *suck* and he definitely said *dick*.

"No," Poppy said very quietly, her eyes still on the teddy, then because she was gutless, she added, "But thanks."

The man floored the accelerator and drove off in a wheelspin with his penis freely lolling. Poppy crouched down to the road and turned over her phone—the screen had splintered into slivers and rainbowed like spilled petrol. It was beyond resuscitation; the buttons didn't work. She straightened then and squinted at the North London houses all painted perfect like a stage set, with wisteria winding over windows and clematis creeping around doors. The world was gross and could be glorious—but Poppy wasn't in it. Every day was just a circle, a loop she had to fall through. It had been two hundred and thirty-one days since Dandelion died and, somehow, it was spring again.

Poppy longed to feel the sun.

2

Sunday, 6th April

"Aloha?" Poppy called to the empty hallway of her sister's flat.

Standing in the kitchen, she unwrapped magenta tulips she'd picked up from the florist on Newington Green, filled a glass jug with water, and nudged the stems around until their configuration pleased her.

"You're welcome. I thought you'd like them," she said, carrying the jug to Dandelion's bedroom and unlocking it. She'd put the lock on so she could rent the flat out as a one bed and leave this room untouched, only the renting still hadn't happened; she couldn't bring herself to do it and, besides, she liked to be able to drop in, hang out, and, if need be, hide.

Often she brought flowers, the kind she knew her big sister would coo at: fat-headed dahlias, fleshy peonies, tulips in different pinks. Sometimes she put music on, pulling an unknown record from Dandelion's vast collection. Or she'd sit with a drink and sink quietly through thought. Twice, both times in the last month, Poppy had stayed the night, sleeping in Dandelion's bed, trying to dream not only that she was with her sister but that she *was* her sister—stretching her own soul into Dandelion's skin.

"I've just come for your phone." Poppy placed the jug of tulips in the center of the dressing table. Through the petals, she could see her reflection in the mirror, slivers of her sister too. "I dropped mine. Exactly, because of that man's dick."

From under the bed, she pulled out the box where Dandelion kept her old devices and nests of tangled cables. Her most recent phone was at the top; Poppy had put it there herself after she'd finished the death admin. The closing of bank accounts and resetting of passwords. Putting an *out of office* on Gmail—writing and rewriting the wording—composing what was, essentially, Dandelion's *out of life*.

That whole phase had consumed the previous autumn, and at the time, Poppy hadn't had the inclination to peruse her sister's apps, the notes, her messages. She'd been in and out of the phone efficiently, tied up tight with shock. But now Poppy's grief was a starvation, and so she sat on her sister's Berber rug and scrolled back in time through the photo gallery, desperate to consume. She marveled at the smiling faces, the dogs, the pubs, the birthdays, the dark blurs of dance floors, the artfully composed plates of food shot from up above. There were so many pictures of Poppy, obviously. Their mother, nearly always in her Levi's. Their dad—back when he could smile. There were photos, too, of Dandelion topless and looking alluring, pictures for her lovers.

"Sorry!" Poppy said, having found herself in an album full of nudes. She glanced up at the door as if Dandelion was already flying toward her, screaming, *Poppet! What the actual fuck?*

On the home screen, Poppy tapped into some of the apps: BBC Sounds, Instagram, Net-A-Porter. There was an app for tracking periods, another for tracking investments, and in the middle of them all an icon Poppy wasn't sure about—a large black *H* in a stark white square. She lingered her thumb over it, then pressed down to find Dandelion in her sequined harlequin jumpsuit, half-way through a cartwheel. She was at Glastonbury Festival, by The Park stage; Poppy recognized it immediately. She'd been there with her sister that year. In the background was the big colorful ribbon tower, a balding hill, some happily billowing flags. So this, Poppy realized, was Hinge—her sister's dating app. And here, the digital version of Dandelion was still alive, being cheeky. Securing likes.

Dandelion had shown Poppy some profiles of potential suitors before (mainly the funny ones), but Poppy had never seen her sister's actual profile, how she marketed herself. It was titled with three sentences that Poppy read a few times, her brain glitching on the facts that were now redundant: *Dandelion. 39. Does Not Want Kids.*

As well as the Glastonbury photo, there was a close-up of Dandelion in bed looking sleepy, her skin prickling pink like it did when she was just out of a hot bath. In the next one, she was in her neon seersucker swimsuit in a deck chair somewhere exotic, a (probable) Negroni in her hand. In the last picture, Poppy saw herself. It was from a recent-ish Halloween party; the two of them and their friend Jetta had dressed up in vintage Adidas and tucked all their hair up into short, curly wigs. They'd been characters from the film *The Royal Tenenbaums*; Dandelion was the dad (Ben Stiller), and Poppy and Jetta had been his two matching red-tracksuited little kids.

In Hinge's inbox, Dandelion had one hundred and seventy-three matches and countless messages. Poppy tapped on a few at random. First, a girl (too young) called Chloe, a dancer. Dandelion had never answered her Sup? To an electrician called Gerald, Dandelion had gone in with Gezza, tell me a joke. He'd come back with one about an Englishman an Irishman and a Scotsman, to which Dandelion had replied immediately: I no like, byebye!

As Poppy scrolled, it became apparent that her sister lied a lot, which was no enormous surprise. She told people she was an exotic dancer and a firefighter and trilingual and super into roller blading—which caused Poppy to huff an appreciative laugh. She gave Hinge's inbox one final, long swipe so that the names of tiny digital people careered past, like the bounty of a slot machine, before slowing and slowing and coming to rest on Jake.

JAKE

14TH MARCH, 2024. 8:24PM:

Dandelion, (good name)

It's weird but

I can feel

9:03PM:

Sorry.

my son woke up

He had a nightmare.

But was going to say -

I can feel your heat.

9:17PM:

(my son is three.

Split custody. No biggy)

The messages had been hanging, unanswered, for a year. Poppy liked the sound of Jake; she liked that he'd felt her sister's heat.

It seemed highly possible that Jake's main photo was a covert selfie, that he'd extended his arm and looked the other way as he'd taken the picture, pretending not to pose. In it, his hair was buzzed short and his eyes were closed, which maybe was the point, because it showed his eyelashes, top and bottom together, unusually thick and pretty in his square-jawed face. In another picture, he was wearing a faded cap pushed back, his dark hair curled behind his ears. He had dimples, or maybe just the one dimple eddying into his right cheek. His profile said he was forty, but he dressed boyish: sweatshirts, worn-out jeans and trainers.

Mainly, the other men Poppy had seen on Hinge were topless in a toilet taking unsmiling selfies, or Lycra clad and bulging, unsmiling on a bike. But Jake was playing Jenga with his son (captioned *My Little Bud*), and grinning wide and silly. In the cap picture, he was sitting with friends, holding craft beers in colorful cans on the crest of a hill, and the last shot wasn't even him, but a handsome sky at dusk.

From a nearby garden the gnawing of an engine started: a mower or a chain saw. Poppy stood, and in front of the long mirror, she looked at herself and frowned. Throughout their whole lives, people had found the sisters to be confusingly similar. And, yes, Poppy knew their eyes (hair, complexion, voice, laugh), and, probably, skeletons, were ostensibly interchangeable, but she'd always felt the comparison to her sister to be overly generous, like comparing a Tuesday morning to a Friday night. Two and a half years older, Dandelion had been more attractive and more confident. More mischievous (nefarious, lightly evil). Later, more successful, pretty much running a hedge fund by the age of thirty-five. Consequently, Dandelion had been considerably more wealthy— bought her gorgeous flat with cash. Mainly, though, and ironically, as it turned out, compared to Poppy and to anyone Poppy had ever met—Dandelion seemed more vital. She'd been filled with much more life.

Poppy smoothed her hair into a ponytail and stepped closer to her reflection. "Yes, thanks, I know I look like shit. I couldn't sleep, so I ran here." She thought of her boyfriend then, waking on a Sunday morning to find her gone; he'd be brewing coffee and, quite possibly, a sulk. "Anyway, better go. Thanks for the phone," she said, through an inhale. Around her the room got bigger, gaped large and painful like an open wound.

In the hallway, Poppy locked the bedroom door and reread Jake's messages. I can feel your heat kept catching like a splinter, though it didn't hurt. It was more that the world hurt and this one line felt soothing. It was so true—Dandelion had been a wildfire. She'd ripped through life. She'd frazzled. Poppy closed her eyes and, next to her, she felt her sister scorching. She felt her sister nudging. Daring. "I guess I could . . ." Poppy whispered, and then she was typing through the trembles and they were back together—stealing lip gloss from Superdrug as teenagers. Smoking on the beach, leaning up against red rocks. They were stripping to their knickers and cliff jumping at sunset, falling, flailing, holding hands, catching a few seconds of HOLY FUCK airtime, before smacking hard through black.

DANDELION

6TH APRIL, 2025. 8:26AM:
Jake!
I'm sorry I've not messaged you
I was kind of busy
with, you know,
Life.
But now I'm here
I'm back.

3

Monday, 7th April

Jake

Through half-closed eyes, Jake gazed at Amisha's hideous, swirling rug as the light in her bedroom moved from black to fuzzy gray. He was wondering how he was going to extract himself without waking her, which, he'd decided, in the long run, was the most polite thing to do. He was almost certain she wouldn't want to see him again, either, so at least this way no one would have to deal with a face-to-face rejection, or attempt any awkward hungover acting, saying what a great time they'd had.

He shifted slowly until he was leaning up against her rattan headboard. He looked down at the heavy breathing mass of hair; that hair had been the first thing he'd remarked upon on Hinge, and then they'd started messaging and Jake had thought he'd felt that brilliant spark—the one that can go on to burn the house down. Over their three-week courtship, which had, up until last night, been conducted entirely through their mobile phones, Jake and Amisha had shared playlists (him), selfies (her), updates on the minutiae of their day: Just made the best toastie with cheddar and . . . wait for it . . . kimchi! (him), and empowering memes (her).

Mainly, Jake had found it lovely to talk to someone so lovely. Someone who kept doing the eye-watering laugh emoji at pretty much everything he typed.

Someone who had instigated text sex, twice.

Having text sex twice was as cutting-edge as Jake's romantic life had been in the last fifteen months, since his divorce. Not that the actual experience had been the smoothest thing in the world, being, as it was, quite hard to maintain the typing, alongside the left-handed wanking, alongside the thinking of good things to say, alongside the manual correct of autocorrect. Still, he'd since dropped the text-sex-twice anecdote into a few different Whats-App and real-life conversations with a couple of old mates, some colleagues, and, most recently, his dad. It wasn't Jake's usual style to be so brash—he just wanted everyone to know how great things were going for him these days. How really, totally great.

Amisha had been in the pub already when Jake arrived, and he'd been pleased to see that she looked almost like her photos. Though when she got up to kiss him, he wasn't very into her rose petal perfume, or the nasalness of her voice. After twenty minutes of chatting, Jake understood the problem to be simple and yet complicated—Amisha was not the woman he had been expecting; she was not the honey that his mind had, almost entirely, made up.

Yet here he was in her stuffy South London bedroom, naked.

When Amisha suggested she get them an Uber, Jake had nodded meekly and downed the rest of his pint. In the taxi, she'd kissed him and he'd found nothing in her mouth. Just emptiness. A place to put his tongue and try to make the best of things. In her bedroom, they'd embarked on a disappointing roll around. Jake hadn't been able to stay hard and so he'd gone down on her, and though she'd made some okay noises, he'd had the distinct feeling that they'd both rather be asleep.

And now, outside Amisha's window, the sky was paling and another night was dead. Jake lifted the duvet off his body and slipped his boxers on, crawled around the carpet holding his breath, feeling for his socks. He dressed silently and tiptoed to the bedroom door, easing the handle, millimeter by millimeter, with all the caution of a hero on telly dismantling a bomb.

"Jake?"

Jake stood completely still, with one hand on the wall and one hand on the door.

"What are you doing?" Amisha asked.

"Just going to the bathroom," Jake said, upbeat. He turned to her and grinned.

"'Cause it looks like you're trying to figure out how to use my door." Her voice croaked low and sleepy, devoid of any amusement.

"I know how to use your door!" Jake opened the door and closed it three times, super quick, by way of demonstration, simultaneously noticing that Amisha had put a white vest on at some point during the night, which now was askew—side boob slipping out.

"And then I thought to myself," Amisha continued, propping herself up on her elbows, "if he can't figure out how to use a door handle, not surprised he doesn't know his way around a vulva."

"Whoa!" Jake took two small steps to the side, in a performative bent-knee stagger. "I'm a forty-year-old man!" he said, as if his age was absolute evidence that he was a fantastic lover. The sentence sounded arbitrary and ridiculous, so he added, "I was married for over ten years!" *And* Jake wasn't going to tell Amisha this, but before his marriage—he'd been kind of a cad.

Amisha looked bored. "Your poor wife," she said. She plumped her pillow and lay back down.

Jake took a step toward the bed and perched on the corner.

"Hey." His tone was soft. He put his right hand on her red-nail-varnished foot. "I know this looks bad—"

"Get off!" Amisha kicked, a vicious little buck. In the distance there was the *nee-nor* of an ambulance rushing to an accident. "I'd love it if you could leave."

"I'm really sorry." Jake stood and took three steps backward. He opened the door again and hopped through it, clearing Amisha's staircase in two long leaps.

On the street corner, he found a bus that would take him in the direction of home, bleeped himself on with his bank card, and swung around a yellow pole like an exhausted stripper. Slumped by the window, he pulled the sleeve of his bomber jacket over his hand and wiped himself a view, watching early-morning London stagger past: kebab shops and bus stops, drunks and their debris. Strangers taking each other home and workers forcing themselves forward.

Jake took his phone out of his pocket and unmatched from Amisha, and then, to distract himself from the great burden of shame, he began swiping through more women—*Yes. Big-time. Yes! No. Too young? Yes. Yes. Absolutely not.* He was a forty-year-old teenager cruising for the endorphins of likes—the rush of a match. The opportunity to imagine a new happy ending. The very first taste of a whole new life. The life that was meant for him and that was going to begin any second, any second, any second now . . .

After he'd been through a whole brood of profiles, Jake went back to Hinge's inbox and scrolled through the tiny ladies' faces, mainly cringing at the last snippets of the chats:

Happy Friday!

Happy Hump Day ☺

Divorced 🙁

Six foot. Why?

Suki, I can feel your heat

Soo . . would you rather hands for feet or feet for hands?

Yous awak? Awake?

There was a new message too. It was from a woman he'd matched with a long time ago, probably one of the first after his split from Zoe. Dandelion had never replied to anything Jake had written to her. But now here she was—over a year later—saying she'd been busy with you know, Life.

Jake held his phone close to his face and zoomed in on all her photos. Sure, he remembered her. She was a babe. Looked fun. And funny. He decided to ask her out immediately—save himself the indignity of attaching to someone imagined and fictitious. He replied, suggesting a date on Friday. He added a kiss, then deleted the kiss. He added a heart-eyes emoji, then deleted the heart-eyes emoji. He pressed send, turned his phone off, rang the bus bell, and, with a surge of hopeful romantic dynamism, Jake sprang up.

4

Wednesday, 9th April

On the school run that morning, Jake had been covertly googling diagrams of female genitalia and then closing his eyes to test himself. "Majora . . ." he whispered. He was sitting on the busy overground train, his five-year-old by his side. "Minora."

Majora and Minora, Jake reflected, would make fitting names for glamorous and lascivious (not necessarily incestuous, but potentially incestuous) sisters. Twins.

"Jeepers!" he said, having clicked through to an anatomical diagram of the clitoris, which was, evidently, a whole big thing inside the body. He twisted his phone to get the landscape view, squinted. "Kinda like a spaceship."

"I want to see!" Billy held out a small scrunched hand, grasping for the phone.

"Errr, sooo . . ." Jake slid the phone into his pocket and asked Billy about his birthday party on the weekend, which Jake's ex had neglected to invite him to. "Who was there, bud?"

"Mummy and Yan and Algy and Archie and Layla and Luna and Lila and Lola and Odysseus and Thrush and Dave."

"Wow! You've got a lot of friends, bud," Jake said, as he reasoned his own best mate was probably his child, and then after that Cindy—his houseplant—then after that Alexa the home operating system, then after that . . . his dad?

"Yan is Mummy's best friend," Billy said, "and he can walk on his hands."

Jake had managed to play it fairly cool in front of their fellow passengers on the overground, nodding affably as if he already knew who Yan was, until Billy landed the real kicker. "And now Yan lives in our house!"

After dropping Billy off, Jake spent the next three hours in a social media hellhole. He'd started with Zoe's Instagram, which had led him to Yan's Instagram, @YanDaYogiBear.

Yan took selfies and used hashtags and captions that said things that included #LetsDoThisLovelies!!! #MotivationMondayPeople!!! He was always asking his (not very many) followers questions like, *Chia or maca in my breakfast smoothie today peeps??!!* Yan used multiple exclamation marks and a plethora of nonsensical emojis—like a juggling man and then a panda bear's head and then a paintbrush and then an avocado and then something that Jake had no idea what it even was but the internet reported as a *curling stone.*

Jake had only brought the research to an end because he had to meet his dad for their weekly lunch in Hampstead. And now, waiting by the Ladies' Pond, he tried to think nice thoughts about the ducks, the sky, the trees. He exhaled loudly; his breath was hiding in him in pockets and escaped in jagged increments. It was useless—he pulled his phone out, swiped it to unlock.

On both their profiles, Yan and Zoe had posted selfies with their faces pressed. They whanged on about being *grateful* and *blessed* and referred to each other as #ThisOne, which Jake found to be immensely green-vomit-face emoji. Besides anything, Zoe wasn't even a sweet goo-goo type of person. Not even in their own honeymoon days of fire had she been one for intertwined fingers, or the *you're so cute, NO, you're so cute* stuff. Jake looked up at the dense sky and squinted; he and Zoe had never been overly lovey-dovey, but genuine passion had been there, and he could still see it quite clearly, unfortunately. He could picture them as a younger couple, in the middle of the night or in the middle of the supermarket, shimmering with pheromones. They'd bone anywhere back then, but they'd been in their goddamn twenties, and the horniness had hurt.

"JAKEY!"

Jake was yanked from this particular tangent of self-harm by his father's booming voice, which caused him to gasp and clutch at his chest.

Through the trees, his dad was on the approach; he had quite a pace on him for an old guy, although his knees didn't bend that much anymore—he swung them out to the sides instead, like a school compass mapping semicircles. He was looking good though. He always looked expensive, having buggered off and left them three decades ago and then, somehow, become rich. In the olden days, he'd been mainly topless with a tan and a barbecue fork, standing on the weed-infested patio, somewhere near their 1980s red egg barbecue. That's how Jake remembered him in his stock memories of Summer Dad. Then there was Pissed Dad, coming in late with a jacket on inside out. Another big one was Leaving Dad, which involved him looking sheepish and putting a suitcase in the boot of the blue Ford Escort.

No Dad, though—that was the version of Jake's father that had been in his childhood the most.

Still, he'd paid child support, sent a generous allowance, and been behind Jake's first job at the London ad agency Fallon (old pals with the creative director on the Cadbury Schweppes account). And so, Jake had shimmied onto the career ladder with a helpful nepotism leg up. He'd taken the money and the favors, but he'd not felt it to be love. And when Jake's mother died, Jake's father had covered all the costs and filled the world with flowers, but he hadn't mentioned coming to the funeral. Their communication had never been hostile, more . . . perfunctory, polite. That was until Billy had been born and Zoe had encouraged Jake to invite his father to come and visit from where he lived in Switzerland, then, BOOM, Jake's dad was back.

It transpired that he was going through a divorce, and it was evident he was going to the gym. And bizarrely, for a man called Roger, had changed his name midlife to Rafe. He bought a house in Hampstead and made a massive effort, intent on making up for lost time. And Jake had forgiven his father, because he'd come to understand that everyone deserves a fourth chance.

"How are you, my boy?" Jake's father walked over to the closest wooden bench and sat down, stretching his arms out long across the back of it; his navy Barbour jacket was crisp, clean, too new. "You look tired."

Jake rubbed his temples and took a seat next to him, noticing how his father was taking up space. "I am quite tired," he admitted. He spread his legs as wide as he could. "I'm not sleeping that well. The flat is pretty noisy . . ."

Three teenagers in school uniform, with short rolled-up navy skirts, walked by. They were squawking looking down at a phone. One of them was laughing so much she bent double. "Stop it!" she was pleading. "Nadine! I said stop!"

"Mm." Jake's father nodded.

Jake watched his father watch the girls, and by the time he spoke again his head had turned in entirely the other direction, so now Jake was looking at the nape of his neck, his slickly combed-back hair. "Were you up all night with that little lady? The sexty-texty one?"

"Um . . ." Jake rubbed his jaw and thought of Amisha; he was feeling bad about how that all ended. "It wasn't a great date. I mean it was okay, just not what I was expecting."

Jake's father turned back to him, furrowed his brow like he was reflecting on something terrible. "It's tough for us romantics, isn't it?" He leaned forward over his legs, twisting at his Rolex, and then clasped his hands. "Have you spied anyone new on your dating application?"

"Yeah . . ." Jake thought of Dandelion in her swimsuit. "I've asked someone out. I've not heard from her, but it was only yesterday."

"So do you pay to meet with these ladies?"

Jake scrunched his face. "No, Dad." His voice had a whine to it.

"It's not a sex thing?" his father clarified, then winked.

The winking actually looked pretty good. Jake coughed, turned his head, subtly winked at an approaching French bulldog, just to practice.

"And what are the sex ones called again?"

Jake looked back at his father, and another childhood collection of memories came to mind, Friendly Dad: his dad sitting on a foldout striped garden chair with a woman on his lap, which was only sometimes Jake's mum. "Why do you want to know about the sex apps, Dad?"

"No reason." Jake's father smiled at him, and it was a smile that had love in it.

"Anyway, I'm starving. Shall we?" Jake stood and took a couple of languorous steps toward the pond. He felt his phone in his pocket and pulled it out to find Hinge buzzing with notifications.

Dandelion was still typing . . .

DANDELION

9TH APRIL, 2025. 12:51PM:
Friday you say?
Friday is my bday Jake
So . . .

In front of Jake, a middle-aged woman walked up to the pond. She was pushing an old man in a wheelchair. His legs were covered by a gray checked rug, and his head was at an awkward angle, chin tilted to the sky. Jake looked back at the message, scrabbled a reply, excited by the knowledge that Dandelion was out there in the world writing to him, right that moment. Two strangers with their strange lives, looking down at their phones, connecting up.

JAKE

12:52PM:
Ah okay
Another day then?
Would love to bang

12:53PM:
Hang!
Damn phone!
Would love ot hang
TO HANG
Apologies.

Jake's father was talking to the woman who was behind the wheelchair. She was laughing and holding on to an earlobe. She hadn't noticed the man in front of her had slumped, totally, to one side.

"He's, um . . . he's . . ." Jake began, but the woman wasn't listening, so Jake lurched forward and helped the man upright—his face had gone quite pink.

"Oh!" the woman said. "Thank you."

Jake looked down at his phone again. Already, Dandelion had replied.

DANDELION

12:54PM

I could do a quickie Friday.

Let's bang out x

5

Friday, 11th April

Poppy

On the morning of Dandelion's fortieth birthday—the first birthday since she'd fucking died—Poppy had been awake, widely, since 4:00 a.m. She tiptoed into the sitting room, wearing a pair of faded purple knickers and her sister's Fleetwood Mac T-shirt, bought at a concert in Rome. She flicked the kettle on, made a cup of weak, sweet tea, then sat on the sofa in front of the window, watching the entire performance of the sky as it moved from black through blues and came to rest in a place of beige. She toasted two crumpets and spread them thick with butter (the way both sisters liked), and ate them looking down at her newly adopted phone.

Poppy scrolled back and back through her and her sister's incessant WhatsApp conversation. They were funny together in a way they couldn't be with anyone else. They were as silly as little girls. They were loving and monotonous. They were crude and catty and mean. After Poppy had read the entire exchange, she cried, had another crumpet, and called her parents.

Her father picked up the phone. He stammered, spluttered like a dotted line. His strong and steady voice had left him the day his elder daughter died, and now it wavered, as if the base of a hand was repeatedly jamming up against his sternum when he tried to talk.

"P-P-P-Poppy!" It took him four attempts to say her name. "We wish you were here today. Missing you, d-darling."

"I know. I miss you, Dad."

"Last night we watched some home videos. One of your old p-plays."

"Oh, yes? I take it Dandelion was the star?"

Her father laughed at this. "N-not at all!"

Her mother took the phone and sang "Happy Birthday" to Dandelion, the entire song—a solo; Poppy just listened and gritted her teeth. They were off to visit the grave soon, apparently. And later, her mother was cooking Dandelion's favorite double-pie meal (fish pie then banoffee). "Daddy's going to make cocktails. Twinkles!"

"Yum," Poppy managed, wiping silent tears from underneath her eyes. "She would have loved that, sounds really fun."

"She'll be with us in spirit."

"Definitely," Poppy agreed.

"Now, darling, what do you have planned? Some sort of little adventure?"

"Not sure yet," Poppy said, because this year's birthday jaunt was a secret she would have to keep from everyone, forever. "Love you. Speak tomorrow. Send pictures of the pies."

Every year since they were teenagers, the sisters had organized a surprise for their respective birthdays. Something wonderful, weird, or wild. The previous year, for Poppy's thirty-sixth, Dandelion had taken her to Go Ape. They'd shared a bar of magic mushroom chocolate on the train to Dorset and, when they got there, Poppy had laughed so hard at Dandelion in her helmet and her harness on the zip line that she'd actually wet her pants. But as this birthday of Dandelion's approached—the only thing Poppy felt was dread.

That was until Jake had messaged, suggesting they meet on the exact day Dandelion would have turned forty. It hadn't felt like a coincidence, more an intervention from her sister. Poppy had debated the ethics with her bathroom mirror and come to an agreement. There were ground rules—it would be for one night only. And she wouldn't feel guilty about Sam, because it wasn't anything to do with him, or them as a couple. It was an escapade she was executing for her sister's birthday. For one night only, Poppy would be Dandelion.

And so she'd responded to Jake's messages with words that she would never usually use, stuck her tongue out as she'd typed. She'd pressed send and died with terror but then, like the violent flashes of a firework illuminating blackness—Poppy's world lit up with a glittering kind of light.

So now, here she was, at the open door of the trendy dim sum restaurant that Jake had suggested, on the edge of Victoria Park. She gave his name to a small woman with a cheek piercing swamped in a baggy white T-shirt standing by the bar. The woman pointed out into the courtyard at a man sitting alone at the furthest table, and then Poppy was walking right over to him, Dandelion's cowboy boots clicking beneath her on the black square tiles.

"Hi," she said when she reached the table. Jake was leaning back on the bench, looking up at the strings of red-and-orange paper lanterns that crisscrossed through the sky. He hadn't noticed her, and so Poppy followed up with a left-field, instantly regrettable "Howdy!"

At *howdy*, Jake turned to her. "Dandelion?"

He stepped over the bench, and Poppy could tell he was going to hug her or possibly kiss her, and she panicked at all the available greeting options and all the ways they could go wrong.

"It's Dandelion, right?" Jake asked.

For a second, Poppy wanted to turn and run, but then she was in his arms, the side of her face smooshed against his shirt. She was blinking at the restaurant: wooden walls, dark green lamps, glossy tables strewn with small colorful plates of food, and all the people being normal on just another Friday night.

"Dandelion," Poppy said in agreement. She heard Jake's heart thump in his chest, or maybe it was blood beating in her ear. "Yes. Hi."

Jake took a step back but kept his hand on Poppy's upper arm. "You all right?" His eyelashes were just as good as they'd been in the pictures, and his eyes were even better, brown with yellow flecks which radiated his pupils, like petals. His eyes were sunflowers. As Poppy looked into them, they unfurled, whirled, turned like spokes, and she had to close her eyes. "I'm feeling a bit weird," she said. What she really was though—was drunk. Much more drunk than she'd planned.

"Good weird, or bad weird?" Jake asked, still holding her arm.

Poppy nodded. Shook her head. She could smell his cologne, and it smelled of something primal but exotic, like afternoon sex on holiday, like body and citrus and storms. "Good weird, I think," she said. And then she thought of her sister smirking, holding two thumbs up. She opened her eyes. Smiled at him. Sat down.

"Well"—Jake sat down too—"very pleased to meet you, finally." His voice was deep and silty. "We matched over a year ago, if you can believe it."

"Yeah, I . . . yeah, we . . ." Poppy's hand was trembling. She fumbled with a bottle of water, pouring it into both of their glasses, drinking hers immediately, refilling it, finishing it again. She picked up the cocktail menu. "Just gonna . . ." In front of her the words danced, fell, and made no sense at all. "Gonna get another drink. I mean, a drink. My first . . ." she lied.

After lunch with Jetta at Dandelion's local (the publicans had known her well and their meal was on the house), Poppy had bought a bottle of champagne from the off-license on the green. She'd let herself into her sister's flat and cracked open the bottle, pouring it into a coupe glass. She'd watched two Goldie Hawn movies back-to-back, laughing and making asides. As the late afternoon ticked into early evening, Poppy had stood in front of her sister's crammed cupboard, her eyes running up and down the jostling hubbub of clothes. For their entire lives, the sisters had teased each other about their respective wardrobes. Poppy wore exclusively grays, navy, black, white, and denim, and Dandelion wore whatever the fuck she wanted. She dressed like a flower bed, Frida Kahlo, a flaneur, a cheetah, their granddad. For the office, she had suits and silk shirts in every color of the rainbow, and beyond the rainbow into neons and stripes and patterns that were LOUD.

Since her death, the sight of Dandelion's clothes could savage Poppy—the hoodie with ragù stains on the cuff, the attention-seeking hats, the silk kimono she'd wear when she was sad. But that afternoon, Poppy had felt bizarrely brilliant as she'd stripped and slipped into a low-backed bodysuit and a pair of shouty trousers that Dandelion had bought from a vintage store in San Francisco and called her *acid trip pants*. In her sister's bathroom, Poppy ran black over the waterline of her eyes the way Dandelion used to, until it shone slick, then she'd clipped her hair up in a milkmaid's braid so that it met over her crown, in thick and doughy plaits. In front of the long mirror, she'd admired her transformation. "Tonight, Matthew, I'm going to be . . ." She'd twirled, finished the bottle of champagne.

Behind the menu, Jake was talking.

Doing her best to hold the paper still between both hands, Poppy tilted it to the side so that she could see his face. He was

27

leaning forward. His hair was tinged gray at the temples and maybe he looked older than she'd been expecting, but also, in the flesh—Jake was very hot.

"I said . . ." He was clearly repeating himself for her benefit. "Many happy returns! I feel very honored to be granted a birthday date. Have you had a good day?"

"Yes. I have. My evening plans canceled . . ." Poppy said, hoping this would be enough of an explanation as to why she was meeting up with a stranger on her supposed fortieth. Her eyes moved to Jake's neck and the chest hairs visible at the top of his crumpled shirt.

"So you had a window. Lucky me." Jake smiled and the dimples swirled through both of his cheeks, seemingly all the way.

"I had a window," Poppy agreed. Though actually, this evening, this date, was her window. For a few hours, she would climb through it to a new place where both she and her sister could breathe. "I'd really love a drink." Poppy twisted and looked over her shoulder and waved the menu like a surrender flag.

"Yes, me too! I can see the waiter. He just nodded at us," Jake said.

Poppy couldn't think of anything to say. She smiled, then made a face that felt too stern, so she smiled again and made another face that felt insane.

"Um. Dandelion, tell me . . . What you been up to?" Jake asked. "How's the birthday going so far?"

"Great. Yes. So, I had some champagne and watched *Overboard* and I . . ." Poppy had no idea where she was going with this; honesty was not an option. "Went to Go Ape." She put both her hands on top of the menu on the table, pushed her lips together hard.

"Go Ape? The adventure playground thing?"

"Mm."

Nothing.

Nothing.

Fuck.

"I went to Chessington World of Adventures for a birthday once," Jake said, in the rushing sort of way people pull at information when they want to fill a silence. "But I think I was ten." He winked.

Dandelion used to wink all the time. Up until that moment, she was the only person who Poppy had ever seen pull it off. When she did it, it looked excellent, perverted but ironic. Basic—obviously, though somehow, sort of smart.

"Sorry," Jake said. "I'm experimenting with winking. Did that make me look like a creep?"

"Yes," Poppy said, inhaling an amused breath. And then another firework—pink and silver shimmers crackled on her skin.

"Right. Noted. Sorry."

"No problem." Poppy looked at her hands and twisted her sister's gold snake ring around her finger. She wanted to show Dandelion how brave she was. She wanted to make her proud, and so she looked up—winked back at him.

Jake was taking a sip from his glass, but at this, his head jerked and his cheeks ballooned like a puffer fish and he blew water out over the table and onto Poppy. "Sorry!" He stood up, took a black napkin from the canteen-style dispenser, and started dabbing at her arms. "I really wasn't expecting that to be reciprocated. You caught me totally off guard."

Poppy took the napkin from him and pressed it to her neck. She pouted quickly. The wink had been terrible, had felt like a lopsided blink. "Did you think I was having a stroke?"

"No!" Jake wiped the table with another napkin. He kept his eyes on his hand. "I liked it very much."

A waiter was there then, and Poppy was relieved because the

situation felt too intense. It was like being in a play, only she'd never read the script. How did people do it? The constant dates, the brazen flirting, throwing themselves in at the deep end of intimacy.

Dandelion had done it all the time. She was always seeing someone, always hooking up. Not just through apps; she asked people out in doctors' surgeries and petrol stations. She'd slipped a policeman her number once when he was giving her a warning; later (allegedly) she'd handcuffed him to his bed. She'd had sex with someone she met at the British Library, in the British Library. And if she was rejected, she didn't care; she'd shrug. *Whatevs. Your loss.* Dandelion would laugh.

The waiter put a fresh bottle of water on the table and pulled a notepad from his apron pocket, took a pencil from behind his left ear. "What can I get you guys?"

"I'll have a mezcal margarita," Poppy said. "Thank you very much."

"Me too," Jake agreed. "I sort of imagined you differently, but don't you find people from apps always look different to how you imagine them?" he said, once the waiter had left.

"Um . . ." Poppy wondered if she should take her hair out of the braids and let it fall over her face in waves. She rested an elbow on the table and covered all of one cheek with her palm. "Not really. Anyway, so—"

"But not in a bad way." Jake reached out and touched her wrist in a quick apologetic gesture. "What I mean is you look younger."

Poppy tried to recall her game plan because, now that she was actually here, sitting with this stranger, the evening was sliding over her and she didn't, totally, have a grasp. She excused herself and stood up, said something about the loo. She needed a very quick breather, or a slap around the face.

Inside, the waiter nodded to a single cubicle, and Poppy jogged over to it, locked herself in. She leaned back against the door and looked at her reflection in the frameless rectangle mirror screwed to the wall. "I can't do this," she said, and then she said, "You absolutely can."

Before, when they'd been messaging, Poppy had thought of Jake as a character, an avatar, and she'd believed—after this adventure with her sister—it would be easy to never think of him again. But now that she was here, she felt something unnerving and exhilarating that she hadn't been anticipating. "It's going great, Poppet. Chill." Poppy inhaled loudly. Exhaled louder. "It's just a bit of fun." She looked at the small sink, the gold taps, the green tiles. Everything felt hyperreal. Everything was *very there*. "You're Dandelion!" she said. "I'm Dandelion. Hiya!" She waved at the mirror, then rolled her eyes. "Stop being so fucking weird."

When she got back to their table, the drinks were there and Jake was grinning, holding up a tumbler of cloudy liquid with a chili-salted rim, a chunk of lime and ice. "Dear Dandelion, happy birthday!"

"Thank you," Poppy said as she clicked her glass carefully against his, took a sip.

"So, how's the dating going?" Jake cleared his throat. "I expect you're rather popular on the apps."

Poppy turned her attention to the small red candle between them. Pushed her finger into the warm soft lip of wax. "Going okay. I prefer to meet people in real life though," she said, speaking her sister's feelings, seeing as her own dating life was a total non-event and she'd been with Sam for nearly five years.

"Old-school, I like that," Jake said. "Do you mean in pubs and stuff?"

"Pubs and, like, petrol stations."

Jake shouted a laugh. "You serious?"

"Deadly." Poppy looked down at her chest, watched the heave

of her breasts in Dandelion's clingy bodysuit. She had the distinct impression that Jake fancied her. There was undeniably a vibe.

"Wow. So petrol stations. Hot. Where else?"

"Um . . ." Poppy scrolled through Dandelion's back catalog. "Well, recently there was a time outside a children's nursery and . . . one of the dads . . ."

"Sorry." Jake put his glass down. "Tell me everything immediately, and feel free to exaggerate and lie."

It had been early summer. Poppy and her sister were leaning up against a wall across the street from a chichi nursery, housed under a railway arch round the corner from Dandelion's flat. They'd bought Twisters from the ice cream van parked up by the square, both using their tongues to remove the yellow ice cream swirl first—a technique they'd developed as little girls.

"Have you ever seen such sexy parents?" Dandelion asked, not looking at Poppy but watching the congregation gathering and chatting at pickup time. Poppy looked sideways and pulled a distasteful face at her sister, who was in a very short slip, showing off her fresh-from-holiday tan. Dandelion lowered her cat-eye sunglasses as a tall man who looked like a Viking crossed the road, holding a toddler's hand. She watched him, pushing her Twister in her mouth and then, in a manner that was distinctly X-rated, slowly pulling it out. "Do you dare me to chat him up?"

The door of the nursery was open, and through it Poppy could see a long rack of tiny colorful coats. "No," she said. She finished her Twister and posted the wooden stick into a nearby black bin as Dandelion skipped toward trouble, out onto the road.

"He was a divorced dad, I should add," Poppy said. She'd relayed the story to Jake, though in this version she was Dandelion, and the character of Poppy wasn't there at all. "So, I wasn't totally husband stealing. But yeah . . ." That man (a tech bro who had started up a start-up) had been in Dandelion's life for a few months. "We dated for a while."

Jake had been nodding excitedly the whole way through this retelling. He didn't seem to think that Dandelion was a hussy or anything. He didn't, at all, seem to be put off.

"Your turn," Poppy said, crossing her arms and holding on to opposite elbows. Behind Jake, the sun was going down and the sky was bleeding from a slit of red. "Met anyone nice?" She wanted him to say *No*. Or, even better, that he hadn't *until tonight.*

"Well, yes, I . . ." Jake told Poppy about a handful of awkward dates he'd been on. How it was fun to get back out there after a marriage and a long time with one person, but now he wanted to settle again. Delete the apps. Find someone to really love. And Poppy found the way he talked to be honest and self-deprecating and, apart from the occasional anecdote and very necessary lie, she'd been able to be herself. A better version of herself—one she actually liked.

When Poppy finished her second drink, Jake ordered them a third. By now, the only light was from the lanterns above them, the deep glow of a nearby heater, and the candles that shone like rubies and large nuggets of gold scattered over the tables. Everyone else had left the courtyard, but still, Jake and Poppy's conversation flowed and ebbed, carried them like a current that was going somewhere. He showed her a picture of his little boy, Billy (long hair, long eyelashes, clutching a dolly). He told her that, recently, Billy had been getting into trouble for calling his teachers Mrs. Bottom Head and Fart Face. He told her that he had a lot more free time now, what with the co-parenting, and was planning on doing some type of course. He had a fantasy of one day being the sort of man who could whittle and make tables. "One day I'll be the sort of man who can carpent."

"Carpent?" Poppy asked. "Fit carpets?"

"Carpent," Jake said. "As in—carpentry."

"Oh!" Poppy laughed. "Is that a word?"

"One day," Jake said, "I'll be the sort of man who knows if *carpent* is a word."

Poppy told Jake about how she'd grown up by the sea in Devon, felt the salt of the water in her blood. She told him how, sometimes, she felt moved to tears by how sweet her parents were together; forty-nine years of marriage, and they still held hands.

"Set an amazing example then," Jake said. "My dad left when I was nine."

"Love like theirs is unrealistic though," Poppy said. "Aspiring to that will only lead to disappointment. Is there such a thing as setting an example that's too good?"

"No," Jake said, with palpable sadness in his voice. "Parents being too in love is definitely not a thing."

"Sorry," Poppy said, ashamed for sounding brattish. "I was lucky. I know."

Jake looked down at his hands and then up at her face. "It's been really nice to meet you finally, Dandelion. I'm the lucky one tonight."

By the time they finished their third margarita, their eye contact had a volume; it was shouting very loud. Poppy had begun to worry that Jake was going to kiss her. She worried how much she wanted him to. She touched her phone, saw the time, and panicked. "Totally forgot," she said, "my friend is throwing me a birthday thing, I'd better go. I'm actually pretty late."

"Now?" Jake asked. He sounded disappointed and, potentially, disbelieving.

"Mm, mm. Yes."

"Okay." He nodded. "Well . . . I'd really like to see you again. How's that sound to you?"

Poppy swallowed. She crossed her legs at the thigh and wound them tight around each other. She had a vision of standing up, walking around the table, and climbing onto Jake's lap in a straddle, turning his head to one side and licking up his cheek—only in the vision she was Dandelion, or she was both of them. Their edges had blurred. They'd fused.

A second date had not been part of the plan, but fuck it. The rules were hers to bend. "Yes," Poppy said. "I'd really like that too."

6

Still Friday, 11th April

Crouched on the street outside their flat, Poppy rummaged through her bag so viciously that when she pulled her hand from it, turquoise nail varnish had chipped from the tip of nearly every finger. She couldn't find her house key. She emptied her bag upside down so that everything spilled across the pavement and a couple walking a squidged-faced pug stopped to ask her if she was all right. She was great. Precariously excited. Alive! Her key was lying spread eagle over some old chewing gum that had been stamped flat on the street, into the shape of a heart.

Poppy held her breath while she unlocked the front door, try-ing not to act like a drunk person. Already she could hear the telly was on.

"Well, look what the cat dragged in." Sam slung his arm over the back of the sofa and twisted to face her. He was wearing his blue-and-white-striped toweling dressing gown. Poppy noticed his hairline, how rapidly the tide was going out. It felt as if she'd been away for a very long time, and now that she was back, he'd aged. Out of nowhere—Sam had jowls.

"Where were you?" he asked.

Poppy pressed one cheek up against the door frame, predicting that she looked all bleary, like someone who'd had a bottle of champagne and three margaritas over the course of eight hours. "I was with Jetta." She'd rehearsed her lies on the bus. Refused to feel terrible. It was her dead sister's fortieth—that was vindication enough.

Poppy had not mentioned the importance of the date to Sam in the preceding weeks, and he had not remembered, which was to be expected. It was Poppy who looked after their joint calendar; she was the one who bought his family cards and gifts. Annually, she reminded Sam of her own birthday and their anniversary, as subtly as she could.

"We were meant to have that chat tonight, Pops. Remember?" Sam's face tightened in the way that he reserved specifically for her, like he was being tested by a child.

"Really?" Poppy played dumb, though she'd known he wanted to talk about big things, scary things: a marriage, a baby, their future. It was as if Sam had set an alarm for the six-month anniversary of Dandelion's death, having deemed a suitable period to have passed. And then, some weeks back—PING! Poppy's allocated mourning time had been up. "Can we . . . how about tomorrow?" she asked.

"I'm going to Dublin, remember?" Sam said. "So, yeah. Quite annoying."

Poppy pushed herself away from the door. "Sorry, baby," she said, in a sweet voice, a meek voice. "Would it be okay to chat when you get back?"

She knew she needed to face all this stuff with him, and, sure, there had been a time—not even long ago—when Poppy had been looking forward to their future. In her mind there'd been a picture in a frame where they were smiling and on holiday and there were children: one, two, maybe even three. A dog. A garden she would do her best with. Intimidating mortgages and conversations about catchment areas for schools. Dinner parties with neighbors she half liked. Elaborate crisps, dips, and too much okay wine. It was what people did, and it was what Poppy had wanted. Thought she wanted—and it had all been about to start.

"Are you in fancy dress?" Sam asked, eyeing the trousers.

Poppy knew what he was implying; a huge issue in their relationship had always been Dandelion. And vice versa. Dandelion thought Sam was snide and basic. She said she didn't trust him. Conversely, Sam found Dandelion to be tiresome and controlling. And, although he never said it outright, Poppy knew—he thought she was a slut.

"I'm just going to change." Poppy made a chewing motion with her mouth as if she had gum—as if she was an innocent girlfriend who felt relaxed. She kept on fake chewing and strolled up the corridor, swinging her arms. In their bedroom, she pulled on pajamas and hung Dandelion's trousers and bodysuit in the wardrobe. In the bathroom, she washed her face, scrubbed her sister from her skin. "I love him," she murmured defensively, looking for the feeling inside of her heart.

The sisters' last physical fight had been an altercation over Sam.

They'd been in the big Nike Town at Oxford Circus. Among the teenagers and tourists, Dandelion had told Poppy that she was ruining her own life by committing so spiritlessly to him. "He's a slimeball. He's a bad dude. You're shrinking and I hate it. He's got zero sense of humor. I've literally never heard him laugh."

Poppy had stormed off, and Dandelion had come at her from behind, shouting, "You're so embarrassingly desperate for a husband, aren't you? It's pathetic!"

With a flourish of high drama, she'd pushed Poppy into a rail of leggings, and Poppy had staggered and fallen over. Gasping and incredibly offended, Poppy knelt, then stood and ran at Dandelion, and there had been a full-blown, grown-woman scrap. At least one person had been recording them on an iPhone. In (self-described) self-defense, Poppy had hit her sister around the face, and her ring snagged Dandelion's eyebrow, drawing blood. They'd been escorted out of the shop by a flustered guard and sat on the Victoria line home with Dandelion pressing a Pret napkin to her forehead. They didn't speak, but Poppy had the distinct feeling she always got when she was forced to fight—that she'd made her sister proud.

"What are you watching?" Poppy asked Sam, sloping back into the sitting room, braless and barefoot in her shrunken tartan pajamas. She rested a finger on the sofa and stood looking at the screen, trying to focus.

"*First Dates.* Reality thing. I'm not necessarily watching it," Sam said. "I was waiting for you. Are you drunk?"

Poppy crossed the room into the kitchen, headed for the sink. She picked up a glass from the draining rack. "No." Their basil plant on the windowsill was withered and too brown.

"What's up with you?" Sam asked.

Poppy finished the glass of water. "Nothing," she said brightly, turning back to him. He'd slumped further down, arms folded, neck totally retracted into his dressing gown.

"You've been acting strange."

"I had some mezcal, maybe I am a bit tipsy." Poppy walked back over to him, did a pirouette like a ballerina and then an elegant backbend with an outstretched hand. Sam didn't look up, so she perched on the sofa arm and leveled her gaze at the screen; two people who looked to be in their fifties were sitting opposite each other at a small white table in a crowded restaurant. They were both dressed as rockabillies. "They look like a good match," Poppy said.

"They hate each other," Sam said. "I'm not just talking about tonight, Poppy. Recently. This last week . . . it's like you've been silent and lethargic for ages, *understandably*, but now you're not replying to my messages and you're being insanely aloof and avoidant—even for you. And . . ." Sam turned his head to her. "I know you're wearing your sister's clothes, by the way, and shit-loads of makeup, and you're letting your hair . . ." He moved his hands over his head. "Be a big mess."

"I'm just wearing eyeliner, Sam," Poppy said flatly. She ran both hands once, twice, over her hair.

"And you're always at her place."

"I was always at her place before."

"Yeah, but she's not there anymore, Poppy. So . . . I don't know, it feels like you're sneaking about. Also, this tone you're using with me—it's hostile, and, really, the point is it's all not very *you*."

The joy, the sugar, her sister's courage, was bleeding from Poppy in life-threatening pumps. How long had she had this head-ache for? She looked down at her hand and twisted her sister's gold snake ring.

Even when Dandelion was naked, she'd been tangled in jew-elry. An arrangement of chains at her neck. A fluctuation of rings. Once, there had been a bar through her nipple and a hoop looped through her nose. In hospital, Poppy had been asked to remove all the jewelry from her sister's strangely still, but still-breathing, body. The snake had stayed, though, up until the end. After the end. Poppy had only slipped it from her finger shortly after Dan-delion's heart had stopped and her soul was curling upward and out of her, like the final gasps of smoke from a burned-out fire.

"It's Dandelion's birthday today, Sam. So . . ." Poppy lobbed the Death card into their conversation like a hand grenade, hoping it would blow an escape route and assuage the mounting guilt.

"Oh, Popsy . . ." Sam held his arms out to her. "Come here." He moved so that he was lying along the sofa, indicating Poppy should be the little spoon. She walked around, then sat, then lay. He belted an arm around her middle. "It's okay, we don't have to talk about this stuff tonight. How about we schedule a proper date night to make our exciting plans?" He kissed the top of her ear.

Poppy closed her eyes. "Okay." She felt guilty for lying. For flirting. She would delete her sister's dating app; of course she would. *Of course.* She turned over so that she was facing Sam and pressed her cheek against his chest. "I'm sorry," she whispered. "I know I've been a dick."

Sam squeezed her. "I just want us to move on with our lives, Popsy."

"So do I," Poppy murmured and then hiccuped. She clung to Sam with the very tips of her fingers. If she let go of him—what would happen? She'd lose another person she loved and then she'd be obliterated.

On the telly behind Poppy, a couple were being interviewed after their date and asked if they wanted to see each other again.

"You go first," a woman's voice said.

"I'd love to see you again, Mikala," a man's voice said.

"I'd love to too," Mikala agreed, all giggles.

After the cocktails, Poppy and Jake had bickered over who would pay the bill and eventually agreed to go Dutch, because Poppy wouldn't take no for an answer. On the street outside the restaurant, Jake called it their *first fight* and then he'd tried to kiss her.

Sam was stroking the side of Poppy's cheek with the backs of his fingers, and his hand smelled a lot like foot. He'd propped himself up on his elbow and was looking at her in a way that, she knew, was meant to communicate sentiments that were heartfelt and arousing. He slipped his fingers inside her pajama shirt and did his go-to move with her nipple. When he kissed her, Poppy closed her eyes and thought of Jake.

It was Jake's stubble scratching across her skin.

Jake's body pushing down on hers.

Jake whispering in her ear: *I can feel your heat.*

7

Saturday, 12th April

Jake

Jake couldn't see a *For Sale* sign outside the house. Surprise, surprise. He shuffled around on the gravel, putting on a show of looking, in case Zoe was watching him from a window. She had said she'd speak to the estate agents weeks ago, though he knew she was in no rush to move out.

Their car was in the drive, with two legs and large bare feet emerging from beneath the bonnet. Jake crunched over. "Hello?"

Hands emerged, a torso, a man bun, a smiling face. "Jake, mate!" Yan stood up, brushing his palms on his tracksuit bottoms. He had a slight Scandi accent. Da Goddamn Yogi Thor.

"Hi?" Jake made his greeting into a question, very much going for bemused but charming Brit.

"Yan." Yan extended his hand. "I'm Zoe's partner."

Jake raised his eyebrows like this was news to him. As if he hadn't already spent hours of his life scrolling through every picture Yan had ever posted and watching YouTube videos of Yan's yoga classes—while he sat topless on his sofa, eating cookies and making disparaging comments to his ficus, Cindy.

They stepped back to survey each other.

Yan was wearing a vest, which seemed pointless, as it sagged down, exposing his pecs and most of his torso, which was patterned with tattoos. His thin cotton tapered tracksuit bottoms articulated the outline of his cock, and Jake put both hands on his hips and looked up at the sky, affronted that his ex-wife's new boyfriend's tackle was so clearly visible to him, without consent. "Lovely weather."

"Dada!" Billy came running toward him, down the stone steps, and onto the gravel. Curls bouncing. Holding his dolly by her hand.

"Hi, son!" Jake said, picking him up. He had never called Billy *son* before—as if it was his name—and he absolutely hated it when his own father called him *son*. Still, in front of Yan, an expression of paternal ownership seemed fitting.

Zoe was behind their little boy in leggings, crop top, and signature sneer. She walked over to Yan and put her arm around him. "Oh, have you two met?"

"We did, yes," Jake said, smiling broadly. He would absolutely not let the bastards grind him down.

"Yan was fixing the car," Zoe said, in a way that sounded a lot like *Just so you know—his cock is bigger than yours and he can go all night.*

"What have you done to the car this time?" Jake forced an amiable laugh and switched Billy to his other hip.

"It's the—" Yan began.

"Absolutely no need, though, Yan," Jake said, speaking over him. He put Billy down and watched him as he ran over to the red plastic slide on the grass. "I can fix the car."

Zoe sniggered, and then in case Jake hadn't caught it, she said, "Hilarious!"

"It's done, man, no sweat."

44

"Thanks . . . *man*," Jake said, looking back at him. "Sorry, still haven't quite got to the bottom of . . . do you live here? Because . . . when did you two meet?" Jake chuckled again, flashed his eyes between both their faces.

"It's not a permanent thing," Yan said. "Zoe's letting me crash until next week, and then I'm running a retreat in Oaxaca, so—"

"A retreat?" Jake looked puzzled, although he knew all about it because he'd read the (poorly worded) summary on Yan's website.

Yan put his hands together in prayer and bowed slightly. "Yoga."

"Jake can't even touch his toes," Zoe said.

"My legs are long." Jake stood up as straight as he could, locking his knees. Yan was still a good couple of inches taller than him, so he clarified, "In proportion to my torso. I'm long-legged."

"That makes it harder," Yan agreed generously.

"Mm." Jake smiled, almost accidentally feeling charmed. "Well, anyway." He looked over at Billy, who was holding his dolly by the legs and hitting her head against the slide, quite aggressively. "Bud," he called. "Have you got everything?"

"I'll get his bag," Yan said.

Jake watched Yan jog (with high knees—*why?*) toward the house that Jake owned. He looked up at the large magnolia tree, where a crow was cawing. He used to be able to see that tree while he was lying in their super-king bed. He'd lie in their super-king bed with their super-king pillows and the expensive linen and nice womanly smelling air and look at that tree and feel sorry for himself. The magnolia was in bloom now. Its deep purple petals were gigantic, silken, incredible. It was actually the best-looking tree Jake had ever seen. But who owned it? Could he dig it up? There was no garden in the flat that he rented, but he could, probably, get a van and take it to his dad's. Jake looked back at his ex-wife. He was pretty sure she'd had something cosmetic done; she was more shiny and taut, and her face seemed—very slightly—less like her original face. Her lips, he was almost certain, were more pouty. And her cheekbones . . . had she had them enhanced?

Jake met Zoe's eye and was struck by the feeling she was assessing his appearance too. He sucked in his tummy. Crossed his arms. "Look, Zo," he said. "If you wanted to move your toyboy into the house with Billy, you really should have asked me."

Zoe scoffed. "Well, you could have asked me if you wanted to shag Ashley Madison in a cupboard." She smiled thinly as she beckoned Billy over and opened the car door. "Or told me, perhaps? Not left me to find out through the indignity of reading my philandering husband's messages."

Jake inhaled long and slow through his nose. Always and forever, Zoe would have this comeback. Always and forever, she'd get Peggy Sue's name wrong on purpose and pretend that it had been sex. Tell everyone it had been sex, when it had actually been a half-hearted blow job and a fullhearted grope.

The enormously regrettable cupboard incident had been the culmination of a brief workplace flirtation. Peggy Sue, a production assistant, had been messaging Jake about a project, and they had got on very well. The messages turned to GIFs and gags, and Jake felt, truly, that he and Peggy Sue had become friends. They went for after-work drinks a couple of times, on Peggy Sue's suggestion. Once, they went to the cinema and Jake pretended to Zoe that he'd gone with a whole gang. Then—*bam*—Jake and Peggy Sue were in the cupboard, literally out of pretty much nowhere. Then—*ahh*—the instant terrible regret and self-loathing. They'd gone for one last drink and Jake had ended it. Peggy Sue had cried, they'd hugged, said goodbye, and both sadly laughed at something sadly funny Jake had said. The very next day, though, Jake had come into the kitchen, having been planting grass seed in the back garden, and he'd found Zoe, panting, holding his unlocked phone in her shaking hand: "*YOU ABSOLUTE BIN RAT! YOU TERRI-BLE FUCK-FACED FROG!*"

It had been bad. But it had also been two and a half years ago.

"Seriously?" Jake said, through an inhale. He was enormously remorseful and ashamed, but he also wished Zoe could begin to let it drop. "Can we please just—"

"Oh, I'm sorry, does poor Jakey get a bit sad when his mean ex-wife brings up his affair?" Zoe hissed quietly through her teeth, because now Billy was trundling over, burping his dolly over his shoulder.

"Dada, Spleen has gas!"

"Who?" Jake glanced at Zoe.

"Lazy Susan is called Spirulina now," Zoe said.

"No," Jake said. "She's not." Billy's dolly had been called Lazy Susan since they bought her when Billy was a baby. Jake, as a small child, had also had a dolly called Lazy Susan whom he'd loved deeply, and he'd always thought it to be a very excellent name. He looked back at Billy. "Right, come on. You and Lazy Susan are getting into the car."

"SPLEEN!" Billy shouted.

"He can't even say the word *spirulina*, Zoe," Jake said, affronted, looking at his ex. "He's literally calling her Spleen."

"No, he's not. He's saying Spirulina," Zoe said.

"Spleen," Billy agreed.

"Fine!" Jake said, in a way that made it absolutely clear it was not fine at all. He reached for Billy and helped him into the car. He straightened, ran both hands through his hair, and shut the door gently. "So, the thing is, Zoe, I'd really appreciate it if you didn't use your creative license when it comes to my life, it was hardly *an affair*. As you well know—"

"Once again: Sex doesn't need penetration, and affairs don't need sex," Zoe said, through a big fake smile.

Billy waved at his mummy and daddy through the window. Both of them smiled like kids' TV presenters and waved back. They were well practiced at having bitter arguments while maintaining looks of moronic glee for the sake of their kid.

"What are you two laughing about?" Yan called, coming toward them with Billy's tiny blue-and-red backpack.

"Just talking about how happy you make me, Babasita," Zoe said. She reached her arm around his body, stood on her tiptoes, and kissed his cheek, with a loud *mwah* sound.

"Actually." Jake cleared his throat, clapped his hands. "You should know, I've met someone too."

"Ah, cool." Yan handed Jake Billy's bag.

Zoe didn't say anything. She had her arms around Yan's waist and was holding him tight, like a koala on a very huge and fucking masculine tree.

Jake walked slowly around the car and tapped the roof, all chipper. "Yeah, she's called Dandelion," he continued, like they'd inquired, which they hadn't. "We had such fun drinks for her birthday last night . . ." Which wasn't a lie—they had! Sure, maybe he was making it sound like he'd been seeing her longer than two days, but that old adage was ringing loud and true like wedding bells: When you know, *you know.*

"You know . . ." Jake said, his face full of sunshine, "when you know, you know. You know?"

Yan was smiling but wincing, visibly untangling this sentence. And, *yes*, grammatically it was potentially perplexing, but Jake had had the best first date of his life. He felt himself swoon at the memory of the previous evening. Dandelion had turned up hammered, which was fair enough since it was her birthday. Before they'd met, he'd presumed she was going to be a bit odd—

48

choosing to spend the evening of her fortieth with a total stranger—but as soon as he'd seen her wobbling around in those incredibly tight trousers, he'd felt a primal magnetism. Sure, she was a tiny bit precarious as a character and he'd had a vague sense that she was fibbing occasionally—but Jake didn't give a monkey's. If anything, he preferred someone slightly off-kilter. He was truly, madly, deeply, already, almost infatuated. He couldn't wait to see Dandelion again. Was already planning date two.

Jake slid his gaze back to Zoe. She opened the car door to give Billy and Spleen a kiss. "Anyway, we'll see ya Thursday!" he said, ducking down into the driver's seat.

Zoe came round to his door before he could close it. "I'm pleased for you," she said, looking disconcertingly earnest.

Jake sniffed, looked past her at the magnolia, nervous that she was being nice and that this was a sincere moment. The crow cawed again, pointedly. Unless this was some sort of calculated mind game? Jake looked back at Zoe's pretty panther face and her dark wily eyes, trying to work it out.

"Are you going to introduce her to Billy?" Zoe asked.

"I wouldn't without asking you. And besides," Jake relented, "it's very early days."

"Okay. Well, look, I'm sorry. It happened quickly, Yan needed a place to stay. It wasn't planned."

"Er . . . fine." Jake's mind was blown; Zoe never apologized.

Yan stepped toward the open car door. "It was nice to meet you, brother. I hope we can hang out in future."

"Okay, bye," Jake said, shaking his hand, very firmly, looking down at his inner arm and the stick-and-poke tattoo that was maybe an Alsatian, or a not-very-good wolf.

"Bye, Da Billy Boy! Bye, Spirulina!" Yan tapped on the window.

Jake twisted around to look at his little buddy in the back seat. "You ready to rock?"

Billy nodded. Jake started the ignition and backed the car, turned it to face the road. In his rearview mirror he looked at his ex-wife and her new boyfriend, standing outside his old house. Zoe was smiling and waving, and then Billy started to laugh hysterically as Yan began walking on his hands across the gravel, in a very impressive display of virility, strength, and youth.

8

Wednesday, 16th April

"Good men do bad things!" Jake held his arms out. He was naked, standing in front of his grotty bathroom mirror.

He'd already put Billy to bed, watched a David Attenborough doc he'd seen at least once before, eaten everything in his flat, even the weird things like some old ginger biscuits that had turned bendy and a pickled egg. (Where had that jar even come from?) He'd cleared his inbox for the first time since email began, and had his first bath since he'd moved out of the family home—all to avoid thinking about Dandelion and the fact she had not been in touch.

So now he was biding his time with his secret hobby— explaining himself to the world, via his bathroom mirror. "Yes, I am a good man. A kind man," Jake continued as he noticed Dandelion in the front row of the vast and impressed audience he had conjured. She was perched on her seat, leaning forward so that Jake could see the very top of her cleavage, a smidge of lace trimming on her red bra.

Jake shook his head and tried to erase her. He didn't need *her* here. At least he didn't need the imaginary version of her. The real her would be fine. What was going on between them? Nothing? He thought they'd had such an authentic connection. And the chemistry had felt reciprocal—excitingly smoldering hot.

But now, obviously, Jake had blown it by being too keen.

Since the date, he'd tried his very best not to message Dandelion about every little thing. The previous day, he'd found himself writing her a message about how much he loved butter, while he was eating toast. He'd managed to delete it. To rein it in. Though he'd spent most of the afternoon staring at his phone longingly instead of working. He kept having to turn it off, only to turn it on again ten minutes later. *No New Messages.*

So this was what it felt like to be ghosted: confusing, shameful hell.

Jake shook his head, banishing Dandelion from his thoughts for the fiftieth time that day, and launched back into his bathroom mirror speech. "Yes, I have learned the hard way that temptation lies in wait for all of us, and when we are low, when we are weary . . ."

Initially Jake had imagined himself giving a talk in the Royal Albert Hall, but now, he'd elevated himself into the center of a stadium, his face smiled outward from massive screens, and he had one of those tiny microphones strapped to his own cheek. It was a TED Talk. On forgiveness. Some of the audience were waving flags. Some of them had those massive pointing foam fingers. Was he in America? Yes. He had broken America. And the internet. *We love you, Jake! We love you!* The audience were pulsing their foam fingers to the beat.

Although potentially, Jake was getting carried away, because in reality, even Billy's rubber bath toys were looking at him skeptically. The leader of them, a multicolored octopus known as Occy the Puss, was straddling the edge of the bath, four legs in, four legs out, and was rolling his googly eyes at Jake, more so than normal. Jake turned back to the mirror and rubbed the condensation off the glass so he could see himself again. He was starting to feel a little cold, a little wrinkly. Shrunken and pathetic. The thing is, everyone hates you once you've had an affair. Jake used to have loads of friends, or enough at least. But since all the Zoe stuff— well, the women sided with her and the men sided with their wives.

"We all make mistakes . . ." Jake murmured, looking down at his feet, his hairy toes. "What matters is that we move forward . . ." He looked up, held his hands over his heart very earnestly. "With grace."

Dandelion was back in the mirror now. She was clapping so much she was sweating, just lightly, just speckles of sexy damp moisture. Jake put the back of his hand to his head and sighed. It was futile: She was refusing to leave his thoughts alone. And, sure, maybe he was being ghosted, but he was also genuinely concerned for her welfare. Because what if this was one of those rare instances when someone goes on a date with someone and then that second someone . . . falls down a well, or is trapped in an attic without a ladder or, like, desperately needs some sort of help? Jake grabbed his towel from the rail and, swinging it around his waist, stalked to the bedroom. The problem was, he didn't know her surname, so searching for her on the internet had proven fruitless. Typing *Dandelion, woman, London, 40* into Google gave him nothing. All he had was Hinge.

Jake picked up his phone and reviewed his post-date messages to her. At the time, late on Friday night, he'd thought he was being charming and lightly suggestive. He'd asked for her number. He'd sent a whole line of winky faces because winky faces felt like a top-notch private joke. Perhaps sending her a song ("Good Time," Donnie and Joe Emerson) on Saturday had been a bit much, and in hindsight, he regretted the second Good Time–themed song he'd sent on Sunday ("I Know There's Gonna Be (Good Times)," Jamie xx), and the desperate third stab on Monday morning ("Good Times," Chic) was, obviously, now mortifying. But looking on the bright side, at least he'd not sent her that *God, butter's the best, yummy yum* thing. There'd be no coming back from that.

Now, weighing it all up, Jake decided there was nothing left to do but to call her. Then he'd know once and for all what the deal was. Because frankly, maybe there was something really up with this woman. Maybe she was a massive player. Maybe Dandelion wasn't even her real name. Maybe on the way back to the station after meeting him she'd been mowed over by the number 38 bus and now, very sadly, was . . .

"Just do it. You can do it," Jake said, steeling himself. He pressed the phone icon in the top right-hand corner of her profile and inside his body cortisol began clenching in tiny fists. It rang once, then again, then—

"Hello?"

"Dandelion?" Jake's heart beat so hard it hurt. He was delighted. "Hi!" No, actually he was terrified. "Just calling because I hadn't heard from you . . . I was worried." He sounded really upbeat. "So, great news you're not dead!" He was practically singing.

On the other end of the phone, Dandelion didn't say anything and, for too long, they were silent.

When it was obvious she wasn't going to speak at all he staggered onward. "Right, so that's established! I suppose all I wanted to say, really, is that it would be most excellent to see you again and so, I guess, call me. Anytime! Through Hinge is fine. I'll be here. Unless you want to chat now?" he asked, realizing it was odd to call someone simply to tell them to call you back.

Dandelion said nothing. Not one single word.

"Right. So, call me anytime!" Jake spoke in a high-pitched voice like a jilted woman in a nineties sitcom. He put down the phone. "Fucking hell."

He had used the phrase *most excellent* for the first time ever. He had started talking in a woman's voice for no discernible reason and totally not pulled it off. He'd pleaded with her to call him, then abruptly hung up.

So that was a mistake.

Jake wished he was the one who was dead.

9

Saturday, 19th April

Poppy

Outside the train window, London gave way to Reading. Power lines, blocks of flats. Poppy's prebooked seat was in first class, and her carriage was full of Americans, middling twenties, glamorous and loud. The woman in the seat next to Poppy hung her arms and chest over the back of her chair, talking to her friends who were sitting behind. She wore very short shorts.

Poppy popped another painkiller, her fourth of the day, and massaged her temples. She'd been working for the last seventy-two hours at an event in Venice and had only had time to go home quickly from the airport, where, in a state of shallow breath anxiety, she'd showered and changed, and now she was on her way to the Cotswolds for another job—a wedding. A fifteen-hour shift.

A woman with a singsong voice and a long, tattooed neck extending from her crisp Great Western uniform came around to check everyone's tickets. "Helloooo!" she said to each person, greeting them like an old friend. A guy with a mohawk, also in uniform, pushed a food trolley past them and Poppy bought a full-fat Coke, a packet of salt and vinegar crisps, a croissant, a flapjack, a coffee, a bottle of water, and three miniature gins. The young Americans exchanged looks.

She opened the Coke, turned to the window, and toasted her reflection. A lot of the time, a lot of her life, Poppy was simultaneously trying not to think about something disturbing or upsetting, while also feeling anxious in a myriad of ways. Since she'd lost Dandelion, she'd been near constantly trying not to think about her big sister and the total insanity of her being dead. Increasingly, she found herself thinking of her own death, the concern it would be too soon, or not soon enough. The death of her parents, which loomed like the next worst thing. She'd been trying not to question how detached she felt from her job, and from Sam. Poppy had been trying repeatedly, relatively unsuccessfully, to pull her mind back from the precipice of despair. That was until last week—until her date with Jake.

Because ever since those margaritas and that flirting and the swirling petals of his sunflower eyes, Poppy had been waiting for the swarming thoughts of him to calm. But it seemed they were only layering and making themselves more substantial so that she could hardly see around them. And now, with her head against the dirty glass of the train window, Poppy recalled how Jake had looked sitting across the table from her in the courtyard of the restaurant, underneath the heater. His neck muscles, his forearms, his crumpled shirt over his chest, the smile before his laugh started, the deep breath as it ended. His brushy eyelashes pushing together as he winked, his hand on her waist as he leaned in and tried to kiss her. The volume of Poppy's lust had been turned right up and life had begun, again, to prickle. Like the fleck of a cigarette ember dropped on silk, desire had burned right through Poppy's grief, and now she could see a new place on the other side—a world she shouldn't know.

Every morning since Poppy met Jake, she'd woken at dawn,

breathless. A horniness stirred within her, and graphic fantasies had turned dizzying—sparked by moments that, usually, meant nothing at all: The smell of weed on the street as she walked past a cluster of much younger men. The way an elfin woman sitting opposite on the tube caressed her girlfriend's neck. Her yoga teacher pressing down onto her shoulders when she was in Savasana lying on the floor of the hot dark studio. A man in a green Hackney Council jacket in her local park with a leaf blower, who looked Poppy right in the eye when she passed him. A few days previously, Poppy had been crossing the Downs and had accidentally stopped to gawp at a group of men playing Frisbee with their tops off—she stood there, alone, having a perv, until one of them waved at her and asked, "What's up? You lost your dog?" Even the pink-and-white spring blossoms that frothed and foamed in all the trees had become an aphrodisiac and made Poppy want to press herself up against strangers. Basically, since she'd met Jake, Poppy had been hot, a lot.

Her plan had been to never see him again. But since she'd heard his voice and his hurt when he'd called her late the other night, she kept coming back to—*But what if?* The only person whom Poppy would be able to discuss Jake with was Dandelion. Her silent coconspirator. Poppy would do anything to be able to call her sister. To hear her actual voice out loud in the world again on the other end of the phone: *Yeah? Popeye? Wha?*

"Glok-es-ter-shi-yre." The Americans had been practicing their English accents. They were traveling to Gloucestershire, had taken on the word, and, so far, Gloucestershire was winning.

"Gluskest—"

"Glawstishir."

If Dandelion had been there, she would have stood and said with all the authority of an orchestra's conductor, *Glos-ta-sha! Glos-ta-sha! Repeat after me!* Instead, Poppy put her headphones in—played the songs Jake had sent her again, looped them on re-peat. She ate the croissant, leaning forward to avoid getting crumbs on her suit, and on the steamed-up window she wrote, *WHAT IF?* And *TELL ME!* And *Pleeeeeeese.*

At Kemble station Poppy was greeted by someone who intro-duced himself as Digby, an uncle of the bride. He ushered her into his vintage Aston Martin and, as they drove, every time he shifted the gear stick, he glanced at Poppy's upper thighs. Thankfully, the first gin, downed at the station, had smoothed the edges of her broken-glass thoughts and she was able to slip into Charming Photographer Mode and titter politely at Digby's off-color jokes.

"And here we are!" said Digby as they turned in to the drive of the bride's family seat, an enormous honey-colored stone house with lots of wings.

"Mummy, it's Poppy!" Astrid, the bride, said, prancing through the front door in a silk dressing gown and Hunter wellies as the car drew up. She embraced Poppy before wordlessly instructing Digby to carry Poppy's camera bags into the house, just by waving at them, then him.

"I've heard you're a wizard with the camera," Astrid's mother said, coming toward Poppy with her hand outstretched, wrist limp. She was wearing a knee-length collarless navy jacket and a massive diamond brooch that blinked and winked at Poppy, like a second head. "How do you do?"

Apparently, Poppy's assistant, Betty, had already arrived, and Astrid's stepfather had taken her down to the local pub, on the edge of the village green, to photograph the groom and the ushers, who were having an early sharpener. It was impossible to do these weddings alone; two photographers were needed to be in different places at the same time, and Poppy and Betty made an excellent team. They'd met four years previously, when Poppy had gone to the graduation show at Falmouth, her former university, and had been impressed with Betty's portfolio. They'd worked together on most jobs ever since.

Poppy followed Astrid into the house and set about taking pictures of her and her friends getting ready, all in silk pajamas and with curlers in their hair. From there, the day unfurled like so many of the English countryside weddings Poppy had photographed. The service in the large fifteenth-century church, the interior of which had been adorned with peonies, irises, lilies of the valley, anemones, and long trailing stems of eucalyptus leaves. Then group shots by the lake—which were not fun to do because, by that point, the champagne had started circling and the family wanted to chat rather than pose; someone kept wandering off.

During the reception on the lawn, Poppy wove through the crowd discreetly pointing her camera at the exquisite tans, long necks, and big-chinned/no-chinned aristocratic (and aristocratic-adjacent) faces.

From the outset, Dandelion had spurred Poppy on with her career. Made good things happen. She'd written Poppy's business plan for her. She'd conducted due diligence on Poppy's behalf—all the stuff that Poppy would never think necessary, or want to do herself. Dandelion had invested to get her off the ground and made lucrative client introductions. She'd built buzz and momentum, and over the years, Poppy had become coveted by the British upper class, wealthy Euros, wealthier Americans, the art and fashion set, and minor, tasteful, celebs.

Traditionally, spring and summer were exhausting, and Poppy was away at events most weekends. Last year, obviously, had turned tragically catastrophic, so this year she'd purposefully planned to be quieter from a professional point of view, knowing she wouldn't be able to handle the manic cadence of it all. Poppy had turned down most inquiries that had come in, and instead of a wedding every weekend, she'd only booked a few for the entire season. Besides, since Dandelion had died, she was in a different financial situation and could afford to slow right down.

As the guests finished dessert, Poppy stood in the corner by the top table and stifled an enormous yawn. She watched an usher prepare the microphone: making it taller, shorter; tapping on it, then blowing on it; dragging it to the left and giving it another blow. Probably, by this point, Poppy had witnessed north of five hundred wedding speeches. Once upon a time, they used to move her, but that was before she had gathered enough data to discern there was a template and a formula. Really, the speeches were all the same and—in a way—the antithesis of genuine romance.

Astrid's stepfather stood up, thanked everyone, and then began the deathly dull chronology of Astrid's life, up until her wedding day. It took thirty-five minutes, for most of which Poppy fantasized about being let loose on the very extensive cheese table, which was manned by a cheese expert the wedding planner had shipped in from Paris and referred to as "the frommelier." Poppy's fantasy developed from being purely about eating cheese to also being about Jake. Jake *was* the frommelier. He had rolled-up shirtsleeves and he kept slicing Poppy slivers, skewering them with his fancy knife and watching intently as she ate them, all the while saying very knowledgeable things about Comté and Manchego in his sexy voice. Then, once she was satiated, Jake swept all the cheese to the floor in one strong swish of his arm and threw Poppy down onto the table, aggressively but also lovingly—the perfect amount of hard.

Everyone in the marquee was clapping now, and Poppy clicked back into reality as the very short and very wealthy groom stood and pushed himself to the limits of his own cringe threshold just to ensure that the bridesmaids and the aunts all kept bleating in heartfelt unison. "I'm the luckiest man alive . . . I don't know what I did to deserve her . . ." He pulled out all the hackneyed clichés that Poppy could have written for him. "Astrid, you've never looked more beautiful than you do today . . ." His audience cooed. Whoo'd. Clapped.

A cymbal crashed, and everyone staggered to the dance floor. The uncle, Digby, began viciously twirling a very young overexcited bridesmaid around by the arm. He let go of her, catching Poppy's eye while the girl ricocheted away, delighted and out of control. There was at least one of these men at every wedding Poppy had ever been to, a drunk who thought jiving with a kid (the smaller the better) made him look alluringly child friendly and approachably shaggable.

Ironically, it was how Poppy had met Sam.

She could still distinctly remember the pictures she'd taken of him as he skipped around in a circle of children a quarter of his size, doing ring-a-ring o' roses. Poppy had known Sam, a stranger at that point, wanted her to look at him, that he was performing, but still—she had been endeared. While she was packing up, he'd come over and asked if she had a boyfriend, or a husband. When Poppy said, "No," Sam said, "Right, I'll get my coat."

That first night, Sam walked Poppy through the city, carrying her equipment and chatting animatedly. He was not an objectively handsome man, but his manner and confidence were attractive. He'd kissed her on her doorstep, taken her number, and pursued her in an old-fashioned, full-on way. He'd turned up at her flat the following day with flowers. Had taken her for dinner. When they slept together, the first time, he breathily told her he was falling in love with her. Sam was always so sure of himself that it was easy to go along with him, and Poppy let him carry her over his shoulder into a relationship. He was very different to her in all the best ways and she liked how he saw things with such clarity, how he said things with such certainty—she found his presence in her life reassuring. Although Sam was totally different to Dandelion, they were both forthright and self-confident, qualities that Poppy greatly admired and knew she lacked.

Uncle Digby sidled up next to Poppy, with two glasses of champagne. He had one of those noses that looked like an organic root vegetable and his face was properly wet. "I've come to your rescue," he said as he put a hand on the base of Poppy's spine. In front of them, the small bridesmaid began to scream, refusing to be put to bed. Poppy lifted her camera and took pictures of the little cherub as she began to scratch and kick.

"I want to do bad things to you," Digby whispered so close to Poppy's ear that she winced at the carcass of his breath.

This was not the first time a drunk wedding guest had shown her unwanted attention, but it was perhaps the most disgusting. Her camera was now hanging from the strap around her neck and she was looking down at Digby's glass below her face and then, as if summoned by the untoward behavior, Poppy heard Dandelion's outraged voice: *Stand up for yourself, Poppet! Go on! Show that turd who's boss!*

Subtly, Poppy coughed spit into her mouth. She was aware of herself—revolted, but she was also aware of her sister—excited, delighted. She tipped her face forward and dribbled into Digby's glass, but he was so consumed with whispering increasingly wanton indignities into her ear that he didn't notice as the spit sank in a globule and came to rest at the bottom of his glass, like a sugar cube.

Reeling, Poppy lifted her hand and held the back of it against her mouth as Digby paused for breath, smirked, and took a sip.

"I think my taxi is . . . I'd better . . ." Poppy didn't finish making excuses, she was too appalled at her own bad behavior. She turned and fast walked around the perimeter of the marquee until she was out in the coolness of the night. She stalked past the stone busts of long-dead children, through the center of the rose garden, past the fountain that trickled a never-ending spurt. She crunched over gravel and then began to run, clutching her camera bag to her body—pretending she didn't see the couple lying half-naked underneath a rhododendron. She ran all the way to the top field, which was being used as the car park, and finally stopped, bent over her legs, and exhaled a ragged sigh.

Alone under an oak tree, Poppy opened the last miniature gin and leaned her back against the rough bark. The music from the disco carried through the night, with the intermittent cheering of tiny voices. Just another party—the running stitch of hedonism through time. People distracting themselves from the slow bleed out of life by getting wasted, getting married, getting laid underneath the stars that have seen it all before.

She still had another half an hour until she'd arranged to meet Betty for their respective taxi pickup (Betty was going to Somerset where she lived, and Poppy was going to a local hotel for the night), and so she fished around in her bag for the first packet of cigarettes she'd bought in years.

She imagined Dandelion's body rolling around the trunk of the oak so they were standing with their shoulders touching. She imagined her sister finishing the last swig of gin and taking a cigarette from the packet, her profile tilting up toward the sky and exhaling smoke so that it grew from her mouth like branches. *Well done, Poppet, liked that gross spit thing a lot. I heard that old bastard say he wanted to taste you—well now, lucky dog, he has.*

Poppy rubbed the half-smoked cigarette down the gnarled skin of the oak and let it splutter into sparks. She opened Hinge and scrolled through all Dandelion's pictures. Then Jake's. "Fine," she said. She would call him. It was what her sister wanted. It was what she would have done herself.

The phone rang, once, twice. A second of silence. "Dandelion?"

Poppy moved her gaze, let it settle on the dark oak leaves above her as they fluttered their applause. "Hi, Jake."

"Well, this is a surprise."

"I'm sorry," she said, "about all the not calling."

"All that frantic not calling," Jake agreed. "Just *not* calling me constantly. It's like . . . chill with the not calling."

Jake's voice reverberated inside Poppy's body, and she tingled. She laughed. "Mm, well, exactly. Things have been hectic. I'm sorry."

"I forgive you. Obviously. What you up to?"

Poppy thought of the spit. She thought of her sister. She thought of the woman who, all Dandelion's life, she'd been coaching Poppy to be. "I just did something mad," she admitted.

"Oh yeah?" Jake asked. She heard a shuffling noise and imagined him propping himself up in bed, putting down a book, a dim lamp beside him casting a warm glow on his skin. "Good mad or bad mad?"

Poppy walked around the tree slowly, watching her feet in her sister's chunky leather loafers that she used to find hideous. These were her shoes now and she was determined to fill them. "Is there a difference between good mad and bad mad?"

"Errrr, yeah!" Jake's voice made Poppy smile. His voice made her feel like everything was going to end up good, or even great. "There's a massive difference, Dandelion," he said. "Huge."

10

Monday, 21st April

"Welcome, beautiful beings." A birdlike woman with a shaved head was sitting on the floor next to a man in a purple felt waist-coat embroidered with mushrooms. They were all in a candlelit sitting room in a top-floor flat on Dalston Junction, and behind them, a shelf jostled with books and an abundance of houseplants and what was clearly a television covered by a batik sarong.

On the floor in front of them were crystals and different-sized bronze bowls. "Singing bowls," Jetta had informed Poppy, with a borderline smug nod as they'd sat down on bolsters next to each other.

"For those who I've not met, my name is Thorn." Thorn had an Irish accent and a low, slow voice. Tiny hands, a big mouth, a sheer top, and lots of earrings. "I will be your guide this evening, working with the energy of Mother Cacao." She began burning a small fragrant stick, turning it over through a candle flame. Once it had started to smoke, she stood and wafted it around the woman next to her, in a cross between a baptism and a dance. On his guitar, the man in the purple waistcoat played a folkie song that didn't have any lyrics—only accompanying moans.

"I think he's forgotten the words," Poppy said under her breath, leaning into Jetta.

Jetta ignored her.

"What's that stick, Jetta?"

"Palo santo," Jetta whispered back, without looking at Poppy, still maintaining the special holy expression she'd assumed as soon as they'd walked through the door. When Thorn started whirling the smoke over Jetta, Jetta basked in it a little too much, and Poppy couldn't bring herself to watch; she closed her eyes and forced a relaxed smile until the welcome smoke had moved over her and come to an end.

As she sat back down, Thorn said she'd love for her "fellow travelers" to introduce themselves. Looking around, Poppy reflected that *fellow travelers* really did feel like a good description for the other people. Six women, two men. "Please find a crystal you feel drawn to," Thorn purred, "and we'll build a spiral of intention as we open the energetic portal."

Jetta had sold this "cacao ceremony" to Poppy by making it sound like a calming hot chocolate thing, where they could lie down in the dark as someone bonged a gong. Historically, Poppy wasn't one for spirituality stuff. Dandelion and Jetta, on the other hand, were always getting enlightened. Taking ayahuasca in Peru. Panchakarma in Kerala. Vipassana in Wales. Poppy preferred to stay at home, receive their gushing, addled, sporadic messages from her sofa, while she took journeys into Netflix and worked with the energy of crisps and wine.

Thorn turned to the woman on her left and nodded, indicating she should start the introductions. "Hello," the woman said in a Glaswegian accent. "I'm Letty. My intention is fertility. I've . . ."

Poppy wondered if Jake had messaged her since she last checked her phone.

That call under the oak tree two days ago had lasted the duration of the taxi ride to the hotel, through check-in (on mute), through a thirty-minute soak in the huge freestanding bath with gold claw-feet (on speaker), and then another hour lying on her bed, in a hotel-monogrammed robe. Poppy had only said goodbye because she was so exhausted that she'd accidentally fallen into a micro-sleep while Jake had been telling her about his ex-wife's new boyfriend's YouTube channel—which seemed like a good point in proceedings for Poppy to tap out. When she'd woken the following morning, he'd already sent her a song ("Got My Mojo Working," Muddy Waters), and since then, it seemed Poppy and Jake's conversation had no end; it merely paused momentarily while they both went about their actual lives.

Poppy thought of Jake's recent messages: his questions, his x's that clung suggestively to certain sentences, and the possible string of new green dots glinting in the depths of her handbag right that minute. On her walk over to Dalston, he'd messaged and asked if she could meet him for a date on Wednesday, late afternoon. Yes, I'd love that, Poppy typed back, with a string of emojis that alluded to the flirtatious private language they were building—the winky face (their go-to), and then some tenuous carpentry imagery: a log, an ax, and the farmer woman in a hat holding a massive ear of sweet corn.

"Hi, I'm Petro," another of the travelers said, "and my intention is Dragon Energy." Petro placed a dark green crystal in the spiral they'd been building on the carpet. "It's hard for me to leave the house . . ." Like the others, misfortunes flowed from Petro and lapped at Poppy's ankles unpleasantly. She looked at the door—she kind of wanted to leave.

And then they were on to Jetta. "Last week was my best friend's birthday. The first since she passed, and so we wanted to mark it by doing something that felt, perhaps, healing." Jetta had been holding a rose quartz and, at this, she placed it purposefully in the spiral. She turned to Poppy, and Poppy could see a reflection of candlelight in her eyes. "I'm here with Dandelion's sister, who I've known since we were kids and . . ." As she talked, Poppy thought back to when Jetta had shown up in their village, having moved with her dad down from York after her parents' divorce. Jetta and Dandelion were in the same school year and had become best friends instantly. The bigger girls had been inclusive with Poppy (when they weren't being bitches), and, mainly, they'd moved through the world, up until last August, as a trio.

When Poppy first came to London, the three of them lived together. Partied together, had seen sunrise after sunrise. Dandelion had been there at the birth of Jetta's children, and Jetta had been there at Dandelion's death. She'd stood next to Poppy—their little fingers linked and shoulders shaking—as Dandelion's casket had been lowered and the rain coughed into their faces, two hundred and forty-seven days before.

"And I think, really, for us, if Mother Cacao can . . ." Jetta was still talking. She'd been talking for longer than anyone else. She was like Dandelion in that way—didn't apologize for her voice. Felt worthy of people's time. And now, as Poppy watched her friend speak—using her hands to mold her feelings—she recognized a gold chain bracelet on Jetta's wrist she knew Dandelion had bought her to mark the birth of her daughter.

Poppy smiled, pleased to see Jetta had reclaimed it, because there had been a strange swath of time last year where Jetta had taken the bracelet off, like the purposeful removal of a wedding band. It had been a very difficult time—just before the worst time—and when Poppy asked Jetta about why she was trying to shut Dandelion out of her life, Jetta had said, "I can't deal with her anymore, Poppet. I'm sorry, I just can't." It had been deeply upsetting and terribly perplexing for Poppy, because although the three of them quarreled often (or rather the two of them fought with Dandelion), the unpleasantness was usually short-lived. Scraps. Scrapes. Flesh wounds. But that last fight between Jetta and Dandelion had felt malignant, and different in the way that neither of them had bitched to Poppy about what had gone down.

"Poppy, we're so pleased to have you with us." Thorn placed one hand flat to her chest. "What's your intention for this evening?"

Poppy's mind was blank. She couldn't speak. She looked at Jetta.

"We'd love to call Dandelion in," Jetta said.

Thorn nodded, sincere, radiant, and said that they would be calling in all their ancestors. "Our four directions of north, south, east, and west, the sun, the moon, the planets, our mothers, fathers, grandfathers, grandmothers . . ." As Thorn continued the extremely inclusive list, Poppy turned her attention to the crystals. She reached for a smooth round stone she felt drawn to because it looked like a pebble from the beach back home and she placed it down in the spiral they'd all laid out. The purple waistcoat man stood, left, and came back with a tray, mugs, and a saucepan of dark liquid cacao. Thorn filled each of the mugs, while the waistcoat man made sonorous sounds by running a tiny mallet around the lips of the metal singing bowls. When Thorn lifted her cup and took a sip, the rest of the travelers followed.

The cacao didn't taste like hot chocolate. It was thick and gritty. In a way it tasted ancient; it tasted quite profound. Poppy drank until she reached sediment at the bottom of the mug. Then, following Jetta's lead, she plumped her bolster and lay down. She closed her eyes, pulled her cardigan sleeves over her hands, and curled up small, burrowing into Dandelion's cashmere scarf. Unsure of what she was meant to do, she pushed her tongue to the roof of her mouth, silently asking the four syllables of her sister's name: *Dan-de-li-on?*

The music in the room was more intense now. Poppy felt stirred. The music was inside of her and outside of her, it had a weight—it held her. London fell away and memories spread around Poppy like a universe of photographs and film. She drew each memory toward her and looked at them in turn, going back and back through time. She was at a bonfire on the beach with friends, singing. Holding hands with Sam on their sofa, watching telly, their legs intertwined. Her parents' ruby anniversary, a summer dinner in the sprawling cottage garden—her dad made a speech, and they all clapped and cried. Dandelion's thirtieth: Studio 54 themed, in the toilets, doing coke. They were teenagers bodyboarding in the sea; Dandelion's bikini got whipped off, and she ran back home shrieking with her bottom out. They were getting drunk on rum straight from the bottle with two Spanish brothers who were in Devon on holiday; that night was Poppy's first kiss.

Then a close-up of Dandelion's hair, her own hair too.

Their hair used to be so wild when they were children. In the school holidays, they'd never brush it, and it would clump weighty like clematis over their backs. To Poppy, her hair had been a habitat, a cloud cover, and somewhere good to hide—until the day Dandelion took the kitchen scissors and their dad's clippers to it. And now, Poppy was back in that day—she was under the kitchen table. Nine years old and patchy bald.

Both their parents were shouting at Dandelion, as Poppy watched three different pairs of feet shuffling over the lino like they were modern dancing.

"The male gaze?" Their father was incredulous. "Dandelion, you've gone too far, my girl. You've gone too—"

"Not the fucking abstract notion of the fucking male gaze, Dad!" The swear words had been shocking. "I'm talking about men, looking at me. At Poppy. Every day. *Every day*. It's not okay! It's fucking gross!"

Beneath the table, Poppy began to cry.

"She has no idea what the male gaze even is, Dandelion," their mother said, her voice rising with an anger that was very rare. "Nor, I think, do you."

And then Poppy was looking at Dandelion; her pale eyes had grown larger and more scary now that she had no hair. "Poppet! Come out and tell them what we're protesting?" But Poppy didn't want to; her sister was a horror film. "Poppet! Come out! Now!"

Poppy slid along the floor, using only her arms to pull the rest of her body, like a dog with worms. She tilted her face so that she was looking at the reassurance of the kettle and rubbed a small hand over her stubbled skull. "We're protesting the objectification of girls as sexual objects for the pleasure of heterosexual men," she recited, having been forced to repeat this phrase over the course of the day, until she knew it by heart.

Their mother pulled a kitchen chair out, fell down onto it. "She's only nine years old, Dandelion."

"Exactly!" Dandelion shouted. "I wish she didn't have to know about it, but she fucking does!"

"OUT!" their father yelled. "I can't even look at you. Out of my sight. Out of my house, you selfish girl."

And now, lying on the floor in Dalston, her head on the bolster, her mouth covered with her sister's scarf, her hair again grown long—Poppy saw something of that day that she had previously never remembered. Dandelion was shaving Poppy's head, actually in the process of it—they'd been in her bedroom, and Poppy was sitting on a chair in front of the mirror.

"Stay still!" Dandelion scolded. "Stay still!"

But Poppy had been trembling, whining, and so Dandelion turned the clippers off and gripped her roughly by the shoulders, in a way that hurt. "One day you'll understand, Poppy." She was flame-faced, impassioned. "I'm doing this for you."

Poppy opened her eyes. She clapped a hand to her ear, sat up. She was panting. Everyone else was still lying down except the purple waistcoat man and Thorn. "Dandelion?" Poppy gasped. She'd been rocked with her sister's anger. She knelt, she stood. "DANDELION?" she called.

Thorn held both her open palms to Poppy. "Just go with it," she said. "Let her come to you—"

Poppy was shouting. Or Dandelion was shouting. One of them. Or both. One of them threw a bolster at the sarong-draped television. One of them trashed the portal, kicked crystals around the room. And then Poppy was out in the hallway, scrabbling with her shoes. As she skidded down the faded carpet of the communal stairs, over flyers for pizza joints and decorators, Jetta was behind her shouting, "Pops! What's going on? Come back!"

Poppy ran over roads, through traffic, across the Downs. If she could run all the way to Devon, back to their childhood, she would have. To save herself. To save her sister. To work things out. To understand. Instead, she ran to Islington, to her sister's home. Up the stairs, into the bedroom, where she slid under all the covers of the bed—the whole time, Dandelion's words pounding in her thoughts in a bullying rhythm: *I'm doing this for you. I'm doing this for you. One day you'll understand. I do all this for you.*

11

Wednesday, 23rd April

Jake

Jake stood in the center of the Millennium Bridge, waiting. He was concerned that Dandelion would find the idea to meet on this spot unoriginal, off-the-shelf romance. But he went ahead and suggested it anyway because he had an image in his head of how it would look cinematically—and this was it. He checked his phone again; he'd arrived early. He could have dawdled, but he was desperate for the date to start.

Already in life, Jake had done a fair bit of waiting for Dandelion. An embarrassing amount of champing at the bit. Obviously, it had taken her a year to reply to his initial message. And then, after their date—not one peep for a week. That first time he'd called her didn't count, because she hadn't said a word. And so, Jake had been in the process of making peace with the fact she didn't like him and he'd got it all wrong, until, UNTIL, she'd called him back and they'd spoken for over two hours, which was something Jake hadn't done with anyone for, probably, fifteen years.

He would have seen her the very next day, if he could have, but he had Billy. And so today was their first chance—two weeks after they met. Of course Jake was not so naive, or un-self-aware, as to deny that Dandelion's sporadic disinterest fueled his fixation. But there was something genuine and intoxicating there as well, outside of the sex appeal and mysticism. In the time that he'd spent with her, or even just reading her messages, Jake felt like he was breathing the purest type of air.

On the river, a long boat was approaching with rows of seats running across it horizontally, in pews. Someone was standing up with a microphone, flinging their arms in different directions, pointing out sights to the spatter of tourists aboard. As the boat passed beneath the bridge, Jake clocked its name: *Lioness.* "Oh, bloody hell," he said, feeling this to be a sign that he should immediately start believing in signs.

"Talking to yourself, Jake?"

He glanced over his shoulder—her face was a relief. He sighed. She looked Parisian, she looked perfect. Belted into a checked coat he liked a lot with the collar turned up and a red beret. Her skin so clear Jake could see all the way in and through. She winked. He winked. *Their thing.*

Jake gave her a kiss on the cheek and a tiny cuddle, pressed into her for a second. "Oh, it's just that that boat is called *Lioness.* So I thought of you. Dandy . . . lion . . . Lion . . . ess," he said, spelling it out, because she was looking back at him, seemingly nonplussed.

She hunched her shoulders up to her ears, turned to the water. "It's so windy!" She lifted one hand to her head, holding her beret. With the other, she pressed down her long skirt, which was dancing precariously, threatening to do a Marilyn.

"Oh, sorry. Let's go." They headed south along the bridge, curving toward the Tate Modern. This, too, was how Jake imagined it. Imagined her: stylish and windswept. "I like your hat," he said as

75

they turned the corner onto the river walk. "Very Prince . . . raspberry beret," he clarified.

"Thank you." She took the beret off and smiled at it. Smoothed her hair down, slowed to watch a street performer, a woman dressed as a ghost—a sheet over her head with cutout eyeholes, waving her arms above her head.

On the escalator to the third-floor gallery, Jake kept thinking how it would feel to hold her hand. She had a ring on every finger. "I like your rings," he said, then immediately mentally reprimanded himself not to give her any more crap little compliments. He wondered if she thought he was insincere. He wondered what she thought of him. He wondered if she went on lots of dates. He wondered how long she'd been single for. He wondered when she'd last had sex, and with whom. He wondered if she was looking for a long-term partner, because she didn't specify on her dating profile, although she did clearly say that she didn't want kids. Was that because she didn't like kids? Because that would, obviously, be an issue for a potential stepmother. Or maybe it was climate related. Or maybe she just didn't want to be a biological mother—which Jake thought was bloody fair enough. Though maybe she *had* children already, which would definitely be better than hating them. "Hey, random, but . . ." Jake said as they stepped off the escalator. She was holding out both her hands, showing him her jewelry, and he realized that this wasn't the right moment for *Sooo, you hate kids?*

"Very cool, I like that gold snaky one," Jake said instead. "Do you have bells on your toes?" And then, in his mind, he was sucking each of Dandelion's toes, popping them into his mouth like a Roman emperor with grapes. Which was surprising, because a foot had never occurred to him as an appealing appendage before, but Jake desired this woman so deeply, the thought of being perverse with her was highly arousing. If she was game—he was prepared to do bad shit.

They joined the queue for the exhibition, Jake passed his membership card to the old guy at the entrance, and they walked in through the open arch. Dandelion turned immediately to the literature about Van Gogh's last three months in Paris, and Jake found he wasn't able to concentrate on reading. He was eager, too quick, whereas she stood in front of each painting for a time, taking it in. He tried to slow himself and went to stand by a painting of trembling rooftops, but all he could think about was the click-click sounds of her shoes on the wooden floor. She was in the left-hand corner of the space, she was moving again, she was standing still. *Do not look*, Jake told himself. *Do Not Look At Her.* But then the clicking was coming toward him and he was panting like a puppy, head over his shoulder, watching her approach. It felt like a very long time that he was waiting for her to get to him, and he was embarrassed by his eagerness and the fact that he was staring. He sidestepped in front of a painting of yellow fields and glared at it—thought exclusively of her face.

She stood right behind him and spoke close to his neck: "Which is your favorite?"

Jake could almost taste her in his mouth; his salivary glands were going ballistic. He swallowed. "Shhh. Would you mind? I'm trying to appreciate art!"

"Sorry." She breathed a laugh, stepped forward so they were side by side. She was holding on to opposite elbows, making a rail across her body; her coat was draped over her forearms and beneath it she was wearing a tight green T-shirt. The tops of her fingers were touching Jake's arm. His actual skin. Her closeness, the silence, their breathing were so erotic that Jake felt certain today he would kiss her. He imagined the kiss playing on a big screen—open mouths, gentle tongues, heads twisting, grasping hands.

"But which is your favorite though?" she asked him seriously.

She was so close to him that Jake could smell the ripe cherries and roasted coffee of her breath, and he wanted to turn and bite into her arm. Take her into a toilet cubicle and . . . see what happened next.

"Jake?"

"Urm." Jake's voice was unattractively strangled. He was looking at her mouth. *Her mouth, her mouth.* It struck him that this could be the first-kiss moment.

"Are you all right?"

"Me? I'm great. Um, favorite, favorite, favorite?" And with his blathering, Jake felt the perfect moment pass. When they went outside again, though, he'd take her in his arms, she'd bend one knee, her leg lifting behind her like a woman on a train platform welcoming back her long-lost lover, and, ideally, she'd have the beret back on.

"If you had to take one of these home with you and keep it forever," she prompted, clearly trying to help, "which would you choose?"

Jake turned to look at the painting right in front of him, then the next one, the next. He tried to consider her question. "Out of everything in here?"

"Yes," she said. "The whole exhibition. The one you'd keep forever."

"Then I'd choose you." Jake crossed his arms and looked back at her.

She laughed so loudly that the gallery burst open and all the paintings leaped from the walls and began to tingle and shimmy in a dance. "Stop it!" She pushed at him and Jake swayed backward and then forward toward her like a metronome, refusing to go away.

"Being serious," Jake said. "Dandelion, I think you're mesmeric. I think you're—"

She looked down at the floor. "Thank you." She glanced back up at him, then turned on her heel and walked away through an arch, into the next room.

Jake jogged through her wake, then slowed to a walk so it was less like he was chasing her, but in his mind he was screaming at the bones of her ankles: *Come back! Let's kiss! Don't leave!*

Outside, they stood by the Thames, both leaning on the wall, looking in opposite directions along the South Bank. It had clouded over so that no actual sky was visible, and the wind had picked up even more.

"Hey, so," Jake said, glancing back at her. "I don't even know what you do for a living?" From their date, their chats and messages, he had begun to build a fuller picture of her—her personality, her humor, things she liked—but he was also aware he was missing some basic, essential facts.

She turned her face toward him with her chin lowered, her eyes cast down to his chest. "Let's not talk about work."

"How come?"

"Maybe I don't like my work."

"No one likes their work," Jake said, aware he sounded gruff, like a real dad.

"Do you like your work?" She pulled her beret from her bag and positioned it on her head at a pleasingly jaunty angle.

"I love it," Jake admitted, and they both laughed a single note.

"I know you're a big success." She looked out at the water, away from him. "I googled you."

"You did?" Jake tried to keep the glee from his voice. "How d'ya know my full name?" Googling him most certainly displayed a level of interest from Dandelion, which delighted him, and besides, Jake had googled himself, obviously, and he knew both the search and image results made him look pretty good.

"Did you not know you'd put your full name on your profile?"

"Oops. I did not. Well, it's only fair you tell me your full name. And, now that I think of it, I'd like your number too."

Her head tilted as she watched a seagull shuffle over shingles. "Isn't talking through Hinge fine?"

"Yes. It's fine, but I'd vastly prefer something more real." Jake opened his palms to the city, the river, the clouds. He needed more of her, as much as he could get.

"Now is real." She took in a big gulp of air like she was drinking. He watched her swallow. "I don't think my number will make any difference."

"Are you married or something?" Jake blurted. "Do you have kids? Do you hate kids?"

"Do I *hate kids?*"

"No, I mean . . . what do you think about having kids? Not with me, I have one already, obviously. I have the best one, but just checking you're into them. Him. Mine. Yours. Um. What?"

"I love kids," she said, laughing the sound of wind chimes. Then, more serious: "And sorry if I seem guarded. It's just I want to take things slowly. If that's okay?"

Jake looked out over the water. The white horses cresting the waves had begun to leap with more panache. He could see the MI6 building, the extravagant layers of it. It looked like a wedding cake. It looked like a tomb. "So, what you're saying is . . . you're a spy?"

"No comment." She took a step away from him and brushed one tiptoe along the pavement like a ballerina. Jake watched her and wondered if he was inadvertently dating a famous person who needed an abnormal level of privacy, or perhaps she had been seriously hurt by someone and was paranoid.

"If I'm honest with you . . ." She was speaking out into the wind, over the water, her words carried back to him. "Sometimes, I worry that I failed at being the person I was meant to be." She laughed a lament.

"Oh. I, er . . ." Jake had not been expecting that level of vulnerability, and it floored him. "I . . ."

"That sounds pathetic," she said. In her eyes, Jake could see some kind of pain; it glinted with a sharpness. "Pretend I didn't say that." She stretched her arms out to either side along the wall, holding on. "I don't really know why I did."

Jake thought of his mother—and how she had fooled most people, a lot of the time. He wondered if Dandelion was depressed, too, struggling with secret demons. "With the greatest of respect," he said. He reached out and touched her back. Beneath her coat, he could feel a shoulder blade. "You've got so much time to do whatever, be whoever. To find the life you want to live, if that's what you're worried about. You're only forty. You're only halfway through!"

"Not necessarily, Jake." She spoke in a way that was surprisingly scolding as she buried her hands in her pockets, raised her shoulders in defense.

"No . . . well, sorry if I overstepped the mark. I just want to help," Jake said, feeling a little offended.

"I know you do. It's fine," she said. She looked away and exhaled.

Jake wanted to make her smile again. "I apologize, I didn't mean to sound—"

"I get it," she said. "I shouldn't have snapped."

"No." Jake shook his head. "I'm *more* sorry."

"You want to win the sorry thing?" she asked, looking back at him, one eyebrow raised.

"Yes. Me." Jake nodded.

"Fine," she agreed. "You."

"Tarzan . . ." Jake pointed at himself. He was freestyling. He nodded encouragingly.

She shook her head.

Jake opened both his eyes as wide as they would go, slid his gaze to his left, back at the Tate, and then across to his right, at the river, insinuating he was waiting for her to play. "Me Tarzan." He pointed at himself again, prompting. "You . . . ?"

"Jake, I'm not going to say *Jane*."

"Okay." Jake reached for her and, without thinking, pulled her into him and gave her a hug. He let his face fall into her hair.

"You're silly," she said.

Jake let go of her and took a step back. She was half smiling. There was a more mischievous glimmer in her eyes now, and he was pleased that they'd moved through a bad moment so quickly.

"I know." He shrugged. "Do you hate it?"

"I don't hate it."

"You like it. I can tell." Jake turned his head to the sky and squinted, although it wasn't at all bright.

This date was very different from their first. Very different to what he'd been expecting. Very different from dates with other women where they'd got pissed as a way to construct artificial affection. But now, standing alone with Dandelion by the Thames, Jake was intrigued by his own fear and fascination. He felt as if he could stand next to her forever if she'd let him, eternally unraveling her mind and trying to make her smile and tell him secrets. He could see them in different moments of a shared future: in an airport queue, on a sandy beach, at a funeral, up a mountain, under the covers and a billion stars.

"You know what?" Jake said after a minute, once he'd clarified his own perspective. "I don't care what you do for work." He would give her all the time she needed to open up to him. "I shall accept your elusivity. Or at least endeavor to accept it. And, if it's any consolation, although I've done fine professionally, my personal life is . . ." Jake whistled and shook his head. "I certainly failed at being the man I hoped to be," he said, adopting her turn of phrase.

"Lots of people get divorced, Jake." She adjusted her hair over her shoulder, and it coiled itself as if someone was winding it around their fingers.

When Jake rehearsed his soliloquies in the mirror, this was exactly the sort of prompt he imagined preceding them: justifying himself to someone he liked a lot. "Well, I guess good men do bad thi . . ." he began, but couldn't bring himself to finish the sentence, because aloud—to her, here, now—it sounded trite and stupid. "What I mean is, well . . . I cheated." This was his biggest secret. This was his greatest shame. "It was once. I'll regret it forever. And although I *did* cheat, I don't want *to be* a cheat. If that makes sense? It was wrong, but things were tough. My ex—she can be cold and, frankly, quite mean. And when a colleague started giving me attention . . ."

"We all make mistakes." She shook her head as if reflecting on a personal misdemeanor. "But what I will say is, even if your ex was difficult, or whatever—don't blame *her* for *you* cheating."

"I'm not blaming her . . ." An acidic sensation flashed through Jake's stomach, a type of anger. A type of hurt. He gulped and rubbed a hand over his throat. "I literally just said it was a terrible mistake and I'll regret it forever. But now, looking back, I do wonder if Zoe had postnatal mood things going on, because she really was—"

"I don't want to know, Jake."

Jake crossed his arms in front of his chest and leaned his weight back into his heels. "Right, so. Well . . ." He pivoted around in a slow circle to gather himself, but he was still annoyed. "If I can't tell you about me and I'm not allowed to ask you any questions, where does that leave us, conversationally? The weather? Well, hey"—he made a show of looking up into the sky—"it's windy!"

"That's completely not what I'm saying," she said. "It's just that I'm a private person and, likewise, I don't need, or want, to know everything, immediately, about your personal life, or past." The wind made a whistling noise as it passed through them, and she did her coat buttons up, all the way to her throat.

Jake must have been looking hurt, because then she said that she was sorry. "This doesn't mean I don't want us to get to know each other. But, I guess, I don't want to rush."

"I can respect that." Jake conceded, realizing that he really could. He was very close to her now, looking into her eyes. They were the palest eyes he'd ever seen and so full of cloud; beneath one of them mascara had slightly smudged. "I promise I won't inundate you with endless questions, but, I suppose, I just want to check that you're okay," he told her. "And I wonder if you're happy?" This was a silly question; the concept of happiness was too broad and the definition too subjective. But watching her bite her lip, Jake realized he'd asked because he knew that she was sad.

"Right now, in this moment"—she pointed at the ground—"yes, I am. What about you?"

"Happy? Yeah! Course!" Although as soon as he said it, Jake had a fear of the happiness ending. "But I guess I feel a little scared."

"Oh, yes?" she asked. "Of what?"

"I'm scared of lots of things." Immediately, Jake thought of his little boy's face. "Like, well . . . I'm scared I've already failed my son.

That one day, soon, my ex will tell Billy that I betrayed her trust." Jake looked out to the water's edge, noticed how it coiled and curved like the body of a snake. "And I'm worried her version of events will turn Billy against me. Just as I resent my father on my less generous days. Pass the pain on, you know? I had an opportunity to break the cycle—not just of cheating, but of fucking up my kid, and I . . ." His voice wavered. He was so surprised at his own honesty that he twisted his head all the way in the other direction and focused on a family taking pictures of each other standing in front of an overflowing recycling bin. He tried to concentrate on them, not to be confronted by the grim reality of himself.

"You're not stuck in a cycle. It doesn't work like that." Her voice was soft behind him.

"I think it does though. Evidence would suggest." Jake turned back to her and gave her a smile. "Sorry. My oversharing is *not* sexy. Let's go and get a drink."

"We're all scared," she said. "At least I am, anyway."

"What are you scared of?" Jake asked.

"I'm scared of my life."

Jake laughed quickly, but only because he felt nervous. "Do you mean your death?"

"No." She touched her ear, glanced up at the sky before looking back at him. "I'm scared of myself, I guess." She looked pale and drowned then, and Jake felt frightened of her too. He turned his head away in case she saw his thoughts. The family by the bin had gone now. He blinked at where they'd been standing, at the yellow chip boxes and water bottles on the ground.

"It's really beginning to blow a gale. Maybe we should . . ." The tone in her voice had changed, and when he looked back at her, Jake knew the conversation was over. It had moved him, though, to talk so honestly.

Emboldened, he pulled her even closer toward him by her coat collar, very gently, so their bodies were touching. He looked down at her wildflower face, and every single thought and memory and terrible fear left him so that there was only her. Smoke was flooding from all the windows of his mind. If there had ever been a moment for a kiss, then this was surely it.

"Dandelion," Jake whispered. The wind snatched her name from him. Rubbish scuttled along the pavement all around them in synchronized movements like a choreographed dance. "Dandelion, I . . ."

"My hat!" She turned and pulled away. "My hat!"

The beret had blown off her head. It was caught in a gust and it was six feet away, then twelve. It swirled upward and swayed, darted over the seawall. She was already running away from him, and then she was standing with both hands to her face.

Jake began jogging toward her. It was amazing how quickly that had just happened. "Whoa!" he said, through a laugh. "The raspberry beret has a life of its own!"

"Where is it? Can you see it?" She wasn't looking at him. Her eyes were darting over everything, and from the stiffness in her body, Jake could tell his amusement had been misjudged.

"It's there!" he said, pointing. The tide was out, leaving a littered area of exposed beach, and next to a brown beer bottle, at the water's edge, was her hat. Jake reviewed the distance down—it was far. Probably fifteen feet, a sheer drop. "There must be some steps somewhere further up. Let's go and have a look." He reached for her hand, but she shook him off and, instead, hoisted herself up onto the wall and pulled her legs over. She launched off, her coat and skirt lifting. When she landed on the stony bit of beach beneath, she fell forward onto her hands and knees, and Jake heard a lungful of air push out in a painful-sounding *ooomfff*. But then she was up and stumbling toward the smudge of red as it lifted and twirled as if it was playing, animate.

Jake pulled himself up onto the wall, but the drop down looked like a broken ankle; it looked like a dislocated knee. He fast walked along the pathway, searching for some steps, calling her name. "Dandelion!" The beret twirled into the water. "Oh no." Jake's body clenched as he watched her rip her coat from her body, fling her shoes off, and then launch toward the floating beret like she was tackling an invisible opponent. Then she was gone, she was under—lost to the shit death water of the motherfucking Thames.

12

Friday, 25th April

When the lift doors opened into Yesness's reception, Jake finished humming, but with a dramatic flourish, to show he wasn't embarrassed about humming to himself in one of the hippest ad agencies in London. Although, potentially, no one would have heard him anyway because the music was always banging, dance floor loud. Today it was a UK garage track that used to be massive, play everywhere, all the time, when he was in his teens.

Karla was talking to the receptionist guy, who was wearing lederhosen, without a shirt underneath. The staff at Yesness had mullets and monocles and, for the most part, did not accessorize with smiles. Karla was Jake's favorite person to work with here, a German producer, who managed, very efficiently, to be both supercool and incredibly nice. She looked up, sprang from the desk, and bounded toward him as the receptionist picked up a ringing phone, as if it was a major hassle.

"Busy morning in the scrap metal yard?" Jake asked, nodding down at Karla's faded boilersuit. She always looked like she'd been dancing all night in a basement in Deptford or had recently emerged from a wild swim in a reservoir, both of which, often, she had.

"Ah!" Karla laughed, ever generous with Jake's jokes. "I was on a shoot until three this morning. Girl, I'm tired. How are you?"

"Great!" Jake followed Karla past the glass-fronted meeting rooms, all named after artists: Schiele, O'Keeffe, Kusama.

At Rego, she turned and used her bum to push open the door. "And how's the dating going?"

"'Mazing," Jake said. "I've met someone I really like."

He thought of Dandelion.

If they stayed together forever, he could tell their future grand-children (or her step-grandchildren, depending on how that kids thing played out) how, on their second date, she'd jumped *into the Thames*. Obviously, it had been shocking to see at the time, but, Jake had since decided, it was extremely courageously hot. She'd front crawled right over to the beret like a total ninja, retrieved it, seemingly with ease. Afterward, once Jake was sure she wasn't in need of a stomach pump, he'd insisted on getting her a taxi home. When she'd got back to hers, she called and said sorry—apparently the beret was very special, had belonged to her granny. From the war.

"You know Skye, right?" Karla asked Jake.

"Hi!" Skye, the account director, had a dyed purple pixie cut and wore a vintage bridesmaid dress (lilac, puffy sleeves, bows, highly flammable). She was arranged on a big double-sized beanbag next to a French creative whom Jake had met a few times, called Colin (pronounced *Cola*), who was a total bellend. A bellend with a heavy-browed vampiric face, like Robert Pattinson, and an accent that made people swoon, regardless of sexual orientation. Colin was a lady-killer who consistently impressed everyone—including the Cannes Lions jury, including Jake—with his work.

"You know Colin," Karla said, "and this is Sydney, who is in-terning with us." Karla nodded at a young woman reclining on a smaller beanbag, wearing a toweling bucket hat with daisies on, cargo pants that were as large as an actual parachute, and a top that was just a wisp.

"Skye, Colin," Jake said, nodding at them. He got a pathetic kick out of pronouncing Colin's name the British way. "Nice to meet you," he said to Sydney as he took a seat on a red sofa in the corner, pleased he wouldn't have to try to look authoritative on a beanbag.

"We've actually met before," Sydney said, propping herself up on an elbow. "I was in a commercial you made for KFC."

"Sydney was a model, but she's moving into production," Karla said.

"Oh, yes, hi." Jake worked with a lot of attractive people; such was the nature of his job. In his mind their beauty fused into one and he wouldn't necessarily ever recognize each of them individually again, and besides, faces were not his forte.

"So anyway—Jake's in love," Karla told the room.

"Again? Weren't you in love last time we saw you?" asked Colin. "With that girl you sent a dick pic to?"

"Ha! Yeah, no. It wasn't a dick pic. It was text sex. Twice. But anyway . . ." Jake forced a laugh. "Also, that was totally different. Also," he said in a reprimanding tone, looking at Karla, "I'm not in love. I just met someone pretty great, that's all."

"Do you use apps, or is it like . . ." Sydney's voice trailed off, and Jake got the impression she wasn't sure how his generation went about things.

"Yip." He leaned down, opened his bag, and pulled his laptop out.

"Visuals. We need visuals," Skye said. "Is she a babe?"

Jake looked between the women's eager faces (Colin was fingering his Fitbit). He didn't want to come off like a lovesick loser, but also, he was proud of Dandelion; talking about her was a pleasure.

He pulled his phone from his pocket and opened Hinge, navigated to her profile, and handed it to Karla.

"I like," Karla said, swiping through the pictures. "Okay. Okay . . ." She nodded approvingly.

Sydney leaned forward, wanting to see, and Karla turned the phone to her. "Is her name Dandelion?" she asked.

"Yeah," Jake said, actively holding his tongue. Though, if Colin hadn't been there and it was just him and the gals, he'd definitely get stuck into a gossip and ask their advice on where he should take her for their next date.

"Such a gorgeous name," Karla said.

"Did you say Dandelion?" Colin asked from where he was, lying totally horizontal on his beanbag. "Let's see?"

Karla handed Colin the phone. After a beat he looked up and said, "I know her."

"No way!" Sydney's body jumped in a gleeful electrocution.

"Oh," Jake laughed, despite the fact he could feel all the blood draining from his heart.

"We met on Feeld," Colin said. "It was a couple years back. But that's definitely her."

"Feeld? The kink app?" Skye asked.

"Not just kink, but for Dandelion"—Colin looked over at Jake, smiled thinly like they were sharing a filthy secret—"it definitely was."

Jake realized his mouth was hanging open. "Oh, wow, so you dated her? That's so . . . funny," he said, though it wasn't funny at all and, potentially, nothing would ever be funny again.

"It was casual. FWB, you know? NSA," Colin said, then clarified, because perhaps it was obvious Jake did not know. "Friends with benefits. No strings attached. Just a super-relaxed physical thing. Cool woman. Poly, right? Tell her the Frenchie says, *Ciao ciao ciao.*"

"Polyamorous?" Jake asked, and then had to work on seeming cool and chill. "She had other partners, did she?"

"Of course," Colin said. He stretched with an enormous yawn. Apparently, suddenly very tired and bored. "She was in a throuple, if I remember correctly. An open throuple, obviously." He put both hands behind his head and crossed his ankles. "Was sad we lost touch, but she had a project on the Galápagos and so . . . no Wi-Fi there, or phone signal."

"A zoologist," said Sydney. "That's very cool."

All the women were still nodding, though now the nods were less enthusiastic. In every single one of their eyes Jake saw a twinkling of pity that they were trying to counterbalance with their smiles.

"I'm not sure we have the same person." Jake shook his head. Because if Dandelion was really a zoologist, then surely she would have, at one point, mentioned an animal. Or, like, a zoo. And also, on the polyamory thing, Jake knew, it was ethical to be up-front with that information. That was the whole point—otherwise it was just cheating. He stood and strolled over to Colin's beanbag, reached down for his phone, wanting Colin to stop touching it and for this conversation to be over and, ideally, to never have happened at all.

"Hombre," Colin said, smirking as he handed Jake the phone, "she used this swimming costume photo on her Feeld profile too. I'm telling you—it's the same girl." Colin whistled and looked up at the ceiling like he was recalling a very rude memory, and then, unfortunately, Jake could see it too—Colin and his devastating face, bending Dandelion over his awards cabinet, in a mirror-paneled room.

Jake went back to the sofa. So, this was a major blow. Out of anyone that he knew, Colin was most definitely the worst possible person to have slept with Dandelion, especially as Jake hadn't even kissed her yet. "Anyway," he said. He turned his attention to Karla. "I know we've got a hard stop at twelve, right? Shall we get going? I want to show you where I'm at with the treatment."

"Are you all right, Jake?" Karla asked. She came to sit next to him, put one hand on his thigh, and gave it a squeeze. "London might be big, but those dating apps are pretty small, people overlap all the time. So don't worry about it. It's not a big deal."

"I'm not worried," Jake said, typing his password into his laptop with his two index fingers. He got the password wrong. "I'm pretty sure it's not the same person." He got the password wrong again. "But either way, I'm really not worried. *At all.*" He got the password wrong again—his computer locked him out.

13

Saturday, 26th April

Poppy

"She's back!" Sam rubbed his hand over his head and pointed at the bluebells in a vase and an open bottle of red. "I was beginning to worry you wouldn't make it home for tagine night. You hungry?"

Sam dusted the tagine off when he wanted to be romantic or was going to put something to Poppy. They'd bought it from a souk in Marrakech, a few months after they met. And Poppy had found it very sweet at the time, how he um'd and aahed over hundreds of colorful clay pots and then bartered, badly, for their favorite. The tagine had been their first co-owned thing, and they had carried it around, dopey like new parents. Taking it in turns at the airport to sit it on a knee.

"So hungry," Poppy said, although she'd stopped and folded a pizza slice into her face on the walk home from the pub.

It had been one of those early hot days when Londoners get excited and unsheathe their winter legs, decide it's time to drink pink wine and pale ale, forget they don't smoke, and sit on the street for as long as possible. And Poppy and Jetta had submerged themselves in all that late-spring glory, spending the afternoon outside The Dove on Broadway Market, like the good old days, when the three of them lived on the north side of London Fields. On Saturdays, they would mooch across the park with their hangovers, get coffee from Climpsons, oysters from the place next door, maybe a vintage nightie or spangled jacket from the market, and then spend the rest of the day in the pub.

"Never seen you that angry, Poppet. It was really horrible." Jetta's glass had been smudgy with fingerprints and her eyes smudgy with wine. "It was like you were possessed." And then, with a note of amusement in her voice: "Possessed by the spirit of your mentalist sister."

"But it was a bit like that, Jets. Genuinely. I was filled with her fight." Poppy let her eyes rest on their wine bottle with a pig's head on it and reflected on the bouts of rage and precarious behavior that had begun surging through her.

"Frankly, in hindsight, now I know you're okay, I kind of loved it," Jetta said. "Very authentic experience to have a live meltdown at one of those things. Really maximized the twenty-quid ticket for everyone. Although of course, it did fuck the energetic field momentarily when you trashed the portal. But Thorn rebuilt it, swiftly. So . . ."

Thorn had been in touch with Poppy. Messaged her on Instagram and told her about a "sober ecstatic dance" event her friend was organizing. According to Thorn, dancing was one of the best ways to release trauma. She said it could be immensely therapeutic for Poppy. And despite the fact the whole cacao thing had been carnage, Poppy had bought two tickets because she loved dancing. Both sisters loved dancing. Always had.

Sam brought a large saucepan over to the table, doling out the rice as Poppy sat down on the wooden bench. "Thank you. Amazing," she said, tucking her hair behind both ears at the same time.

"You been with Jetta?" he asked.

"Mm."

He observed her pointedly. "You drunk?"

"Teensy bit tipsy. Delighted to be fed. Thank you so much."

Sam nodded at Poppy's downturned phone. "Please don't tell me you're still using Dandelion's?"

"Mine was smashed to smithereens." Poppy rested her elbow on the table and touched a drooping bluebell, curving from the vase.

"You just needed a new screen, Poppy."

"But this phone's great, Sam. It's better than mine. I put my SIM card in and it works as good as new."

"It doesn't have any of her stuff on it, does it?" Sam reached for the phone, but Poppy pulled it onto her lap.

"Just the things that were downloaded. Some apps and stuff."

That afternoon Poppy had longed to come clean to Jetta about how Dandelion's phone had taken her through the looking glass. She'd wanted, more than anything, to slip her sister's adopted phone from her sister's adopted bag and show Jetta Jake's profile—ask what she thought. Debate options. Seek vindication. Make a plan.

"Okay, Poppy, that's . . ." Sam articulated each word with amped-up gravitas. "Really weird that you're still using it."

Poppy picked up her knife and fork. "It's absolutely fine," she said to her plate. The portion he'd given her was passive-aggressively large—all she'd be able to do with it was fail.

"I'll get you a phone from work tomorrow." Sam worked at Facebook and was always pilfering their kit: bulging ergonomic keyboards, zingy watches, awful branded T-shirts. Anyone they knew who gave birth would get a babygrow with *Meta* on the front, which, Poppy could only assume, and hope, immediately got binned.

"It's all good. I like using this phone," Poppy said through a mouthful. She needed the phone for her sister's Hinge profile. She needed it for Jake.

And then Poppy was thinking of him again, and a shooting star arched through her body. The chemistry between them was like nothing she'd ever known. They'd spoken for a long time on the evening of the Tate/Thames disaster; afterward Poppy had a shower, and when she'd come back to the bedroom in her towel, she had a message from him saying, I wish I was with you, and another saying, I cannot wait to kiss you. And another saying, I think of little else, and Poppy had had to get into bed immediately and have a long, very hard think. Then another. Then a third.

"So how was Jetta?" Sam asked.

Poppy could feel the warmth in her cheeks. She was still looking down at her plate as she arranged another mouthful, knowing that Sam was looking at her face. "Great. The usual. But, um, tell me about the stag do," she said, wanting to move Sam to safer ground. "Was it really fun?"

"Mental." Sam took a swig of wine. He reached for his phone from the end of the table. "That's me at Quasar Laser in Norwich after an all-nighter," he said, showing Poppy a picture of him wearing pink shiny leggings and a dinner jacket with nothing else underneath. Glitter on his face. "That's Bonners, on his fourth dirty pint . . ."

Poppy moved through different amused chewing-nodding faces while Sam showed her more photos of middle-aged men looking semitragic. She turned her thoughts back to the pub—she'd told Jetta how it had been the head-shaving memory that had come to her before she'd flipped out at the cacao evening. She'd told her how she'd heard Dandelion's actual voice, like she'd been in the same room.

Jetta wiped a tear from a green eye with her finger, then howled a delighted laugh into the afternoon sunshine. "God that was good." The head-shaving anecdote still amused. "Just really sums her up."

"Yeah, I get it's funny *now* . . ." Poppy watched a group of young men at the table behind Jetta who were getting rowdy. Tank tops, rouged shoulders, wishy-washy eyes. Jubilant with the evidence that another winter was on the way out. Never had Poppy known a summer without a sister—could her bones still get warm? She pulled her gaze back to her friend and her mind back to her questions. "Why did Dandelion do it though? Was it really all *for me?*"

"She did it 'cause of the science teacher," Jetta said matter-of-factly, taking a knowing sip of wine. "Dandelion was a vigilante, wasn't she. Always fighting back."

"Fighting back against the . . . science teacher?" Poppy asked, seizing on this wisp of information that she had not been expecting. "*The* science teacher?" Poppy knew who the science teacher was. Everyone did back home in Devon. He'd taught at their school, been sacked for being a perv, or possibly a pedo. Poppy wasn't sure on the specifics because she'd been about nine years old when it all went down. But the science teacher was no-torious. Unfortunate local lore. "What the hell did it have to do with him? That's hardly the male gaze!"

"Look, your big sis was a card-carrying badass, Pops," Jetta said, quite hurriedly. "End of." She leaned over the table and took both of Poppy's hands, shook them. "I don't want you getting up-set about the nuances of her psyche *now*. And, yes, you know so much of what she did was for you. She wanted to make the world a better place for you and she was hypersensitive to you being around bad dudes."

"It's not just bad dudes, Jets. You know what she's like with Sam. Was like . . ." Poppy corrected.

"Please, Pops, don't deep it. Not now! Dandelion was who she was and let's just love her for it and accept that we can never know everything about her. Or understand all of what she did."

Poppy dropped the topic, but she had a strange feeling that Jetta was still colluding with her sister. Like the older girls knew something, that Poppy, thirty-seven but still a child, wasn't privy to and didn't understand.

"Hello? Earth to Pops?" Sam waved his fork in front of Poppy's face. "I said," he said, "how you feeling?" He took a large swig of wine.

Poppy brought herself back to the present moment, to their kitchen, to her boyfriend's face. "I'm feeling great," she said, though actually the preplanned impending life convo that she knew Sam was about to launch into was glinting at the top of her field of vision like a guillotine. What excuse could she make this time? She didn't have the strength to say *Yes, Sam, let's give it a go! Let's start a family*, and she didn't have the courage to say *No, Sam, this feels bad. Adieu!*

"I'm so pleased, Popsy," Sam said, putting his knife and fork down. "You've not felt great in . . . Do you think things are starting to shift? Because I've been worried. It felt like . . . we lost you both."

Poppy was chewing on a patty of lamb, which was now just sinew. It niggled her when Sam spoke about Dandelion as if she was someone he was close to. Twice since she'd died, he'd posted a heartfelt tribute to her on Instagram and, silently, Poppy felt like he was using her sister's death for likes.

"Okay, so, well, in that case . . ." Sam tapped the table in a drumroll. "We need to decide what to do with Dandelion's flat?"

Poppy lifted her glass and used a swig of wine to wash her mouthful down. She had absolutely not been expecting him to start there. "What do you mean?"

"Well. Soooo . . . what if we moved in?"

"We live here!" Poppy choked at him. Something that was potentially a prune fell from her fork and splatted meat juice onto the table.

"It's so small here. And it's ridiculous having that big empty flat. You love it there!" Sam pressed his fingertips together in a steeple. "You go there *all the time*."

"But we're cozy here!" Poppy tossed her gaze around the cluttered, sticky kitchen. "And anyway, I'm going to Airbnb her flat, remember? I've put a lock on her bedroom door and everything, to keep her stuff safe. I've done the photos. They look . . . really great. It's totally ready to go. So, thank you for reminding me, I'll put the listing live tomorrow." Poppy picked up the phone from her lap, started navigating to Airbnb. She'd put it live tonight.

"Hold on!" Sam said. He laughed at her like she was being hilariously hasty and endearingly thick. "Another option is—you could put Dandelion's place on the market and we could go in together. A house, imagine! A garden. A spare room. Stairs! More space for, you know . . . the sprogs. It would have to be further out, obviously. Heathrow, I heard, is up-and-coming. Great investment . . . on the Elizabeth line and—"

"Heathrow?" Poppy's jaw jutted; her face was tight. "There's a fuck-off-massive *airport*."

"Jesus, Poppy. Chill!" Sam was not used to her raising her voice. "Fine. Well, we could go *out* out, couldn't we? The Midlands are meant to be very . . . central and—"

"I mean, yes, the Midlands are in the center of England—"

"OR, POPPY, OR . . ." Sam projected, holding a hand up, "coastlines are really huge these days, aren't they, so, we could . . ."

Poppy's eyes moved to the kitchen window. Dandelion was in the reflection, twisting with reproval: *Did he just say . . . coastlines are huge?*

Poppy looked back at Sam—for the entirety of their relationship he'd made all the decisions. It was only recently she had started pushing back, and he hated it. They never used to fight, because she used to let him get his way, and for the most part—she wanted his way too. "Absolutely not, Sam," Poppy said now, talking over him as he explained St. Leonards-on-Sea to her. She wasn't even sure exactly what she was disagreeing with, or why. She only knew that she didn't feel the same.

Sam stopped talking. His mouth opened and closed twice, silently, like a fish yanked from water. He wiped his forehead with his napkin, then put it down, scrunched on the table. "Fine, Poppy, I was trying to be fair about things, but realistically, you're the one who is minted these days, so why don't you buy us a house in Notting Hill if my ideas aren't good enough for you?"

"I don't have access to Dandelion's money, Sam. It's all—"

"Of course you do! It's your money now, Poppy. You just need to deal with it. Talk to those accountants. Cash in some shares. Sell her pimp-ass flat. Let's move somewhere lush." And then, a little softer: "Dandelion wanted you to look after yourself and to live a lovely life, Popsy."

"I'm not ready!"

"Do you want us to rent this flat forever?"

Poppy looked sideways at the fridge like she was interested to hear its opinion. *If I hunch my shoulders in a sort of "Possibly?" way,* she thought, *then he'll actually hit the roof.* She moved her gaze from the fridge back to Sam. Shrugged her shoulders.

Sam's eyes rolled up, then down, then sideways. "What is going on? We're not thirty anymore, Poppy! We're forty years old! You do get that, right? You do get . . ."

"I'm thirty-seven." Poppy put her knife and fork together, pushed the bench back, stood, and walked over to the sink. "And anyway, we're lucky! We're lucky to be this old!" Poppy felt young. She felt like she was getting younger. Just as Jake had said, theoretically, she was only halfway through her life. And even if death was around the corner—she wouldn't let it be the boss.

"Poppy," Sam said from behind her.

Poppy scraped the remains from her plate into the bin, her eyes on their basil plant; it had been overwatered in an attempt to bring it back from the brink, but now the soil was growing mold.

She turned around and Sam stood, finished his wine, put the glass down, and leaned forward, pushing his fingers into the surface of the table so hard that the tips of them went white. "Why are you acting like our life is something you don't want? We were, pretty much, already trying for a kid. But now it's like you're pushing me away on purpose. You're trying to antagonize me all the time . . ."

And it was true—there had been an appointment to remove Poppy's contraceptive coil. Only Poppy never went to it, because it had fallen in that most strange sliver of time that comes after a death and before a funeral. On her phone, she had a list of baby names: Willow, Ted, Fern. They sounded foolish to her now, like make-believe creatures from a children's storybook.

"Plenty of people get pregnant at forty, Sam," Poppy said. She was holding on to her upper arms, her fingernails digging into the flesh.

"FUCKING HELL, POPPY!" Sam really shouted, and it shocked her. A muscle in her neck caught and pinged with pain. "You're always talking about your one random friend's sister who had a kid at forty-two—"

"Forty-six! Betty's sister was forty-six!" Poppy pinched the tendon on her neck between two fingers, rubbed it hard.

Sam exhaled. "Okay. Fine." He exhaled again. "But I don't want to be a geriatric dad. I want to play football with my children and carry them on my shoulders and see them grow up. I want to be a granddad."

"That's totally fair enough, Sam. But I don't want to enter motherhood when I'm feeling like this. My sister . . . It's only been half a year. It's only just happened and . . ."

"I've been very patient." Sam shook his head in a small unimpressed movement. "All my friends think I've been a frickin' saint, by the way. Honestly, they all think . . ." Sam was always bringing his friends' opinions into his and Poppy's conversations for extra validation, but most of the time she strongly suspected he'd made them up. He rubbed his hand over his face. He was trying to look less cross. "I'm so devastated that Dandelion isn't here anymore, Poppy. Everyone is. Of course. But we need to carry on. I want us to get married. To get a bigger place. And to have kids, okay? Soon. I'm ready. *You're ready.* I know you are. This isn't something I'm springing on you. These were all joint decisions that we'd come to after years of talking about it, and you can't suddenly just change your mind. We're doing it. It's time."

Dandelion was sitting on the counter and she was leaning in the doorway and she was behind Poppy and beside her; she was shouting in Poppy's thoughts.

"I think we should go on a break, Sam," Poppy said, still holding on to her arms, looking down at the floor.

"*A break?* What does that mean?"

"A break from this!" Poppy raised her voice, moved her eyes to his face.

"A break means a breakup. So, if that's what you want . . ."

In the silence that followed, Poppy knew Sam was waiting for her to back down, but she didn't say anything and instead turned away from him, stretched her arms out along the kitchen counter, let it steady her. Inside her heart and her mind, there was a mounting sense of strength.

"You're so selfish, Poppy. I cannot believe what a self-centered bitch you're being right now."

"Please stop gaslighting me, Sam."

"Stop gaslighting me!"

Poppy spun around to face him; she poked a finger toward him. "You know that in this relationship, you're the patriarchy? You make all the decisions and—"

Sam hit the vase of bluebells from the table and they fell across the floor like soldiers on a battlefield. "The patriarchy? Now? Here? What the fuck, Poppy? You sound like your sister," Sam hissed. "The only difference is—you can't pull it off." He spun and left the kitchen with heavy feet.

Shaking, Poppy knelt, picked up each of the bluebells. She reached for a slender ceramic vase from the shelf over the fridge, slipped the stems into it, filled it with fresh water. She swept the broken glass vase into a dustpan as Sam slammed their bedroom door. Drying her hands on a tea towel, Poppy walked over to the kitchen table, picked her phone up, and took it over to the sofa. Sitting on the far end of it, she tucked herself in with the peach merino blanket she'd taken from Dandelion's flat. She looked up at the door, then down at the phone. She opened Hinge. Messaged Jake.

14

Wednesday, 30th April

Poppy had stayed at her sister's flat for the last four nights. She'd had an efficient day working at the desk in Dandelion's sitting room; she'd been through all forty rolls of film from Astrid's wedding, having got them back from the lab. She'd finished editing and sent Astrid the files to choose from. She'd called her parents. Her father updated her on the war against the slugs in the garden, and her mother told her about the amazing savings at Holland & Barrett. In the background, her father shouted, "Mum's bought t-t-ten tons of nuts!"

Poppy told them she would come and visit on the weekend— she hadn't been back to Devon since Christmas. Hadn't been able to face it—the pain of missing her sister in their family home was too excruciating; everywhere, there was a visceral sense of sad. But now she was feeling more resilient.

Bathed, moisturized, all dressed up, Poppy put her handbag over her head, let it hang across her body. Before she left the flat, she stopped in front of the big photograph of Dandelion on the wall in the sitting room, a portrait Poppy had taken and had framed in pale oak. "Still not heard from Sam," she informed the picture, "bet you're over the moon about that." She gazed at her sister's face and thought back to that day in Devon.

Their mum had made a Sunday lunch, all the trimmings, crumble and custard. Afterward, stuffed, the sisters had forced themselves out for a walk along the cliffs and Poppy had taken her camera, as she so often used to. As they climbed the steepest crags, their hair whipped wildly in a way it never did in London, and their faces lit up, autumnal. At the peak, Poppy took several photos of the sea, then turned to her sister, who was looking into the distance. The sun had collected as heavy gold in the clouds behind her and, as Poppy focused, she swore she'd seen her sister's soul.

In this photo on the wall, Dandelion's mouth was closed, but drawn out long in a way that said, *I know a million things and I have a thousand secrets.* She looked like a pre-Raphaelite beauty, a siren on the rocks, and Poppy had loved the image so much that she'd blown it up and had it framed as a gift for her sister's birthday. And now, standing in the sitting room alone, Poppy recalled Dandelion unwrapping it. They'd both been cross-legged, facing each other on the sofa, and Dandelion said she loved it, "Truly, Poppet." But, also, she wasn't sure if she could hang a portrait of her own face on her own wall. "Bit much?"

"It's not a portrait," Poppy had told her, standing by the coffee table, exactly where she was standing again today. "To me, your face is a view."

Poppy turned away from the picture, left the flat, and ran down the stairs. She walked, with pace, across the Downs, listening to TLC's *CrazySexyCool* through her headphones—an album Dandelion used to play from her bedroom as a teenager, up loud. When Poppy arrived at Hackney Church, Jake was already standing outside, waiting. He waved. He was wearing a tie-dye T-shirt. Poppy nodded at it as she came toward him. "Nice top."

"Well, I thought it might be on-brand?" Jake said, picking at the T-shirt with his fingers. His eyes ran over her body. "I like your top too. And your . . . everything else."

Poppy had not known what to wear; in the end she'd opted for Dandelion's leopard-print vest, acid-washed jeans, and her new favorite cardigan. Her hair was in a ponytail with a pink scrunchie. She looked and felt like a lot.

Jake put his hand on Poppy's waist and stepped into her so their pelvises were almost touching. "Hello," he said. He kissed her on the cheek, and she looked down at the gravel, then up at his mouth, and smiled.

"Hello." Poppy took a very purposeful step backward, fighting the pull toward him. "It's nice to see you."

"Yeah," he said. "I was excited about seeing you, a bit nervous of this whole dance thing, but I'm game." He looked over his shoulder at the other people who were behind them, then back at Poppy. "Hey, so, listen. First up . . ." They shuffled forward with the rhythm of the queue. "I need to ask you something, a few things . . ."

"Oh," Poppy said. His tone made her feel shaky. "Shoot." She pretended to be fascinated by a woman walking past them carrying a baby in a fabric sling. The woman looked very young, barely out of her teens.

"I wanted to ask you face-to-face, are you a zoologist?"

Poppy turned back to him, moved her eyes from side to side. "A zoologist?" she laughed. "I'm not."

"Okay, right." Jake nodded his head in different directions, like he was bopping to a beat. "And so, totally cool if you are, but are you polyamorous? I've been wary of asking, I know you're into the whole secretive thing. But . . . I feel like we've got to a place where . . . well, are you looking for something monogamous, or . . . ?"

"I'm not polyamorous, Jake." Poppy wiped a finger underneath the waterline of her eye, as if she was collecting an amused spilling of tears, though actually she was feeling stressed.

Jake pursed his lips. Swallowed. "Because I work with this guy, a creative, and he said he's dated you."

Noo. "Who?"

"Colin Dubois." Jake's accent implied the guy was French.

Poppy shook her head. "Nup. Don't know him." She did remember a French creative Dandelion had dabbled with though. *Un pervers narcissique*—which, coming from Dandelion, was saying something. "Never heard of him." Poppy smiled, trying to think how an innocent person might act in this situation and what they might do with their face. In her shoes, her toes were clenched.

"You sure? 'Cause he said you went to sex parties together," Jake said. "I don't mind, by the way, I'd just rather know the truth. I think you know how much I like you . . ." He paused, looked up at the church roof. "But I can't do the poly thing, I'm afraid. I'd get jealous, I'm not evolved enough," he added, with kindness in his voice.

The truth was that Dandelion had worked in finance for the best part of twenty years. She was monogamous, when she wanted to be. Couldn't be arsed to be poly. Too busy. Too selfish.

"Ummm, that name's not ringing any bells." Poppy shook her head, feeling that this probably was the same French guy, and that, yes, her sister had told him that she was a polyamorous zoologist—because Dandelion spun yarns for her own entertainment, added frills and sequins to the truth. "Did he say anything else, out of interest?" Poppy asked, looking down at the pale stone steps into the church as they climbed them. Soon they would be in the dark.

"He said, *Ciao ciao ciao*, and he said you were . . . nice." Jake landed on *nice* after a few seconds, which indicated to Poppy that may have been his own choice of word and that Colin had said something else.

"Reckon we could talk about this later?" Poppy asked. She put on a mock-stoned voice. "It's just I'm really trying to get into the ecstatic zone." She raised a hand and almost did a peace sign, but then thought better of it. She stepped in front of Jake; the queue was thinning to get inside. Unzipping her bag, she pulled out her phone, slid open the tickets. Realized that on them—was her actual name. *Poppy Greene x 2.*

"Actually, we kind of need to talk about this, Dandelion. I've been feeling a bit upset, if I'm honest with you." The couple behind them were definitely listening, enjoying the real-life drama; they were making eyes at each other, not saying anything at all.

"Jake, look, I . . ." Poppy began in a whisper. She was feeling robbed of the truth that she'd created, really scared that the extravagant house of cards that she'd been building (was hoping to move in to) was about to topple down.

"Can I have your tickets?" a bearded man behind a table in the entrance hall asked. He must have been six foot six. Poppy flashed her phone at him, and he ushered them into the coolness of the church, a large, dark, open space with colorful stained glass windows at one end, and wooden floors. Poppy stopped in front of a gold statue of Jesus in a robe looking welcoming, arms outstretched. Jake was standing right behind her, very close, and she turned back to him, let three of her fingers press into the inside of his arm. The yellow petals of his eyes caught the only light there was.

"I'm a photographer," she said. Poppy wanted to give him something that was real—not just to appease him, but because she needed him to know her. *Her.* Start to stack up truths alongside all the lies. "I'm a straight, monogamous photographer." Because now that things were ending with Sam, then maybe she and Jake could get to a place, one day, when the only lie would be her name. And maybe, if Poppy started the story at the beginning—right at the beginning, not even at the end of Dandelion's life, but at the start of her own—then Jake might understand that not all lies are terrible and sometimes they are a way of getting closer to the truth. Sometimes, lies are necessary to stay alive. "Do you believe me?" Poppy asked.

"Welcome, brothers, sisters," a woman purred over the microphone. The church was nearly full of people now.

Jake turned in the woman's direction, and Poppy stayed looking at him for a moment, then shifted her gaze forward too.

"Remember, there's not a right or wrong way to move. Allow your body to lead. Free your soul and let it be your guide." Poppy knew this woman was Thorn's friend, also Irish. "If you're not sure what to do," she said, "I recommend shaking to activate kundalini." Poppy stood on her tiptoes, lifted her chin; she could see the woman, a redhead, jiggling both of her hands roughly in demonstration, like a dog shuddering its fur after emerging from a pond. "So you really become aware of your life force."

Poppy was feeling anxious about what Jake was thinking. Concerned her story was getting too confusing to be credible. But then he took her hand and intertwined their fingers, weaving a bridge between them. When she looked at his face, he bent his head and kissed her on the mouth, and Poppy closed her eyes. It was only a few seconds, but she felt all that she was rise to the surface of her skin, and she knew herself and she knew him. When she opened her eyes—the world looked like morning. Like waking. Something of it was brand-new.

"I believe you." Jake pinched her waist, and Poppy squirmed and yelped with pleasure. She felt a smile spread through her collarbones, down her arms, into her wrists, her fingertips. "Now," Jake said, "I'm in the mood to dance."

All around them, people were standing in dark anticipation. "When we start the music, we'll have two hours to move through five states: flowing, staccato, chaos, lyrical, and stillness," the woman told them all. "So plenty of time to dissolve the ego."

"Two hours?" Jake whispered. "I can see how some of these cats might need that long to dissolve their egos, but . . . I'm feeling nervous about my catalog of moves."

"You'll be fine," Poppy reassured him. The music had started, so she stepped away, knowing she'd be too distracted if she was near him. "I'm going over here."

"Well, I guess, good luck?" Jake put his hands on his hips. He winked.

Poppy moved through the crowd and found a corner, next to a candelabra. The music was trippy; over a bass line, a thing that sounded like a keyboard pinged and called. She sidestepped back and forth, concentrating on the candle flames, and tried to tune in to her body—tried to stop thinking about that kiss and when they could do it again. She shunted her thoughts away from Jake and reflected on the woman's instructions: Let the soul be her guide.

Poppy shook her arms and legs for several minutes, and when she stopped a fuzzy energy ran over her skin; her breath was coming fast. Around her, fragments of bodies swayed and then dissolved. Poppy was dancing in a way that wasn't quite free, though was certainly getting there, until she became aware of another person—a man's bare feet. She wondered if she should turn immediately and pretend she didn't know that someone was trying to dance with her, but her curiosity got the better of her. She moved her eyes up the man's legs, the three-quarter-length trousers and then the purple waistcoat, with the embroidered mushrooms.

He didn't have his guitar with him this time, but it was the same guy from the cacao circle. His arms were open wide, and he was staring right at Poppy. When they made eye contact, he moved his hands together in front of his chest and made the shape of a heart with his fingers. He started beating the finger heart back and forth to the rhythm of the music, and then he lifted the heart to his face and closed one eye and looked at Poppy through it, like a telescope.

Poppy's dancing was now hardly happening at all; she was very slightly swaying her shoulders, but mainly trying to calm because she was in a place where someone thought she was Dandelion, and someone else knew her as Poppy.

From Instagram, Poppy knew that Thorn was at a tantra training retreat in Topanga and, perhaps naively, believed tonight would be a safe place to bring Jake; none of her fellow travelers had occurred to her. She glanced at where Jake had been dancing but couldn't see him, and when she looked back up at the purple waistcoat man, he'd moved the heart telescope to the center of his forehead and was holding it there. He was twisting his hips and biting his lower lip, really feeling the music. The panic in Poppy's body was making her feel woozy and faintly sick as the man stepped in toward her. "Let go," he whispered in her ear. "Become one with the rhythm . . . let it inside you."

And then Poppy was lost, not to the rhythm or the music, but something much greater and much worse. Her mind ripped from her body, and she was looking down. She watched herself hiss at the purple waistcoat man through gritted teeth, shove him away so he stumbled backward. Poppy was rising and rising through the church, while she was simultaneously pushing through the crowd beneath. She was at the altar; she had both her hands on it and she was crying, while she was also looking down from the ceiling, where she was numbly calm.

And then Poppy was back in the hospital, and she was staring at her sister's body in the bed, after Dandelion's heart had stopped and had run out of all that life. She was holding her sister's hand and she was taking the gold snake ring from her finger and pushing it onto her own. Her mother closed Dandelion's mouth, kissed her hair. Her father was standing in the corner and, at this, he left the room—walking like he'd been in a car accident and his body was badly hurt. Jetta was on her knees on the other side of the bed, silent, not moving, an atheist in prayer.

In the church, at the altar, Poppy was clutching Dandelion's gold ring; it pinged off and then she was totally back in her body and she was scrambling over the floor on her hands and knees. Desperate. Grabbing at people's feet, until Jake was there, crouching beside her.

"Dandelion?" He held her by her arms, pulled her up, but she fought to get away from him. "It's okay," he said. "I've got it."

Jake held the ring out to her and Poppy snatched it back. She was crying hard for her sister and for all the people who had died, and for all the people who were left, and all the pain she had no idea how to cope with. Her hands were on Jake's face and then her mouth was on his mouth and they were kissing. When she pulled away, they looked into each other's eyes, and she knew he knew they had to leave. Jake tunneled them out through the swarming crowd—like it was his job to save her. Like he was her bodyguard.

15

Still Wednesday, 30th April

Jake

"You ready to see the Palace?" Jake asked, turning to her outside the front door of his flat. "Sorry, it's not the most glamorous."

"Please, don't apologize. I should apologize for being such a wreck." Her face was still mottled and puffed from all that crying, though her voice was back to normal. Maybe Jake was frowning, because again she reassured him, "I promise. I'm okay."

Jake hadn't been able to stop himself from looking for Dandelion at the dance thing and, initially, had been quite moved because she seemed to be really embracing it. After his own brief attempt at "ecstatic" dance, which he did not enjoy at all, Jake turned and read the gold panel of the Ten Commandments he was next to, then the creed, which made him feel more anxious, and so he decided to jog around the church, because exercise seemed like a good use of time.

That was until he'd come across Dandelion again, who was dancing with the very epitome of a hippie. Jake stopped dead, openly stared, surprised to see Dandelion push the man away and stumble off. Jake tried to get close to her as she bashed into people, and then she was on the floor, and by his own foot; there was a glint of gold—her ring. Jake swooped and saved it, then helped her stand, and their foreheads banged. She'd kissed him. Then howled, and he'd had to, pretty much, carry her out of the dance disaster—thirty minutes in.

"Very trendy, isn't it? Very Hackney Wick warehouse," she said now of Jake's Hackney Wick warehouse.

Jake closed the door behind them, unsure of what he was meant to do. She'd been the one to ask if they could come back to his place. Was he meant to push her up against the wall immediately? Was what she wanted sex? She was smiling at him in a way that potentially meant *come hither.* Jake held on to the radiator behind him, clutched it with both hands. He wasn't totally sure about the ethics of getting it on with a woman who, not long ago, had been publicly hysterical.

"Can I have a tour?"

"Right, yes, of course." Jake stepped past her and into the hall, which was only as big as a cupboard. "This is the bedroom," he said, nodding at the open doorway, "where the magic doesn't happen."

"Do you sleep in here with your son?"

"Yup, or I sleep on the sofa when he's here. It's a sofa bed, so . . . And this is the bathroom, but it's an eyesore so let's skip it. And this," he said, stepping back to the sitting room, "is the main room, and that hob and shelf and fridge over there is what I like to call the kitchen."

"I love it." She didn't even sound like she was lying.

"I'm probably one of the oldest in this unit," Jake said loudly, because next door it sounded like someone might be starting a party; there was a drumming thud of bass. "It's a bit of a community. I like them, mostly. Though obviously they're cooler than me and stay up late, taking cool drugs."

"Good ficus too." She stroked one of Cindy's leaves, and now Jake was in a fantasy where Dandelion was moving in. They were sitting on the sofa in their pajamas, getting takeout and working their way through every season of *The Sopranos* again. Or *The Wire*, or one of the classic box sets that were the foundation of all good middle-aged relationships. They'd spoon. They'd laugh—loads. At Christmas, they could dress Cindy up in tinsel, fairy lights. Then fuck.

"Can we open this?" She'd pushed off her shoes and was nestling into one corner of the sofa. She held up the bottle of red he'd bought from the natural wine place downstairs. "And would it be okay if I smoked?"

"Course." Jake hopped over to the kitchen, began digging around for two glasses that matched. Something she could use as an ashtray.

"You don't take cool drugs then? At the cool parties?"

"Urm . . ." Jake was on his knees, emptying the kitchen drawer looking for the corkscrew. "Found it!" He stood, leaving much of the cutlery on the floor as he opened the bottle, glugged it into glasses. He nudged the kitchen window open and repeated her question to himself. "Drugs? No. Allergic." He brought over the wine and sat next to her, put a saucer down for an ashtray.

"Allergic to drugs?"

"Well . . ." Jake knew it sounded ridiculous to claim to be allergic to something that was essentially toxic. "Yeah, either that or I have the constitution of a hamster when it comes to narcotics." He could count the number of times he'd done drugs on one hand, and each occasion had ended with disaster—starting with a house party at uni when he'd had three tokes on a spliff, got extremely paranoid, and kept thinking he'd pissed himself. Eventually, he did. "Booze? Fine. Know where I am with booze. It's really not a huge problem, though, was never really into the whole clubbing thing. What about you?"

"I probably still go *out* out a few times a year," she said. "When I was a kid though . . . I went to raves and clubs on the regular."

"*A kid?*" Jake repeated with too much force.

"Not an actual child. But my big sister always took me along for the ride, and she was kind of a party animal."

"Oh yeah?" Jake asked. He was pleased to have her chatting, not crying. "Tell me more?"

"Well . . . we went to local clubs in Devon when we were dramatically underage—especially me as I'm younger. But I was more like fifteen, sixteen when we started going to London. We had this whole routine where we'd go up for twenty-four hours and hide in the train toilets or move carriages, shirking the ticket person," she laughed. "In the afternoon, when we arrived, we'd go straight to the National Portrait Gallery, or Tate Britain and moon over Pre-Raphaelites. *Ophelia* I always loved in the permanent exhibition, or *La belle dame sans merci,* which was kind of my sister's vibe." She took a long thoughtful inhale through her nose, closed her eyes, and leaned back, like she was physically falling through memories. "We'd spend a few hours taking in the art. Then go and find a corner shop that would sell us booze. Buy a liter of Strongbow and, like, a family pack of Hula Hoops or something. Sit in the park and roll cigarettes. At an acceptable time that wasn't too eager, we'd go to Fabric, The End, The Cross." She opened her eyes and looked at him. "One of those clubs. Maybe a couple of them. Dance all night. Get the first train back to Devon and make it home for a late lunch with our parents. Tell them about the exhibitions and friends we'd seen. For the most part, they believed us. Occasionally, obviously, we'd get busted. In deep shit. Though, to be fair, my sister always took the rap."

Jake laughed, a bit impressed, a bit uneasy, a bit bemused. "Glad we didn't meet back then, because you would have thought I was an enormous loser." He thought of himself as an adolescent—sucking at an Um Bongo carton through a bendy straw at Chess Club. He'd been a late developer.

"I would never have done any of that if it was just up to me, I don't think . . ." She paused; she seemed almost entranced. "We thought the world was ours. Or maybe I thought the world was hers. For a time, it really was."

"Wow," Jake said. Accidentally, his gaze had settled on the outline of her breasts in the tight leopard-print number, as she breathed—they heaved, it was marvelous, and he was entranced too. Catching himself, he looked up quickly. "I'd like to have fun with you, Dandelion. I've always loved live music. Tends to be more bands than DJs. Always been into soul. And funk. But . . ." Jake remembered the Yesness summer party. "I am going to a techno thing next month. Not exactly my usual bag, but it's with a whole bunch of people from work. If you wanted to join, we could attempt a less devastated dance." She'd finished her glass of wine already and was refilling it. She was looking much better now, he thought, more shiny. Like a present to unwrap. Jake reached for her thigh and spread his hand over her jeans. "But anyway, you okay now? I was really worried about you back there."

"I know." She nodded. She was looking at her glass. "I'm sorry."

"What's up? What's going on? Can we talk about it?"

She stood and took her glass over to the vinyl. "What a collection," she said. The shelves were custom-built—for his old house. But they still looked good in this flat, running in two levels along the far edge of the room. "Almost as good as my sister's." Her voice quavered. It nearly broke.

"So, your sister is John Peel?" Jake joked. The sassy sister was getting a lot of airtime this evening. Dandelion had never mentioned any siblings before; he'd thought she was an only child.

Their eyes met, and she smiled at him with a face that looked like an apology. They fell into a silence that felt not comfortable, but full—like she was using it to clarify her thoughts. Twice she opened her mouth to begin a sentence, but said nothing. Jake's own anxiety was swelling. Was any of this to do with him? Did she want to be just friends? Maybe her photography wasn't going well. She had no clients; she was in debt. A sick parent? The possible catastrophes were endless.

"Jake, I have something . . ." She cleared her throat. "I need to tell you."

"Okay," Jake said. He put his glass down. Held on to his own hands.

"So, my sister's records are mine now." She came back over to the sofa slowly. Glanced at him as she sat down, then back at the records. "She left them to me." She pulled at the scrunchie that was holding her hair in a messy topknot, and it fell down around her face in tumbles. She brushed it from her cheeks and leaned down to her bag, pulled out a cigarette from the open packet, lit it. "She left me everything. All her stuff. Her flat. Her clothes . . ." A single tear had escaped one eye and fell fast to her cheekbone. "Because . . . she died."

"God! I'm so sorry." Jake lifted his hand and put it on her thigh, then moved it to her shoulder. He felt a stabbing in his heart and he had to look away and focus on the pattern of the rug. "I had no idea."

"I wanted to tell you because—"

"Was it recent?"

She exhaled. "It was two hundred and fifty . . ."

Jesus. Was she going to say it *in days*?

But then she shook her head. "Eight months. I just need to tell you because . . . well, that's why I was upset this evening. Like, I'm fine! I was having a lovely time and . . ." Jake could see she was using all her effort to speak, to get the words out. "Then, reality comes back to me and I realize the most unbelievable thing that could ever happen, *happened*. That she's . . ." She took a hard pull on her cigarette like it was oxygen and she needed it. "No longer here. And so, and so . . ." Her words were coming out with smoke, and Jake found it horrible to watch, like she was internally on fire. "This is her ring and I thought I lost it in the church, and that was her beret, in the Thames—that's why I jumped in, I mean, I couldn't lose that too!" She looked desperate and Jake felt desperate for her. "I owe you an enormous apology and—"

"Don't be sorry!" Jake reached for her hand, brought it to his lap, looked down at the beautiful ring. "If there's anything I can . . . I don't have a sibling . . . that I know of," he added, because he'd always felt it unlikely a man with as many wild oats as his father would have sown only one kid. But he had lost his mother. He had lost his mother in a terrible way. "I lost someone and . . ." Still, it was too difficult to talk about. To think about. "I guess I've never really recovered. Yeah, I . . ." He could do it though. He could tell her. Of all the people he could talk about this with, it was Dandelion, it was Dandelion right now. "My mother died, quite young. Ages ago, but . . ."

Her mouth was open, the inside of her lips stained with frills of claret. In her hand the cigarette was uncoiling into ash. "Oh, Jake," she said. "I'm so sorry."

"It was a long time ago. Nearly twenty years." Jake shook his head. How could it have been that long? "Anyway, look, I don't want to talk about me, I want to—"

"And you don't think you've recovered?" she asked. She wiped away another tear.

"No. I mean, I have. I have." He had not. But he did his best not to think about it. About her. About what he could have done. "It's just that it's never the same again. It's something you adjust to." He wanted to give Dandelion hope. "You come to understand that you live a different life to what you had before. And that doesn't mean it's all eternally terrible. Just because you're grieving doesn't mean that life won't, again, be good."

The way Jake saw it, the world was divided into those people who had experienced a serious loss and those who hadn't—those who still walked through an ignorance they didn't even yet realize was blissful. And Dandelion was another of the unlucky ones. On some deep level, had he known this all along?

Next to him on the sofa, she wiped at her eyes too roughly, as if she was cross with herself. She bent her cigarette into the saucer, wiped her hands on her jeans, got up, and walked fast to the bathroom, hit her shoulder into the door frame; her movements were all slurred. She shut the door, and Jake heard the extractor fan turn on with the lights. He slumped backward, ran both his hands through his hair, and exhaled. He'd said the wrong thing. He'd said too much. Why had he talked about himself? In the flat next door, the bass continued pounding, as persistent as a worried heart.

Jake stood and went over to his records. He got to his knees and ran his fingers over the spines, and by the time she came out of the bathroom, Joan Armatrading was singing and Jake was back on the sofa. He could tell she'd washed her face; she looked pink and scrubbed.

"Do you mind if I stay awhile?"

"Please. I want you to. Would you like to stay the night? We could cuddle. Or talk. Or we could just be quiet. How about a toastie?" Jake asked. "I make very fantastic toasties by the way, it's really one of my skills."

"Would you . . . tell me about your mother?" She filled her glass with wine. The bottle was nearly finished. She sat at the other end of the sofa, lit another cigarette, and curled her feet under her body, resting her head down on the arm.

"Why don't you tell me about your sister? I'd love to—"

"Please," she said. "I want to listen."

Jake closed his eyes.

His mum was running, pulling him along the pavement, holding his hand, and he was holding Lazy Susan's hand; they were late for something, they were meant to be somewhere, but they were laughing. The sun was bright.

His mum was drying glasses behind the bar in the pub where she worked and he was playing solitaire with a pack of cards that had naked ladies on the front. He looked up at her and she was watching him. *I love you*, she mouthed, and stuck out her tongue. He stuck out his tongue back.

His mum was crying, again, about his dad. About her dad. About her heart. About her head. About money. About the hoover breaking. About being tired. About nothing she was able to talk about. About nothing at all.

"Well, my mum was very funny. Silly too. I think she was the funniest person I ever met, to be honest with you. She was always, like . . . jumping out at me and stuff. We'd make practical jokes all the time and we'd howl with laughter. She was beautiful. People said she looked like Bianca Jagger." Jake looked at Dandelion's face, and although her eyes were red, she was smiling with a softness, like she was being calmed. He moved his gaze to his feet on the rug, and in his mind he opened his mum's bedroom door and it was daytime but the curtains were drawn.

With hindsight, it hurt a crippling amount that although Jake's mum had spent days in bed, he had accepted it as the way things were, hadn't realized she'd been quite that level of seriously badly sad. He should have shown his love more. He could have asked for help from his dad, his teachers, doctors, social services, friends. Anyone.

He'd been told she'd taken around a hundred pills. Jake had this feeling she'd counted them out one by one, sitting at the tiny kitchen table with the blue-and-white oilcloth. It came to him like a memory—like it was something he'd actually seen. No one had been there though. She'd been all alone, until the following day when a neighbor had popped round to borrow something, some kind of dried herb, as Jake recalled, at which point it was too late: "She was my whole family. She was my mum and my dad and my sister and, sometimes, when she was having a bad patch—she was like my child. Even though, I guess, I was only a kid myself."

Next to him, Dandelion put both hands to her face, and her shoulders began shaking. The cigarette was still between her fingers, and the ash fell from it like snow from the branch of a winter's tree. Jake took it from her and stubbed it in the saucer, pushed the saucer away. He sat back and pulled her gently toward him, her face dropping against his chest. He could see how she was clenching against the anguish, as if something was physically hurting her. He picked up a cushion for her head and eased her onto it, then put both hands by his side and laid his head back and looked up at the ceiling. In the far corner of the room, murky clouds of damp blossomed and bloomed and almost looked pretty, despite the fact they were made of mold.

At the time that Jake's mum was dying, lying on the kitchen floor, he'd been in Berlin with an ex-girlfriend. It was disgusting to him that while she'd been ebbing from life, he'd been having a romantic time. He could see both scenes simultaneously in his mind: a split screen. He was laughing, his arm around his ex, both very drunk, in a dive bar, and his mother was all alone, crying, dying. In an internet café the next day, he read an email from his aunt: Please come home immediately. The first flight. Please.

In his lap, Dandelion opened her eyes. His feelings toward her had layered and looped again—a new ring inside the trunk of a fledgling tree. An orbit of the sun.

"What was your sister's name?" Jake asked quietly.

She whimpered something that he didn't hear. And then, with more force, "Pop-py."

"Oh, that's beautiful," Jake said. Another flower. "I love that name." He reached for her clenched hand, brought it to his lips, and kissed it. He glanced into the corner of the room, because, for a second, he thought he'd sensed someone there.

"Do you, Jake?"

Jake looked at her, let his eyes wander over her face. She'd been crying so much that she was different. She'd changed.

"Do you love that name?" she asked.

In his mind, Jake saw a whole field of delicate, crepey poppy petals, bloody and brilliant. How sweet and fitting—the symbol of remembrance. "It's a beautiful name," Jake said softly. He ran the back of his finger against her sticky cheek. He smiled at her. "I love it, Dandelion. Yes."

16

Thursday, 1st May

"We couldn't get a meeting room"—Karla was halfway up the spiral staircase—"so we'll take Vicky's room. She's in Amsterdam for a meeting today."

Jake followed Karla up to the long mezzanine that Vicky, Yesness's managing director, used as her office. There were views out over London that stretched wide down the river, a large concrete desk, a pale green bouclé sofa, and more scattered beanbags, each a different shade of pink.

"Hej!" Sydney said. "How's love?"

"Super. It's official now, so—"

"Official love?" asked Skye. She was leaning over an open Moleskine notebook, perched on the sofa, wearing a long prairie dress. Today her hair was the color of tangerines. "You sure move quick."

"We're officially going out, is what I mean. We're in a relationship," Jake said. He sat next to Skye, with an exhausted but contented exhale. It seemed things moved faster when you were older, like dog years. The level of intimacy he and Dandelion had achieved in a month as forty-year-olds would have taken him a whole lot longer as a younger man. He'd told her about his mother already, and the only other person he'd ever really spoken about his mum to was Zoe.

Jake thought back to the previous night. They'd listened to records, and he'd impressed Dandelion with a serrano ham, mozzarella, and rosemary toastie. She'd fallen asleep in his arms, and he'd woken that morning with a face full of her hair, the boner of a teenager, seized-up knees, and cramps in three different places. He'd negotiated himself over her and left the flat to hunt and gather breakfast: potato sourdough, eggs, coffee. When he came back, she'd kissed him, and it had been the sort of kiss that feels like it could change a life. They ate, all smiley, giggly too.

Before Dandelion left, Jake said, a bit joking, mostly serious, "So, listen, question for you?"

"Mm?" she'd hummed. Without any makeup her face was an apricot. Her skin prickled with pinks, with peach. She looked highly lickable.

"If you're not polyamorous . . ."

"Mm?" she hummed again, but this time he could hear the wind chimes of her laugh.

"How do you fancy being monogamous, with me?"

She was standing in the open door. "Oh gosh, Jake."

Jake's stomach dropped like he'd flung himself from a bridge, but then she'd winked her agreement and turned with a speed that made her cardigan whip through the air like the cape of a sorceress. At the kitchen window, Jake waited until he saw her leave the building—watched his new girlfriend run fast for the bus that had pulled up at the stop. She waved down the driver, leaped on. And Jake had been struck by the feeling that he had found her and now everything made a more peaceful sort of sense. He'd been wound up for many years; his heart had been a tangled knot pulled too tight, too small, but it was releasing, unfolding. It felt like the start of love.

On the mezzanine, Karla, Skye, and Sydney were all saying *wooooo* and *cuuute*.

When Colin came up the stairs, Sydney announced, "Jake's got a girlfriend."

"Ah, yes?" Colin was wearing a tight roll-neck top. He threw his phone in the air, and it twizzled twice before he caught it. "Dandelion?"

Karla plugged her laptop into the big screen so that the presentation they'd been working on came up. "I want to meet her. Bring her to the pub sometime, will you?"

"Definitely. I will," Jake said.

"Hey, did I tell you—I know someone else who dated her?" Colin dropped onto a beanbag. "My friend Cynthia. They went out for, like, a year."

"Cool," Jake said. He didn't give a fuck. It was all bullshit. Probably. He clapped his hands. "I'm excited to see how everything is looking, Karla."

"Her surname is Greene, right?" Colin asked. "Not a zoologist, as it turns out, according to Cynthia. I guess she lied about that."

"No, she's not." Jake was talking to the big screen on the wall. He realized he still didn't know Dandelion's surname, which actually was ridiculous. And the phone number thing needed resolving, which definitely would happen, because they'd be deleting Hinge, obviously, now they were exclusive. He decided to ask her for dinner later, maybe cook an osso buco or something low-key impressive, and elicit from her these exciting, basic facts.

"Works in finance," Colin said. "She's minted. Apparently."

Jake looked back at Colin to see his expression, but Colin was looking at the big screen too. He'd put glasses on. Jake presumed they weren't prescription because he'd never seen Colin wear them before; they were probably a fashion thing. They looked ridiculous. Why were they so big?

"Oh yeah, wow." Sydney was looking at her phone, frantically scrolling. "Total girlboss." She turned her phone to Skye. "I just googled *Dandelion Greene*. That's her LinkedIn."

Jake pulled his laptop out, opened it. "Right! Shall we? Let's!"

Skye nodded. "A finance girlie, is it, Jake? Didn't see that for you, but, sure, why not."

"Right, gang," Karla said. "I think we're in a good place with this . . ." She clicked the presentation and it moved to the agenda slide. "Obviously we'll start with intros. Then, Jake, let's dive straight into your show reel."

"She's a photographer," Jake said, wanting to set the record straight, once and for all. "And monogamous. With me. Anyway . . ." He let his voice trail off and squinted at the screen again, like it was far away.

"There's a seriously gnarly rumor about her though," Colin said, tapping his pen against the beanbag. "Cynthia heard she was dead."

Jake stood up, exhaled, and flapped his hands, and then put them on his waist. This was incredibly inappropriate. "You know what, Colin, it was unprofessional of me to bring my private life into work and I regret it. Reckon we could park this one?"

"Fuck. FUCK," Sydney said loudly enough that everyone looked at her. "I'm on Dandelion's Facebook page and it's all condolences. From, like, last year." She began to read some out. "*A great light has been extinguished, Dandelion was a trailblazer, a mentor, a game changer* . . . Yeah, and then this one says, *I'll fucking miss that biatch, I met her on Chatroulette*, and this one says"— Sydney was using different voices for each message—"*Lion, how will we cope without you?*"

"Okay, thank you!" Jake said loudly. It was hot on the mezzanine and very stuffy. "Karla, can we get on with our work, please, and stop all this poking around on the World Wide Web?"

Sydney and Colin both laughed. Probably because Jake had said *World Wide Web*. Which was quite embarrassing. But he was stressed! He sat down on the sofa—moved his arm along the back of it, but that felt wrong, so he crossed his legs. Uncrossed them. Reached for a bottle of water.

"Okay, everyone . . ." Karla didn't sound as stern as Jake wanted her to. She was looking over at Sydney.

"Let's see." Colin held his arm out, wanting Sydney's phone.

"I'll share my screen . . ."

A nanosecond later Dandelion Greene's Facebook page was on the big screen. In the profile picture there were two women sitting on the edge of a cliff, turning back to look at whoever had the camera. They were sisters, obviously, different versions of the same thing.

"That's her, that's the woman you showed us from Hinge, isn't it?" Skye pointed at the woman on the left, wearing a vest, denim cutoff shorts, and pulled-up socks and trainers. She was smiling, eyes closed, her hair tied into two long plaits.

"Yeah," Colin said. "That's Dandelion." He stood, touched the screen, tapped the woman's face.

From inside Jake's body came a loud gurgle as his internal organs communicated their discomfort. Skye ran a hand over her hair, fluffed it up. Sydney clicked at her laptop, and the name tags came up on the picture: *Dandelion Greene* and *Poppy Greene*. In the picture, the tagging was the wrong way around, and the woman wearing leggings and a hoodie with her ponytail pulled over her shoulder—whom Jake had made scrambled eggs for that morning—was tagged *Poppy Greene*.

"Jake! Hey, Jake!" Jake's face snapped to Colin. "You dating either of these chicas, or have you been totally catfished?"

"I, uh . . . I . . . I . . ."

"Right, that's enough," Karla said, coming to Jake's rescue. "Kill it. This is not a good use of our time together."

And then the Facebook page was gone, and they were back on the agenda of their presentation.

Karla moved through more slides, and the others chimed in with their thoughts. Jake pulled out his phone. He kept it on the sofa next to his thigh, looked down at it, and, with one finger, searched *Dandelion Greene finance*.

A stream of links came up. He clicked back into her Facebook, and the death messages were endless. He scrolled deeper and deeper through them. He opened Hinge and looked at Dandelion's pictures. It was the same woman as Facebook and LinkedIn. The woman that he'd first messaged on the dating app last year was, according to the internet—dead.

"Jake?" Jake looked up at Karla. They were all staring at him. In the center of the slide on the screen was typed, *THANK YOU! ANY Q'S?*

"So . . . um . . ." Jake lifted the back of his hand to his head and wiped away a layer of sweat. "God, sorry, guys." His mouth tasted awful, like he'd been sucking metal. "I'm actually feeling a bit bleurgh all of a sudden." He stuck his tongue out of the side of his mouth like a dead dog and then stood up. "Gonna go to the . . ." He was already on the rickety staircase, jogging down it. "Carry on without me! Don't worry, I'll be . . . absolutely go ahead."

In the toilet cubicle, Jake sank down the wall so that he was sitting on the gray speckled floor, his legs bent up. He googled *Poppy Greene photographer* and then stared at the back of the door, too nervous to look at the results. "It's okay, you can do this," he encouraged himself. "Just look."

The first link was a website; the domain was her name. On the home page was a carousel of aggressively tasteful tables adorned with bright place mats, enormous candles, glasses in every shape and size, photographed up close. There were vines trailing over terraces in sun-bleached hills with patchwork fields and waify women in tight white dresses staring into the eyes of jacked men. There were trays of champagne, fireworks with barefoot dancing, discos that sparkled, cascading flower arrangements in churches with vaulted ceilings, and children dressed in silk. Jake flicked through the photographs, not breathing. He clicked on "Our Founder, Our Philosophy" and was taken to a picture of Dandelion looking exquisite in a loose black trouser suit, underneath the name *Poppy Greene*.

Jake scanned the three paragraphs. A degree in photography from Falmouth, *always been an observer . . . obsessed with the psychology of human dynamics . . . emotionally collaborative . . .* Blah. Et cetera. Blah. On the "Kind Words" page, there were testimonials hailing her as *an artist, a curator, the personification of harmony and serenity* and a dozen other very gushing compliments. There were cuttings from *Harper's Bazaar* and American *Vogue* and pictures of her looking like a celebrity. On the "Contact" page was a phone number. Jake saved it, then opened WhatsApp. He enlarged the profile photo. She was in a black strapless top and gold hoop earrings. Her hair looked wet and was pulled into a ponytail. The table in the foreground was covered in a red-and-white-check tablecloth, and it looked like she was in a Greek taverna. There was a candle in a bottle. A carafe of red wine. A generous bowl of chips. A fuck-off-massive dead fish on a plate stuffed with sliced lemons. On the chair next to her, a douchey-looking man was leaning in—his hand was on her upper thigh. Behind them were strings of colored light bulbs, glowing yellow and red.

"What the fuck?" Jake said aloud to the toilet cubicle. He navigated to Hinge, to Dandelion's profile. He zoomed in on the photo of her in the bed. On the deck chair. And then: "Fuuuuck."

In the *Royal Tenenbaums* photograph, both of them were there—he could see that now. He'd only ever really looked at the woman in the middle—the main event—but crouched on the floor, face half-hidden under the very curly wig, was . . .

Jake was shaking. Properly shaking. Last night, she had told him that her dead sister was called Poppy. He believed her, obviously. The whole evening felt like one of the most truthful interactions of his life. Somewhere, there would be an explanation, and she needed to give it to him. Immediately. Jake clicked out of Hinge and onto the newly saved telephone number. Pressed call.

Part Two:
More Lies

ONE MONTH LATER

June 2025

17

Wednesday, 4th June

Poppy

Poppy cast her gaze around the small, hot wine bar and reasoned that it was Sam's engagement party really. He had organized it and invited all the guests—though it was Poppy who had proposed.

She placed a whole smoked salmon blini on her tongue, closed her mouth around it in a manner that felt comically uncouth, chewed once, swallowed, and reached for another.

"Not on a pre-wedding diet then!" Sam's sister, Hayley, said and added a small scream to make it seem like a joke. She put her glass down on the bar and wrapped her coral nails around Poppy's arm. "I actually think you look gorgeous like this." She nodded at Poppy's cleavage. "You've got such a lovely figure, so why not put it on display?"

From her brief flirtation with the confetti cannon that was Dandelion's wardrobe, Poppy had gone back to wearing monochrome COS and Arket numbers and dressing like the background rather than the stage. Though she had gained a little weight, which, ironically, had given her her sister's tits and ass—not only in size, but also in temperament—intent on breaking free and shouting, *HEYGUYSLOOK!*

"Can't help noticing you're not drinking, either, Pops?" Hayley said, eyeing Poppy's tumbler of iced sparkling water, then looking down pointedly at her own stomach. Hayley was six months pregnant, though she still had her marathon runner's physique, all tawny biceps and sinewed neck. Like Hayley herself, her bump was petite, neat, and hard looking. She kept one hand on it at all times, communicating that *yes* it was a pregnancy and *no* she wasn't fat. Tonight, she had pinned a *Baby On Board* badge to the strap of her bag, just in case anyone could be in any doubt.

Hayley was right—Poppy wasn't drinking. Obviously, she wished she could get sloshed at her own engagement do; she missed the feeling of alcohol greatly, how it made her amorphous. How it let the sadness blur and sometimes sparkle. But after everything that had happened . . . Poppy couldn't let her judgment get even fractionally impaired or fall under any sort of influence.

"There he is!" Hayley blinked at her husband. Daniel was talking to a willowy woman from Sam's company in a micro satin dress. He said something as close to her ear as he could get, straining for a millisecond on tiptoes. "Daniel!" Hayley called, beckoning him over violently when he glanced back at them.

"My favorite ladies," Daniel said as he pushed through the crowd. He reached for Poppy's waist, squeezed. "Hubba-hubba! Looking smoking hot, sis."

Since hearing the news of their engagement, Daniel had started calling Poppy *sis*, which she loathed. So as not to betray her revulsion, she let her eyes fall to her glass, away from Daniel's face, which had been filmed, as it so often was, with a layer of pallid sweat.

"No!" Daniel scolded. "Don't look away when I give you a compliment. You really are too shy for your own good, sis. Say, *Thank you very much, Daniel, you look smoking hot too.*" Daniel paused, his chin lowered. "Say it," he repeated. "Say it," he sort of growled.

"So, Poppy . . . did Sam tell you about my new role at Haus?" Hayley asked. Her neck sinews twinged; a ripple moved over her jaw. Poppy wasn't sure if Hayley was trying to help because she sensed her unease, or if she was grossed out by her husband too. "You've heard of Haus, right?"

"Yes. It looks amazing there, Hayley," Poppy said of the new Sussex hotel where Hayley had taken up a position as head of marketing and PR. "Clever you."

"Big dog, she's a big dog!" Daniel said. Then barked. He leaned through the middle of them, replacing his empty wineglass on the bar and picking up another full glass of red. "Very progressive place. Hired her when she's up the duff and everything."

Poppy turned her head to the large window at the front of the bar; outside it was clement. A black bird was sitting on a phone wire which traversed the sky, now dusky and fusing violet. It was an attractive evening and Poppy longed to fling herself into its arms and smoke a secret cigarette. "So lovely to see you guys, thank you so much for coming." She took a tiny step backward with one foot. "I'd better . . ."

"Not the easiest place to get to, is it?" Daniel said. He snorted and then Hayley snorted, and Poppy asked them if anywhere was easy to get to from Penge. She kissed them both before the retort, turned, and wove through the shoulders and the spines, keeping her eyes away from other eyes, focusing on her Mary Janes stepping over the pretty patterned tiles.

Outside the door, a couple who Poppy vaguely knew, but wasn't in the mood for talking to about her ring or the proposal or her happiness, were vaping. She walked around the corner, leaned her back against the wall, and slid down to a crouched position, taking a cigarette from her clutch. She lit it and admired the row of beautiful Hackney homes opposite. Different-colored doors. Glass boxlike extensions presumably designed by expensive Swedish architects. In one of the front gardens, two small children in smock dresses ran down a path with a miniature wirehaired dachshund on a red lead. A man stepped out of the house then, and for a single beat of Poppy's heart, her body iced—he looked just like Jake. Same height and shoulders. Same jeans, same trainers. But then . . . No. *No.* It wasn't him.

Poppy's legs still went weird when she thought of their final phone call: Jake and all his questions, leaving a silence that gaped wide for her to fill with explanations, justifications, excuses, and some kind of sense—none of which she'd been able to give him. As soon as she'd picked up her phone that afternoon to a number she didn't know and heard Jake call her *her own name*, Poppy had been crying. Dandelion had died again that day, for both of them. And Poppy was hiding from two ghosts now.

"Who are you?" Jake had asked her slowly. "Where's Dandelion?" Already, though, there had been shock in his voice and Poppy could hear he knew the truth.

"She's dead," Poppy whispered, and she'd felt like an evil person. Twisted and malicious. She fell to her knees on the station platform at Highbury & Islington, her phone pushing hard into her ear. "I'm so sorry, Jake. She's dead, she's dead, she's dead," Poppy had repeated, like the chorus of a terrible song. "I'm not her. She's not here. She's not anywhere. Dandelion is dead."

A freight train had passed then, fast and terrifying. And the people on the platform had moved away from Poppy—the lady wailing about death, on her knees, much too close to the edge. Poppy had hung up. Or Jake had. He blocked her. She blocked him. And then nothing. She'd gone through the rigmarole of changing her number. Bought a new phone. Turned her sister's off and slid it back in the box under her bed. The next day came. Then the next. Poppy hoped that Jake had put the whole thing behind him and had gone on living his life—safer, happier, better—without her. Without them.

For Poppy, though, it had been grisly. She'd been fearful of every single thing in the world, including everything she saw and thought and felt. The first week she'd been convinced that Jake was going to turn up at any moment and accost her. Or that one of his hip, scary colleagues would track her down, or troll her. Section her. Arrest her. Humiliate her on the internet.

In the mornings, Poppy had been scared of checking her emails, in case Jake had come through the inquiry form on her website, sending her aggressive messages in capitals, calling her a PSYCHO BITCH. Anytime she went anywhere, she thought she saw him. He was coming round the corner. He was sitting in the seat behind her on the bus and working on his laptop in cafés when she bought coffee. For a split second, he was the dad in a cat food advert on telly. It was his voice reading the news. He hurried toward her through every crowd. He was at Poppy's work events, swaying in her periphery. For weeks, Poppy had been continuously fearful and jittery with anxiety, self-loathing, and desire. For the tiniest second Jake was everywhere, but then he was nowhere, and the whole thing, again, was all a madly gorgeous nightmare. A totally terrible dream.

"And here she is!" Sam was on the approach, wearing a new navy linen suit. He looked very suave, had taken longer to get ready for the party than she had, by quite some way. Poppy gave him a closed-eyed wide-mouthed smile.

"Smoking? Really? I thought we—"

"I'm just finishing this pack. Once this pack is done, then . . ." Poppy sliced her hand through the air sideways, signaling that the habit would be finito. She took one last long toke, enjoying the sizzle in her lungs, then flicked it into the road.

Sam's mouth and nose drew close together in a pinch. He nodded. "Are you coming in?" He dropped a hand to her.

Poppy reached for him. When she was up on her feet, she turned her head to look back at the not quite Jake and those two small sisters from the dream house, just as they walked around the corner. The dachshund was tottering after them, tail wagging hard and rhythmic like the thrashing of a whip.

In the bar, they joined a circle of Sam's colleagues. Sam wrapped his arms around Poppy as she tried to tune in to the latest workplace anecdote that was being relayed. Poppy was grateful both to Sam and for him. Through all her wobbles and terrible times, he'd been there like a sheepdog—to nip and herd her toward the safety of the pen. She'd been lost and wrong, and he'd remained stable and committed. After everything that had happened with Jake, the shame was monstrous, and so, eight days after it all imploded, Poppy got down on one knee and apologized to Sam for being strange, distant, selfish. She pleaded a proposal. She was sorry and she couldn't lose him. *This* was her real life.

Sam had been over the moon and he'd instantly forgiven Poppy. He'd put it all down to grief, and so had she. They'd walked to the jeweler's in Hatton Garden hand in hand, and Sam had bought a diamond ring and Poppy had taken all her sister's jewelry, including the gold snake, off. For good.

"Speeeeech," someone in their circle hollered. "Speech! Speech!" Other voices joined in.

Poppy opened her eyes, looked up at the underside of Sam's chin. She'd specifically requested no public speaking. It had been her only request. "Sam . . ." she whispered. She squeezed harder around his body. Over the side of his arm, Poppy could see people turning toward them to look.

"Shit, babe." Sam unfastened her grip, took a step away. "It looks like this is happening."

Someone, potentially Daniel, shouted, "I can't see Poppy! Poppy, stand on the bar!"

"Stand on the bar!" another man agreed.

"Stand on the bar," Sam said. Poppy shook her head, but then hot, strong hands were lifting her up, and she was perched on the bar, feet dangling, looking out over everyone's heads.

"On behalf of my fiancée and I . . ." Sam said, and the room ripped into a cacophony of cheering and whooping. "I'd love to thank everyone for coming," he continued, projecting his voice expertly over the noise. "I know for some of you Hackney is a bit of a trek, so—"

"So far north I've got a nosebleed!" someone shouted with a guffaw.

Poppy concentrated hard on her own face, trying to summon the expression of one of her serene and amused bridal clients. She was aware of people holding up their phones and taking pictures, videos, stories, reels.

"Popsy," Sam said, turning to her. "It's been a tough year for us, hasn't it?"

Poppy smiled at him like there was a yummy taste in her mouth. Thankfully, Sam didn't dwell on tragedy and instead said something about how Poppy had tamed him. People laughed and he said, "No, but seriously . . ." He had both his hands over his chest, the center of it. He looked like a man about to sing. "Poppy, my soulmate—you're my other half and . . ."

Poppy could feel her face twitch. The skin above her lip was damp. She blinked repeatedly, in quick succession, then blurred her vision at the faces staring at her. In the middle of the crowd, Dandelion was slinging an invisible noose around her neck and pretending to hang herself for comic Sam-hating effect—one hand pulling up to the ceiling, her tongue hanging down to the floor. People were clapping, and Poppy shook her head once with a small deletion, a backspace. Her sister had not been invited. Since the whole Jake debacle, every time Dandelion entered Poppy's mind, Poppy banished her. She didn't want to think about her, speak about her, speak to her, see her, or—most of all—feel her fury, or her heat.

"Poppy! Speech!"

"Do you want to say anything, Popsy?" Sam asked, touching her thigh. His eyes widened; he was nodding.

Poppy pulled in a deep breath. "Thanks, everyone, for coming," she said as she glanced at the people surrounding her. She tried to speak loud, but her voice strained. Her mind washed clean of words. Someone coughed. Someone went outside, actually left. Poppy looked at Sam. He was nodding still, urging her onward. "I love you, Sam," she said.

Love—Poppy understood—wasn't passion, romance, laughter, or lust. It wasn't happiness, or Jake, or other people's relationships on social media, or at the cinema. Love meant Not Being Alone and it didn't have to feel nice every minute of the day, or most of the day, for Poppy to have to want it. Love wasn't red or pink or chocolate or heart shaped. Love could be boring and was, ultimately, uncertain. Love led to babies, which kept things turning. Love was someone to get annoyed with and cook for and hide from and hide with and to talk to about TV. Love was having someone to snuggle, spoon, grate, grind. Love was having someone who loved you back and who was there for you when everyone died, left, got sick. Love was having someone to like you, still, when you'd been a bad person. Love was having someone to upset you and irritate you and look after and care for and think of as a big fat distraction from the inevitability of the total obliteration of everyone in the world and the actual world itself.

Poppy had no clue what love was truly, or exactly, but she was climbing up its branches—with intention. She was moving through its ranks. She looked out at the faces of the people whom she vaguely knew, looking back at her. The bar jostled with their thoughts and wants, which used up all the air. Poppy reached for a half-drunk glass of water on the bar. Still, no one was talking, or clapping. They were waiting for her to say the next thing, make some sort of moving romantic declaration. Clearly, *I love you, Sam* did not sound like enough.

18

Friday, 6th June

It was dark, with a few floodlights set in the outside walls of the North London warehouse club that used to be IKEA. Poppy and her friends had been there for hours, arrived in the late afternoon, queuing next to a motorway, in long rows, like livestock separated and herded by metal fencing. All waiting to get to the front and have their bags and pockets and wallets checked for drugs. Weapons. Dates of birth. After a few hours of dancing, they'd settled outside in the smoking area.

"Commiserations, pal!" Stefan held up his plastic glass of gin and tonic.

Jetta lifted her glass too. "And good luck!"

Stefan and Jetta were both zipped into oversized fleeces, their pupils massive, tunneling into their souls. It was their first night out together since their youngest had been born; the kids were at Stefan's sister's for the night, and they were very much leaning into the respite from parental responsibility.

"Oh . . . thank you," Poppy said. She was sober. "How moving. Remind me not to let either of you near a microphone on the day."

"The Big Day," Jetta said. She pouted, gave a nod.

Jetta was the first person Poppy told about her engagement after her parents, and she'd found her to be disappointingly unenthusiastic. No squealing, no hugging, no questions about dresses, or dates, or cakes.

"The Big Bad Day," Stefan said. From the outset, Stefan had been more readable than his wife on the subject of Poppy's forthcoming nuptials. They'd been standing in a queue outside the Indian restaurant Dishoom a couple of weeks previously when she told him she was engaged, and he'd choked on literally nothing, then wheezed at her: "You sure?"

"No, I'm sorry," Jetta said quickly. "But what I will say is—"

"It's not too late to . . ." Stefan cut in. The effing double act. Years ago, they'd dressed up as the Chuckle Brothers at a house party for some reason, and a bit of Poppy had seen them that way ever since: mustaches, yellow trousers, bow ties. Collaboratively annoying. Setting up each other's jokes, finishing each other's sentences in their Yorkshire accents (Stefan was from Leeds, and Jetta, pre-Devon, had grown up in York and never lost her twang).

Poppy pushed her jaw forward, took a sharp inhale of air through her nose, and, without looking down, felt around in her bag for her tobacco.

"Sorry, Pops." Jetta leaned forward over the wooden slatted table and touched Poppy's forearm. "Only teasing."

Stephan was nodding, in a manner that looked distinctly sarcastic.

"All these snide comments, these jibes . . . Where's this coming from?" Poppy's chest was tight. She pressed the tobacco down onto the table, hard. "Sam and I have been together for a long time and—"

"Where's Sam this weekend, again?" Opposite Poppy, Stefan was framed by wisps of cloud, orange from all the lights on the adjacent motorway. He touched his phone and a picture of Jetta and their kids on a large inflatable unicorn in an electric-blue swimming pool flashed up on the screen.

There was a beat of silence, then Poppy coughed a tiny noise of outrage. "He's on a work trip until Sunday. I told you. Not all couples want to live in each other's pockets, you know." Poppy was officially not having a good time. "I actually think I'm gonna go home, leave you to it."

Stefan looked at Jetta, and something passed between them; he leaned right over the table and took both of Poppy's hands. "Noooooo."

"Absolutely not allowed. I'd like to make an apology and a toast!" Jetta grinned, showed her teeth, the sweet gap between the front two. "Here's to our little Poppet."

"Sam is a lucky man!" Stefan added. "We wish you every happiness."

"Thank you." Poppy touched her glass to their glasses, her agitation slightly thawed.

"I keep getting this feeling that Dandelion's here." Stefan was looking around them, at all the other people. "Like, right now, she could be on a mission to find the dodgy blokes who bring in laughing gas."

"I reckon she's in the mosh pit grinding with strangers," Jetta said, turning her face back to the arched entrance, as if she could see all the way to the dance floor and had spied her friend.

"Any second now," Stefan laughed, "she's gonna sidle up next to us with some random dude's shades on."

"*You'll never guess what . . .*" Jetta said, doing her disconcertingly good impression of her best friend. "*Guysguysguysguysguys!*" And then both she and Stefan were really laughing. He slung his arms around her, kissed the side of her head, and then called up into the sky, "Dandelion? Come back!"

Watching them, Poppy exhaled with such heaviness that Stefan was prompted to offer her mushroom oil for the third time that evening. "Coupladrops?" He untangled himself from his wife and pulled the small brown bottle that he'd smuggled in from the zipped top pocket of his fleece. "Go on . . . all aboard for Mummy and Daddy's big night out."

Poppy curled her lip, shook her head. "Really, I'm fine."

"Honestly, micro-dosing will really help with . . ." For the last couple of years, Stefan had been shroom-splaining the (seemingly endless) benefits of micro-dosing to the girls. As far as he was concerned, mushrooms were a panacea.

"Stef, you've macro-dosed, be quiet," Poppy said.

"Maybe stop pushing drugs on everyone, my love," Jetta agreed. "I saw you getting that bottle out about ten times on the dance floor."

"People ask!" Stefan objected. "I like to share."

Jetta stood up, adjusted her bag across her chest. "Think we need to move, I'm getting chilly. Drink, then back for a boogie?" She pointed at both of them in turn. "Gin and tonic and a lemonade." She'd only taken a few steps before doing an elaborate one-eighty, her body crouched. "You gotta see this," she said, coming back to them. "I know *we're* having fun, but not nearly as much fun as that dude over there." She nodded her head in the direction of the bar.

Poppy followed Jetta's eyeline and noticed that people at other tables were also looking at something. Someone. A couple, both in parkas, were pointing. Equidistant between them and the main door, a man was staggering in circles all by himself.

"Is it just me, or does he look even older than us?" Stefan stood up.

The man crumpled to his knees, fell to all fours. The parkas started a slow clap.

"Ah!" Jetta clutched her stomach. "He's not very well. He's vom-ming."

Poppy placed her fists on the table and pushed herself to her feet. She leaned forward, focused her eyes on the man who was floundering, alone, on the ground. He had Jake's hair, but longer. The same sort of build. A very similar profile. Poppy was holding her breath, waiting for the inevitable confirmation it definitely wasn't him—but with every passing millisecond the man on the ground became more Jake, and more Jake, and more.

"Why is no one helping him?" Stefan asked. He jumped the bench and slow jogged over.

The man pressed his cheek against the cement, and Poppy could see that it was Jake's face. No doubt. "Nooo . . ." She opened her mouth and then covered it with both her hands as if she was trying to keep her secrets in and that, already, just by virtue of seeing him, she was going to scream every terrible thing she'd done, out loud.

Jetta reached out and pulled Poppy's wrist as she started jogging over to the action, but Poppy shook her off, roughly enough for Jetta to stop and flash her a surprised look.

"What's wrong with him?" Poppy asked. It made no sense.

She had known that one day she would see Jake again; she'd felt it innately. But now that it was actually happening, it was to-tally wrong. Out of all the possible scenarios, never would Poppy have imagined this—with Jake so visibly spangled and sick.

Another man was standing with them, too, now. A big guy, wearing a black shirt tucked into black trousers: a bouncer. Jetta turned her head to speak to him, while Stefan helped Jake sit up.

Okay, so, *good*, he was being looked after. He was in safe hands. Poppy turned to the bar. She could leave and go home. The only reason she was here was that Stefan and Jetta had bought her a ticket and then guilted her into coming with the whole *Mummy and Daddy never have any fun* thing, but this would be a perfectly acceptable time to slip off. Her friends would definitely make sure Jake was okay, Poppy knew they would.

But instead, she took a few tentative steps toward the little group clustering around Jake, like a moth drawn to a flame. And then a few more. With every step, she murmured a single-word question to herself, her lips barely moving: *How? Jake? What?* Because it couldn't be drugs. He didn't do drugs—he'd told her that last time she'd seen him at his flat, and she'd heard in his voice how much he meant it. So, was he just really drunk?

Poppy was standing right behind Jetta now, and she watched as Jake pulled himself up Stefan's trousers, clutching with his fists. "I'm coming out," he said, and it was still his voice—but rasping, like his lungs were packing up.

"He's coming out!" Stefan repeated loudly, informing the spectators. "The man's in a possible, suspected, alleged K-hole and he's coming out!" Some people at a nearby table cheered. "Look at that," Stefan said to Jake encouragingly, as if talking to his toddler. "Standing and everything."

"He's pissed himself," the bouncer said. He nodded to Jake's crotch, the darkening of his khaki trousers. The smell of vomit and maybe piss cut through the air around them with a musty acidic bite. "I'll radio for a stretcher." The bouncer had a walkie-talkie clipped to the front of his shirt. He held down a button on the top of it and spoke with his chin to his chest.

Jake's eyes moved over Jetta and Poppy, but there was no recognition there at all. He slid to the dirty concrete floor again, onto his back, coughed.

Stefan crouched down and felt over his pockets gently, while Jake's face contorted into insane iterations. "We have keys, we have a phone . . . but it's dead," Stefan said, holding up Jake's things.

"So which one of you is going to accompany him to the medi-cal unit?" the bouncer asked.

"Just to say," Stefan said, "we don't actually know this guy. I have no idea where his friends are. I asked him, but . . . yeah." He looked down at Jake. "I'd be surprised if he knew his own name right now."

Poppy knelt right next to Jake. He didn't acknowledge her at all. Obviously, she was worried about what would happen if he started spitting accusations, but more than anything—she was concerned about how seriously sick he was. Seeing him in this state was aw-ful. She touched his hand, quickly at first, and when he didn't move, she held his arm. She squeezed it, whispered, "You're going to be okay. I promise." She looked up at the bouncer. "I think we should call an ambulance."

"Stop touching him, Poppy!" Jetta scolded, grimacing.

"He's just had too many disco biscuits, Poppet, don't stress," Stefan said. "He'll be grand in thirty minutes."

"GAGAGAGAA!" Jake shouted, as if he was trying to commu-nicate very important news.

"Maybe . . ." Stefan corrected himself, "more like an hour."

"We'll get him assessed in the medical unit," the bouncer said. "Stretcher's on its way."

"I'm going to come with you," Poppy said to the bouncer. She kicked over Jake's vomit-filled shoe, let it drain, then picked it up, holding it by a lace.

"We don't need a stretcher, he can walk. You can walk, right?" Stefan pulled Jake onto his feet and slung one of his arms over his shoulders. Jake staggered, but his eyes were open. He looked at Stefan, and then his head sagged down. "I'll bring him," Stefan said.

The bouncer lifted Jake's other arm over his shoulder. "Fine," he said. "This way."

Poppy and Jetta followed the bouncer, Stefan, and Jake's floppy body to a metal door with a big sign that said *NO ENTRY*. Once they were through it, inside the warehouse, they wove through a series of dark corridors, Jake intermittently groaning or saying something nonsensical.

"What was that? What did he say, my love?" Jetta asked.

"I think he might be a carpenter," Stefan said. "He's talking about—"

"No, he's talking about carpets," the bouncer corrected.

"Carpets!" Jetta was having a great time. "Pop, did you hear? Carpets . . ."

"I heard," Poppy said.

The medical unit was a large room with foldout beds on metal legs and wipe-down plastic covers. The lights were on bright and there were no windows, potentially because they were underground. In one corner, a girl with a tearstained face lay curled in a ball, on a bed. Two others were sitting on chairs right next to her and they were chatting, hoods pulled up over their heads.

The bouncer introduced Poppy, Jetta, and Stefan to the guy who worked there, Deo. Then he handed Deo Jake's phone. Jetta gave the bouncer a hug goodbye. "You're the best! Thank you so much!"

"Behave. Okay?" the bouncer said, quite obviously endeared to them. He tilted his face into his walkie-talkie, started speaking into it as he turned away.

Deo was in pale green scrubs, had one pearl earring, and looked very tired. "Who's this?" he asked.

"Ja—" Poppy started. She caught herself. Put her hand to her mouth and looked thoughtfully at the floor.

"We've got no clue, pal," Stefan said.

"No clue," Poppy repeated, nodding. "We found him alone, upstairs."

"Can you tell me what he's taken?" Deo asked as he lifted Jake's eyelids one by one and shone a small torch into them.

"Fuck knows," Stefan said. "Ket? 'Cid? Fourteen pingers?"

"And what are you on?" Deo asked, standing up straight, turning to them.

"Us?" Jetta blinked, all innocent. "We're just high on life, Deo."

"Unless you're into mushrooms, in which case can I offer you . . . ?"

One of the girls who was sitting in the corner started sniggering.

"Do you know what, guys—you go. I'll stay," Poppy said. "I'm sober anyway and . . ."

"We're not leaving you, Pops," Jetta said.

"Honestly, I'll wait until I know he's okay and . . . maybe you could look for his friends?"

"Yeah, I guess . . ." Jetta was swaying from foot to foot. Poppy knew the idea of a task, a little mission to carry out, would capture her imagination. And they'd both definitely want to get back to the dance floor, before they totally sobered up.

Stefan had closed one eye and was trying to focus on the lineup on his phone. "We could still catch Bicep, they're playing 'til half ten."

"Are you sure, sure, sure you don't mind if we go?" Jetta asked.

"Totally." Poppy put Jake's shoe on the floor. At the side of the room was a sink. She went over to it to wash her hands. Dried them on blue paper towels, turned back to her friends. "Seriously, I'm perfectly fine, promise. I wasn't feeling it up there anyway."

They didn't need any more persuading, and once they'd sandwiched her in a suffocating hug and left, Poppy felt slightly calmer. Deo instructed her to get a blanket from a pile. He cleaned Jake's arm and hooked him to a drip, without Jake even noticing.

"What should I do?" Poppy pulled out a gray plastic chair.

They had those chairs in the hospital last year, the exact same ones.

"Just sit with him. He needs to get these fluids into his system," Deo said.

Poppy reached for some wet wipes on a shelf behind the bed and took one of Jake's grubby hands, cleaned his palm. His head turned from side to side and he started kicking his legs. Poppy stood and whispered, "Shhh, shhh." She tried her best to soothe him. "Shhh, Jake. It's going to be okay. I promise. Calm down. Just calm . . ."

Jake stopped thrashing and turned his head to her. His eyes didn't look like his anymore. They weren't yellow and petaled and smiley; they were glossy and black, a night sky without any stars. He opened his mouth. His lip was bleeding. "It's you," he said.

"Oh." Poppy felt herself start to get upset; she gasped a small sound of pain, of shock, of deep and twisting remorse.

"Dandelion?"

"Jake, I . . ." Poppy shook her head and looked away from him. She wasn't going to lie. Not this time. Never again, in fact. She looked back at his face, into his eyes. Took both his hands in hers. "I'm not Dandelion."

19

Saturday, 7th June

Jake

When Jake came to, he was in the bath of his childhood home. Pink tiles, white textured walls. His mother was there. She was kneeling on the floor, and she was showing him how to play with a blue plastic submarine that had a small propeller. His mother was wearing her yellow halter neck, and her hair was tied up in a dotted scarf. Jake reached out to her, but her face melted to her shoulders and her shoulders melted out of sight and when he leaned over the bath she was nowhere and the floor tiles were swimming, circling like piranha—ready to kill.

The bathroom changed into another bathroom and Jake was somewhere else. Everything was in hyperfocus: the cleanness of the light, the gray swirls in the marble, the fluffiness of towels on the rail. There was an intense pain in his mouth, in his stomach, his eyes, and a yanking down his spine as he pulled himself out of the bath and turned to a large window that had a blind drawn over it. Was he in a hotel? There were birds outside and they were shrieking—*Pathetic, pathetic, you should be dead.*

Jake clutched his hands to his stomach and looked down at his naked body. His dick had shrunk to an actual acorn. He screamed, fell to his knees, crawled into a long hallway, and then he was in a sitting room. There, too, was Dandelion, her long hair blowing gently in a breeze.

Quite overcome with relief, Jake crawled toward her, got to his feet, and let his fingers touch her face, but she was cold and hard. "Fuck," he hissed—because she was just a picture, a torso hanging on a wall in a room he didn't know, and he was naked, caressing the picture's frame.

Jake staggered backward over a rug, and the patterns of it whirled in a wind around him as strong as the mistral. He was Van Gogh. No, he wasn't. He hoisted himself onto a sofa and covered his body in a blanket he found there. He looked up at the ceiling and watched the wind as it morphed and split and joined. He didn't have an ear. He had an ear. Two. His eyesight had shattered like a brick through a window. The pain had layers and fingers and claws. The blackness pulled at his ankles, and then he was falling through a place that wasn't sleep and wasn't wake and, maybe, wasn't life.

Noises filtered through. Muffled clatter. There was an opening and closing of doors, the running of taps, the creak of a floor. Someone else's breath. The room got bright, dark, bright. Maybe a lot of time passed, and then Jake was looking at a person through the open doorway. She was on her hands and knees scrubbing the floor. He tried to move between thoughts like stepping stones. Go forward—stability, facts. He closed his eyes, and when he opened them, she was in front of him, perched on a large, low coffee table, bent forward, hands clasped. "Jake? Are you there?"

She had freckles that were strawberry seeds and eyes made of sky. Her hair was pulled back into a ponytail which exploded out behind her, from shoulder to shoulder. Her hair was every different color that had ever been invented. Her hair was wildfire. The room around her burned.

Jake focused. She was in black leggings and a hoodie. There was a teapot with spots on, red and orange. There were mugs with bright green handles and an open carton of milk. She poured the tea, not looking at him, and Jake knew he was a man in a body, and his body was in a room, and also in the room was . . . her. Dandelion's sister—Poppy. It was Poppy Greene.

A crowd of questions shouted in Jake's mind, and he tried to reach for one of them and make it into a cohesive sentence and push it out of his mouth. "Where am I?" he managed, although his voice sounded awful, clagged with goop and phlegm. He cleared his throat. "What day is it? What happened?" There was a glass of water and he reached for it. "Why you?" As he drank, water dribbled over his chin. He lay back again, exhaled with the exertion of it all. He would not be able to move or run away, even if he had to. He touched his lower lip; it was crusted in scab and swollen. He felt around his ribs because it hurt very much to talk and also just to breathe. Someone had kicked the life right out of him. Had they? Who? Her? No. Was this a punishment? For what? Which bit?

"How are you feeling?" Poppy asked. She was holding on to her own wrist. That wrist. He remembered how the bone of it raised and circled into the smallest island. He remembered the skin on her arm, the skin that held her all together, how it was sugar and cream. "You've been asleep for a good long while. It's six p.m. Saturday. So . . . how you feeling?"

Jake covered his eyes with a hand and fell into his thoughts, looking for lost time. "Saturday," he repeated. His mind, for a while, he knew, had no longer been his own, or even a mind at all. But now . . . Jake was becoming a person again.

Tomorrow, Sunday, he was seeing Billy, and whatever it was

that had happened needed to have stopped. "I don't remember . . ." He kept his thumb and finger pushing down into his eyes so that he didn't have to deal with the complication of Poppy's face.

"Jake." She touched his arm and he pulled it away from her, rubbed his skin as if she'd scalded him. "Sorry. Don't worry. Everything's fine. I was at the club yesterday with friends and we bumped into you." She was speaking quickly, trying to get the explanation out. "You were very high. Beyond high. I took you to the medical place and they said you needed to go home and sleep it off. There's nothing seriously wrong with you, you're going to be fine. Only you'd lost your friends, so . . . don't you remember? We got a taxi here."

Jake rolled into a fetal position and took a long inhale of breath. None of what she said sounded familiar, or possible. He lifted the blanket covering his body and saw that he was naked. "Where are my clothes? My clothes, where . . ." The words dried up, his breath ran out.

"You must have undressed yourself." Poppy was composed. Angelically serene. "I brought you round here and left you to sleep, and when I came back, you'd obviously had a bath because all your clothes were in there and you'd been sick a bit in the hall, so . . . yeah. I've put your stuff on to wash, it's drying next door. Hope that's okay."

Jake closed his eyes, and there, again, was a dance floor slashed by razors of light. He remembered the feeling of his heart beating in his temples, thumping out his eyes. *Okay. So. Yes. The club.* And what happened before that? He concentrated on a piece of the puzzle, pushed it up against another piece, clicked it into place— the previous morning came into soft focus.

He had gone for a run, bought a cinnamon roll and a coffee from the café on the canal, and done some work at home. FaceTimed Billy. For lunch, a whole group of them met at the restaurant Brat in Shoreditch, colleagues from Yesness and their favorite clients. Jake remembered—it was the work summer party, and it had been planned for months. After, there'd been a string of pubs: sitting on tables outside, standing in groups on pavements. Tokes on cigarettes. Cold pints. Snippets of conversations about work. Flirting. Walking down the street with arms around each other. London in summer. People had been everywhere, sunny, bright, skirts showing flesh. Then a taxi. Queuing. Laughing. A round of drinks, plastic cups. The hard hit of bass, pulping his insides. The crowd had swollen. Severed heads had been calling his name. All around him—a horror show of lights.

"I can remember some stuff . . ." Jake said, his eyes still closed. But how had he got so drunk?

Much later, there'd been a bathroom and he'd been all alone, throwing up. He'd managed to run a bath, hallucinating—thought he was a child again, thought he was with his mother. *His mother.* Jake felt a desperate swell inside of him. He rolled onto his back, opened his eyes, and looked at the large windows, the wooden shutters. All the books on the floor-to-ceiling shelves, the enormous record collection. He recognized the flat from Instagram now, from the intense Google research he'd done, in the weeks after he'd lost her.

Dandelion Greene death
Dandelion Greene images
Dandelion Greene boyfriend
Dandelion Greene dating
Dandelion Greene net worth
Dandelion Greene Instagram
Dandelion Greene sister
Dandelion Greene kids?

"I remember her," Jake said, tilting his face to the pale wood frame on the wall, the large photograph of Dandelion—her hair still moving, very slightly, in some faraway, potentially hallucinated (through incredibly realistic) breeze.

Back when they'd started dating, Jake had been in the process of falling for Dandelion, hard, but then reality had been pulled from under him and, for a moment there—things had got quite dark. The first night after the phone call with Poppy, when the truth was revealed, Billy had come into the sitting room late, because again, the neighbor had woken him with an all-night Tuesday party. Billy had found Jake crying, actually sobbing (he'd had three-quarters of a bottle of white wine), and the following day Billy told his mummy that Dada was sad, and then the whole caboodle—Zoe, Yan, Jake's father—were alerted and concerned. And so, under duress, Jake had told them that there had been a death. A sudden one. He had found himself spinning a yarn, convincingly—with genuine tears in his eyes—about how his new girlfriend, Dandelion, was gone. *Dead.* And perhaps he'd wanted his family's sympathy, rather than the pity he'd got from his colleagues, who all knew the mortifying actual truth. So, *yes*, Jake had admitted to Zoe, Yan, and his father that *of course it was all very new*, but he hadn't felt that way about anyone for a long time. And they'd been shocked and had felt terrible for him, and Jake, in turn, had felt terrible about his fibs.

But he'd been lied to, and worse. By Poppy.

Initially, Poppy's deception had made Jake feel a fool, of course, but it had been more than just shame and anger; Jake had felt as if his future had been stolen from him. From *them*. But not from him and Poppy, because she had been playing a part, and it was the character Jake had fallen for—the sister.

And so he had taken that premise between the palms of his

hands and molded it into a shape that he could keep around forever: a tragic, short-lived, powerful connection. Poppy's lie became Jake's truth and, like a method actor living a fictional reality, he'd barely let himself think of the actual, real-life Poppy since. Dandelion was the woman Jake had fallen for and whom, maybe one day, he suspected, he could have truly loved. But she'd slipped through his fingers, like she'd slipped from her life.

"Jake?" Poppy touched Jake's arm, and his eyes whipped back to her. His vision was still fucked, and she was glistening. Little sparkles pinged from her skin. "Do you remember what you took?" she asked. "At first, they thought maybe ketamine, because you couldn't really move, or talk. But then it went on for so long, the medical person said maybe acid—which can last for days, apparently . . ." She caught herself and tried to backtrack, pressed her hands together in a soundless clap. "They fully examined you, though, and said you would be fine. So don't worry. The doctor one hundred percent said it would pass, you just overdid it and need to rest, drink plenty of fluids. So . . ." Her voice trailed off. "No one lives here at the moment. You can stay as long as you need." Poppy held out her arms to Dandelion's flat. "Islington, so it's not too far from your place."

"Can't be . . ." Jake said slowly. There was no way he'd be so stupid as to take anything. No matter how pissed he was. "I don't do drugs."

"Right, well . . ." Poppy raised her eyebrows at him in a kind way, though he could see she was skeptical. "We're probably not going to get to the bottom of it now, and the main thing is you're really improving. How do you feel?"

"Definitely a bit better than I was . . ." Jake admitted.

"That's such good news, Jake. What a relief." She smiled at him, and her amped-up radiance made him feel worse, more mad. "Your phone is plugged in to charge." She nodded at his phone, which was on the floor next to his keys and wallet. "I'm sorry," she said, looking back at him. "I know this is a crazy situation. I'm not sure when the right time for a real apology is. I want you to be able to understand it. I want—"

"Not now," Jake said. No way. What he really needed was food, painkillers, fluid, and a lot more sleep.

"There's food," Poppy said, like a psychic. "It's in the kitchen. Shall I bring it? I got ibuprofen, rehydration sachets, and Lucozade for you too . . ." She left the room, came back with two full plastic bags, and put them on the low table. "This is my new number." She'd already written it on a yellow Post-it note, which she stuck to a large coffee table book. Reading the title of the book felt like intense brain exercise. Jake squinted at it: *A Woman's Right to Pleasure*. There was a massive pink shiny mouth on the cover. A mouth in a mouth in a vulva. Or was it a vulva in a mouth? Or was it a flower in a stomach in a . . . ? Jake closed his eyes. This was a terrible day. Or was it one of the best?

"I've gotta go, I'm afraid. Will you be okay to rest here for a bit?" Poppy asked. Jake heard her move further away; the floorboards creaked.

"Yes," he whispered, then managed, "Thank you, Poppy." He was grateful he was going to be able to stay still and quiet.

"No one's going to be here, so you can recoup all week if you need to. No rush, okay . . . I left a key." Then, from the hallway, she called, "There's a bedroom. Well, there's two, one's locked, but the other's all made up for you. Ring me anytime. You're going to be fine, Jake. I promise."

Jake was getting hot and, again, nausea curdled in his stomach. A door slammed loud, and when he opened his eyes, Poppy was no longer there. He missed her. Almost missed her. What he felt was scared. Maybe she'd never existed. How was he meant to be certain which of the things he could feel and see were real?

Jake moved his gaze to the picture of Dandelion on the wall. She'd found him, that's what had happened—fate had brought them together once again. He pushed himself up and shuffled over to the picture. She was speaking, but he couldn't quite hear the words. Behind her there was sea and it was crashing; seagulls were screaming. Everything was very noisy. Her world was impossibly bright.

"Okay, yes," Jake said, because he understood what she wanted. He lifted Dandelion off the wall and carried her in his arms. He rested her on the sofa, took a cushion for his head, and lay on the floor. He stared at her face until his eyes dried and he was pulled into a sleep that was bluer and better. Next to him, Dandelion pressed her fingertips up against the glass of life. And so did he. They weren't that far apart.

20

Sunday, 8th June

"Jakey! Better late than never!" Jake's father called from where he was standing in his expensively landscaped garden, next to a barbecue as big as an open coffin.

Jake lifted his hand in greeting, and another of the flashes passed through his head—from temple to temple—a fuzzed bolt of electricity. They didn't hurt, but for a millisecond the only thought he had was *phzzzzzz*. Still, he was four hundred times better than he had been yesterday, which, it sounded like, according to Poppy, was four hundred times better than he had been on Friday night.

Of the previous twenty hours of his life, Jake had been asleep for fifteen on Dandelion's floor next to a picture of her in a frame—which, yes, he realized when he woke up again was niche. In the remaining five hours, he had eaten two takeaway pizzas and drunk three liters of water, had a glorious shower in Dandelion's exquisite bathroom, holding his face up to a brass showerhead the size of a Frisbee, feeling himself palpably perk up, like a thirsty plant. His penis had regrown, thank Christ, and he had been brave enough to leave the house and take on the overground.

"Dadaaa!" Billy bolted over, wearing swimming trunks with purple turtles on.

Jake swooped him into his arms, pressed his cheek against his sweet-smelling head, and noticed that his son's hair was tied into a boy bun. "I missed you, buddy."

A couple of meters into the garden, near the barbecue, was a long table with a large canvas umbrella. Zoe was sitting in its shade in a wide-brimmed hat and a caftan the color and consistency of porridge. Yan had pulled his chair back into the sun. His long dark hair was piled right on the very top of his head, and he was wearing a pair of board shorts and a gold chain necklace, which looked undeniably sexy, glinting just above his sculpted pecs.

"You nearly missed the food, brother." Yan stood up, Jake put Billy down, and they did their hugging-backslap thing. Zoe stayed in her chair watching them, then Jake kissed her on the top of her sun hat. She placed her hand on his hand, a little pat, the type of affection that would have previously been unfathomable, but things were different between them now—there had been an enormous improvement in relations.

Since Jake had told them his girlfriend, Dandelion, had died, Zoe had been worried and, really, very kind. It was a kindness, Jake knew, which wouldn't have been wholly available if Yan hadn't been in her life. Zoe was in love, and that love had flooded the banks and drenched the surrounding area, so that now Jake felt her love too; not in a romantic way, but something almost deeper. It was a post-love love—an acknowledgment that they had tried, and they had failed, but, together, they'd made the world's best thing. After years of bad blood, it felt relieving for the insidious resentment to have subsided and exposed new good ground.

Billy squatted on the floor by Jake's chair, interested in some ants, and Jake closed his eyes, trying to soak up some serotonin, joy, vitamin D.

"Jake, your lips. Is that a cold sore?" Zoe asked.

"They're just chapped," Jake said, head back, eyes still closed.

"Looks nasty."

"It's fine," Jake said.

"You're trembling." Zoe reached out to hold his arm. Jake opened his eyes and looked back at her, scrunched his nose up as much as possible. Everything was good between them, but also, Zoe irritated him in a very unique way. "You're looking quite . . ." She lifted a hand and moved her fingers over her own face. "Sallow."

"Yeah, I . . ." Jake slipped a pair of sunglasses he'd found in Dandelion's bathroom from his shirt pocket and pushed them on. "Had a big weekend."

"What does that mean?" Zoe asked. "Whose glasses are those?"

"I went to a club," Jake said as Yan passed him a cold lager. Instead of reaching for it, Jake sat on his hands, and Yan put the bottle on the table in front of him. He wasn't quite ready to be in contact with alcohol.

Billy looked up from the grass. He had some ants in the cupped palm of his hand, which were zinging around, all panicked. "After-school club?"

"A different type of club," Jake said.

Zoe had lowered her chin and was looking at Jake over the top of her sunglasses. "Clubbing?" She blew a raspberry and reached for a tortilla chip. She never used to eat crisps, chips, crap. She barely used to eat.

Jake leaned forward, reached for a chip, and admired Yan's necklace, which had nestled itself into his dark chest hair. "Nice chain, man," he said, nodding at it, and then his mind flashed with another electric current and for a split second he saw Dandelion sitting on one of the other chairs, smiling at him in his mother's yellow halter neck. Though actually it was Poppy. Though actually . . . it was just the light, the heat, his mind. It was Billy's dolly, Spleen, creeping him out.

Jake closed his eyes again. It was safer in the dark. He felt his lip ooze scuzz. Maybe he should get a chain necklace too? Maybe he should call Poppy. Or just message her and thank her again for letting him stay. Unless she'd drugged him on Friday. Unless this was the next articulation of her evil plan. Though, even if she had—and Jake felt innately that she hadn't—recuperating in Dandelion's flat had been an enormous blessing. Like living in the pages of an interior's magazine, which, in comparison, made Jake's flat look like an actual squat. He really needed to move out of the Palace. The novelty had massively worn off. He was too old to be in the mix with all those kids; he wasn't down with them. And if it hadn't been hectic enough, now there was a new nocturnal neighbor who was, apparently, majorly big on TikTok, and even when she wasn't hosting an after-party, she was home alone, "dropping tracks, making beats," which were not at all relaxing to listen to through the wall. Billy hated being there too. And it wasn't even like Jake was broke; he could afford somewhere much nicer, he'd just not got round to looking. He'd been too busy and now it was summer and, anyway, he was spending most weekends here, at his dad's, and was planning on booking a solo holiday—maybe Menorca. Lie around. Get a tan. Actually read a book.

Being at Dandelion's felt amazing though; maybe he could rent it from Poppy for a holiday instead of going abroad? Jake felt around on the table in front of him for the beer. A beer would give him the courage to call her, but first he needed to work out how he was meant to feel. Was Poppy calculating? Was she kind? She was certainly very attractive, more so than he'd remembered, which was not ideal. Unless it was?

The beer was helping already. Soon, Jake would be able to face the Yesness WhatsApp chat—all those messages that he'd been avoiding. Hopefully, his disappearance from the club hadn't been a massive deal. Hopefully, none of his colleagues had really noticed. Although maybe . . . what if it was food poisoning from their lunch, perhaps other people had got sick? He'd had mussels for his starter. Could shellfish make someone flirt with insanity for roughly twenty-four hours? Alcohol poisoning, potentially, could get that bad . . . Maybe it was both? A poisonous clusterfuck.

"Please stop muttering to yourself, Jake," Zoe said, "it's really unsettling."

Jake opened his eyes. "I'm not."

"You are."

"I wasn't, Zoe."

"Jake, you were."

"This looks amazing, Rafe," Yan said as Jake's father put two large dishes on the table. One was piled with kebabs and different types of sausages, and the other was barbecued veg and hunks of charred Halloumi. "Gracias, amigo."

"Grazyasmigo," Billy repeated, bouncing up into the chair, his bun bobbing. Billy, too, was smitten with Yan. On Yan's suggestion, Zoe had enrolled him in gymnastics class, and now Yan and Billy always seemed to be bonding over backflips—Jake's little boy was fast becoming Da Yogi Cub.

"So, Rafe, tell us who you're dating?" Yan asked Jake's father, who had taken a seat at the head of the table.

"Yes! Well, I must thank Jakey for introducing me to the apps," Jake's father said. His linen shirtsleeves were rolled up, his forearms tanned, crinkled, and marked with age spots, his Rolex glinting in the sun. "I've met a really lovely little thing. Extremely smart and very adventurous. *Liberal*," he added in a tone that implied he was not referring to her politics.

"Oh, fucking hell," Jake said, rolling his head to Zoe, then rolling it back to his dad. "How old?"

"I don't know how old she is. I would never ask a lady her age," Jake's father said as he lifted a bottle of Viognier from a cooler.

"Dad, I know you know," Jake said, glancing at his empty plate and wondering what the army of angry ulcers who had set up camp that morning in his mouth were going to have to say about this food. He looked at his father again. "All the apps specify age, so there's no use pretending. Is she younger than me?"

"She's in her thirties," Jake's father said, swiping at a wasp that was buzzing at his plate.

"Right. Well. That's disgusting." Jake definitely would not be able to eat.

After lunch, Jake gave Billy a swimming lesson in his dad's pool. He was holding him under his tummy, saying, "Kick, kick, kick, kick," when Zoe came over in her swimsuit. Jake watched her slender legs lower into the water.

"Your dad's showing Yan his new car."

"He's got a new car?" Jake asked.

"I want to see the car!" Billy said, blinking wet clumped-together eyelashes.

Jake steered him through the water toward Zoe, and she helped him out, wrapping a towel with a hood and little ears around him. "How did your dad become so rich again?"

"Investments. Stocks. Shares. Stuff I don't fully understand," Jake said. "I ask him about his business and then thirty seconds into the answer I realize I'm thinking about the sky. Or food.

Or . . ." Jake pulled himself out of the pool and sat next to Zoe. He looked at the cloudless sky. It looked exactly like the swimming pool, but endless. He thought about dinner; maybe good old pesto pasta was what he was up for tonight. Like he used to make for his mum when he wanted her to eat. "Um, sorry . . ." He moved his gaze back to Zoe. "What were we talking about?"

"CARRRRR!" Billy's patience had expired.

"Baba!" Zoe called across the lawn to Yan. "Babasita! Can Billy come and see the car?"

"Hey, da Billy boy!" Yan shouted. "Come see!"

Zoe turned back to Jake as their little boy charged off. She stroked some hair behind his ear. "I think it's really lovely we can all hang out like this, Jake."

Jake looked down at their feet resting on the second step. "Yes. Who would have thought? We made it to a good spot." He put his hand on the center of her back.

"I wanted to ask . . . do you ever think about talking to your dad about any of your stuff?"

"*What stuff?*" Jake tipped his head away from Zoe, took his hand off her, and squeezed his own thigh.

Zoe leaned back on her hands, her collarbones tilting up toward the sun. Her skin shone with a white cast of sunscreen. "I mean have you discussed any childhood stuff. About how he left you guys. About your mum . . . feels like now might be a really good time?"

A good time? Of all the times, this one would certainly be the worst. Jake shuddered at the thought of having to talk to his father about his childhood. "There's nothing to say, Zo. Everything's fine." Across the lawn, Yan lifted Billy onto his shoulders. "I appreciate the concern, but that's all water under the bridge."

"You're a good dad, you know that, right? Billy adores you,"

Zoe continued, patronizing as hell. "He looks up to you so much. And once upon a time, you were a good husband—"

"ZoZo," Jake interrupted, his jaw clenched and really hurting. "I am still in the grips of a hangover, and I'm not in the mood to self-reflect. I feel enormously remorseful for every misstep I've ever taken, and I'm giving myself a hard time already, I promise. Could I respectfully ask you to leave me alone?"

Zoe was silent for a few seconds, and although Jake was looking down at their feet in the water, he imagined her back arching like an angry cat's. "Leave you alone?" she repeated, overarticulating each word.

"It's really cool that we're acting like old friends." Jake slung his arm over her shoulder, rocked her a little. "We *are* old friends. The oldest. The friendliest. So, please may I ask you to leave out the heavy chat for today? And just . . . drop it. Please?" And then he added, "For once?" *Fuck.*

Zoe slid backwards and changed the angle of her body so that now they were adversaries. "You've turned up here in a total state, Jake. You look, frankly—like you've been sleeping under a park bench for a week and, apparently, you've stolen some ridiculous sunglasses off a teenage girl."

Jake sniggered a laugh. "Okay, well—"

"Obviously, you've been through such a horrid time losing your girlfriend," Zoe continued forcefully, "and, obviously, it's going to bring up a lot of stuff to do with your mum's death. So why don't we try acknowledging it and stop ignoring it?" She paused. "I want you to be well. For you and for Billy. For all of us."

Unfortunately, they were all a little *too* worried about Jake. Back in May, when Zoe had asked him about the cause of Dandelion's death, he'd moved his gaze dolefully to the horizon instead of answering. And, so, yes, Jake *had* intended for them to take his silence to mean suicide. Because he, too, felt Dandelion's death had been something she'd done to herself. The internet said nothing of the cause, but Jake had a gut feeling about it and, after all, he knew about this stuff. He had pictured Dandelion at her kitchen table with pills, in an apron, exactly like his mum. And maybe that's why he'd still felt so devoted to her even after he knew she was a dead person—because Dandelion, too, obviously, was a wonder of a woman who had struggled desperately with her mental health.

"I'm fine," Jake said, smiling at his ex-wife, although his heart was panting and he had the distinct, terrifying feeling that he might actually cry. He smiled wider, rubbed his hands into his hair, tried to snap out of it.

"Oh, Jake . . ." Zoe could see that he was upset and clearly she felt bad.

"I am fine. Okay? I've just got the worst hangover of all time and possibly some sort of hallucinogenic gastric flu or, like, a life-threatening shellfish thing. Can we forget it and move on? Okay? Yes? Please? I promise you I'm just hungover after the Yesness party and this is not a cry for help."

"I don't think it's a cry for help, Jake. I think you've not dealt with your total abandonment issues and this recent thing with Dandelion has triggered . . . I don't want to say a midlife crisis, but—"

"A midlife . . . ? Fucking hell, Zoe!" Nope. Not acceptable. Way too far below the belt. Jake shook his head. "You're the one boning a teenager and yet, somehow, I'm the one having a midlife crisis? How's that work? You're eight months older than me!"

"Take that back, immediately, Jake."

"You take your thing back!"

"I'm genuinely not joking."

"Sorry, Zoe, but we're not married anymore, so stop . . . bloody . . . bossing me about!"

"We're actually going to get to the point where Billy is more mature than you. You know that, right? Talk about arrested development."

Jake felt like putting his fingers in both his ears (*Lalala!*) but managed to restrain himself. He couldn't think of anything good to say—a tumbleweed blew across his father's lawn.

"Yan and I are in love," Zoe continued. "He's a wonderful, sage soul and he isn't going anywhere. Unlike you." She stood and stepped down into the water, swam to the other side of the pool in a long-necked high-and-mighty breaststroke. She always *had* to feel like she'd won every single interaction. Not just with Jake. She was in a nonstop competition with everyone and everything, from the car next to her at the traffic lights to the other stupid names on the Peloton leaderboard. "I absolutely murdered the shit out of @chelseamilf52 this morning!" she'd say, staggering into the kitchen, sadistically delighted, soaking and puce.

"Wow," Jake said, under his breath, and then, louder, over his breath, "Wow! I forget what a bitch you are when you've been on the wines. The"—this would really rile her—"lady petrol."

Zoe was swimming back toward him. She stood, walked up the pool steps. When she was out, she reached for a towel that was on a sun lounger and wiped her shoulders. "Not only have I not been drinking today, Jake," she said, looking down at him, "I'm not drinking. *At all.*" Once she was sure the implication was evident, she called for Yan, all upbeat. "Baba! Babasita! We need to head off soon. Billy, time to go, baby. Please go and find your clothes."

Jake was in the shallow end of the pool now, crouching so the water came up to his shoulders. He let his gaze move up Zoe's legs, onto her tummy.

"I'm only eight weeks," she said, coming back to the edge. "I'm sorry. I didn't mean to tell you like that."

Jake opened his mouth wide, but it took a few seconds before he could get the word out. "How?" It sounded a lot like something had hurt him and he was saying *Ow!*

After Jake and Zoe married, she'd started talking about children almost immediately, and Jake hadn't really been up for it at that moment in time, but then it didn't happen and didn't happen and didn't happen. *Unexplained infertility*, the doctors called it. They had their first round of IVF on the NHS, and it hadn't worked, so the second two they'd paid for, which had crippled them financially, but then the embryo stuck and grew and eventually became Billy.

"It's a big surprise," Zoe said, and Jake could see she pitied him and she was pleased she wasn't with him anymore. "So . . . I guess the pullout method doesn't work." She shrugged. She was trying to be amusing. She absolutely failed.

"*The pullout method?*" Jake repeated. He almost gagged. "Have you told Billy?" he asked, straightening, water chasing itself in droplets down his chest.

"Of course not. We'll tell him in the second trimester."

Zoe saying the word *trimester* booted Jake over the edge. "Right!" he said. He turned away from her, lifted his arms above his head, and dived into the deep end. He let himself sink down through the water with his eyes open, hoping the chlorine would burn out all the tears.

21

Tuesday, 10th June

Poppy

Poppy took on the gray carpeted stairs of the communal hall and, although she was incredibly nervous, the thing to remember was that Jake had been the one to ask if he could see her today. It was Jake who wanted to talk. His message had been cordial, which boded well. Obviously, there was the possibility that he still had romantic feelings, and, if so, she'd have to tell him: *No, sorry. I'm engaged!* Poppy held her ring finger up in a solo demonstration, flashed it at the stairs.

"Hi," Jake's voice said above her. Poppy whipped her hand behind her back, hid it, hoping Jake hadn't seen her being weird because, clearly, he'd come out of Dandelion's flat and now was on the landing, looking down.

She decided she wouldn't launch straight into the engagement news and instead would start with something totally casual. "Fancy seeing you . . ." Poppy began, although when she did round the corner of the staircase and see him, she was so surprised at how terrible he still looked that such trite congeniality seemed drastically misplaced, and instead of finishing her sentence, she leaped up the last three stairs and gave him a massive hug.

For a second, Jake was stiff in her arms, but then he bent a hand around her back and placed his open palm between her shoulder blades. "Hi," he said. He smelled of the Jake she had met in spring; his cologne, or deodorant, or whatever it was, filled Poppy's body with warmth. She wondered what the brand was—if she knew, she'd buy it for Sam.

"You okay?" she asked, stepping backward. Jake's stubble had grown scraggy, his lip had blistered badly, and his shoulders were too hunched.

"Still a bit ropy." He was in pale green Bermuda shorts and a gray sweatshirt. No shoes or socks. He reached for the front door of the flat and pushed it open for her.

"Well, you smell nice at least," Poppy said. Then, cringing at how lame that sounded, she walked fast past him into the sitting room, lapped the sofa by the window to calm, and then sat down. "Oh." She pointed at the picture of Dandelion resting on the floor. "Did that fall off the wall?"

Jake turned to the picture and put his hands on his hips. "Not sure?" He went over for a closer inspection. "The string seems fine." He glanced up at the wall, at the nail. "Shall I put it back?"

"Okay. Yes. Weird." Poppy watched as Jake lifted the frame and rehung it. He adjusted the picture in minuscule movements, stepped back, then adjusted it again.

"This is obviously Dandelion, right?" he asked. "Great picture of her, really captures—"

"Mmm." Poppy smiled. "I took it." It had dawned on Poppy that, these days, she never took photos when she was off the clock. She used to always take her beloved cameras out and about, capturing clouds, streets, strangers, people she loved. But since

Dandelion had gone, Poppy's passion for photography felt almost nonexistent. She worried it was dead too.

"Beautiful," Jake said. "It's a really beautiful photograph."

"Thanks," Poppy said, though she felt awkward—like she was accepting a compliment that was not meant for her. She exhaled with a long hum, then busied herself with finding her water bottle in her bag. "So, you're on the mend?"

"I'm getting these buzzing feelings in my head." Jake held one finger to his temple. "And my lips shed like snakeskin. And I did cry yesterday."

"Oh, I'm sorry. Sounds horrid." Poppy watched as Jake lifted one brown, hairy calf and took hold of his foot with his hand. She unscrewed the lid from her water bottle and took a long slow sip, using the opportunity to take him in. Although he still looked un-well, Poppy found him to be simultaneously handsome and very pretty. He was big and strong and delicate too. He looked like a grown man, of course, but she had seen the boy in him. When she'd negotiated him into a taxi back to Dandelion's after Deo had discharged them from the medical unit, he kept calling for his mother and it had broken Poppy's heart.

She had an urge to hug him again. She wanted to be sitting on the same sofa as him and link every single one of her fingers through every single one of his. She wanted to crawl on top of him. Lay her head down on his chest and breathe him in, feel his body between her thighs, take off his sweatshirt. Imagine? Imagine. He'd run his hands up her back and then pull her down toward him, then kiss her, quite noisily, passionately hard . . .

Ooops.

Poppy glanced away from Jake and her own inappropriate fantasy and focused, instead, on the door handle that led back into the hall. "Sorry," she said, "that all sounds rough."

"So, yeah, obviously, more than anyone, you know that it was dicey . . ."

Poppy nodded, leveled her gaze back at him. He was massaging his foot with both hands, and she was feeling unsure of how she was meant to be with him and unsettled about the fact that, clearly, she still fancied him. As part of the *We're Getting Married and Not Hiding from Our Future Anymore* phase, Poppy had agreed with Sam that she would get her contraceptive coil out. And so they'd gone to the doctor together and, eagerly, Sam had begun tracking Poppy's menstrual cycle on an app. Poppy hadn't thought too much about it, until earlier that morning when Sam strolled into the bathroom naked while she was brushing her teeth—he showed her the app on his phone with a graph she didn't understand— and he told her that her ovulation window was opening. Then he just gawped at her as if he expected her to drop everything and hop on (which she did not). So that might explain the distracting Jake fantasy, because ovulation-induced horniness was a very natural thing. The *most* natural thing in fact.

"And now my colleagues seem to be avoiding my calls, which is giving me massive fear." Jake let go of his foot, lifted a striped linen cushion next to him, and brought it onto his lap, and Poppy relented to the idea that just because a person loves someone doesn't mean they don't still find some other people occasionally arousing and objectively dreamy and hot. "And then there's some personal stuff with my ex. So . . ." Jake ran his fingertip over the frill that bordered the cushion. "Don't ever get married is all I can say."

Poppy held on to her left hand with her right one, covering the engagement ring. It dug into the skin of her palm. "Haaaaa," she said in a faint attempt at laughter. She slipped the ring off, bent, and zipped it into the front pocket of her bag while Jake was still looking down at the cushion, totally engrossed. Did he still fancy her? Not that it mattered either way. But, as yet, Poppy couldn't tell.

"Anyway, I'll be fine. Really, I'm feeling a lot better. But this certainly cements the fact that clubbing is not for me, what a monumental disaster. Christ knows how that all happened, I can't get my head around it." Jake cleared his throat. "And on that point, Poppy, I do want to thank you. I really appreciate you bringing me here." He looked past her, exhaled a massive sigh. "Sounds like you saved me. You went above and beyond—"

"Course!" Poppy interrupted. After all, she was the one who needed to grovel. "Jake, I actually . . ." She'd had this apology on her mind since Jake left her life, or really, since he'd entered it. "I obviously want to say sorry," she continued tentatively. She was palpably anxious again, clammy. "And explain . . . as much as I can . . ." There was such an enormity of things Poppy could tell him, but she had no idea where precisely to start. "I guess, you should know, that whole Hinge thing wasn't premeditated and I'm not a psychopath." She laughed nervously, but Jake didn't say anything.

Poppy glanced over her shoulder and followed his gaze—he was looking, again, at the picture of Dandelion. "So, yes, she died seven and a half months before I met you. And one day I needed her phone and, somehow, I saw your message and I replied. I don't know why. It was a spur-of-the-moment thing and then it became . . . something else."

"Did you message other people?"

"Just you."

Jake moved his gaze back to Poppy. His eyes were interested; they examined her face, and she had to look down at her lap. "I get that you were grieving, Poppy. But that was bad. You duped me and played me for a fool. And you only came clean because I found out."

"I'm so sorry," Poppy said in a small voice. As well as a heartfelt apology, she had planned to fess up about Sam today. Tell Jake that she'd been with someone for a very long time and now they were getting married. She wanted to be totally honest, had promised herself she would be. Though now, looking up at him, she couldn't help thinking that Jake wasn't quite up to it. "Just so you know, that whole thing was so out of character for me. I don't go around doing unhinged things like that. And I won't, ever again." Poppy pushed the air out of her body in a shocked type of laugh—it was so embarrassing and horrible having to talk about it, but the only way out of this mess, she understood, was by tunneling through.

"Well, obviously, Poppy," Jake said. "It would be out of character for most people."

Would it have been out of character for Dandelion? No, in all honesty, Poppy knew it would not. She thought of her precocious sister causing mayhem over the decades, and a flood of memories came back to her. She winced, blinked them all away. "So, with us two, me and my sister, I've always been the one who was more straight down the line and maybe that's . . ." Every single time Poppy had lied in her whole life—or done something wild—it had been either because of, or with, Dandelion.

"Are you saying you felt like *you* were *her*?" Jake leaned forward over his knees, a flicker of light in his eyes. "Channeling-her-energy type thing? Because I feel it, I see it," he said. He nodded. "You seem like a different person to me now, it's bizarre. Today, it's like, you're Poppy, *definitely*." He let his hand fall toward her. "But before, when we met—you were Dandelion." He moved his gaze back to the picture of Dandelion on the wall, and in his eyes Poppy saw a misty affection. "Or she was you, I guess."

"Oh, I . . ." Poppy stood and walked toward the mantelpiece, placed a hand on the stripped wood, and glanced into the mirror, first into her own eyes and then at Jake's reflection.

So there it was—he wasn't attracted to her as Poppy, only as Dandelion. Was she surprised? No, she wasn't, but in her chest, there was a deep muddling of sadness.

"I guess?" Poppy said. "Yes. I suppose I kind of was her." Though as soon as she'd agreed with him, it felt like a lie—it felt like she was trying to please him. Poppy could tell this was what Jake wanted to hear, and maybe that was fine—to be able to tie the whole thing up with a bow as neatly as possible, in the way that he most liked.

Overcome in the sudden and unexpected way that happened sometimes, Poppy took an inhale of breath so sharp it hurt. Jake stood and came over to her, put his hand on her arm, and Poppy looked down at where he was touching her skin. "Of course, it was horrible for me," he said in a soft voice. He crossed his arms in front of his chest. "And it was wrong of you. But I've been thinking about it these last couple of days, and I don't regret meeting you, and I don't regret meeting Dandelion."

"Okay," Poppy said, looking at her arm where his hand had been. She tried to make her thoughts calm and clear. She didn't regret meeting him either—meeting Jake had been the best thing that had happened to her since her sister's death and—although it was totally bonkers—meeting Jake had shocked Poppy back into life and forced her again to feel things that were good, and even new. "Did you tell anyone else about Dandelion?" Poppy asked, looking up at him. "Did you tell anyone else what I did?"

Jake opened his mouth and moved it through the shape of different vowels, silently. "No," he said, after a stressfully long pause. "But my colleagues know, that's how I found out. That French guy that presumably your sister slept with was kind of a sleuth about it all. Took great delight in the big reveal."

"God," Poppy said. "And what are you going to tell them now?"

"Nothing. None of them have even mentioned anything about it since, I think they've forgotten," Jake reassured. "Yesterday's newspaper is today's fish-and-chips wrapper and all that." He changed his tone. "But I sort of . . . forgive you, I think, Poppy. And you've been so generous letting me stay." He rolled his head, taking in the room. "It's such a magical hideaway. Why don't you live here? *This* really is a palace! I'm dreading going back to mine, I never would have recovered if I'd been there. I need to get my shit together and move out."

"Well, I suppose . . ." Poppy looked down at the mantelpiece again. Next to her fingers was a domed glass paperweight with a seeded dandelion head suspended in it, never to blow away and multiply. Her sister was everywhere, in everything. It was too much, but it was also not enough, nowhere even close. "Well, if you wanted to stay a little longer, then you're very welcome." Poppy looked back at Jake and exhaled a smile. She was calmed by his friendly mouth, his jaw, the line of his shoulders, his very gorgeous eyes. And she was so pleased to find they still liked each other, that still, there was something between them, something inexplicable.

"I'd love to stay on for a bit, Poppy!" Jake's face lit up; his shoulders had pulled back. "Do you think . . . would my son be able to stay a night with me? Or even . . . I've got him from tomorrow until Sunday. I know he would love it. We could pretend we were staying in a fancy hotel, on holiday."

Poppy lifted a hand to her forehead, gauging her temperature. Did Jake want to move in? Because she wasn't ready to live in her sister's home and, anyway, she could never live here with Sam, but she also wasn't ready to put it on the market and she definitely couldn't deal with packing up Dandelion's belongings and working out what to do with everything. "No one lives here, Jake. I've been meaning to rent it out for months, but if you'd be interested in staying on longer, then that could be good for both of us?"

"Really?" Jake asked, blinking quite manically. "Because I could go and get my stuff and, pretty much, move in today. I mean it would be incredible, Poppy. But only if you're sure?"

"I'm sure," Poppy laughed; she was sure. She was thrilled. "We could do a short-term contract. See how it goes?"

"Yes, definitely. And rent-wise . . . what you thinking?"

"How much do you pay now?" Poppy asked.

"A thousand, before bills. I could double that, though, or even—"

"Why don't we match that, make it easy." Poppy would be able to get a lot more on Airbnb, but this would only be short-term. And this would be Jake, on tap.

"Do you want to sleep on it? I don't want you to feel coerced."

"Why don't you sleep on it, Jake? You're probably still addled after the other night. It might be weird for you?"

"Absolutely not, this is an offer I couldn't possibly refuse." Jake put his hand out. "You got yourself a deal, Poppy Greene."

Poppy gave Jake her hand, but instead of shaking it, he pulled her forward into him, rocked her back and forth in his arms. "This is so funny," he said. "What a turnup for the books."

Pressed against Jake's body, Poppy closed her eyes. Something in the very center of her body lit, glowed like the striking of a match. They'd been brought together, that's what it felt like, and then they'd been brought together again. Poppy understood it on an instinctive level—in a place that was deeper than conscious thought or rationale. Yes, she fancied him, but that was okay because she *loved Sam*, and, anyway, Jake seemed to be totally over the romance of it all. Which was fine. Which, actually, was good.

She let go of him and took a step back. They were looking into each other's eyes, and Poppy reasoned that the flame inside of her body, the tiny raging fire, would burn out, and in its place a paler, cooler, but more enduring light might illuminate a new path and show them the way—as friends.

They were smiling at each other now, twitching mouths, bigger and bigger, until they were both laughing like they had shared a secret brilliant joke—which, in a way, Poppy supposed they had.

22

Thursday, 12th June

"Your mum's in a good mood," Sam said as Poppy's mother flung herself from the door of the house and leaped toward their car. Through the windscreen they watched her do an embarrassing waving dance, which morphed into the Charleston. She was wearing her Levi's 501s, as she had been for the past forty years. *Good jeans. Good genes*, the boys used to murmur to Poppy at school, though they were too scared to say it to Dandelion.

"See, I told you," Poppy said. "It's like she thinks *she's* getting married."

Sam turned the car engine off, but neither of them moved. They were both exhausted; the five-hour drive to Devon had been filled with Life Chats. Crossing London, they'd started with the wedding, a conversation that had, previously, repeatedly been aborted, because every time they attempted it someone got upset.

"What about if we throw a mini festival?" Sam said. Already they'd found themselves in standstill traffic and it was only Euston Road. "Pop & Samstival? Wedstock? Lovefest?" The ideas rolled from him in a manner that implied a fair bit of prior thought. "I feel like there's something in Pop Star . . ."

"Ha." Poppy hoped he was joking. "Funny." She looked out of the window, watched all the people on the Central London street. She colored in their lives, gave them wives, lovers, funerals to attend, hangovers to eat through, emails to feel anxious about, lurid secret buried crimes.

From the driver's seat, Sam snorted a laugh. "Mad idea, but what if I arrive at our wedding on a white horse!" Another snort. "Really make an entrance!"

"Ummmm . . ." Accidentally, Poppy's thoughts returned to Jake. How quickly life can flip and zag and spark. And now he was living in Dandelion's flat—fully moved in! She wondered what he would say when she told him she was getting married. She wondered if he'd get upset. She swiped her phone to unlock. Over the past couple of days, she and Jake had fallen into a rhythm of messaging again. They discussed actual practicalities: a rental agreement, Wi-Fi, what day he should put out the bins. And although there was no overt flirting, or winky faces, she felt like they were kind of showing off to each other, in a fun way. There'd been some really silly jokes.

Looking down at WhatsApp, Poppy saw Jake had sent her a video of his little boy, in Dandelion's sitting room, dancing with his dolly in a joyful way.

"What's that?" Sam asked.

"Nothing. No one. Instagram." Poppy put her phone back in her bag. She reached for Sam's thigh, squeezed. "So, anyway, where were we?"

Through Hampshire, they talked about their finances, and Poppy found herself telling Sam photography was making her feel weirdly alienated from herself, and he suggested antidepressants.

In the obligatory slow stretch on the approach to Stonehenge,

Sam asked about Dandelion's flat. "Are we moving in, or selling? Discuss."

"Oh, didn't I tell you? I've let it out," Poppy said. "Great news, huh?"

"You what?"

"Only short-term." She flicked on the radio. "And then we can . . . next year, after the . . ." They were passing a field of lying-down cows.

"Who's in it?" Sam asked.

"Huh?"

"Poppy, who is living in Dandelion's flat?"

"An old friend, he needed a place for a few months. He's been through a tricky divorce and—"

"Who?" Sam turned the radio off.

"You don't know him." And then, because she'd decided this would be the best possible explanation: "He's an old flame of Dandelion's." She turned the radio back on.

At the first sign for Glastonbury, Poppy hid herself in memories of festival trips; she'd been with Dandelion nine times. She smiled thinking back to the year when she'd been otherwise engaged in a festival love affair, having taken up with a Northern Irish man, and when she'd reunited with her sister (speaker, front left, The Park stage), Dandelion regaled her with stories of smoking opium with someone called Bilbo, *inside* a tree. She'd had some very strange photographs on her phone.

Sam and Poppy had fallen silent, but at Exeter, he brought up Project Baby. Poppy was not averse to indulging this conversation as an exciting future concept, but she also wasn't desperate to immediately get pregnant and take on parenthood. Sam, on the other hand . . .

"Will you find it weird conceiving at your parents' place this weekend?"

"Not happening," Poppy said. "They'll be in the room next door. And I thought we'd agreed that we were going to wait until after the wedding before we start properly trying. I need to let my body regulate, after years of contraception." Poppy had no idea if this was true, but it sounded legit.

"It takes a while, though, doesn't it, and we're in your ovulation window, still, so, I really think we should get in the habit of—"

"Sam, can I track my own menstrual cycle, please?" Poppy cut in. "I don't love these bulletins from you."

"You can do it, too, if you want. I'm not stopping you. But I think we need to take every opportunity to . . . Otherwise, if we move at your pace, then three years will go by, you'll be infertile, and we'll be fucked."

"Maybe you'll be infertile, Sam," Poppy said, which was not a helpful comment, but she was finding the biological clock–pressure cooker thing extremely irksome. "Maybe you already are."

"Think not," Sam scoffed. Then added, "Look at the Rolling Stones . . . they're all still having twins."

Poppy had to turn her head to the window so she could roll her eyes without him seeing. The verges jostled with cow parsley and red campion. "Please stop tracking my menstrual cycle, Sam," she said, turning back to him. "It feels a bit dystopian."

"I'm being a modern man! Literally cannot win." Sam gripped tight to the steering wheel and tensed all the muscles in his face and his neck.

Outside of her parents' home, which used to be *their* parents' home, Poppy and Sam were still sitting in the car with their seat belts still on and Poppy's mum was still doing leg flicks.

"Right, well, let's." Sam opened his door, and Poppy watched her fiancé kiss her mother on both cheeks, and then her mother pulled him in for a hug. For a second, Poppy thought she was going to make him dance with her; she was all bouncy on her feet, holding one of his hands.

"Come on, darling!" Poppy's mother came over, flung open her door.

From the boot, Sam retrieved their bags and took them into the house. Poppy undid her seat belt, stood, and then she was in her mother's arms. "Getting married," her mother cooed, "our little girl."

Poppy closed her eyes and breathed in the honeyed scent from the lime trees all around them and her mother's nurturing talcy smell. "Hello, Mum."

In the kitchen, Poppy's father and Sam were standing on opposite sides of the wooden table, and Poppy couldn't be sure if they'd opted for a handshake, or any greeting at all.

"Hi, Dad," Poppy said. She kissed him on the cheek, and he rubbed her back once, smiled, and nodded. He looked at her briefly and then looked past her, out of the window above the sink.

"Have you said congratulations to Sam?" Poppy's mother asked her husband.

"Yes, absolutely, thank you," Sam said, replying as if Poppy's father had spoken.

"Now, is it too early for champagne?" Poppy's mother asked, opening the fridge, bringing out a bottle of Pol Roger. "We are just so thrilled about you two. Aren't we, darling?"

Poppy's father nodded again. The tap was dripping and he went over to tighten it, while Sam and Poppy followed her mother and the bottle down the hall.

"How very modern for the woman to propose!" The champagne flutes were laid out on a hand-painted tray on the table in front of the window which looked all the way to the beach.

"That's not really how it happened," Sam said through a laugh. "I've been on at her for months."

"Years." Poppy grinned at Sam as he sat down next to her on the sofa, tugging up his trouser legs.

"Well, I was going to officially propose," Sam said, "but that was when . . . well . . . last year and . . ."

Poppy watched her father walk around to his green velvet armchair and lower himself into it. His eyes were chalk, his skin craggy. He was getting paler, fading like a photograph that had been on a mantelpiece for decades, bleached from too much light.

"Well, of course. Everything was on hold . . ." Poppy's mother was nodding fervently, perched on the very edge of the sofa opposite them, like she was waiting for a start whistle and, any second, would pounce forward, sprint across the room, and smash through the French windows, not bothering to open them.

"And then, well, we were in the flat one day," Sam continued, "and I woke up to Poppy on one knee, on my side of the bed . . ."

When Poppy proposed to Sam, foolishly, especially considering her profession, it had not occurred to her that it would be an anecdote that would get wheeled out for life. But since that moment, she'd heard Sam relay the story about twenty times, and even though he had a tendency to embellish it slightly, it still always sounded crap. She knew he wished he'd been able to hike her up a hill, or organize a treasure hunt, or get a turtledove to shit the ring onto her lap, or . . .

"And Pops said, *Babe! All I want is you! Let's do this!*" Sam said. Which is not what she'd said at all.

Poppy slipped her sandals off and folded her legs underneath her on the sofa, looked down at the olive pincered in her fingers, flecked with unspecific herbs. She had the urge to disagree with Sam so her father would know that's not what she'd said, but she resisted and put the olive in her mouth and made an *mm* sound.

Poppy's mother was clapping as if this was the most romantic story she'd ever heard. As usual, she was doing the enthusiasm for both her and her husband. Though obviously her lust for life had been dulled with the death of her eldest daughter, their mother was someone who found palpable pockets of delight in each and every day. Even as Dandelion was dying, their mother was still able to take pleasure from baking white chocolate and macadamia nut cookies and bring them in for the nurses. Pointing at the luminosity of the sky through the hospital window on that last day, Poppy remembered her mother saying, "Isn't that stunning? Such a glorious fuchsia pink."

Still, Poppy had not seen her mother quite this animated in ages. Imagine what she'd be like if Poppy was pregnant. It would be all cartwheels and cabaret every day for months.

"So have you decided on a date?" Poppy's mother sang at them.

"We were thinking New Year's Eve . . ." Sam said, his hands clasped in front of him, chin in the air.

"Oh, really? Well, we'd better talk to our lady vicar soon and see when the church is free. We could even go down tomorrow morning and . . ."

Poppy and Sam exchanged quick glances. Neither of them wanted to do it in the church. Sam didn't want to because he was an atheist, and Poppy didn't want to because the last time she'd been there it had been for her sister's funeral.

"You were christened there. You get m-married there. You have your funeral there," Poppy's father said, clearly sensing the trepidation. "That's what we've been d-d-doing for seven generations. Half the graveyard is related to us."

"We haven't discussed it," Poppy said, with misleading diplomacy. She stood, went over to the bottle of champagne, and began refilling everyone's glasses.

"Well, anyway," Poppy's mother said, reaching over for her husband and patting his knee, "did Daddy tell you he's been cataloging the home videos? Such a huge task!"

"Yes, I know," Poppy said, her smile feeling strained. She kept imagining her sister walking in. She wondered if they were all as acutely aware as she was that there was someone missing from the scene.

"They go back to our wedding in '76. Just takes ages to go through all the films because we keep getting distracted and watching them, don't we, darling?" Poppy's father didn't say anything, and so Poppy's mother turned and addressed Sam. "Then from the nineties we have hundreds and hundreds of films because the girls were always recording each other. Poppy was the camera lady, obviously. And they wrote these very elaborate scripts and put on very grown-up performances."

"Oh really?" Sam asked. "How so?"

"Well, they were never about princesses, or, you know, puppy dogs," Poppy's mother said, holding her own throat with one hand. "But instead often about terrible men . . ." She moved her hand and held it in the air, pausing for dramatic effect. "But the super-girls always saved the day in the end." She looked at Poppy. "Right?" Then back at Sam. "You must watch one tomorrow. They're brilliant, very girl power."

"Sounds hilarious." Sam grinned at his future mother-in-law, then turned to Poppy. "I'd like to see that."

Poppy finished her glass of champagne, not wanting to commit. "What's for dinner, Mum?" she asked, standing up. "How can we help?"

Poppy's bed was a single, so, after dinner, she and Sam took their things to the spare room. They read their books in bed for a while, then Sam turned his head to Poppy. She could feel him waiting for her to look at him; she could see him in her periphery. Eventually he cleared his throat. "I know you've said that Dandelion and your dad had a fractious relationship when she was younger, why was that? Was there . . . like . . . an incident, or . . ."

"No! Sam. What?"

"Merely asking a question, Poppy. Relax." Sam exhaled loudly to show that he found it exhausting communicating with her sometimes. He tilted his head slightly, pretending he was taking in his book. He wasn't, though; he'd only turned two pages in the past half hour. Poppy knew Sam so well that she had vantage points to his thinking that he was unaware of; he thought she was in his audience, looking up at him, but actually, she was backstage, in the wings, watching him talk into the lights. She kept on looking at him, her book on her lap, waiting for him to say the next annoying thing; she could feel it coming and had guessed at what it might be.

"His voice is getting better, isn't it . . ." Sam continued eventually. He turned to Poppy, tapped his Adam's apple.

"Yes, Sam. I told you. He's been seeing a speech therapist," Poppy said.

"Weird how that happened, wasn't it?"

"Not at all. He had a stammer as a boy, and then the trauma of Dandelion's death triggered it. You know all this."

"Awful. Poor guy. But . . . just thinking . . . when your mum said you guys put on plays about terrible men. Maybe Dandelion got her inspiration from things that were happening here . . ."

Poppy got out of bed. "What the hell are you implying?" And then in an angry whisper because her parents were next door: "He was the best husband! The best father, and you know that. Dad and Dandelion were *fine*, they just butted heads when she was a teenager, that's all. She was rebellious. She was Dandelion, right? Really sorry to have to tell you that there's nothing salacious here, Sam."

"Stop being mental." Sam looked down at his book. "Completely bit my head off. Again."

Poppy turned and left the room, crossed the hall, and went to the bathroom, locked the door. She looked in the mirror with the driftwood frame that her father had made, hanging above the pale green, very eighties sink. "I genuinely don't know what to do," she said, no idea whom she was talking to. "What am I meant to do?"

She stayed in front of the mirror for a long while, waiting for some answers. She could hear her own heart, and she thought about her sister's heart, which was silent now, and rotting. Worms and maggots feasting on her skin. Poppy smacked a tear from her face, and then she saw a baby, *her baby*; a tiny bundle, gurgling, kicking on a blanket on a patch of lush grass in the garden, just outside.

She could picture her dad nearby, kneeling by the flower bed, deadheading roses, singing to himself with a strong voice—like he always used to do. Her mother was there, too, sitting at the garden table, looking down at her grandchild, and she was pulling funny faces to make the baby smile. It felt like a premonition—a happy future photograph. Poppy put her hand on her stomach and looked down. A new life for a lost life. A little girl. A troublemaker. A sunbeam. Something to hold on to. Someone to love as much.

She turned the light off and went back to the bedroom. "Sam?" She shook him gently until he murmured. "Let's do it."

He rubbed his eyes. "What?"

"Let's go down to the beach and . . . make love." The idea of conceiving down by the lapping sea seemed, suddenly, quite magical to Poppy. She thought of a teeny drifting seahorse. Of a sparkling darting fish.

"Now?" Sam asked. But he was already sitting up.

23

Jake

A heat wave turned London volcanic, and Jake had opened all the windows. He'd been playing his guitar for most of the evening, wearing a pair of boxer shorts. When he got to the end of "English Rose" by the Jam (nailing the barre chords up and down the fret), he went and got a beer and lay on the sofa—facing Dandelion, his captivated muse.

"So, yes, work stuff is giving me the heebie-jeebies. Karla is being pretty vague in her emails. The whole thing seems a little . . ." As he spoke, Jake's eyes fell on the writing desk by the door, an old-fashioned bureau-type thing, and it occurred to him that he hadn't yet examined its compartments.

In an attempt to get to know Dandelion better, Jake had been exploring her home. Contemplating her taste in art (great), furniture (wouldn't have chosen it himself, but totally worked), and literature (highbrow, with a distinctly feminist tilt). He'd squinted at all her photographs on the fridge and in the frames in the hall. He'd examined her music collection for hours, supremely impressed. He'd perused the shelves in all the rooms aside from her bedroom, which Poppy kept locked.

There was a seriously warped romance to the entire situation now that Jake had officially moved in; it was as sad as the very best ballad he could play on his guitar. *Man meets woman. Man falls for woman. Woman is actually dead. Man has totally justifiable fleeting meltdown.* Then what? Jake thought of Poppy and how quickly they'd picked up a new thing that was good. *Woman's sister is not as psychotic as man perhaps thought, is potentially very charming, and she . . . becomes his landlady . . .*

The ending needed work, but still, Jake was pleased, very pleased to have Poppy in his life because, frankly, he liked her. Possibly quite a lot.

The other day when she'd come round, Jake had been struck by how it felt for his breathing body to be close to her breathing body, alone in the same room. She made him feel jittery, but in a smiling way. They'd started sending funny messages again; they were at it all the time. And so, all things considered, Jake had decided to put the seriously embarrassing sister-catfish situation behind him. Besides, he had both sympathy and empathy for Poppy—he knew, firsthand, how grief was a mental illness all its own, and he didn't doubt her when she said that all that lying had been a behavioral anomaly. And, besides, the truth was, Jake had had an incredibly tantalizing spring because of Poppy, because of Dandelion, and now, as a totally acceptable consolation prize, he was here—in the heaven of this flat.

Jake looked down at Dandelion's bureau. He touched it tenderly, as if it was her skin. It was the type of cumbersome dark-wood piece of furniture that he didn't care for, but in this sitting room, on the bright rug, under an abstract painting of blue squares, it stood majestic. He sat on the velvet chair and eased open the long thin drawer, finding the usual crap people squirrel away: cel-lotape, an ancient Oyster card, a set of headphones, hair bands, a packet of sunflower seeds. Jake turned his attention to a small compartment with a key and a knotted red ribbon attached. Inside were more keys. He looked over his shoulder, gripped the back of the chair as a thought flashed into his mind. "Is one of these . . . ?" He shook his head. "No. I couldn't." He couldn't. Could he?

Jake stood and approached the picture of Dandelion on the far wall. "Your bedroom is private, obviously, so I won't go in. Unless . . ." He paused. Surely it was unlikely that any of the keys would work.

He took the small drawer of keys out of the sitting room, leaned against Dandelion's door frame, and slipped the first into the lock. It didn't turn. He tried another and another. On the fourth go, the door swung away from him softly. "Oh," he said, genuinely surprised. "Shit."

Jake went back into the sitting room, stood in front of the picture of Dandelion again. "Right, well," he said, with one arm around his own waist and the other held out to her. "Your bedroom is unlocked now. I won't go in though." He paused. "Unless . . . check if everything's okay?"

Dandelion's room was exactly how Jake imagined it would be, large and chaotically chic. The greeny-blue paint on the walls had been applied in vigorous, visible brushstrokes. The color wasn't uniform and in some areas it was darker, like the shadowy patches of clouded sea. Jake let out a sigh and turned to the bed; there was a quilted throw and two ikat cushions, pink and white. He lay down on it; it was extremely comfy.

And then: *Hmm. Interesting.* Jake was horny, and when he closed his eyes—there was Dandelion.

No, actually, it was Poppy.

No, definitely—Dandelion.

She was in the doorway, watching him. Wearing a faded gray T-shirt. Her legs were bare and long and Jake could just make out some pink lace knickers. Her hair was loose and hanging down over her shoulders in mermaid tendrils. She put a hand on her hip. *Hey, sexy,* she said. She was really pleased to see him.

Jake opened his eyes. "Fuck." He sat up. He blinked in different directions. He lay down again, and when he closed his eyes, Dandelion was still there, only now she was slinking over to him, very slowly, dragging bare toes over the shaggy rug. Jake said something to her like, *So, I was just checking everything was okay in here. My apologies.* And she said something like, *I want you to be in here, Jake. Please never leave.* And then she crossed her hands over her body and lifted her T-shirt over her head. She wasn't wearing a bra.

Jake thought about opening his eyes again, standing up and leaving. Locking the bedroom behind him. But before he could, Dandelion said, *I really want you, Jake. Can't we kiss, just for a minute? Please? PLEASE. I really am so desperate to . . .*

"No. We shouldn't. We mustn't!" Jake said, aloud to her bedroom. "We shushn't!" Which wasn't a word, but he was getting jittery and then, fuck, yes, his hand was in his shorts and he was stroking his cock and Dandelion was crawling over the bed and then she was lying right next to him. The look in her eye was sugary and sweet, but also mischief. She bit her lip. She was obsessed with him. *I'm obsessed with you, Jake.*

Jake was very hard. He shook his head, unsure, but she said that she'd do anything for him, *anything*, and she also wanted to make it clear that he didn't need to feel guilty about this situation because he was such a good man and anyway, she'd invited him. She was consenting, wholeheartedly. In fact, she'd lured him in. This was all her doing—if anyone asked. Which they wouldn't, because it was a secret.

Their little secret.

And she really, really wanted him.

And then she was saying . . . she was saying . . . what was she saying? She was saying that she'd searched through secret mists and that no matter where she roamed no bonds would ever . . . and then she stopped speaking because Jake realized that she was actually reciting the lyrics to the song he'd been playing next door. So then he was panting and stroking himself but also trying really hard to think of things Dandelion could be saying that weren't lyrics, which, in that moment, was very difficult to do. But then, phew, she was sucking him off expertly. She paused to look him right in the eye and say, *Jake, you're amazing and strong, but also kind, and manly . . . not too manly, obviously, Jake. Jake, you're just the right amount of manly, and you are the best lover and . . .*

From next door, Jake's phone started ringing, and he jumped to his feet—electrocuted by reality—and staggered, dazed, out of the room.

"Hi? Dad?" he asked breathily into the phone, wet with sweat and shame.

"Jakey!"

"Yeah, hi." Jake tucked his dick back into his shorts.

"How are you? What are you up to?"

"Num, I'm . . . playing my guitar."

Jake's father launched into the necessary observations about how it was so hot, how even in the swimming pool he was sweating, and Jake sloped back to Dandelion's bedroom door, looked in, reflected how relieved he was he hadn't jizzed all over her bed. What a sleaze! He'd absolutely got carried away . . .

"Come to France with us, will you? Bring your guitar!" Jake's father said. "Bring someone."

"Mm-mm-yes," Jake said as he tiptoed into Dandelion's room, straightened the bed.

"Longing for you to meet Mish," Jake's father said.

Jake looked down at Dandelion's bedside table, the lamp with the bobbin base and the pleated shade. A blue flower painted on a circular coaster. A dusky pink silk eye mask, with the remnants of mascara smooshed in, which he picked up, stroked against his cheek, and then slipped over his head. He wore the eye mask there, above his eyes, all the while making encouraging noises to his father, who was talking about how he'd made it official with his girlfriend and saying other things about how great she was, and how she made him feel so young and how this and blah and that and something else. Jake's toes brushed against a hard thing under the bed. He put the phone on loudspeaker and crouched to look at what it was.

"Recently got a degree in sports massage," Jake's father said. "And she . . ."

Jake pulled out a wicker box. He'd just have a quick peek, then he'd leave the room and lock it again. Inside the box were phones and chargers and boring cables. He pushed it back and noticed that next to it was a blue Adidas shoebox, which he really wasn't sure whether to look in or not, because his first thought was that it was probably going to be a den full of dildos and, like, crazy nipple clamps and . . . But inside was a mound of letters, carefully slit open across the upper edge—all addressed to Poppy. Jake put the lid on again.

"You can get the train all the way from London to Avignon, did you know that?" Jake's father said. "The Eurostar."

"Yes, good idea, definitely, Dad," Jake said. Though actually, why did Poppy have letters under her sister's bed? He reached for the box again.

He unfolded the first letter carefully. Scanned the black inky swirls, his eyes settling on a sentence near the bottom of the page. *We were remembering the time she thwacked that boy in the playground because he'd been mean to you.*

Jake turned the letter over. *You were so brave at the funeral, so strong, Dandelion would have been so proud. She always was.*

"Gotta go, though, Dad," Jake said, interrupting his father, who was gushing about his girlfriend again. "Will call tomorrow to discuss France. Bye!" He hung up and carried the shoebox into the sitting room, put it on the coffee table, next to the bottle of beer. He had a wild urge to shove all the letters into his mouth, to suck them, chew them up, digest them. He knew he should step away, but also, he definitely couldn't—so he sat and reached for another letter, holding his breath.

I can't imagine how you must feel.

And another: *Can't begin to imagine how difficult this all is.*

Dandelion's eye mask was still on Jake's head, and he pulled it down so, for a moment, he didn't have to see.

Had there been condolences after his mum had died? He couldn't remember any. Not that they would have helped him at the time. It was only lust and tenderness that distracted him then; even if it was for one night—he'd lose himself, fade his anguish with kissing and touch. He cheated on his girlfriend so often, so brazenly, that eventually she left him. Then, even the constant lovers couldn't slow the bleed, his mental hemorrhaging.

Jake had been so depressed that he'd had to leave university; he'd hardly been able to string a sentence together, let alone write clever things down. His early twenties moved fast and slow. Things changed and things got better. Life was the weather—grim as fuck, but then again it brightened up. His job had helped hugely, a kind of calling. He'd met Zoe (a razor-sharp in-house media lawyer) at his work Christmas party, and they'd married quickly, excitedly, and Jake had bloomed and wilted through the different seasons, and with each passing year his mother had become further from him. Until she was hardly there at all.

Jake blew air out through his mouth in a whistle, trying to get a hold on his emotions. "Ayeayeaye!" He removed the eye mask from his head and looked at the picture of Dandelion on the wall. They stared at each other. "Would you like me to read some to you?"

The next envelope was blue with a brown splodged stain over Poppy's address; Jake gave it a cursory scan, turned it over. It was signed, *Love ALWAYS. Jetta.*

He cleared his throat. "*Dear Poppet, I remember the first time I ever saw you two maniacs. I was so devastated to have left York. Left mum.*" He skipped ahead. "*Your big sis taught me so much about life. How to have mad fun. How to fiercely love. How not to give a flying fuck about what other people think. How important it is to be your actual self. And every single time I look at you, Poppet, every single time—I see that love, that bravery. You're her and she's you and death doesn't change that. I'd like to see it fucking try.*"

Jake dropped Jetta's letter and looked up at the picture that was watching him. It wasn't Dandelion anymore—it was his mum; he'd tried for half his life not to think about her, because the tragedy of it made him angry and have thoughts that were scary, the worst type of thoughts to have. "I miss you, Mum, so much," he said, and his mouth muscles hurt because he was trying to talk and keep his face all normal, not cry. "Don't think I don't, because I do." His eyes were full of tears. "I know how harrowing things could get and I didn't want you to be in pain, Mummy." He wiped hard at his nose.

The world around Jake flooded, and his tears choked.

They choked until they drowned.

They drowned until Poppy sent him a message: Is it just me or does this terrier I'm with look A LOT like you?

Jake spluttered and he smiled.

Poppy had flung the message to him like a rope, and he clung to it, pulled himself out of the devastation and the grief. He replied,

Ha, yes, it's the eyelashes. And then he typed, I can't wait to see you Poppy.

He hovered his thumb over the send button—almost, almost—then, no. He deleted the last bit. Too much. He was sordid. He was sorry. Jake looked back up at the picture of the woman on the wall, and her face looked exactly like Poppy's face. It was mental how the photograph did that. Like a magic eye. Like a mood ring.

Poppy Poppy Poppy.

Jake pulled Dandelion's soft, expensive-feeling eye mask down over his face as he imagined a life wedged full and better with different decisions, and he was lulled to sleep.

24

Sunday, 15th June

While Jake and Billy circled the occupied swings in the playground, Poppy went to buy them ice cream from a van she'd spied deeper in Clissold Park. She came back with a 99 Flake for Billy, a Cornetto for Jake, and a Twister for herself.

Billy's mouth fell open as he took the ice cream with both hands. His pupils rolled around the perimeter of his eyes like the turning of a big wheel at the fairground, and Jake anticipated vomit. "What do you say, bud?"

"Thank you very much, *Poopy.*" Billy did a side-to-side bum move, having recently picked up how to twerk.

"Billy!"

"What?" Billy pulled a grotesque old man gurn.

"Daddy's friend is called Poppy."

"That's okay," Poppy said. "I don't mind being called Poopy. I actually think it's a very pretty name."

"YES! POOPY!" Billy twerked again.

"Okay, Poopy, well, it's your call." Jake shrugged.

"No! Only I call her Poopy!"

"Yeah, only Billy," Poppy agreed.

Jake smiled down at his Cornetto. He liked how Poppy had bought each of them a different ice cream. He liked how she was with his kid. "Well, thank you. Cornettos are my favorite."

"I had a feeling you'd be a Cornetto man."

"Oh yeah? How come?"

"Your age, I think."

Poppy had suggested she meet up with them and show them around the neighborhood. They'd walked together from the flat, up Green Lanes, and then onto Church Street, where she'd pointed out her favorite greengrocer, restaurant, pub, florist, and now they were in Clissold Park. "Really pleased you've settled in okay," Poppy said. She was wearing a short denim dress and, as she sat on a bench, Jake could see a shine on her collarbones and the swell of her cleavage.

"Oh, yes . . ." He focused on his Cornetto. "We love it there." He thought back to that very morning when he and Billy had made pancakes in the kitchen, danced around listening to the entire Chappell Roan album *The Rise and Fall of a Midwest Princess* (because it had joint first place in Billy's affection along with Poopy Man's album, on which Billy's number one track was "Everybody Farts"). They'd danced, eaten, watered the plants on the balconies. Billy hadn't requested any screen time, and life had felt like a montage from a nineties movie where Jake was someone grounded and together. Living in Dandelion's flat—Jake was Tom Hanks and everything was building to a happy ending, with a jaunty soundtrack, a sunset, possibly a snog.

The three of them (and Spleen) sat in silence on the bench, negotiating the angles of their heads, licking. Poppy removed the Twister's soft yellow ice cream swirl with her tongue. Jake could see she had a technique, which pleased him—he had a technique too; he was orbiting the outside of his Cornetto, nibbling down, layer by layer.

"The swings are free!" Billy yelled. He had white ice cream covering his cheeks and his chin, and an impressive amount in his hair.

Jake took the remnants of Billy's cone, deposited them in the bin. "Go on then."

After his kid bolted to the belly of the playground, Jake felt aware of an awkwardness or an emotion sitting between him and Poppy, a whole personality of feelings.

With his eyes still on Billy, Jake pictured Poppy and her sister as little girls. Making up their own meanings to words. Sibling wisecracks. Hanging upside down on the climbing frame and giggling. In his mind, they had almost identical temperaments; although Dandelion, presumably, at points, had been very mentally unwell. But Jake knew she'd been sweet like Poppy, and definitely funny too. After all, the sisters had been so close, two peas in a pod, as far as Jake could work out. Their eyes, from all the pictures, seemed almost indistinguishable, and they both had the same hair and so much of it; in some places it twizzled in rings, and in others it fell straight or bounced into curls, and, honestly, Jake didn't know if they were blondes, or brunettes, or redheads. They were all of them, if anything. Their hair was sand and fire and bark.

Subtly, Jake glanced at Poppy—her eyes were bright today, summer skies. She smiled at him, but she didn't say anything, and Jake noticed how her lips had got darker, swollen from the coldness of the lolly. He smiled back at her. It felt easy to be sitting in silence together, and he really liked just . . . looking at her. Looking at Poppy made Jake feel gratefully surprised at life, which in turn made him feel alive, which in turn made him feel happy, which in turn . . . And it went on like that, a building of nice feelings, a staircase going up. The thing between them now was not romantic, obviously. How could it be? A romance would be morally inappropriate, psychologically difficult to navigate, and emotionally chaotic. And, besides, Jake was excited to get to know Poppy better—he wanted to be friends with her and, really, he felt like he already kind of was. Not in terms of a shared history, or any great factual knowledge of her, more . . . a feeling. A relaxation. A warmth.

He slung an arm over the back of the bench, bent a leg up. A few feet away there was a patch of wildflowers and weeds—poppies, dandelions, forget-me-nots, nettles. "Look," Jake said, "it's you guys."

Poppy turned to them. "Mm," she said. "It's our season."

"Your parents are really into flowers, huh?"

Poppy nodded. She'd finished her lolly and tapped the stick against her bare thigh. "My dad used to be a landscaper and my mum still is a gardener. She's known for her cottage gardens in Devon, and a very meadowy aesthetic." Poppy was still looking at the scattering of flowers, which were swaying in a breeze that Jake couldn't feel. "Did you know," she said, as she squinted at him, "that dandelions are the queen pollinators? They keep a lot of insects going, especially bees. I don't know why I love that fact so much. But it's just *so her*. She gave out life and power, and . . ." Poppy pulled in a breath that sounded serrated, had jagged edges.

Jake nodded; he looked at her knee, the hem of her dress, then up at the profile of her face. "Sounds like you two were really similar."

"Oh," Poppy said; she put her head on one side. "We weren't actually that similar. I mean we were very close, crazy close, but—"

"Yeah." Jake nodded in agreement. "Crazy close. Crazy-crazy close."

Poppy wrinkled her nose at him in a way that Jake couldn't

quite interpret, then stretched and posted her lolly stick in the nearby recycling bin.

"Do you want to talk about her, Poppy? Because if you do, I'd be so happy to." The truth was that Jake wanted Poppy to talk about Dandelion. He wanted all the good, but more than that—he wanted to know the shape of her misery. He wanted to hear if Poppy had known how she got to be so sad and if Poppy carried the sort of guilt he did about his mum.

"Oh, not sure . . ."

"Not the end bit," Jake clarified, feeling bad because he knew firsthand how unpleasant it was when people kept circling a death, like buzzards looking for morbid morsels to devour. "Unless you want to. They say it's good to talk." He was so embarrassed by how feeble he sounded (he was pretty sure he had quoted the tagline of the nineties British Telecom ad) that he turned his gaze back to the playground. Billy was off the swings now and making his way over to a kid sitting on the seesaw. He pointed at the free seat, checking if it was okay to get on. The other kid kicked both his legs through the air in a giddyap kind of way, gave Billy a nod.

"Actually, Jake, there was something else I wanted to talk about . . ." Poppy huffed a smidge of a laugh. She glanced over her other shoulder, as if she was summoning strength, then she turned back to him and held her hand up, looked at it pointedly. Jake took in her wristbone, all the bangles, her short, clear fingernails. And the diamond ring.

"I'm not sure if you noticed? But . . . I got engaged in April, after everything. With us."

"*Engaged to be married?*" Poppy nodded, and in the pause that followed, Jake was conscious of the fact that he needed to say something else. The ring was not nice. "That . . . is . . . shiny!"

"I'm sorry I didn't tell you before, I figured you knew I had a boyfriend . . ." Poppy's new WhatsApp profile was a picture of her and her sister, much younger, on a beach, and, based potentially just on that, Jake had presumed the man from the previous profile picture was no longer around. "We've been together for a long time." Her voice faltered. "Sam. He's called Sam."

"Well, does he know about me?" Jake asked, and then immediately felt ridiculous, like a spurned lover. He stood up and took a step away.

"I said someone's moved into the flat. One of Dandelion's friends."

Kids had begun to buzz everywhere, swarming over the playground, their screams piercing the peace; why were there a hundred of them all of a sudden? It was a frickin' beehive. Or a birthday party.

"Jake, I feel terrible about everything I did to you. And everything I've done to Sam," Poppy said behind him. "But I'm not going to tell him what happened. I don't want to upset anyone else anymore. Is that . . . okay? I don't know what's best. What do you think? I feel like you and I have been through a lot together, strangely. Or, I guess, we've been through a strange thing together and—"

Jake screwed his entire face up, and it felt like a fist. He turned back to her. "Yes, Poppy. It was a terrible thing that *you* did to *me*." He genuinely wondered if she was trying to upset him—because maybe she enjoyed pulling the rug from under his feet at the precise moment that he was having a nice time.

"I know, yes, it's my fault. But, maybe, we're pleased about how everything has worked out now, are we?" She was gripping her own hands, wringing them. "And, I mean, you said the other day that you see me differently to how you did before, and so I thought you wouldn't be upset—"

"I do see you differently. I do!" Jake nodded furiously. "You were Dandelion and . . . and now Dandelion is . . . is Dandelion and . . ." Jake thought of himself talking to that picture on the wall—maybe that had been about his mother. Had that been about his mother? And then the whole thing on the bed—maybe that had been about Poppy. Had that been about Poppy? *Fuck.* Women confused him. Life confused him. And there was nothing more confusing than love. "No, I'm happy for you, Poppy!" Jake shouted. He felt a slap of embarrassment about getting too riled up. "Really it's the lies that upset me," he clarified. He felt better for having said this, because maybe it was true.

Jake sat back down on the bench, exhaled heavily, managed a smile. "But hey-ho, anyway. I guess . . ." He could say it. He could say it. Was going to say it. "Congrats!" Yup. He was fine. He was calm. She'd caught him off guard. But—whatever. She was a liar and a cheat, but so was he. This scratching hurt was an ego thing. A silly thing. A selfish thing. It was nothing at all. "Don't bother telling Sean," Jake said, batting a hand, like it was no big deal.

"Sam."

"Sam. It's in the past. I agree." Jake hissed a *tisss* sound. "Three dates? Was it three dates?" The best three dates of his life. "Something like that. One insignificant little kiss." He'd kissed her at the ecstatic dance thing. He'd kissed her when she was crying on his sofa. The next morning he'd kissed her a lot, a lot, a lot, and each kiss, at the time, had felt seismic, shifting the shape of his heart, maybe even his life. But . . . that had been lust, probably. And grief. Confusion. Delusion. That whole thing had been Not Real.

"Whatever next, Poppy? Whatever will you do or say next? Really, I'm on the edge of my blimmin' seat!" Jake laughed, but he knew he sounded quite angry. He leveled his gaze back at the playground, ran his hand through his hair. Billy was on the seesaw, but it still wasn't bouncing; the two little boys sat, at opposite ends, silently staring each other out.

"That's the last thing I need to tell you, Jake. If you still want to be friends, I promise I'll never lie to you again." Poppy was sorry—he could hear in her voice that she was maybe going to cry. "But if you don't want to have any sort of relationship, I understand. You can keep living at Dandelion's, I'll honor our contract until Christmas, like we said, and . . ."

In his pocket, Jake's phone buzzed, and he answered it immediately, without looking at who it was.

"Jake, can you talk?"

"Karla! Hello! Hi!" Jake shouted. He put one finger in his other ear and looked down at his trainers. "Yup, absolutely. What's up?"

25

Still Sunday, 15th June

Poppy

After watching Billy on the seesaw for a time and finding herself in a conversation with the mum of the other little boy, in which Poppy pretended she was Billy's mum (it had been assumed and she went along with it), Poppy and Billy moved closer to Jake, mainly so she could hear what was being said on the phone. Even when they were in his eyeline, he didn't acknowledge them. He was waving his free hand side to side. "I AM SO NOT A CREEP!"

Jake had told Poppy it was an urgent phone call and asked her, despite the fact that they'd been having a difficult conversation, if she could watch Billy *for a sec.* That was thirteen minutes ago.

"Poopy! Let's do yoga!" Billy said, tugging on Poppy's hand.

Poppy looked down at his face: almond eyes that tilted upward at the corners, framed by lush eyelashes that might potentially, one day, be even better than Jake's. He wasn't at all shy like Poppy had been as a small child, hiding behind Dandelion, or up her mother's skirt. Billy was a twerking, joking little heart melter. "Okay," Poppy said, "let's."

Jake was pacing now. He shouted, "HER NOONI?" and then,

"MY FACE?" and then, "ABSOLUTELY NOT!" with such vigor that he threw his phone into the air by mistake and then bent to pick it up from the grass. "Karla, are you there?"

"Why is Dada being so funny?" Billy asked, chuckling. He had tucked his dolly into his shorts and was carrying her there like a baby kangaroo.

"I'm not sure . . ." Poppy said. "Why don't you show me your best yoga move?" She sat down on the grass, feeling a tad panicked for Jake, who was now using the word *vehemently* along with the word *deny*.

In front of her, Billy said, "You go like this!" He flung his body forward onto his hands, and his legs swung up into the air; he stayed upside down briefly, before rolling out and crawling toward Poppy, grinning, his dolly still wedged in place.

"Wow!" Poppy didn't even know it was possible for a kid that size to do a handstand. The arm strength. The core! "Billy, that was amazing."

"It's really easy." Billy shrugged. "You do it."

Poppy stood. Glanced at Jake, who was sitting cross-legged and pulling at strands of grass in front of him and then chucking them, blade by blade, over his shoulder. She looked back at Billy. "So I go like . . ." She lifted both her hands above her head and bent forward—"This?"—and then kicked her legs into the air. Her dress attempted to fall off over her head, then her feet landed back down on the grass.

When Poppy straightened, Jake was off the phone. "I saw your pants," he said, though he didn't smile. Poppy mentally congratulated herself for picking out a pair of reasonable-looking knickers (French, black) that morning. Billy had both hands clamped over his mouth, trying to hold in his laughter. He bounced up and down, then shouted, "POOPY, I SAW YOUR PANTS TOO!"

"Oh, embarrassing." Poppy pulled a joke awkward face. She

glanced at Jake, who was clutching his T-shirt with one hand in the place where his heart was, looking very fretful. "Everything okay?"

"You got any plans now?" Jake asked. "How do you feel about the pub?"

Later, Poppy was having dinner with Sam's family, and she should really get back and tidy the flat, be a good fiancée. "Could do a quick one."

"Phew, because I'm canceled. So, I could do with a drink." Jake used a hushed *don't let the kid hear* voice. And then he said to Billy, "Fancy the pub, bud?"

"Yes!" Billy clapped. He twerked. "Shots!"

In The Rose & Crown on the corner, directly outside the park, Jake lifted his pint glass and swirled his beer around, looking down into it like it was tea leaves bearing prophecies. Poppy took a sip of lemonade, and Billy downed another water "slammer" from a shot glass, then started sidestepping toward some bigger kids who were sitting on stools at the bar.

"This is not a cancellation," Poppy said again.

"My contract is suspended," Jake said.

"Frozen," Poppy corrected. She felt confident that this was going to be a firm wrist slap from Jake's bosses, not the annihilation of his entire career. He'd taken her through what his colleague had said on the phone—apparently, he'd collapsed on an intern when he was totally wasted the other week. The sentence *He face-planted in my nooni* had been used by the woman, unfortunately. So, yes, Poppy understood why Jake was freaking out—a successful director's face in a young colleague's lap sounded very bad.

"Do you think I should call her?" Jake asked, looking up from his pint. "Sydney, the girl, should I message her?"

"No. I don't think you should contact her directly, not until your HR people have properly looked into it, right?"

"I could send her a message saying, *Hope you're okay?*"

Poppy was making a skeptical *nnn* sound.

"Right." Jake nodded. Sighed very loud.

"So, we know this is more of a 'he-was-totally-wasted' thing, rather than a sexual complaint, right?"

"It's been reported as inappropriate behavior, not like . . . *abuse,*" Jake said, visibly struggling with the word. His forehead was furrowed. Since he'd heard the news, his cheeks had become pinker than Poppy had ever seen them—presumably burning with shame. "It's all grotty, though, isn't it? A creepy old man's face in his nubile colleague's crotch." Jake put a hand to his stomach, like he was feeling queasy.

"Maybe don't refer to her nubile crotch again," Poppy said, unable to stop herself from grimacing.

"*I* don't think she's nubile," Jake said. "I was using that word for the purpose of what other people might think I think. And, also, Poppy"—Jake leaned over the table, whispered—"in the past I did actually have a thing . . . a consensual thing, with a younger colleague—a dalliance, for, like, five minutes. So . . ."

"You mean your affair?"

"Yes, that. And if my ex hears about this, she'll . . ." Jake took the last gulp of his pint. "I really, really want you to know that I would never touch a woman just out of the blue. Ergh! And as for the fact I was *on* her . . . that's the most embarrassing thing I've ever heard."

"I know. But it's gonna be okay, okay?" Poppy reached out and held Jake's forearm, wanting to reassure him.

"Like, when I'm pissed, or whatever . . ." Jake was shaking his head. "I'm not struggling to keep my dick in my pants. It's not who

I am, *at all* . . ." He was still whispering. "Do I seem like that? Like a . . . like a . . . like a . . . sex pest?"

"You don't," Poppy said. She heard her phone vibrate again. She really needed to go. Sam had messaged half an hour ago asking her to pick up some lemons on her way back. "Jake, I really do need to head off. Is there someone else you can be with?" She reached for her bag.

But Jake wasn't fully listening, he was massaging a temple with his finger, both elbows on the table. "Besides anything," he said, "I definitely would not have been feeling sexual. My dick, pretty much, didn't exist that night."

Poppy busied herself with getting her stuff together, not wanting her face to betray that she had seen Jake's dick, and it definitely *did* exist; when she'd come back over to Dandelion's after letting him sleep it off, she'd found him starkers on the sofa, the blanket on the floor. His dick was exactly how she imagined it might be— quite thick and friendly looking with lots of pubes in a tangly nest. Poppy had said, "Oopsie," and covered him up.

"I'm bored," Billy said, coming back over to them, clearly tired of being ignored by the bigger kids and doing forward rolls on the swirling, sticky carpet all by himself.

"Yeah, sorry, bud," Jake said through an inhale. "You must be pretty blotto after those slammers? Let's go."

Poppy held out her hand, and Jake took it.

"I'm so blotto." Billy was swerving out through the pub ahead of them. "Whoa, whoa!" he said as he wobbled, being a comedy drunk.

"I'm going to wear my 'I'm a Feminist' socks to the meeting with HR next week," Jake said as he held the pub door open for Billy, then Poppy. "Maybe the matching goddamn hat. Because I have them, by the way, I actually—"

"Don't do that, Jake," Poppy said, squinting at the sudden sun. "I'm not sure the feminist outfit, for this situation, feels quite right."

They let Billy walk ahead as they strolled, very slowly, on the pavement behind him. Jake had both hands clasped behind his back. "Really? Feels like exactly the right message. And I am a feminist, so—"

"Great." Poppy spoke over him. "But you're going to need to be a humble feminist in that meeting, Jake."

As they walked, Poppy recalled the time she and her sister had been at a day festival in Finsbury Park and kept passing the same guy with an *I'm a Feminist* T-shirt on. Eventually Dandelion had gone up to him and said, "Thanks for the feminism, why you into it?" And he'd said, actually, he wasn't too fussed, but it was his lucky T-shirt, always got him laid. Dandelion nodded. "Can I give you my number?" And on the inside of his arm, in lip liner, she wrote, *Suck My Dick.*

"Soo, anyway," Jake said. "You'll be my character witness though? If I need one." He glanced sideways at Poppy, stuck his lower jaw out. "You were there after all."

"Come on, Jake." Poppy was determined to be positive. "It won't come to that."

"But I don't remember anything, Poppy. So my version of events is going to sound so suspect, when in reality my mind is a black hole."

"Just tell the truth. Be as honest as possible. Also," Poppy said, as a new idea came to her, "we can get the medical records from the club? The medic on duty was called Deo."

They had reached Abney Park Cemetery, and Jake stopped walking. "That's not a bad shout. Poppy, thank you *so much* for being great about all this. I don't want you to feel roped into a shit show."

"It's fine," Poppy said. "I want to help." She did.

"Well, thank you, sincerely. You're a very nice person." Jake cleared his throat quietly, looked at Billy, who had his face pressed up against the window of a restaurant called The Good Egg. "And I'm really sorry if I was rude earlier—about your engagement. I was surprised, I guess. And maybe the tiniest bit . . . But I'm happy for you and . . . yeah. So tell me about him? What's he like? Ssss . . . am. Great, obviously." In Jake's voice there was a softness, but his eyes looked tired, quite sad. He pulled at the neck of his T-shirt, adjusting its position, then put his hands in his pockets.

Poppy thought of what it would be like in that moment to not answer his question at all, and instead to step forward and kiss him. "Um . . ." She realized she was looking down at his shorts. "Um . . ." She glanced past him, into the cemetery. "Sam's great. We've been together a long time." Then because, out loud, this sounded shamefully unromantic, she said, "And we're very happy."

And they were quite happy. Averagely happy. Normal-level happy. Which, really, maybe meant trying not to be sad. Long-term love was a choice, though; all relationships needed work, and Poppy and Sam were committed to trying, to working. Also, they'd been through so much together. They'd come so far.

"I'm glad you're happy," Jake said. "That's the main thing. It really is."

"And weddings are fun, aren't they? They cheer everyone up. I think it's going to do wonders for my parents."

"Your wedding?"

"Yeah."

"Your wedding is going to do wonders for your parents?"

"Well, I mean, my marriage. What I mean is . . . it's been a shit year, obviously. The worst year. My dad, he . . . he . . . I just want them to focus on something positive."

"Of course," Jake said. "You all deserve something happy. I'm pleased for you. I am."

From where Poppy was standing, she could see a lot of wonky, crumbling headstones through the wrought iron gate. Abney Park was one of London's Magnificent Seven cemeteries. Poppy had woven through the muddy paths and the trailing ivy and leaping squirrels many times with Dandelion, gossiping, arguing, pointing at trees. How naive they had been not to have ever considered, or discussed, the fact that one day one of them would leave the other, that one of them, then both of them, would lie down in the earth.

"You okay?" Jake asked.

"Yup," Poppy said. She looked up the street; Billy was tap-dancing, holding his dolly on his hip, like a baby. He got distracted by a passing fox-red Labrador and pointed at it, called back to them, "IT'S A COCKAPOO!"

Poppy smiled. "He's a real cutie, Jake."

"He is. He likes you."

They both took a big step forward, began walking again. "Wanna come have dinner with us?" Jake asked. "Because I was thinking of making Bolognese. Billy's absolutely wasted, obviously. The man needs carbs."

"We've got Sam's sister coming over, and her awful husband. So . . ." They were approaching Whole Foods now. Poppy would go inside and buy lemons. Lemons for her fiancé. And maybe a delicious tart.

Billy came running back over, and Jake swooped him into his arms and flung him over his shoulder. "Another night? How's your week looking?" he asked, Billy dangling behind him in a fireman's lift.

Poppy's week was looking busy. She was going to Haus, the chic hotel where Hayley worked, with Sam, and then she had an event in France. "I've got a wedding in Provence next weekend, so I'm heading there."

"No way. Whereabouts?"

"Arles."

"Is that near Aix? My dad's taken a château there for a month. I'm definitely going to go for a few days. Could you come after the wedding? There's a pool. If you're close, I'll pick you up."

"Oh," Poppy said. She'd love to take a couple of days off after the wedding and hang with Jake, but what would she say to Sam? It would mean more lying. It would not be, in any way, appropriate. "That's a lovely offer. But I really can't."

Jake put Billy down and held him by the hand. "Well, if you change your mind . . ." He kissed Poppy on the cheek and said quietly, "I appreciate you showing us around today and watching Billy and . . . stuff. I feel like we're friends. Do you feel like we're friends?"

"I do, yes." Poppy ruffled Billy's hair. "It was so nice to meet you," she said, smiling down at him. "And Sheena."

"NOT Sheena!"

"She's called Spleen," Jake said.

"NOT! DADDY! NO!"

"Very sorry . . ." Poppy glanced at Jake; they smiled at each other.

As Jake and Billy turned to leave, Poppy waved and watched them walk down the street, blurred her eyes as they rounded the corner. Once they were out of sight, she set off too. Whole Foods. Lemons. She'd buy flowers. And wine. She'd buy a pretty card from the art shop next door and write on it, *I love you, Sam.* And write on it, *I'm excited for our baby*, and write on it, *I'm feeling terribly scared about life and what if we're making a huge mistake*, and write on it, *I MISS MY SISTER. WHY DID THIS HAPPEN TO US?*

And then Poppy was running down the street, the wrong way, and when she turned the corner, Jake and Billy were there and she had to come to a sudden skidding halt, like a woman teetering on an edge.

Jake was crouched down in front of Billy, wiping his face with a tissue, and Billy saw her first: "Dada, Poopy is back!"

Jake stood. "You all right?" He squinted an eye at her and it looked like a wink. He held his head on one side. "What's up?"

When Poppy was with Jake, life pinched, but in a good way. She was a bad person, but in the best way. "I . . . I . . ." She didn't want to leave him. "I know you probably have lots of friends and stuff, and obviously you've got Billy and . . . Spl . . . Dolly . . . who are excellent company, but I thought, maybe, I could come with you too . . . after the day you've had . . . seeing as we're friends now and everything."

"We're having meaty pasta," Billy informed her.

"What about your dinner thing?" Jake asked.

"Sam will understand, we see his sister all the time," Poppy said. Which was half-true.

Jake put his arm around Poppy's back and squeezed his gratitude. "We'd love it if Poppy came and had Bolognese with us, wouldn't we, bud?"

"Well . . . do you know how to twerk?" Billy asked, looking up at her. "I can teach you when we get to Daddy's house?" He put his small warm hand in Poppy's, and the three of them set off walking together, in the direction of Dandelion's flat. Everyone who passed them, Poppy thought, as a calmness descended over her, would see them as a family.

26

Wednesday, 18th June

Sam fixed them both a drink, tonging half-moons of lemon into crystal glasses, stirring in gin, crackling in the tonic. This evening had been the first time Poppy had drunk alcohol in nearly two months, and she was feeling dazzling after two cocktails that tasted of smoke and money mixed and sipped in the dimly lit, exquisitely interiored bar at Haus, followed by a three-course meal, with a crisp, dry bottle of white in the restaurant.

And now they were back in their petite room, one that Haus called a Cubby. Next to the bed, a low midcentury side table was wedged up against the wall. At one end was a cherrywood lamp with a cream linen shade, and on the other was stainless steel cocktail-making paraphernalia, an icebox, crystal glasses, and a bowl of citrus fruits.

They were both very tipsy. In good spirits. Sam had forgiven Poppy for missing dinner with Hayley and Daniel—the silent treatment had lasted all of Monday—but since being at Haus, they hadn't squabbled, seethed, or disagreed. They had discussed their wedding quite lovingly in the bar, and then, in front of the other chatting hotel guests, they'd kissed, and public displays of affection were not something they'd done in a very long time.

Historically, traditionally, Poppy had never seen herself as a very sexual person; most of her sex life had been vanilla and, secretly, she'd always favored masturbation to intercourse—she'd never had an orgasm with anyone even close to where she got to by herself. It was true that at the start of her relationship with Sam, as a new and enamored couple, amped up on dopamine and oxytocin, they'd kissed for hours and had sex frequently—hungover on the sofa on Sundays, in the sea on holiday once or twice, and a few times in Sam's parked car. But then, as they moved further into their relationship, the cadence slowed to a bimonthly shag. For the last couple of years, it was more like monthly, max, and on special occasions. Of course they'd done it alfresco in the moonlight, up against the rocks the other night in Devon, and maybe that had been a turning point for them, because now it would be more regular, seeing as they were kind of, or totally, trying for a kid.

This trip had been positioned by Sam as a dirty night away, and after an initial, instinctual feeling of reticence, Poppy had got herself on board. In an attempt to evolve their entrenched foreplay routine she'd hatched a plan to sprinkle on some spice. She'd made a lusty playlist and splurged on some lingerie and a whole load of makeup from Charlotte Tilbury's Pillow Talk collection.

In their Cubby, with its sensual pools of warm lighting, Poppy connected her phone to the Marshall speaker, undid the buttons of her shirt to reveal her lace bra, and spun around. "I've got a surprise for you."

"Oooh la la!" Sam was delighted. He put his drink on the side and leaped onto the bed.

"I'll be right back." Poppy took her drink into the bathroom and shut the door. She was already wearing her new Agent Provocateur bra and knickers and had hidden the rest of the ensemble.

She took her clothes off, unfolded the pink tissue paper, and lifted the delicate suspender belt out of its box and fastened it around her waist. She took a large sip of the gin and then carefully unrolled sheer stockings up her legs, clipped them to the belt (difficult), and stepped back into her skirt and heels. The plan was to do a striptease, which was not something she'd ever done before, but she figured tonight would be a good time to start. She'd loosely choreographed a raunchy, tongue-in-cheek routine.

"How's it going in there?" Sam shouted from next door, over the music.

"Just a minute!" Poppy called back.

The mirror ran horizontally across the width of the bathroom, above a double marble basin with antique brass taps. She stepped closer to her reflection, reached for her nude lipstick, and applied it with an open mouth. She pressed her lips together. Spritzed herself with scent. Pinned her hair up so at one point during the dance, she could take it down and flick it around. "Ready?" She shimmied a response and smiled as she imagined walking through the door of the bathroom to find him on the bed, shirt open, shoes off. Though now she was picturing it all playing out and the man on the bed wasn't Sam.

It was Jake.

"Fuck." Poppy shook her head and a long curl of hair fell out of the clip. She tucked it behind her ear, pulled in a very long breath. "Sexy, sexy, little night away!" she sang at herself encouragingly. "This is exciting! And fun. And . . . This is . . ."

"Popsy?" Sam called again.

Poppy finished her drink and put the glass down hard on the marble. She smiled massive at the mirror. "Go on then!" She swallowed a sudden feeling of terror. "Go on, go on!" she geed.

Sam was lying on the bed and he wolf whistled when he saw her. "Baby, baby, baby!"

Poppy didn't look at him. She stalked straight to her phone in her stilettos and pressed play on the track she was going to dance to, "Foxy Lady" by Jimi Hendrix. She reached for the bottle of gin and took a swig directly from it as the guitar intro filled the room. She walked to the opposite wall to the beat of the music. Ironically, for someone who was trying their best to be sexy, Poppy felt like a kid. Accidentally she thought of Billy. Then, again, of Jake. "Hold on, no. Hold on." She jogged back to her phone. Restarted the track. Took another swig of gin. Her face was feeling hot, and fake.

When Jimi began singing about a cute little heartbreaker, Poppy whipped around to face Sam and began undoing her buttons. She let the silk shirt drop from her arms to the floor.

"Woah-fuuu . . ." Sam was nodding and saying appreciative bits of words as Poppy shimmied into the corners of the room. She shimmied five or six times, really trying to get into it, then grappled with the fastening of her skirt and let it drop too.

"You naughty little bitch cat!" Sam yelled.

Sorry, what? Poppy winced as she unrolled a stocking, whipped it off, and waved it around her head in a very half-hearted lasso. She flung it at Sam's face and he grabbed at it and draped it through his mouth. They were at the chorus now, and Poppy was meant to be doing the silly hand movement (bunny ears) like Garth does in the *Wayne's World* movie, but instead she was repeatedly circling her hips in a figure of eight, not feeling sexy or funny at all. She stared at Sam as he undid his trousers, rapturous, and it struck her—she wasn't remotely attracted to him. She had absolutely no idea what she was doing there. Not just in a suspender belt at Haus, but in their relationship. She began shuddering with an uncontrollable, full-bodied type of ick. An existential revulsion. She only had one thought and it pounded louder than the music: *Not him. Not him. Not him.*

"Come here, you naughty, minxy . . ." Sam growled. Unfortunately, he'd got his penis out.

"I want to break up!" Poppy blurted really loudly. She turned and paused the music. "Sam, I think we should break up."

Sam stopped rubbing his penis but kept hold of it. "What? Is this . . . part of the . . . ?"

Poppy came over to the bed, perched on the edge, one stocking on and one stocking off. "This is a big mistake, Sam. I just . . . we need to break up."

"You are absolutely kidding me . . ." Sam said, pulling the bed-sheet over himself. "Again? You're doing this *again*?"

Poppy put her hand on top of his hand, but he shook her off.

"I think . . . I'm sorry, but I proposed to you, Sam, because I wanted something positive to happen. And marriage and babies sound nice and normal and . . . distracting . . ." She took a big breath and course corrected. "But the truth is we won't make it, will we? I think we both know—this just isn't love." Poppy slid her engagement ring off and put it on the side table.

"You've drunk too much." Sam stood up and pulled on the hotel robe, put his hands on his hips.

But Poppy didn't feel drunk; it was more that she felt wholly sober. Her thoughts were not trembling and uncertain, her vision was crisp and clear. "I'm sorry. I'm not really sure how people are meant to do this. I'm really sorry about how . . . unfortunate this is, but I think I should probably go."

Poppy felt a frenzied need to get away from Sam. She stood and walked, fast, over to the wardrobe. She flung it open and pulled on a sweatshirt over her lingerie, then crouched to the floor and stepped into her skirt. "I'll get a cab. You stay. I'm so sorry."

And she *was* so sorry. She'd been a total bitch cat—that much was undeniable. But she couldn't be in the relationship for another minute. Already it had been far too long. She grabbed her suitcase and began stuffing it with clothes with the clear realization that sometimes you need to be a bad person to become a good one.

"If you walk out of that door, Poppy . . ." Sam was thrusting his finger toward her. Even in the mellow lighting, she could see the sweat and rage. "If you walk out of that door then I'll . . ."

But Poppy was already in the corridor. She was running to reception in high heels and her sweatshirt—so she never heard Sam's threat.

27

Sunday, 22nd June

Jake

Poppy crunched over the gravel toward the 1970s soft-top red MG Jake had hired from a dealer at Avignon (knowing he'd need to compete with his dad's sports car). A leather tote was slung over one of her shoulders and a camera bag over the other. She was wearing a long white dress, brown leather sandals, and a big hat.

Jake got out of the car and went to give her a hug. "Provençal Poppy! You look just the part." He felt smug as hell picking her up; she was a bohemian film star. "Is that all your stuff? You travel very light."

"Betty is kindly taking our equipment home and getting the film developed and so . . . I'm officially on holiday!" Poppy grinned at him. "Sexy car," she added as she climbed in, putting her bags in the small back seat, taking off her hat and clasping it between her knees.

"Excellent," Jake said.

Since Poppy had left him and Billy the previous weekend, after Bolognese, Jake's thoughts kept returning to her with the sort of devotion that worried him, a physical yearning to be near her, to study her face, to know her thoughts, to hear her chiming laugh. And so he was inordinately pleased that, last minute, she'd decided she could come to his dad's place after all. She'd messaged him yesterday, said her plans had changed and that, if the offer was still there, she would love to have a break.

Jake put the address into Google Maps, and as they set off, he asked about the wedding that she'd been photographing, which, by the looks of the venue, must have been extremely lavish. "Get any ideas for your wedding then?" he asked, which was meant to be a joke.

Instinctively, Jake presumed Poppy would want to do something fairly low-key (he could see her in a vintage dress with flowers in her hair in a registry office and then, afterward, with pink cheeks at a table in a rowdy pub with friends). Instead of laughing, though, Poppy made a *hm* noise and didn't seem to smile.

They were winding down the pale gravel drive, through a tunnel of tall cypress trees. "When are you tying the knot again?" Jake flicked the indicator, which clicked pleasingly, and he turned onto the main road a tad too fast.

Poppy leaned into the door, then swerved back over to him with momentum. "Umm, hmmm. Not too sure."

Jake thought, perhaps, he should ask more about Poppy's fiancé, show an interest, but he couldn't bring himself to—didn't feel like hearing her talk about him. He knew what Sam looked like because Jake had befriended Poppy on Instagram, and although it was mainly a grid full of artiness or work events, he'd found one deep snap of Poppy and a man standing in front of a large mirror; she was taking a photo of their reflection with an old Nikon camera. From this photo, and from her previous profile pic on WhatsApp at the Greek taverna, Jake had decided Sam was almost certainly a chump.

"Dare I ask, is there any update on that whole *situation*?" Poppy turned her attention from the landscape to Jake's face. She shifted in her chair slightly, so her knees were pointing toward him.

Clearly, she was referring to the disastrous face-in-nooni fandango, which was very much not rectified. Jake inhaled. "Yup. I had a call with HR and took them through what I remember, which is basically nothing, and I had a chat to the producer I work with." Karla had been friendly, though her language more formal, her accent more German. "We're going to talk again after HR finishes their report. She assured me again that Sydney, the girl, was extremely disappointed and shocked, rather than traumatized."

"Phew," Poppy said. They looked at each other quickly, and then Jake turned back to the road.

"Phew, yes, but it's still all really shameful. Deeply unprofessional. And, more than anything, it's a head fuck as to what even happened. No one else was off their tits, apparently. Anyway . . ." Jake glanced at Poppy again—her hair was caught in the wind and was lifting up in strands like she was underwater. She grabbed at it and tied it into a knot and Jake made his brain focus hard on the road as he took another breath. "First week of July is when I find out my fate. In the meantime, my plan is to push it down."

"The old Push Down method," Poppy said, with what sounded like approval.

"You know it?"

"Know it well."

"What you pushing down then?" Jake asked.

"Everything." Poppy laughed, although her laugh was tight, quite strained.

"Are you? Really?" Jake had an urge to pull the car over and squeeze her really hard. "Like what?"

"Well, I mean, we could definitely start with my job."

The MG was coiling up a hill, toward an ancient stone village set into a cliff. All around them were fields and vineyards, every different type of green.

"You take pictures of rich people in castles looking sensational, eating caviar," Jake said. "How bad can that be?"

"Course, it's lush, but I don't know . . . it's started to feel inauthentic. I put on a persona to do it, obviously. I have to be bossy and shout things like *Beautiful! Give me Strong Face*, while simultaneously being consistently charming—even when people are rude to me, which they are, by the way. All the time."

"Are they? Like what?"

"Well, it's rarely the couple who are getting married. They're usually a delight, but, say, at this wedding yesterday, the older family members kept clicking their fingers at me and Betty when they wanted us to come over, not even like we were staff—like we were dogs. And there was that handsy uncle recently, which isn't uncommon either; people get trashed at weddings and often misbehave. I just feel massively over the whole wedding thing, generally, I guess."

"Okay. Right. Well, it sounds to me like you need some time off work to regroup," Jake said. "Do you have any savings? Can your fiancé help? You don't have kids—which takes a massive pressure off. And you've been through so much, Poppy. It's important to work out how you can best live your very precious life."

"I only have two more weddings booked this season," Poppy said. "And I usually would have one every weekend, so I'm having a more chilled summer already, but I also feel guilty about that."

"Don't feel guilty! You can use the time to think about how you want to evolve your business. You still want to be a photographer, right? Or are you thinking of a total change?"

"Still photography, yes," Poppy said, seeming somewhat encouraged. "But maybe move away from events? It's just hard when that's my whole brand. I guess an evolution is the right idea, it doesn't have to be a totally new thing," she said, with more energy in her voice.

"Exactly," Jake said, "an update is normal. It's needed. And I can help you think about it? We could brainstorm ideas this weekend: your vision, your goals, and—"

"Jake, that's very kind, but we're on holiday in the South of France, so—"

"Honestly, I find this shit fun," Jake said. He did.

They stopped at a T-junction, and the car next to them had a woman behind the wheel with apple-red hair. From her stereo, a record that Jake's mother used to play all the time was blaring, "These Days," the Nico cover of the Jackson Browne song. The memory of her then was visceral, and Jake felt not the pull of tears in his throat he usually got when he thought of his mother, but a small celebratory explosion of happiness for the brilliant woman she was.

"I love this song," Poppy said.

"Ah, Poppy, me too," Jake agreed, glancing at her, feeling quite moved.

The strap of Poppy's dress had fallen slightly from her shoulder, and Jake watched as she reached for it, and then, without really knowing why, he was helping her, pulling up the strap, and their fingers were touching. Embarrassed, Jake moved his hand away quickly. "Sorry." They looked into each other's eyes, and Jake was floored by the desire to kiss her. He felt like he might. He felt like *she* might. But then the woman in the car next to them at the T-junction drove off and the song slipped away, and the car behind beeped and so Jake turned his attention back to the road and accelerated, moving off with a wheel spin. "Anyway . . ." he said, in a loud and singsong awkward way. He checked Maps. "ETA six minutes!"

"So, I'm about to meet your dad?" Poppy asked. She was looking down at her lap, maybe feeling shy.

"Yup," Jake said, "and his new girlfriend. We're both about to meet her. She's from Hinge," he added. Jake had been feeling a tad nervous about mentioning the dating app aspect to Poppy, all things considered, but actually, she just snorted with amusement.

The only other potential disaster Jake could think of was if Poppy mentioned Dandelion, and then his dad might put his foot in it and launch into some whole thing about Dandelion being Jake's dead ex—which wasn't at all a conversation Jake wanted to get into in front of Poppy. He hoped she'd never know about how he'd dramatically embellished that story, and so he'd texted his dad that morning: Don't mention that whole Dandelion thing, dad. Not a good thing to talk about in front of Poppy. Thnx.

"I think this might be it?" Jake slowed right down and leaned forward so he could peer up a dirt track. He drove carefully over the loose uneven stones and turned in to a yard where there was a Porsche and a huge fig tree—twenty feet high and just as wide. Laden with fruit, like it was crying juicy dark tears.

Poppy stepped out of the car, slinging both bags over her shoulder and pressing her hat back on.

Jake pushed at a low wooden gate painted in a greeny blue and followed a path to the house, through lots of chatting insects. The château was even more charming than it looked on the website. Dappled in light, surrounded by lush plants in terra-cotta pots. Each window—of which there were many—was stacked evenly and symmetrically, and the shutters were painted the same color as the garden gate. The large wooden front door was also the same color, as was a small circular breakfast table they passed, which had someone's paints on it and a paintbrush in a jam jar of black water. Behind Jake, Poppy made admiring dovelike coos.

"Hello? Rafe?" Jake called as he opened a second screen door that took them into the kitchen. The room was very dark and cool compared to the temperature outside. All the shutters were closed.

It smelled of overripe fruit and powerful cheese and, faintly, of food on the turn. A background note of sun cream. Almost, vaguely . . . sex?

"Bonjour!" Jake's father came out of the room next door in a white linen shirt, shorts, bare feet, and reading glasses. He had a large hardback book in one hand (another old man's memoir). Jake felt sweaty in comparison, too much like the teenage scruffy son. He wanted to go and wash, to comb back his hair, to put on cologne and change his shirt, immediately. After they had maneuvered the back-patting hug that Yan had brought into their lives, Jake introduced Poppy.

"Rafe, hi," Jake's father said, with a slightly mannered voice. "What a treat to have you."

Poppy took off her hat and ran a hand over her hair. "Lovely to meet you," she said as she was kissed on both cheeks. "Such a gorgeous house."

"We like it," Jake's father said. He took his glasses off and slipped them in his top pocket. "Mish popped out on the bike to get some bits for lunch, she'll be back any sec."

"I bought a few things from the market this morning," Poppy said, putting her tote on the table and pulling out a crumpled brown bag. She looked down into it. "Peaches, honey, and olive oil."

"How sweet you are," Jake's father said, in a way that Jake found embarrassing. "Right, now you're absolutely free as birds for a couple of hours, then we'll have a relaxed lunch. I can recommend the pool, I give it a high rating and review."

"I'll make supper later, Dad, if you want," Jake said.

"Oh, well, that's very kind, Jakey. Thank you." Jake's father smiled at Poppy. "And you're in separate rooms, did I get that right?"

"Yeah, we're just friends," Jake said, aware of Poppy nodding next to him.

Outside, the garden gate squeaked and they all looked through the screen door. "Here she is!" Jake's father said.

"Hi! Hi, everyone!" The girlfriend was coming down the path toward them, a very full basket over her shoulder, overflowing with vegetables, a long baguette. She was wearing a small floral sundress. Masses of dark hair. Jake dipped his head to one side and held out his finger toward her as he tried to place her. He had that nervous mental scrabbling-around feeling. Had he worked with her before?

"Jake, Poppy, this is Mish," Jake's dad said as the girlfriend came into the kitchen. She gathered her hair up behind her with both hands and tied it into a ponytail, long and sleek.

"Lovely to meet you," Poppy said, and they kissed each other twice.

Jake's mouth became so dry that he had to lift a hand to his throat and manually encourage a swallow. His dad's girlfriend was staring at him with her finger pointed out in a way that announced that she definitely knew him too.

"Hi." Jake grinned.

"We've met." Amisha was looking at him through thinned and scornful eyes as if he was the sort of man who might run away after a one-night stand, delete her on a dating app, and never contact her again.

Jake's father kissed Amisha on the side of her head, put his arm around her. "Oh?"

"We went on a date," she said, in the nasal voice Jake remembered now, very clearly.

"Did we?" Jake wiped sweat from his forehead; the kitchen had got hotter. He looked longingly at the door. He billowed air down the front of his T-shirt. "Oh yes! Aaaages ago. That's right."

Poppy had discreetly tasked herself with unloading peaches

from the paper bag and arranging them in a bowl in the center of the table.

"Springtime. Remember, you—"

"Oh, what a coincidence!" Jake's father said. "Well, I never! Fishing from the same London dating app river, I suppose."

Poppy crunched the bag up and walked around the table, opened the recycling bin.

"How have you been though?" Jake asked, throwing his arms wide. He was prepared to break into a musical theater number. He had a very strong urge to click his fingers to a jolly old beat. Do a spin. Moonwalk through the door, along the path, and then turn and start sprinting down the road. Do another runner.

"This is your son?" Amisha asked, turning to Jake's father. "You're kidding?"

"This is my son. Funny old world, eh?"

"Should I . . . ?" Poppy had taken herself closer to the door. "I might go to the pool? Yeah, I think I'm . . ." She picked up her tote, pointed at the outside world. "Just going to go to the pool."

"That's a good idea. I'll come with you." Jake clapped his hands as if he was totally psyched the last woman he'd actually spent a night with was now SLEEPING WITH HIS DAD.

"I'm going for a shower," Amisha said. "Nice to meet you, Poppy," she added, in a voice that sounded a lot less hostile.

"See you later!" Jake said, waving.

"Well, that was unexpected," Jake's father said, once both the women had left through opposite doors.

"Dad, I literally showed you her photos. How do you not remember?" Jake put his hands on his hips.

"Well, as long as you were a gentleman, that's all I care about."

Jake glowered. "Dad! What?"

"Mish did seem a little caught off guard there," Jake's father conceded, "so if you weren't a gentleman, then you sure as hell are going to be one from now on. I like her a lot, okay? She's a lovely lady. So, I'd appreciate it if you could be on best behavior, and I am sure we can have a splendid time and all get along like grown-ups."

Jake crouched down by his bag, pulling out his tattered book and his balled-up trunks. "Yup. Yes. Gentleman. Got it," he said, very much not up for a chivalry lecture from the original lothario. Very much not hoping that he'd gone down on a woman who was going to become his stepmother. "I don't get how you don't remember me showing you her Hinge profile, Dad? She's a physio, right? I mean we discussed her at length."

"Well, we didn't meet on Hinge," Jake's father said. He picked up his book from the table.

"Where did you meet?"

"Feeld."

"Are you joking? The sex app?"

"It's not solely for sex, Jakey. It can be for love too. Love for sexually positive, explorative people. Honestly, it really is the most fabulous forum." Jake's father slapped Jake on the back. "Life in the old dog yet." He winked, and with that—Jake knew he would never wink at anyone, even in jest, even at Poppy, ever again.

"Please." Jake put both hands in front of his eyes. Why the hell couldn't his father be like other dads? An impotent, kindly, selfless grandpa. "I don't want to know any of this. I'm going outside."

Jake pushed through the screen door, out into the thick heat. He stalked over the lawn, through the call of the cicadas, to the swimming pool, which glinted as bright as a Hockney painting. Poppy was standing by the edge of it, looking out into a field, at a donkey. She was in a red swimming costume, which had a low back, and Jake could see the ribbon of her backbone. Her swimming costume was being eaten by her arse; she had a serious wedgie. Her bum was very juicy, swelling out from her waist and curving into her thighs, which were long and really wonderful. Jake had an urge to grab her, to take her in his arms, to lick her neck and make her gasp and laugh.

"No, no, no," he said under his breath, chastising himself. This attraction to Poppy was not helpful and needed to be quashed. Poppy was grieving and pushing things down and she was getting married to a man she loved and whom Jake knew, innately, that he hated.

Jake kicked off his Birkenstocks and yanked his shirt over his head as Poppy turned toward him—a vision in red. He thought of the woman on the Special K ad that he used to wank over before Pornhub had been invented. He thought of Pamela Anderson on *Baywatch* running in slow motion. He thought of Poppy's sister in her swimming costume with a Negroni. He thought of Amisha, scowling, upstairs. He thought of Zoe and her pregnant tummy getting Yan to do things for her. And then Poppy smiled, waved, raised a hand to her face to shield her eyes from the sun, and all these other women and all Jake's troubles—his fucking dad, his work disaster—evaporated into nothing; he breathed them out. He smiled.

"Well, that was a tad awkward," Poppy said.

"Not ideal," Jake agreed.

Poppy crossed one long leg in front of the other, and Jake could tell she felt self-aware being seen without her clothes. She put her hands on her hips, then smoothed her stomach.

"Right, well . . ." Jake dropped his book, sunglasses, T-shirt, and the trunks he was carrying on a sun lounger. "There's only one thing for it . . ." He ran at her, and Poppy shrieked a laugh as he scooped her into his arms and leaped into the luminous baptism of the swimming pool.

28

Still Sunday, 22nd June

Poppy

After lunch, which hadn't been too awkward—considering the revelation—Rafe and Mish had a siesta, then went for a cycle, and Poppy and Jake stayed out by the pool until the sun sank into haze. They finished a bottle of rosé between them, opened another, and, despite the tumults of her life, Poppy had that languorous holiday feeling, when the day stretches long and soft, and the sharp edges are rounded and can't cause pain.

"You're very prolific on dating apps then?" Poppy stood and moved to a lounger under the large canvas umbrella, noticing she had burned around the edges of her swimming costume, cutting over her hips and bum.

"Things are going really well for me right now," Jake quipped sarcastically. He was lying on a striped towel by the side of the pool, in swimming trunks, sunglasses, and a chain necklace, his hands behind his head. He had dark fuzz over his chest and then again running from his belly button, into his trunks. His body was not intimidatingly chiseled and did not look as invested in as

Sam's—but he was giving strong, fit, capable dad, and Poppy was, increasingly with each glass of wine, very much appreciating it.

"How long did you date?" Poppy had been waiting for Jake to bring up the Mish thing all afternoon, but he hadn't. The questions had been swilling inside of her, until this one sloshed right out.

Jake pushed himself onto his elbows. "It was one date. Just before we . . . in spring."

"Right." Poppy wondered if this meant they'd kissed. She reached for the Ambre Solaire and resprayed her legs, pulling it over her skin from ankle to thigh. "Guessing it didn't end amazingly?"

"*Amazingly* is not the word I'd use, Poppy, no. More like an averagely awkward one-night stand. I didn't behave fantastically and now, well . . . is this what they call karma? Anyway," Jake continued quickly, "glad she doesn't seem to hate me, she seemed friendly at lunch, don't you think? I think it's all fine. Do you think it's all fine?"

"Oh, right," Poppy said, surprised to hear they'd slept together. She sprayed her arms with the sun cream, not looking up at Jake. "Well, she's very pretty." And then, by mistake: "So is she your type?"

"No comment."

"No comment?"

"No. She's not. But I mean, I don't really have a type. Do you have a type?"

"I, er . . ." *Yeah. You.* "Not sure." Poppy watched Jake as he hooked his thumb under the waistband of his trunks, pulled them down a centimeter, examining his tan. Already, there was a distinct contrast in color.

"Anyway, how's the wedding planning going?" Jake asked,

looking up at her. "You haven't told me anything about it. Am I invited? I could snog a sexy bridesmaid."

Poppy finished her glass of wine. "So, actually, Jake . . ." Now she was tipsy, she could tell him. Before, she'd been too scared to say the words aloud. Too nervous about his reaction. "The wedding's off. We're not together anymore."

Jake sat all the way up, bent forward over his knees. "*What?*" He lifted his sunglasses so she could see his eyes. "When? What happened? How? Why? Are you okay? Is he okay? Actually, don't care about him. Are you okay?" Jake asked again. "How have you not told me this, Poppy?"

"That's a million questions, Jake."

"I know, I know, I know." Jake was talking quickly. He put his sunglasses on again. Lay back on his elbows. "I'm really surprised. Why? How come?"

Poppy swallowed, thinking back to Haus. To the cataclysmic implosion of her five-year relationship. "I don't love him anymore."

"Fair enough!" Jake said loudly, and Poppy was relieved to hear that, perhaps, he sounded pleased. "And so, what happened? If I can ask that?" Jake bit on his own lip, with evident anticipation.

"You know how I said we were going away to a hotel? Well, it was kind of meant to be a dirty night away—"

"Right," Jake said, his mouth twitching into a grimace.

"I mean," Poppy said quickly, "our relationship wasn't really like that, but I was trying to spice it up, maybe? And I had this whole plan to do a striptease . . . Like a funny striptease, to a funny song."

Jake held his hand up, indicating Poppy should pause the story, and she used this as an opportunity to pour more wine into her glass and take a massive gulp.

"What funny song were you . . . ?"

"'Foxy Lady.'"

"I-can-play-that-on-my-guitar!" Jake said in one fast breath, the words running together. And then, more casually: "I can play that on my guitar. Anyway, sorry, so is the funny striptease funny because of *Wayne's World*?"

"Yes, I had originally planned to do the bunny ears during the dance."

"I think they're probably fox ears, but, anyway, amazing. Right." Jake sat up again. "So there you are, the show is about to start and—"

"Well, 'the show' never happened," Poppy said, using air quotes, "because, before, when I was getting changed in the bathroom—"

"Getting changed into . . . ?" Jake was clean-shaven, his dimples were very pronounced, and he was clearly trying to suppress a smile.

Poppy swallowed a smile too. "Getting changed into lingerie, obviously."

Jake tilted his body so far to the side that he toppled right into the pool. He pulled himself out, sat back on the towel. "Right, that's better. Was feeling a bit . . . hot. Sorry, yes, continue . . . we were at the lingerie bit."

Poppy was so encouraged by such brazen flirtation that she had to look down at her feet, aware her expression might be too uncooly delighted. "So, there I was in the hotel bathroom, getting changed, and I realized . . ." She wanted to tell him that at that moment she had thought of him. She swallowed. "I realized . . ." But she couldn't do it. "Well, I realized I didn't want to go through with it. Not the striptease, or the wedding, or . . . the rest of our lives."

Jake rubbed his eyes with his fingers and then he rubbed his jaw, his mouth open. His body was glistening and wet. He wiped his hair back from his face, pushed his lips together thoughtfully, nodded slowly. Eventually, he said, "This is major news, Poppy."

"It is pretty major," Poppy agreed.

"And are you okay? Are you feeling really sad and heartbroken?"

"Not really. It should have happened a long time ago." What Poppy could see now, so clearly, was that over the years, she and Sam had both changed, or perhaps they'd changed each other—she'd become more avoidant, more withdrawn, and he'd become more aggravated by her, more passive-aggressive, and they'd both become more selfish and resentful of each other. But it had happened so slowly that, day to day, she hadn't noticed, like a flower wilting—it would have only been visible to the human eye played back at high speed. Everything seemed normal. Everything seemed fine. Everything seemed okay. But then—*oh shit.* "I think what happened, honestly," Poppy continued, "is that things started to go wrong a long time ago, and we just presumed we were still in love. My sister always hated Sam and, maybe, I felt protective of him. Annoyed by how annoying she was about him, how controlling she could be."

Sometimes, Poppy wondered what her life would have been like, what she would have been like, if Dandelion had never been there at all. Maybe, Poppy could have been both of them—a yin and yang together—better than each of them alone. Maybe, it all would have felt like this: a holiday. Though, really, she knew, life without ever having her big sister would have been bland and joyless and it was better, now, to live with the searing pain of grief and the ragged scars of loss, because at least she'd got to stand next to her and laugh with her and fight with her and learn from her. And now, here in Dandelion's wake—was Jake.

"If it's any consolation, Poppy, most people break up a long time after the point they really should have. So well done for doing it. There are some other people I know"—at this Jake coughed, to demonstrate he was alluding to himself—"that can never even pull the trigger, and so maybe they act like a total twat so that they get dumped. Ending things always takes some guts."

"Mm." Poppy nodded, half agreeing with him. It was true she did feel proud of herself for breaking up with Sam, but she wished she'd done it sooner and she wished she'd done it in a better, more compassionate way. And obviously she'd cheated on him emotionally and physically with Jake—so she couldn't feel proud of that. "I guess," she said, "it's for the best, but I do feel a bit scared of the unknown, and sad, I suppose because I wanted the things people want from life, like a family. We'd been talking a lot about a baby . . ." Luckily, Poppy's boobs were tender and swollen now, and she had the lower-abdomen-stapling pain, meaning her period was on the way, which definitely was a relief. "But then I was struck by the knowledge that a big part of my desire for a child was the need for a way to counterbalance my grief, and maybe a distraction from my ailing relationship—and those are not the right reasons for a baby, they're bad reasons . . ." Already, Poppy wondered if later, more sober, she would regret this level of honesty, but in that moment—it felt liberating to admit it all, even to herself. "I guess, after Dandelion . . . really for a very long time, I've felt drugged by my own grief . . ." *And then I met you, and things changed and I changed.* "But, yeah, maybe now, I'm coming back to life."

Jake stood up. He walked over to her lounger and sat on it, next to her legs. "You can still have all the things you want, Poppy, and a baby, and a family, of course you can. And you're one step closer to your future happiness now, because you've broken up with thingy." Jake laughed then. "I actually feel quite sorry for the guy; so he thinks he's about to get a striptease, and instead you dump him? That's devastating. How did he react?"

"Um. Okay?" Poppy said. "Considering." After abandoning

Sam at Haus, she'd taken an extortionate cab back to London and spent the rest of the night in their flat. "We haven't really spoken since. The next morning I packed a bag and flew to France."

"Wow. So, it's really over?" Jake asked.

"Yes," Poppy said. "Totally." She looked down at Jake's chest, still wet from the swimming pool. She looked at his face, his sunflower eyes.

"And so . . . you're single?"

"I suppose so," Poppy said. "Yes, I am."

"Right, well . . ." Jake tilted his head to the swimming pool, then back toward her. "Can I ask you a personal question?"

Poppy's heart was beating at the very base of her throat, which had made it harder to breathe. "Mm?"

"That lingerie you mentioned . . . did you bring it with you out here?" Jake asked this question with the exact same tone and seriousness that he'd asked the other questions, and it took Poppy a second to work out that he'd pivoted, smoothly, to a very suggestive place. She inhaled a quick laugh, quite shocked, quite embarrassed, and pushed at his shoulder, lay back down on the lounger, covered her face with her forearm.

Jake stayed totally deadpan. "Only because, did I mention, I can play 'Foxy Lady' on my guitar and I would hate for this funny striptease to go to waste. So, if you wanted, later . . ."

Poppy moved her arm off her face and rolled her eyes at him. "Thank you for the offer, Jake. Shame you don't have your guitar, isn't it?"

"Well, I do have my guitar actually, Poppy. So . . ."

Poppy laughed, but he didn't. "I don't think me doing the striptease I was going to do for my ex-fiancé is very appropriate, do you?"

"I think it's fine."

They looked at each other, hard. Poppy's whole body was rushing with an acute sensitivity. The breeze on her skin was ridiculously erotic. The swallows dipped and looped through the sky above them like they were writing love letters. Even the distant buzz of a passing car was soft and kind of perfect. Poppy felt connected to all her surroundings in that moment, but most of all she felt connected to Jake. She felt their thoughts were synced and the world turned around them. Just them. It was like there was nowhere else she was meant to be, and nothing bad, while they sat there alone together, would be able to reach her. She could tell Jake was thinking about kissing her and she almost didn't want it to happen because the anticipation was so exquisite. How long could this moment last? "I, er . . ." Poppy said quietly. Jake was looking down at her legs. He put one hand on her shin softly, and she shivered. "I might go and have a shower."

"Yeah." Jake nodded; he moved his gaze to her eyes. "Good idea."

Poppy's mouth spread slowly into a smile as Jake ran his hand up her leg, to her knee. Embarrassed by how turned on she felt, she moved her arm so it covered her face again; she hid in the crook of her elbow and breathed in the smell of sun cream, chlorine, hot skin. Jake leaned forward and moved her arm away; their faces were close now, he was holding her hand, and she knew he was going to kiss her. Her body arched toward him instinctively. She drew in a breath and closed her eyes—

"Hello, you two." Poppy and Jake both looked up at Rafe, who was looking down at them, a towel over his shoulder. They hadn't heard him cross the lawn toward them. "What's the plan for dinner, Jakey?" Rafe asked, seemingly unaware that he'd interrupted a very horny moment. "What time shall we eat?"

"Errr . . ." Jake began. "Dad, um . . ."

Poppy swung her legs off the lounger and put her things back in her bag hurriedly. She pulled her dress over her head and slipped on her sandals. She stood and, without looking back, walked into the house and up the stairs, though all she could see in her mind was Jake.

Alone in her room, Poppy put a hand on her heart. She was panting; she was tipsy. In her bathroom, she turned on the shower, took her clothes off, and stepped in. She pressed her back up against the tiles and twisted her head, looking in the mirror, watching the water run over her face and clump her hair into tendrils. She closed her eyes and let herself slide down the tiled wall until she was sitting on the floor of the shower, rushing with emotion, overcome by lust.

29

Still Sunday, 22nd June

Poppy tied her wet hair back into a ponytail and ran oil through it to stop it from frizzing in the humidity. She slipped on a dress of her sister's, one she used to borrow when Dandelion was alive, too, a long black slip, slit to the thigh. Outside the house, she found the others underneath a canopy of vines, around the table covered with a pink-and-white Indian block print cloth. Rafe stood and asked Poppy if she wanted an aperitif. He had the same lovely dimples as Jake, the same wide mouth and certain jaw. Though, much more so than Jake, he seemed to take pride in being debonair.

"I'd love a glass of wine, thank you, Rafe." Poppy took the seat next to Mish and complimented her on her bright-colored silk shirt and matching trousers that looked like very expensive pajamas.

"You look gorge, gorge," Mish said. "Such strong arms. Pilates?"

"Actually, I think it's because I'm always lugging around equipment for my job. So good upper-body strength." When Poppy glanced at Jake he was already smiling at her, and the look in his eye made her heart jangle, and she almost gasped. He nodded at the small plates of food on the table between them. "Can I interest you in some saucisson?"

Poppy shook her head slightly. "Think I'll . . ." She reached for a crisp.

Rafe handed Poppy a glass of wine, and a contented silence descended as they all turned their faces to the sky, which flowed gold and luxurious like an exotic cocktail. The sun was a slice of orange just above the horizon.

"Did anyone see that fox?" Jake said. "Just ran by. Really lovely-looking fox. A . . . lady, I think."

"Bet it wasn't as manky as the London ones," Mish said.

"No, it was beautiful. Lovely . . . legs." Jake looked at Poppy. "A real fox . . . lady. A foxy lady, if you will."

Poppy rubbed at her nose with her hand, tried to hide her smile.

"Could have been a male, though, Jake," Mish said. "Foxes do all look the same, don't they?"

"Mm, good point." Jake nodded.

"Talking of foxes and ladies." Rafe reached for the bowl of pistachios. "Have you heard of Feeld, Poppy? F-E-E-L-D." He spelled it out for her. "It's an app. And it's where Mish and I met, and now we're on it as a couple." He threw the tiny shells over his shoulder and popped a nut in his mouth, then another. "I'm just obsessed with it, aren't I, Mish?"

"Oh my God, honestly. He's obsessed." Mish nodded. "He's been on it out here, looking for some southern French action."

"Absolutely not." Jake stood up. "Let's have some boundaries, shall we, Dad?" He walked to the edge of the paving stones. "Shocking as it may seem, we're not interested in your sex life. Actually, I'd say, more the very opposite." Poppy watched Jake's back, his baggy shirt. He put both his hands in the pockets of his trousers, and she imagined his face, the sunflowers in his eyes looking out at the sprinklers on the lawn, the flower beds that bordered the garden, and beyond them—the field with the donkey, the horse, and the olive grove.

"Well," Rafe continued, unfazed. "I had always presumed I was totally straight, but actually—"

"You're bi," Jake cut in, spinning back to face them. "Cool! We're happy for you. Anyway, moving on . . ."

Poppy glanced at Mish, who had her legs crossed and shoulders back, her face majestically tilted upward to the vines.

"No, Jake," Rafe said. "I'm hetero-flexible, and that's only in group scenarios. So, for example—"

"We know what *group scenarios* means!" Jake said loudly. And then: "Jesus!" And then: "I'm sorry, Poppy." And then: "I'm going to check on the food."

Mish laughed, though not in a mean way, and it was true that the delivery of Jake's protest was quite amusing—Poppy couldn't work out how upset he actually was. She watched him walk around the corner, back to the kitchen. When he was out of sight, she turned to Rafe and said, "I know about Feeld. Sounds quite fun." She smiled at both of them, and Rafe topped up her wine.

Dandelion went through a phase of using Feeld; Poppy had banned her from talking about it, though, because she had less than zero interest in her sister regaling role-plays and things that had happened with ropes. Jetta, though, had enjoyed pressing Dandelion on the specifics and terminology—there was a whole load of acronyms for different kinks and desires that brought her enormous delight. Dandelion went to sex parties sometimes, and Poppy knew that Jetta had gone with her on occasion; once Poppy had pre-drinks with them at Dandelion's flat and they both looked incredible, in latex, thigh-high boots, and black stringy tops—their nipples caught in nets.

"Have we stopped talking about gang bangs?" Jake asked, coming round the corner with a laden tray.

"So we thought, after dinner we could . . ." Mish laughed; she had a real hee-haw. "No. Only kidding." She stood up and looked down at Rafe. "I think it's time for us all to talk about something else." She turned to Jake. "Shall I lay the table?"

And then they were all up on their feet, bringing food from the kitchen on trays. Cutlery, pretty napkins. Two long and crispy baguettes were sliced into big chunks and brought out on an olive wood board. A water jug was filled with ice and fresh mint leaves. In the center of the table, Jake placed a large, speckled ceramic bowl, full of enormous artichokes, the biggest Poppy had ever seen. There was a dish of langoustine, hollandaise homemade by Jake, a bright green curly-leafed salad dressed and tossed by Mish, and a very good-looking assortment of cheese. They all sat and helped themselves to food with a quiet fervor, clearly excited to be eating something substantial, after an afternoon of drinking, flirtation, and sun.

As they ate, Rafe and Mish told them about their holiday so far: the markets they'd been to, the things they'd bought, and some local historic ruins that Rafe had found interesting and Mish had found a bit dull. When Rafe moved the conversation on to the pressing disasters of global politics, Mish turned to Poppy and said quietly, "Did I hear you two are just friends? I'm very confused about this." Since they had begun eating, the sky had scattered with silver stars, and Jake had lit two tall candles on the table, as well as the lanterns that hung from the vines above them. "I call enormous bullshit," Mish said, with an enthusiastic note of gossip in her voice. She twisted a langoustine's head off.

"I'm just out of a very serious relationship," Poppy said, though her mind darted forward to after dinner. She was almost certain that something would happen between her and Jake, and she felt a melting excitement at the thought of being pressed against him, feeling his hands, hearing what he'd say, the tone of his voice . . .

"Whatever. Don't believe you," Mish said.

Poppy was pleased it was dark, because she felt quite flushed and woozy. She glanced at Jake. In a way, it would feel like a first kiss all over again—both single this time, both themselves. So much had happened since spring. It was all quite dauntingly real, though it felt, simultaneously, like an unfolding dream.

"So, Poppy," Rafe said, projecting his voice over the table as Jake stood up and headed back toward the house with the bowl of langoustine shells and an empty wine bottle. "Remind me how you and Jakey know each other?"

"Oh, um . . ." Poppy thought about what an acceptable start to this story would be. "We met through my sister."

"And your sister is?"

"Dandelion Greene," Poppy said. And then, through a big sigh, hoping to move the conversation elsewhere, "I'm so full!"

"Dandelion?" Rafe seemed startled. "Goodness, sweet girl, I'm so sorry. Well, please know how much we all wished we could have met her. Jake was heartbroken to have lost her. Truly, he was a terrible mess." Rafe leaned his shoulders over the table, toward Mish, and said, in a respectful murmur, "Dandelion was Jake's girlfriend, the one I told you about, who . . ."

"No," Mish gasped. "That's so awful!" She reached for Poppy, snatched both her hands up. "You poor angel."

Every muscle in Poppy's body clenched. She looked down at her hands in Mish's hands, trying to untangle what exactly was being said and where she fitted in.

"Then there was the funeral, obviously. It nearly killed him," Rafe was still explaining to Mish, "and Jake had to speak at it, didn't he—"

"Speak?" Poppy repeated. "At the funeral?"

"Tarte Tatin!" Jake called, walking back over to them. At the table he stopped and looked at each of them. "Everything all right?"

"We didn't realize Poppy was Dandelion's sister," Rafe said. "I wish you'd told us, Jake. Although of course that explains why you asked me not to mention her, and now I've gone and done it."

"Huh? What?" Jake put the tarte on the table. He didn't look at Poppy but stayed blinking at his father.

"Well, I'm so pleased you two are friends now, Jake was so taken with Dandelion," Rafe informed Poppy. "How shocking for everyone."

And with that, the magic that had been circling Poppy all evening, all day, was ripped away. It was true that Jake sometimes spoke about Dandelion as if she was someone he knew, but Poppy didn't realize he'd been saying all these lies to his family. He was hooked on her, was he? Still? Poppy looked at Jake, and there, in the shadows behind him, was her big sister—Poppy could see her dancing in her black latex bodysuit; she was writhing, flickering through candlelight.

A silence and a palpable sense of awkwardness had fallen over the table. "No. I see. Well, we won't talk about it anymore," Rafe said. "All I will say is that Dandelion sounded like an incredible woman, and although we never met her, she'll always have a special place in our family's thoughts."

And then Dandelion *was* the candlelight; she was dripping from the lanterns, sprawling over the tablecloth. Licking everyone and lighting them up. Poppy was invisible. Poppy was the shadows. She looked down at her legs in the darkness and she couldn't see herself.

"You know," Poppy said quietly, "I might head up to bed." She moved her chair back. "Thank you so much for supper."

In the kitchen, she didn't turn the lights on. She moved quickly up the staircase, feeling along the wall with her hand. In her bedroom, she pushed the door closed and slid down until she was sitting, her knees bent up, on the sisal carpet.

Jake was outside. He tapped on the door. "Poppy?"

"I'm really tired," Poppy said loudly. "Please leave me alone."

"Let me explain why Dad said that."

"I want to go to sleep!"

From the bedside table, Poppy's phone purred and shimmied. She crawled over to it, picked it up.

The door opened, and she could feel Jake standing there, but she didn't look at him. "I don't want you to be upset," he said. "Can we talk about this?"

On her phone, Poppy had a string of new messages from Sam. They began earlier in the evening and had been arriving, intermittently, over the last two hours. It seemed, certainly, that he was drunk.

Need to speak. Call me.

You can't just end things like this.

I'll forgive you.

It's the grief Popsy

Don't throw all of what we have away

You're gonna be my wifey!

You're lucky to have me. Everyone says it!

There's something you should know about your sister btw. She betrayed you. Real bad. Might be time to stop the hero worship.

"Poppy, look at me," Jake said, still in the doorway.

"Leave me alone!" Poppy flew at him, pushed him backward, slammed the door. She fell to her knees. "Go away!" she said aloud to the empty room.

She called Sam, but he didn't pick up. She replied to his messages—asking what he meant about her sister—but all she got was silence. Now he'd hooked her in, he'd leave her hanging. So maybe it was a way to manipulate her. Or get revenge. It was about getting her attention. A surefire way to get her to speak to him. Was it?

Poppy lifted her dress over her head and lay on top of her bed. Stared at the ceiling. It had been three hundred and nine days since her sister had died, but somehow, still, she was wreaking havoc. All the men in Poppy's life had always been, would always be, beguiled by Dandelion.

30

Friday, 27th June

"Honestly, it's like, we're exhausted all the time," Stefan said, too close to Poppy's face.

"I get it." Poppy nodded at him.

Poppy was wedged between a powdery pink sofa arm and Stefan, who'd been talking at her for ages, eyes almost closed. For his birthday, Stefan had wanted to throw a proper party like the ones they all used to frequent every weekend, a long time ago. The type of party where people bump and grind and snog and smoke and make new friends. And mostly, they'd achieved this. In the corner, a woman was dancing all wafty on her own—doing her best (though not good) Kate Bush. The neighbors had complained, and earlier someone had fallen down the stairs and broken a banister. It was an episode of the noughties TV show *Skins*, except everyone's actual skin was wrinkled and the cast was much more married, quite bald.

"But it's a whole different tired when you have children," Stefan said. Stefan and Jetta's kids had been shipped off to their grandparents' for the night, but still, Stefan had been sucked into a parental conversational sinkhole and had spent the past forty minutes explaining to Poppy how their holidays were *not* holidays anymore, and now he was on to how Poppy could *not* understand real tiredness or, apparently, simple maths. "The thing about two kids is, it's literally double one . . ."

Poppy's gaze slid to the far wall, where someone with gray hair was doing a handstand up against the piano; for about three seconds it was impressive, then he crumpled onto his head in a way that looked painful and sat up and the three women who were watching him all clapped.

"Stef," Poppy said, turning her gaze back to him. "Can I ask you something?"

"Anything, Pop." Stefan smoothed a freshly rolled joint between his fingers and tapped the end of it a couple of times on a big Taschen book on his lap with a hologram of Bowie on the front.

"What do you *really* think that message from Sam was all about? The betrayal one."

"Anything but Sam chat is what I meant . . ."

"Such a weird thing for him to say, though, wasn't it?"

"You need to wait until he gets back from his trip and talk to *him* about it, pal. Please not with me. Not tonight."

Sam was at a sales conference in Vegas and, since the string of emotional messages he'd sent while Poppy had been in France, his comms had become vague. Poppy had been staying in Jetta and Stefan's spare room, spending all her time trying to look down at the labyrinth of her life from up above, to no avail. Jetta had been up against a deadline and Poppy had barely seen her. She'd mentioned Sam's messages to her and Stefan in passing, and they'd both essentially just said, "Sounds shit," then shrugged.

"I just have a very uneasy feeling, Stef. This week's been awful. I'm feeling constantly sick, and . . ."

Stefan lifted a lighter. Sparked up. Through an exhale he sang at her, "He's a dick. He's a cheat. We hate him. Good riddance. Bye-bye!"

"He's not a cheat, Stef," Poppy snapped, feeling he'd gone too far. Sam was a lot of things, but an adulterer was not one of them. Sure, he was a flirt, and, yes, embarrassingly, he liked sexy, scantily clad young women's pictures on Instagram. (Dandelion would screenshot them and send to Poppy with a vomit emoji and a comment like: *SHE'S 21! That's rancid*, or *ickkkkk*, or *he needs to gooooo!*) But Poppy had always believed these examples were just an ego thing and she pitied Sam for it, if anything. The bottom line was—he was always telling her how much he loved her. And planning their future. Poppy trusted him.

Stefan very obviously didn't say anything else. He raised his eyebrows and took a toke on his joint.

"Stef?"

"What? Nothing!" Stefan exhaled a cloud of smoke and coughed. "Shall we find Jetta?"

Poppy pushed up and away from him, masking her anxiety with agitation. "I'll find her. You stay here." She picked her way through people sitting on the floor, in bare feet—her shoes still under the sofa.

On the way past the kitchen, which was now the dance floor, Poppy ducked her head to look for Jetta, but she wasn't there, or in the garden, so she went upstairs, past the spare bedroom, to Jetta and Stef's bedroom in the loft. A side light was on, but no one was in there. Poppy shook her arms around a little, walked over to the far side of the bed, touching the sheepskin throw. On the wall in front of her, framed photos hung all higgledy-piggledy in an artful formation. Stefan and Jetta on a beach, on another beach, in a crowd at a festival, sepia on their wedding day. Half a dozen cherubic pictures of their devilish children in face paint, with birthday cakes, sitting on their grandparents' laps. A picture of Dandelion and Jetta in a pub—laughing. The *Royal Tenenbaums* fancy dress photo of all three of them. All three of them in their London Fields flat fifteen years ago. All three of them on the bench by the seafront, at the very start of their teens.

Poppy rubbed her sternum; she had heartburn, she'd drunk too much warm wine and hadn't eaten food. In her mind, voices were clamoring. There was Stefan's: *He's a cheat. We hate him. Good riddance.* And there was Sam's: *She betrayed you. Real bad. Might be time to stop the hero worship.*

"Pops! There you are!" Jetta came in, kicked her shoes off. She belly flopped onto the bed and lay still for a second, face down, limbs outstretched in a starfish, before rolling over. "Stefan will be up 'til dawn, I'm gonna leave him to it. Do you want to sleep in here with me tonight?" On the bedside table was a bottle of tequila without a lid; Jetta reached for it. "Fancy a nightcap?"

Poppy sat down cross-legged on the cream carpet. She watched Jetta pour the tequila into a mug with Mickey Mouse doing a thumbs-up on the side. "You got some color in France, didn't you." Jetta handed Poppy the mug. "Was it a good wedding?"

"Fine, just . . . busy." Poppy took a sip and rested her forehead on the base of her palm.

She thought of Provence. In the middle of the night, unable to sleep, she'd changed her Eurostar ticket home to the following morning. Booked a taxi, and before anyone else was up—she left. Jake had called her every day since and she was yet to call him back; she'd been too muddled up. Poppy missed him, though, hugely; inside her throat, inside her tummy, there was a constant ache, a longing. She'd been hurt to hear he'd told his family extensive stories about his "girlfriend," Dandelion, dying. But Poppy knew that she had confused Jake, and maybe Dandelion had confused them both. It wasn't his fault he'd got tangled up with them, and it was Poppy who had been the first to lie. Really, what had he done wrong? He'd not cheated on her. Like she had cheated on Sam. Like Sam had . . . maybe? Poppy looked up at her friend. "Jets, Stefan just called Sam *a cheat.*"

"You're joking?" Jetta lifted the tequila bottle, took a swig.

"Did Sam cheat on me? Or am I being paranoid?"

Jetta made a face like the tequila had burned. She swallowed with her eyes closed. "What did Stef say, exactly?"

"Why?"

"I just want to know."

"Jetta! Has something happened?"

Jetta took in a long slow breath, mouth open.

"You're kidding me?"

"I didn't say anything!"

"The fact you're *not* denying it, Jetta! Who with? When? How do you know? Tell me everything. Now."

Jetta wasn't looking at Poppy—she was looking past her, at the photographs on the wall, and Poppy couldn't bring herself to look over her shoulder and follow her gaze. "This has nothing to do with . . . with . . . Sam's message, right? This isn't a Dandelion thing?"

A silence cut and dug and cut and dug, and neither of them blinked or moved or even breathed, until Jetta said, "This is a Dandelion thing, Poppy, yes."

"*WHAT?*"

"They . . . She . . ." Jetta spoke to the tequila bottle that she was holding in her lap. "Last summer. The very start of it. Dandelion and Sam . . ."

Poppy's mind was full of vignettes, the glimmering ignorance of the previous year before their lives had swerved and crashed. "That's not true," she protested through a whisper. But Jetta said nothing. "Jetta?" Poppy said, with more force. "What are you keeping from me?"

Jetta inhaled slowly through her nose, and held the breath inside her body. "Dandelion thought the only way she could get rid of him once and for all was to . . ." The words flooded out through an exhale, the breaking of a dam. "She just couldn't get past the fact he was wrong for you. She didn't trust him. She said he looked at her in a way she found repulsive. She said that, not only would he never make you as happy as you deserve to be, but at some point—he was going to make you really sad." Jetta's green eyes winced like they were full of smoke. "And so, yeah, I think the plan was to burn your relationship to the ground by . . . by getting with him."

"That's RIDICULOUS!" Poppy shouted. She was blinking and blinking. She was shaking her head. The world, again, was different. Poisoned. Fucked. "How could she have done that? Gone that far! I . . . I . . . are you sure? Why couldn't there have been a conversation instead of—"

"Pops, there *were* conversations. She was always on at you. It's not a surprise she felt like this."

"Of course it is! How could this not be a surprise, Jetta?"

Jetta slid from the bed, knelt in front of Poppy, and reached for her shoulders. She tried to rock them both gently, but Poppy pushed her away.

"Where?" Poppy whispered, though in her mind she could see it all playing out: Dandelion turning up at their front door when Poppy was working away somewhere. A little drunk. Intimidating. Angry. Beautiful. The puppet master, manipulating her little sister's life.

"I think . . . in your flat."

Poppy pushed further backward, made more space between her and Jetta. "Why didn't you tell me?" Her voice careered across an octave and finished right up high.

"BECAUSE DANDELION FUCKING DIED, POPPY! SHE

260

FUCKING DIED!" Jetta threw her arms around her own shoulders, hugged herself. "I was worried what the truth would do to you. And then when you got engaged, Stef couldn't stop going on that I needed to tell you. He said you deserved to know what your fiancé was capable of. But I just haven't been sure what to say, how to say it. I'm so angry with her for putting me in this position." Jetta cleared the mounting tears from her throat with a cough. "And then you guys broke up anyway, and Stef and I have been so happy about it that we decided you'd never need to know. But then Sam sent that stupid message mentioning betrayal."

"That's not good enough, Jetta!" Poppy took a hard swig of tequila and then another. Wiped her mouth with the back of her hand. "What a psychotic bitch. What a twisted—"

"Poppy! Don't say that." Jetta's voice was pleading. "Please don't let this come between you. Not now. Not without her here. It was an awful and misguided thing to do, but it all came from her deep love for you. She thought she was doing the right thing and she—"

"Seriously?" Poppy was up on her feet and her fists were balled. "You're going to take her side? How could you not have told me?"

"*She* was going to, that was the whole point. It wasn't meant to be a secret! Dandelion wanted you to know, Poppy. She did it specifically for you to find out because how could you ever stay with him after that? I mean, it wasn't from a place of desire." Jetta's laugh rattled. "She hated his guts, obviously. She thought he had a dark heart and she thought he was controlling and she thought you were shrinking and she thought she was losing you and she thought he was cheating on you, or would cheat on you, and so . . . she decided to prove it. Sacrifice herself." Jetta shook her head. "And when she told me about this whole plan she'd hatched, we had such an epic row and then . . . and then everything!"

Poppy's face was aflame, her nose running. She spun around, and in her mind she saw another version of herself rip each of the photos from the wall and frisbee them in different directions, until they were all smashed up. She saw herself yank the bedside lamp free and hurl it at the window, shattering the glass—decapitating a twat smoking a vape and chatting bollocks in the garden below. She saw herself karate kick Jetta in the face so that her delicate head snapped clean off her body and she was dead, too, and she would never let her down again.

And then Poppy was tripping down the stairs, and she was out on the street—running all the way to Jake.

31

Saturday, 28th June

Jake

Jake sat up and blinked at the wardrobe at the far end of Dandelion's room, waiting for whoever it was who was ringing the doorbell late at night to stop. They didn't, though, so he creaked to the hallway and spoke into the intercom. "Hello?"

"It's Poppy. Can I come up?"

"Poppy?" Jake rubbed an eye, tried to figure out what sort of time it was. He pressed the buzzer and heard the main door on the ground floor click open. He was only in a pair of boxers so he grabbed a T-shirt, pulled it on. When Poppy turned the corner of the stairs she was all dressed up, with a very short skirt and a blazer that was oversized. She lifted her face to him and he could see streaks down her cheeks, as if she'd been crying black tears.

Jake held his arms out and then she was in them and he was giving her a big cuddle. He noticed how she clung to him, the tips of her fingers pushing into his back. "Hey," he said, feeling her unsteady breathing. "What's going on?"

When she let go of him, Jake put his hands on her shoulders

and steered her toward the sitting room. She went over to the sofa by the window and lay back on it.

"You're not wearing any shoes, Poppy?" Jake turned on the lamp by the door.

"I ran," she said. "All the way." She closed her eyes.

"From where?" Jake sat on the sofa opposite her, wide-awake now.

"I'm sorry about France, Jake. About leaving early."

"I'm sorry my dad said that stuff to you. I'm sorry *I* said that stuff to my dad. I've really wanted to apologize to you this week, Poppy, and explain why and—"

"I had a lovely time before I left, Jake. It was so nice to be there with you and to meet your dad and Mish and—"

"They loved you!" They were both talking over the top of each other now and Jake felt thrillingly happy to see Poppy's face and to know she didn't hate him. Because it was true, they'd had a wonderful time in France. Incandescent, really. Until his dad said those things about Dandelion, which had been extremely annoying of him, and deeply awkward. And then Poppy had really yelled at Jake up in her bedroom and so he had left her to it, feeling things would be calmer in the morning, but in the morning—she'd gone! And he'd heard nothing from her since. She'd ignored his calls. Ghosted. Again. Until this. Jake glanced at the clock on the mantelpiece. It was just past 2:00 a.m., five days later.

"This is such a mess." Poppy inhaled a breath that was loud and full of trouble. "It's like . . . I think everything is as bad as it can be and then—"

"Poppy! It's all good. It's all absolutely fine!" Jake stood and went over to her sofa, sat next to her. "It's so good to see you. I missed you. I was worried that my landlady hated me."

"Your landlady?" Poppy repeated, practically spitting the words back at him. "That's what you were worried about?"

Right, so, it was clear she was in a dangerous mood. Jake looked down at her dirty feet. Where had she been? He looked at her legs, her skirt, her tearstained face. "What have you been up to tonight, Poppy? What's going on? I don't like seeing you like this."

Poppy shouted a laugh. "So . . . Funny story . . ."

"Ookay," Jake said, bracing himself.

"Dandelion fucked Sam!" Poppy slapped both her bare thighs, hard.

"What?"

"Last summer. She did it on purpose to hurt me and to prove she could and—"

Jake shook his head. "Naa."

"I was at a house party tonight and my friend told me, Jake. It's one hundred percent true."

Jake pulled a big grin, though he didn't feel happy anymore. There was a pressure in the room and it was starting to strangle. "How about we talk about everything in the morning?"

Poppy's eyes thinned. "Did you hear what I said?"

"Yes! But obviously there's no way Dandelion would have done that. Of course not. There'll be an explanation. Everything's always awful in the middle of the night. Are you tired? You look tired. Why don't you take the bed and I'll sleep here and . . ."

Poppy's lips were pushed together so hard they had paled around the edges. She was studying Jake's face in a way that made him feel way too looked at. "Are you saying you don't believe me, Jake?"

"Of course I believe you. But it's late and you're pissed. Are you? And . . . look, we'll figure this out. Sounds to me like an exciting house party melodrama."

"You don't think Dandelion would have done it, do you?"

"Of course not!" Jake shook his head. "She would never do that to you."

"Because Dandelion was your girlfriend and you knew her so well?"

"Oh, come on, Poppy," Jake said, "you know that's not what I meant."

"You understand that you never met her and that you don't know her, right?"

Jake tried to study Poppy's face in the same intense way she'd been looking at him. "I don't know her like you know her, but I do have a sense—"

"Jake, *what*? No, you don't. Not at all. You don't know anything about my sister. She was a sociopath and—"

"Poppy! Of course she wasn't." Jake stood up, quite affronted by her vitriol. "Please, calm down." He put a hand on her shoulder. "Hey," he said. The last thing he wanted was to fight with her, or upset her any more. "In the morning, let's go out for breakfast, and I want you to talk me through everything and . . ."

"Did you miss me this week?" Poppy asked, and it sounded a lot like a test. A scary woman test, one that was almost impossible to pass.

"Yes. I did," Jake said cautiously, and he had, loads. He was starting to feel the intoxicating attraction creeping into his blood, and the overwhelming urge to take her in his arms. Which, considering the state she was in, would not be appropriate. *Would it?*

"Did you think about me?" Poppy took off her blazer. Underneath she was wearing a silky top that clung to her body.

"Course, yes." Jake moved his gaze to the coffee table, to that big shiny book about women's pleasure.

They had flirted so intensely in France and he had been lost in a sea of his own desire, and an elation at Poppy's engagement ending. He'd been sure, certain, that they would end up in bed together. He'd been sure, certain, that Poppy had been desperate for him too. But then she left. And he'd been gutted and he'd called her every day and he'd thought of little else.

Jake stood up, took a step away. This situation felt too precarious. She was angry about her ex. "Let's order you a taxi, shall we?" He took another step. "Or shall I call one of your friends?"

Poppy lay down on the sofa and Jake looked at her legs stretched long. She turned her head away from him and made a sobbing noise, and so he went to her—as if a fishhook had sliced deep through the beating meat of his heart and now she was reeling him in. He sat on the very edge of the sofa and took her hand. "Please don't cry. I'm sorry things are difficult for you. I do believe you. But you woke me up and I was confused. Can you take me through it all properly in the morning?"

Poppy turned her head and stared at Jake, and although she was upset, there was a determination to her expression. Slowly, she shifted her legs, stood up. She looked down at him, her hair falling in her face, a strand of it caught on her top lip. He watched as she pulled her silk top over her head and dropped it to the floor.

"Fuck, Poppy . . ." Jake said with serious hesitation.

She stood in front of him in her skirt and her bra. Things had taken a turn.

Jake picked her top up and held it out to her. "I don't think this is a great idea . . ."

"I really want to kiss," Poppy said.

"*Huh* . . ." Jake nodded, looked over at the bookshelf as if he was considering this interesting proposition, when actually, obviously, he was powerless to resist. He looked back at her. "I see."

Poppy laughed a breath, then pushed him with the tips of her fingers. She climbed on top of him, her skirt hitching all the way up, and Jake could see the crotch of her black knickers.

He reached a hand to her face and rubbed his thumb over her cheek. "I'm worried about how drunk you are."

"I'm not drunk."

"Poppy . . ."

"Don't you want to? It's okay if you don't. Just tell me."

"You know I do, Poppy. More than anything. But you're drunk and emotional and hurt, it sounds like. And I don't want you to feel confused in the morning."

"The only thing in my whole life I'm not confused about, Jake, is you."

"Right," Jake said, feeling deeply moved. He couldn't believe how strongly he felt about her face; her bewitching eyes, the pink speckles in her cheeks, the curve of her mouth, how she bit at her lips nervously. He could see exactly who she was. He could see right into her mind. He could see that she was sorry about everything, about all the things, and she knew that he was too. It felt as if, silently, they were making an agreement to do something together, to be something together. Something secret. Something strong. Something that would last longer than just that evening, and maybe even forever, because that's what they both wanted. It was such an overwhelming sense of knowledge and wordless communication that Jake felt emotion catch in his throat, and in Poppy's eyes he could see the soft blur of tears that he believed were there for him.

He pulled her down toward him. She tasted of booze and cigarettes, and the wet warmness of her mouth made him very fucking horny. They kissed so deeply it felt like he was falling into her, and she was giving herself to him. They kissed until Poppy sat up and let her eyes fall to Jake's boner raging against his boxer shorts. She smiled and Jake shrugged. A laugh burst from each of them, the escaping sound of this new joy. Jake moved his gaze to Poppy's breasts; they looked bigger than they had in her swimsuit. The bra pushed them upward and toward him, like an offering. With one finger he traced the lace that ran around the edge and pulled it back until her nipple sprang into his fingers. She was watching him, her eyes dewy, dilated. Jake bent his head so he could take her nipple between his teeth, a small wild strawberry. He heard her gasp. He moved his hands around her back and found the clasp of her bra, pushed it together, and it unfastened easily, not putting up any resistance, and Jake felt the quick flutter of relief. He pulled the straps down one by one and slipped her bra off, and Poppy crossed her arms over her breasts, held them, like maybe she was hiding herself.

"You're so beautiful, Poppy," Jake said, taking her in. "I don't think you understand."

Poppy shook her head and Jake moved his hands to her waist, lifted her off him, and laid her on the sofa. He stood and looked down at her. Time slowed, and each second that passed felt so languid and intense that he kept having to close his eyes and inhale, then open them again to take in more of her body, her neck, her mouth, her loose long hair, her eyes. Her eyes. Her eyes. "Fucking hell, Poppy."

"Jake!" Poppy covered her face with her hands. "Stop looking at me! It's embarrassing."

He knelt down next to her. "I can't agree to that, I'm afraid."

She turned her head from him in an invitation, and Jake breathed in the skin of her neck. He kissed down over her collarbones, rubbing the flat of his palm over one breast as he moved his mouth to her other nipple. He felt her body arch toward him, then smooth down, slowly, as he ran his tongue over her stomach, the skin that he'd thought about so much, the softness of her waist, the sweetness of her belly button. He pulled her skirt up further and ran his hands over her thighs, pinched a little, and when he looked down at her knickers, he felt less tender. His breath was coming fast, and he had the innate sense that things were about to get very fucking primal. He pulled his T-shirt off with this new urgency, and when he moved back toward Poppy, she scrambled away from him.

Jake sat back on his heels. "Poppy?" He was panting, the arousal turning quickly to something else because she looked so startled, maybe even scared. "What is it?"

"The . . . you . . ." She wasn't looking at him, but squinting at the open door into the hallway, and then Jake was gripped with a physical sensation that was similar to the sudden hot sweat onset of food poisoning because, yes, *FUCK*, across the hall, Dandelion's bedroom door was very slightly open. He hadn't thought to close it properly. He'd been half-asleep.

Jake watched as Poppy sat, reached for her top, and pulled it back on over her head. She walked to Dandelion's door, nudged it. Turned on the light, went in, and stood at the foot of the un-made bed.

Jake's mind ran through excuses frantically. "Hey, so," he said, "Poppy, I . . ." He got up, grabbed his T-shirt, pulled it on as he walked to Dandelion's bedroom door. His clothes were on the chair. His phone was plugged in on the bedside table, next to a glass of water. "Let me explain."

"Have you been sleeping in here?" Poppy asked. She was still staring at the bed.

"So, listen . . ." Yes he had. He'd been sleeping in there for a fortnight.

Since he'd found the key, Jake hadn't gone back to the spare room. Dandelion's bed was large; the windows let in so much light. It was stylish and, yes, quite sexy, and, really, it was the nicest room he'd ever slept in. And so he'd just stayed, night after night, despite the fact he knew it was wrong.

"Let's go back into the sitting room," Jake said, "so I can explain."

"This room is private. I told you that. It was *locked*."

270

"So what happened is . . ." Jake didn't want to be tried for this new crime, not now. Not after everything that had just happened between them. "I came across her key. It fell out of that desk"—he threw an arm back toward the sitting room—"and so I had a little peek, and the bed looked so incredible that I . . ." What could he say? How could he possibly explain? "I . . . lay down."

"What's *wrong* with you?" The accusation in Poppy's voice was monstrous. She looked down at her body and adjusted her skirt. She wasn't wearing her bra underneath her top, and she crossed her arms over her chest, shielding herself from him. "I cannot believe you would be this disrespectful."

"It won't happen again, I promise. I'm so embarrassed." Jake tried to hug her, but she flinched away from him.

"GET OFF ME! Don't touch me!"

"Can we not make this into an enormous thing?" Jake was pleading. "Let's go back next door. This has all got out of hand. This has all been a big mistake and I—"

"Tonight? Tonight of all nights! First Sam and then . . . and then . . ." A single tear rolled down Poppy's cheek and came to rest on a freckle, magnifying it. She sniffed, pushed her feet into her sister's suede clogs under the dressing table. They looked too big. "Get all your stuff out of here, Jake."

"Course."

"Now! Right now."

Jake hurried to his phone, gathered his clothes, and followed Poppy out of the room. In the hallway she used her own key to lock Dandelion's bedroom. She turned the handle to make sure the door wouldn't budge. "Don't go back in there."

"I won't. I definitely—"

"I want you to move out."

Jake rubbed at his forehead with his fingers, mentally trying to grab hold of the freewheeling situation. He reached for Poppy again, but she pushed him away. "Let's talk this through. I'm sorry, Poppy. I fucked up."

"I want you to move out," she said again, her eyes so large they were silver moons.

"Okay," Jake said, hoping to appease her. "But I've got Billy here from tomorrow for the week. So, could we maybe wait until after that?"

In the sitting room, Poppy picked up her bra and shoved it into her bag. She pulled her blazer tight around her body. "Fine," she said. She didn't sound like his friend anymore. She hated him. He'd hurt her at the worst possible moment—when she'd come to him upset and looking for his care and maybe even love. "Take this as your notice; two weeks from today. Leave the key on the table when you go."

She walked past him, with as much distance as she could. In the hallway, she paused. "This isn't a love story, Jake. For a second I thought . . . maybe, but . . ." She cleared her throat. "You're never going to get the girl. Dandelion is dead!" She spat the words at him. She lifted her bag across her body. "Leave us both alone."

"Poppy, Jesus, it's not like that! Please, don't make this worse than it needs to be! I don't want you leaving like this. Not before you've calmed down."

"Why? I'm not going to apologize to you, Jake, or accept your apology or tell you it's all going to be fine. Because obviously, it's not!"

Jake blinked, unsure of what to say, feeling that anything would be twisted and thrown back at him. He shook his head, looked down at the ground. This was an epic disaster.

"I wish I'd never met you." Poppy reached for the latch of the door and pulled it toward her. "Never contact me again."

Her footsteps moved fast down the main stairs, and then the front door slammed. Jake felt selfish and carnal and wretched.

He felt how much she hated him in his own body; her hatred was infectious. In his mind he could see Poppy's long legs, her little skirt, the big jacket, her sister's clogs, and her full moon eyes walking away from him down the street. Hair flowing in ribbons, tears starry and huge.

Jake spun around to the picture of Dandelion on the wall; she was smirking. Mona bloody Lisa. He couldn't blame her. He didn't know her. She wasn't really there. No one was. Again. They'd all left him. He'd made them up. "FUUUUCK!" Jake shouted at the wall.

32

Sunday, 29th June

Jake took the Victoria line to Walthamstow. It was the early afternoon, and he still had time before he was meant to pick up Billy, so he went to a pub, sat at the bar in his sunglasses, and ordered a porn star martini for the first time in his life, because it was on the top of the drinks menu and he was feeling bold. When it arrived, it tasted of cheap perfume and had something questionable floating in it, so he ordered an espresso. He fell off his stool (the stool malfunctioned / he was paralytic). Then he threw up burning liquid in the pub toilet that petered into bile. It had been a rough thirty-six hours.

Jake approached the house with the wide-legged, swinging-arm swagger of a Gallagher in the nineties. Being a total *lad*. "What the fuck?" He leered at a *For Sale* sign that had been bashed into the front garden, all proud and hideous. He grabbed at it and staggered backward until it was out of the ground.

"What are you doing?" Zoe shouted from their old bedroom window.

"We're not selling!" Jake called back, pleased that the vandalism had been witnessed. He continued the swagger toward the house across the gravel, the sign over his shoulder.

The front door opened and Yan was coming toward him. "Hey, brother, what's up?"

"I'm not your brother!" Jake swiped the *For Sale* sign at him. It was big and difficult to wield, but it was also quite fun.

"Yan!" Zoe shouted, both hands on the windowsill, leaning out. "Do not give him Billy. Jake! Are you pissed?"

"Put the sign down, man," Yan said, all hostage negotiator.

Jake threw the sign down, flung his arms open. "You know what, Peter Yan," he said and then paused to make sure Yan had heard his clever name. "You know what," Jake said again, because now he had forgotten what. "Well," he said, "I do not care if your dick is massive and vegan." This had not been his original point. "I do not care, at all!"

"Baba! What's he saying?" Zoe was still in the window.

"Nothing! All fine, Babasita!" Yan shouted up to her, then turned back to Jake. "Want to come inside and have a coffee?"

"You're inviting me inside my own house, to drink my own coffee?"

"It's my coffee, man."

"You know what, Yogi Da Yanni Bear?" Jake ripped his T-shirt off over his head, which threw him off balance; he staggered to the side. "Let's solve this once and for all—mano a mano."

"Solve what?" Yan asked.

"We're going to fight, Zoe!" Jake called up to the window, then ran toward Yan, head down, charging like a bull.

Yan stepped out of the way easily, with his hands up like a very confused matador. "Listen, brother, come inside. Let's talk."

"Oh, fucking whatever," Jake said, darting back and forth on his toes, suddenly remembering what people did in fights. He lifted his loosely curled fists. He jabbed one fist forward and it felt like it looked real good. He rolled his neck one way, then the other.

Zoe was there then in white shorts with the top button undone, a tanned tummy, a miniature bump, and a strapless bandeau bikini top. "Get inside now, Jake."

"Move, Zo, I don't want to accidentally hurt you or da baby bear." Jake was jabbing his fist with a sideways stance; he'd found his beat. *Jab, jab, shuffle, jab, jab, shuffle. Hook. Hook, uppercut!*

"Did I miss something?" Zoe asked Yan.

It was infuriating how neither of them seemed to be acting afraid, or even vaguely nervous. They clearly did not realize what he was capable of. That he was a wild beast. "I'M A WILD BEAST!" Jake roared and then he beat his chest to prove it and howled up to the sky.

"I opened the door and he was like this. He's absolutely wasted," Yan said.

"Come on, bruddah! Come to Mumma!" Jake said, swinging his right hook so hard that he spun around, too, with the momentum.

"You're going to have to hit him," Zoe said. "Just knock him out. This is the most tragic thing I've ever seen."

And then Jake was on Yan's back, legs wrapped around his waist, pulling his forearms into Yan's neck. Yan flung him forward so that Jake rolled in the air over Yan's head like a wrestler. He landed flat on his back on the gravel, the wind knocking out of him.

Zoe turned on her heel. "Bring him inside."

Yan bent and started to scoop Jake up from underneath his armpits, but Jake shook him off. "I can do it!" he said, though there was no volume to his voice. Slowly, he got to his knees, panting,

276

trying to work out how many bones had broken. Yan picked up Jake's T-shirt and put the *For Sale* sign back in the ground.

In the kitchen, Zoe had her hands stretched along the marble-topped island. "Want to tell us what's going on?"

"My neck hurts. I think you've broken all my ribs. My entire rib cage . . ."

"What's got into you?" Zoe ran the tap, filling a glass of water, then strode over to him. "Go home, okay, sleep it off. I'll have to tell Billy you're sick. Let's talk tomorrow."

Jake downed the glass of water and gave it back to her. "I don't have a home." He fell to his knees. "No one wants me." He lay all the way down on the polished concrete floor. "Please can we not sell the house? Maybe I can live here with you guys?" Jake suggested. "It will be really . . . modern. And . . . blended."

"Dada!" Billy's little feet were coming toward him, a bit hesitant. He was holding Spleen's hand.

"Your dad's showing me a new yoga pose," Yan said.

Billy looked from Yan to Jake. "What's it called?"

Jake sat up, held his hands out to Billy, and almost cried with how heavenly his little boy smelled, but also—how much his little boy was crushing his newly shattered skeleton.

"It's called Pathetic Baby pose," Zoe said.

"Patefic Baby," Billy repeated. "Cool!"

"Billy," Zoe said. "Daddy came round to say that this weekend isn't going to work and we're going to have to reschedule."

"NOOOOOO. DADA'S HOUSE!" Billy threw himself down next to Jake, smashed Spleen's face into the floor. Then hurled her so she twizzled in circles and hit a chair, where she lay still, limply smiling.

"I'll be fine, Zo. This is my weekend. We'll get a cab," Jake said loudly, over the escalating tantrum. The shame had hit hard, and it was sobering. *Oh dear.* That fight thing had been weird. "Could I possibly trouble you for another glass of water?"

Billy got to his knees and ripped his T-shirt off too. "DADA'S HOUSE!"

"What about if he stays the night?" Yan suggested, walking over to Zoe. He rubbed his open palm up and down her back.

"Fine." Zoe had one hand splayed over her forehead, like she was trying to measure the width of it. "Jake, do you want to stay the night with us?"

"I would love to," Jake said, keenly nodding his head in immense gratitude and opening his eyes incredibly wide to demonstrate his candid remorse.

"Would you mind taking Billy up for his bath?" Zoe said, smiling apologetically at Yan.

"I'll come and read you a story, bud," Jake said to Billy as Yan picked him up. Billy's face was red, but he looked happier now. He was able to move through emotions very quickly, and Jake wished he could emulate that. Flick a switch so everything could immediately move from mortifying and go back to fine.

"Right," Zoe said, once they'd left the room. She sat down at the table. "Turning up drunk to get your child is unacceptable."

"I know. I didn't really . . . realize I was drunk."

"Jake, you were topless and screeching out the front of our house, pretending to be a meerkat."

"*A meerkat?* What? A . . . a . . . gorilla more like. A silverback—"

"What the hell is going on?"

Jake crawled toward the table, pulled himself up onto a chair. "I hate myself. I'm sorry."

"Shut UP!" Zoe shouted at him. "Stop feeling sorry for yourself, it's so boring! Sort it out! Stop all this wallowing. Where the hell have you been?"

Jake looked at the ceiling and tried to determine exactly how it had all come to this.

After Poppy left, he'd been in tatters. Hardly slept. Dreams had rippled across his mind, warped and threatening. He'd been in a nightclub surrounded by women who said they wanted him, but when he looked close, they were molding and misshapen, teeth rotting out of their heads. And so, he'd got up and poured himself a whiskey. Sat drinking, listening to records. Elliott Smith. This Mortal Coil. Beck. He'd tried to jam along with his guitar. Failed. Time ebbed and the color of the sky outside the window had fallen darker. He'd lost an entire day, feared getting into bed again and the terrors that he might find again in sleep. So he'd gone out and picked up another bottle of whiskey, wanting the world to blur, for everything to mute and dull and fold and wilt.

He must have passed out for a few hours, because when he opened his eyes, he was still on the patterned rug. The picture of Dandelion was off the wall, leaning on the floor, turned away, but he couldn't remember doing that. His head hurt. He'd had another drink and decided that there was a euphoria to it all; there was something totally invigorating about pushing down hard, with both hands, on Self-Destruct. And then the Victoria line with people looking at him, avoiding him, the pub, the porn star hell drink. The bile. The fight!

"I can't believe I just had a fight with Yan," Jake said, looking back at Zoe.

"I wouldn't call that a fight," Zoe said. At this, though, she smiled, and Jake did too.

"Can I have another glass of water and a lot of painkillers, please?"

Zoe stood up and went to the sink, filled a glass. Opened her first aid drawer. Back at the table she asked him again, softer now, what was going on. She crouched down next to him, looked up into his face, watching as he took the pills. "I'm worried about you."

"This is rock bottom," Jake said. "Don't think that things are worse than this when I'm not with you. They're not. This, right now, is the absolute worst it's been, and will get."

Zoe stood, went back to her chair. "If ever I saw a rock bottom it was . . ." She pointed at him.

"I'm sorry," Jake said. "I drank too much."

"No shit. Why?"

Jake could see himself back on the sofa, kissing Poppy. He could hear the rhythm of her breath. The memory replayed and then sped up, and she was screaming at him in her sister's bedroom; she was leaving. "I upset someone I really care about. Not you . . ." he clarified. "I mean obviously you, but . . . another woman, a friend, who I . . ."

"What did you do?" Zoe asked, drumming her fingers on the table. She was disappointed, clearly, though not surprised.

"I didn't cheat. I did not cheat on her, Zoe," Jake said. He was nervous that this conversation was going to bring up all Zoe's gripes and she'd say mean things that he wouldn't be able to handle. "We're not together, or anything, me and this woman, not really. Or at all. But I did betray her trust and I let her down and she hates me. And I hate myself for hurting her. I ruin everything, don't I?"

"Jake, I really can't stand all this victim shit. Just do better," Zoe said, exasperated. "You're not an alcoholic, or a drug addict. You're absolutely fine!"

"How do you know?" Jake spluttered, although he knew he wasn't too.

"Because I know you and I see you twice a week and we message most days, and also, *I just know.*"

"Well, fine, but what if I'm a love addict? And a . . . woman addict?"

During his solo bender, Jake had searched the depths of his

soul, looking desperately for answers as to why every relationship he'd ever had with a woman had ended tragically: blood, guts, and dust.

"You're not . . ." Zoe laughed dismissively. "And nor, by the way, is your father. That's just a persona he likes."

Jake scoffed, shook his head. "I think Dad definitely is, Zoe." He stood and took his glass back to the sink, filled it up.

"Stop trying to diagnose yourself with labels that you can use as an excuse for acting like a shit." If there was one thing Jake could rely on Zoe for, it was speaking plainly. "Of course, I see that you want, desperately, to be loved, but you simultaneously don't truly believe you're worthy of it. And when you are loved, you sabotage it as a means of control; you hurt the person who cares for you because then you won't get hurt. And, obviously, both your parents and your childhood have really shaped that behavior . . . but you must start rising above it. Please? I know you can. If I didn't think you could, I wouldn't say it. But your problems aren't as big as you think they are, Jakey. Don't throw away all that you have for absolutely no reason at all."

Jake gawped at Zoe, his brain working hard to catch up with how she had gone, so quickly, from insulting him, to being so observant and sage. He wasn't at all sure how to react, and so he reached toward the fruit bowl and lifted a banana. "Okay, well, thank you." He started unpeeling it.

"I will always love you, Jake," she continued. She was speaking with determination, really willing him to hear. "Despite the fact you took a wrecking ball to our life. Despite the fact your behavior has been so terrible recently. Everyone loves you, you do know that, don't you?"

"Zo!" Jake had to disagree. "That's so . . . kind of you to say, but not everyone loves me." He laughed, picturing himself chatting to his houseplant of an evening. "I've got no mates."

"You've got loads of mates, you dick," Zoe snapped. "You just never get in contact with them. You've made some weird narrative in your head about being ostracized, and it's simply not true. I don't even know anyone who doesn't like you. Even after you cheated on me! It's been incredibly annoying—I try and slag you off to anyone who will listen, and most of the time whoever I'm talking with will say something sympathetic toward you, or remark upon how we weren't right for each other—as if that's an explanation for infidelity! Even my new boyfriend loves you, and he's heard every example I can remember of what a self-centered attention-seeking baby you really are."

Jake choked on the banana, put it down. Swallowed. "I'm speechless," he said eventually. He took another bite of banana, and Zoe rolled her eyes. It didn't feel at all like an argument though. It felt like they were on the same side. "I suppose it's not that shocking to hear that Yan likes me," Jake conceded, through a mouthful, "because he's so kind and perfect in every way."

Zoe nodded, color in her cheeks. She pushed her chair back and put her legs up on the table. "True."

"Is he actually perfect in every single way, Zoe?"

"Most ways, yes." She rubbed her tummy, looked down at her bump.

"Can you tell me one way that he's not perfect? Just to make me feel better?"

Zoe glanced at the door, probably making sure Yan was still upstairs. She beckoned Jake toward her with her finger, as if she was going to share a secret. "Just this once. Because you need it."

Jake nodded eagerly in agreement and leaned forward so their faces were close.

"I don't love it when he talks about himself in the third person," she said, "especially when he's calling himself Da Yogi Bear."

She sat back up straight, brushed invisible crumbs off the surface of the table.

"That's it? Nothing else?"

"Apart from that he's perfect."

This was very pleasing. Jake's heart bounced. It had nothing to do with Yan, though; it was because Zoe had confided in him with a tiny, tiny secret. They had known each other for fifteen years, she'd seen Jake at his absolute worst, and, still, she was his friend and she loved him; he knew she always would.

"Well, he's a very lucky man," Jake said.

"Yeah, I know." Zoe drummed her fingers on the kitchen table. "But you could be quite perfect, too, you know."

"That's ridiculous." Jake shook his head. "Look at me! I'm a state."

"It's ridiculous *today*. You're a state *today*, but make the decision to do better and start now. We're all on your side. The only person who isn't on your side is you. Okay? Stop sabotaging yourself. You're surrounded by love, and you have a life so many people would kill for. *Please appreciate it.* And stop upsetting women because you're being a coward and you think it's your destiny to be a scumbag. It's not. You're a successful, funny, kind man, and you're still reasonable to look at. Do better. Start now. I'll help you. So will Yan. And . . ." Zoe continued, "never, ever, ever get drunk around our little boy again, or pull a stunt like that. There's no more chances, Jake, do you understand? I'll do anything to keep Billy safe, even if that means stopping him from seeing you."

"Yes," Jake said gravely. He looked her right in the eye. "I agree. I'll do better. I'll do good. I'm so sorry, Zoe. Thank you for everything. From the bottom of my heart."

"Okay," Zoe said. She spread both hands wide over her belly. "Now, do you want to talk about this woman you're upset about? Who is she? What have you done?"

"Umm . . ." Jake rubbed at his sternum with two fingers. *Poppy, Poppy, Poppy.* "Well, she's kind of become, quite quickly, enormously important to me. You'd really like her, Zo."

"Billy met her, didn't he?"

"Yes. But that's when we were just friends and—"

"I'm not going to have a go at you, Jake. It's okay. What's happened?"

"Well, we had a fight. A terrible one. She said she wished she'd never met me and to never contact her again."

"Jake . . ." Zoe shook her head, unable to hide her disappointment.

"I know, I know. I did something *not great.* But what do you think I should do now?" Jake asked, feeling quite desperate for his ex-wife's counsel. "Because I want to contact her, obviously. Can't really . . ." He cleared his throat. "Imagine not talking to her anymore. She means so much to me, Zo. She's amazing. She's really funny and I find her so uplifting, like a, like a really clever . . . sunbeam and . . ."

Zoe looked up as Yan came into the kitchen. He walked over, stood behind her, and started massaging her shoulders. "Everything okay in here?" he asked.

"All good. Jake's kindly offered to make us dinner," Zoe said, leveling her gaze at Jake, "as an apology."

"Thank you, brother, Da Yogi Bear is pleased to hear you're feeling better," Yan said. "Billy's ready for his story, by the way."

"Thank *you,* brother." Jake stood up and smiled at Yan, delighted to have heard him refer to himself in the third person. Yan hugged Jake then, in an encouraging, loving way, and Jake hugged him back so hard, so happy that he was in all their lives; he was da force for good.

"Guys, enough . . ." Zoe said after a moment of watching them, and the two men let go of each other. Jake pushed his chair in under the table, looked back at her. "So, should I maybe send flowers? I could find where she's staying, somehow, and go and—"

"To the woman who told you to never contact her again?" Zoe asked. "No, Jake. Do what she wants, not what you want. Yes? Listen to what she said to you. Respect her wishes."

Jake nodded. "Right. Okay." He didn't want to make Poppy sad ever again and so he would give her space to move on from him, even though it would be agony for him. He knew already he would think of her every day, and he knew that he would never find anyone like her. Or anyone who made him feel the way he did when he was around her, like he was in exactly the right place, which—despite all the lies—was somewhere true and real. But it wasn't about him anymore. It was about what was best for Poppy, what she needed, what she wanted. He'd let her down; he'd made her sad. Jake slapped his cheeks in small claps, wanting to rid himself forever of the horrible hangover and the heartache and all the other badness. "Okay," he said. "I will leave her be."

Part Three:
The Truth

ONE WEEK LATER

July 2025

33

Saturday, 5th July

Poppy

Poppy had been awake for much of the night, her brain chewing on dark, unhealthy thoughts. She'd slept with the windows open, and now she watched the curtains as they breathed in a new day, like lungs. On the other side of the bedroom wall, she could hear her mother making morning tea in the kitchen: the click of the kettle, the clatter of cupboards, the beep of the fridge as she opened it for milk. She was unloading the dishwasher; she was letting out the cat.

Poppy rolled over, looked at her phone on the bedside table where it had been all week, turned off. She reached for it, pulled it toward her, and pressed the button on the side so it shimmied into life. Missed calls. Messages. Jetta. Sam. Stefan. Betty. Clients. Friends. But nothing from Jake. Nothing at all. Poppy inhaled a tiny yelp. She had hoped there would be some sort of apology, or declaration. If he'd cared for her really—he would have fought.

She tapped on his WhatsApp picture. Jake and Billy sat side by side on a wooden bench at a garden table; someone sitting opposite them had taken the photograph. It was a summer's day. From the food spread before them, it looked like a barbecue. Poppy zoomed in on Jake's face; she had the feeling he was going to be one of those men who kept on looking good until they got properly old, annoyingly. She was desperate to stop thinking about him. But she kept replaying everything, particularly the kissing. The kissing. *Jesus.* That kissing. She had never, ever wanted to have sex with anyone that badly before. But *thank God* she hadn't, because now she hated him. She hated him with passion. Did she? It wasn't totally clear to Poppy, at all, where the boundaries were—how to determine hate from grief from shame from hurt from rage from total drowning love.

Poppy turned her phone off without tapping into any of the messages, let it drop from her hand to the floor, and rolled back to the window. She moved her attention to the seagulls' feet clattering on the roof and closed her eyes, scrunched the white duvet, scattered with small pink roses, tight up under her chin. Any moment now, her mother would come in—it used to drive Poppy bonkers when she was a teenager, how she would wake up to her mother at her door, asking if she was awake.

The door creaked as it opened a fraction. "Poppet?"

"Yes."

"Just seeing if you're awake?"

"I am, yes."

"How did you sleep?"

"Like shit."

"Oh dear, what can we do about that?"

"Buy Valium off the dark web."

"On Radio Four they were saying how the blue light from mobile telephones interrupts the sleep hormone. The phone gives off . . ." In the pause that followed, Poppy could tell her mother was trying to recall the specifics. She eventually concluded, "Bad juju."

"My phone's been off for a week, Mum. I can assure you—this is not about blue light."

"That reminds me, Jetta called again last night after you'd gone to bed. She's sounding a bit desperate. I promised her you'd be in contact today."

"Erf!" Poppy contracted her stomach muscles tightly, pushing out an annoyed sound. "I told you I don't want to talk to anyone."

"I said I'd take some flowers up to the church for the ladies arranging today, will you come with me?" Poppy's mother had a real knack for selective listening. "I do think we need to get you out of the house."

"No thanks."

"Did you say yes?"

"Nnn!" Poppy grunted in the negative and rolled over to face her mother to land the full clout of her hard stare. Her mother was belted into her long dressing gown, cream with dark birds flying across it. Dandelion had brought it back from India. Poppy had one too: pale yellow with gold tigers in various stages of pounce. "Where's my dressing gown?"

"Hmm?" Her mother was turning away.

"My tiger dressing gown." Poppy sat up. "Where is it?"

"Check Dandelion's room, darling. Sometimes things get muddled in the system still."

Poppy pulled on her tracksuit bottoms and T-shirt, discarded on the floor from the previous evening. No bra or knickers. Her topknot was baggy and skewed at an angle, having slipped to her neck during the night; she yanked it in alternate directions, resurrecting it to half-mast. She couldn't recall brushing her hair since she'd been in Devon. It was so dirty she suspected if she was to take the scrunchie out, it would stay greased into a bunch. There had been the occasional toothbrushing, and a few nights ago she'd been in the bath for over two hours, but that had been the extent of her personal hygiene and self-care. Extravagances like deodorant and moisturizer had fallen by the wayside. Poppy felt tight, dry, and cracked; looked gray, blotchy, and sixty—but she was perversely enjoying the metamorphosis into a spinster hedge. A woman on the turn.

In the olden days, there would be music blaring from inside Dandelion's bedroom, which was helpful to determine what sort of mood she was in. Despite the silence, Poppy knocked once—force of habit—then pushed down on the wooden handle. She took in the posters of Blur and Blondie. Barbie was still in a box under the bed. Still, there were textbooks and lever-arch files on the shelves. Rimmel eye shadow palettes in too many colors that would never get used up, that would outlive them all.

Poppy crossed the room to the wardrobe and threw it open. On the back of the door was her dressing gown. "Bitch," she whispered, whipping it on over her clothes as she turned to look at the neatly made bed.

In the kitchen, Poppy ate homemade granola with her dad, in a mutually respectful silence. He was reading an article about deep-sea fishing, while Poppy surveyed the dresser; the shelves were stacked with cards, invites, receipts, pots rammed with screwdrivers, nail files, and felt-tip pens—only some with caps. Her mother came in, wearing jeans and a white T-shirt, and an open blue shirt over the top. She had curled her hair and there was one forgotten roller still pinned in.

"So you're coming to church with me, Poppet?"

"I guess . . ." Poppy said. Apart from taking long walks alone along the coast with just her dad's old camera for company, Poppy had been doing nothing. The previous day, she'd spent the entire morning in the larder, sitting on the floor, hiding from her life.

"Go and get dressed then, darling."

Poppy looked at the dressing gown. "Pretend it's a housecoat." She stood and gently pulled the roller from her mother's hair, put it on the pile of catalogs on the kitchen table.

"She's f-fine. She's fine like that. Just needs sh-shoes," her father said, looking at Poppy, a half smile. Dandelion was in his face, and Poppy turned away.

Although it wasn't far, they drove slowly to the church, the back of the Land Rover laden with cut flowers and foliage in buckets of water that sloshed.

"What's going on, Poppet? Why so blue?" Poppy's mother asked predictably.

"What do you mean?" Poppy was holding on to her chin, looking out at the verges of the lane she'd looked out on all her life.

"We love having you, so much, but how long are you planning on staying?"

"Mum, I don't have anywhere to go!" Poppy exhaled.

"But what's happened? I wish you'd talk to us."

What was Poppy meant to say to her parents about all this? Where could she even start? Her sister had betrayed her, then left her. Her career was growing cold. Her ex-fiancé, the man she'd lived with for years, was despicable, and she wasn't *great* herself. And on top of all that, her heart had been pulverized by Jake. Pulped through a juicer. "Believe me when I say everything is awful, Mum."

They pulled into the church car park, which was full of cars. "Oh, it must be choir practice." Her mother nudged the nose of the Land Rover into a space and turned to Poppy, her high cheekbones islanded and smooth in her wrinkled face. "Well, I'm all ears."

"You don't want to know, Mum. Trust me."

"I assume you've broken up with Sam and moved out of the flat, and if that's what you want to do, then that's okay with us. The only thing we want, Poppy, is for you to be happy." From the glove compartment, Poppy's mother took her lipstick, folded down her mirror, and applied it with precision. She pressed her lips against each other, then offered it to Poppy—as if perhaps a starlet's pout would help.

Poppy took the lipstick and, without looking in the mirror, drew a massive, clownish smile on her face. "How's that?"

"Poppy!" Poppy's mother snatched the lipstick from her. "There's no need to act like a child."

But Poppy did want to act like a child. She no longer wanted to have to be an adult and navigate the monumental challenges of life all by herself. "Mum! Fine, Okay, fine! Well, Dandelion had sex, like, actual intercourse *with Sam*."

"Oh dear, I'm sorry to hear that." Poppy's mother put the lipstick in her bag and pulled out a checked handkerchief. "Well, I can understand why you wouldn't want to get married anymore, though I would understand, too, if you decided to work it out." She dabbed the hankie on her tongue and tried to take it to Poppy's face.

"Sorry, what?" Poppy snatched the hankie and threw it onto the back seat. "No! What century do you live in? I hate him. And as for *her*, well . . ." Poppy hissed a bitter laugh. "Congratulations on raising a sadist bitch. And you know what . . . maybe it's a good thing that she's not even here anymore. Maybe it's a good thing she's—"

"POPPY!" Poppy's mother shouted, and Poppy jolted in shock. For the briefest of seconds, she thought her mother was going to slap her. "Pull yourself together. You really should be ashamed of yourself talking like that. *I'm* ashamed of you." Poppy's mother undid her seat belt, opened the door, and climbed out of the car. When she looked back at Poppy, her face was full of something awful—which was frightening, but also perversely enlivening, because Poppy had made her mother react in a way that she had never seen in her whole life.

"I'm going to tell you, like I've had to tell your sister..." Poppy's mother's voice was firm but fraying at the edge. "The best advice I ever received is *to forgive*. Regardless of if the other person is sorry. Or whether they've apologized, or ever will apologize. Forgiveness is something we must do because our own souls deserve that peace."

"Did you hear what I said?" Poppy was shaking. She felt like she had been sucked into a parallel universe; her family was fading from her. "Dandelion fucked my boyfriend. On purpose. Premeditated. And she hated him. It wasn't as if—"

"Did you hear what *I* said, Poppy? The only thing you can change in this scenario is your emotions." Poppy's mother was a stoic. "Dandelion doesn't get to continue her wonderful life, but *you do*. So you need to let this go." Poppy's mother pulled at each of her shirtsleeves in turn. "Now, will you wipe that Chanel lipstick off your face, please, and help me unload these flowers?"

Poppy turned to look the other way, made it clear she wasn't going to move. She still had her seat belt on.

"Fine," her mother said, closing the door.

Poppy watched her mother struggle to the church in the rearview mirror, with the buckets of cut flowers. That whole forgiveness thing was easy for her to say—she'd been born psychologically privileged, perennially, supernaturally serene. And besides anything, what did her mother know about forgiveness? No one had wronged her; her life had been a pretty little poem. And, really, what did Dandelion have to forgive anyway? And why had her mother even said that? *Like I've had to tell your sister...* Dandelion was at the epicenter of every single storm.

Poppy clicked down the mirror. The lipstick on her face was drying and felt nasty. She looked like the Joker, but worse. She licked her fingers, began rubbing at her face.

Her mother was coming back. She opened the boot. "I've bought some lavender to plant on your sister's grave, will you come with me?" There was no indication of bad feeling in her voice, or in her face. She was soft and kind again.

"No," Poppy said flatly. From the church, she could hear the choir singing now; their voices soared. She recognized it as "Panis Angelicus." The sisters had both been in the choir and they'd sung that anthem at school.

"When was the last time you visited her grave? We've got a headstone now. Please come with me."

"I said *no*, Mum."

Still belted into the passenger seat, Poppy watched her mother leave the car park and weave through the dead people. At Dandelion's grave, she knelt, took her trowel, and planted the pot of lavender among the other flowers—she had made Dandelion's grave into a flower bed. Poppy could see how it bustled and danced with white daisies, blue cornflowers, yellow lupines, and pink cosmos. Her mother had been training a climbing blush rose to rise over the headstone. And now Poppy watched her prune and tidy, fuss over it all—the place where her elder daughter slept.

When they pulled up outside the house again, Poppy's father was standing on the doorstep holding out the portable house phone.

"It's Je-Jetta," he said, when Poppy opened the car door.

"I'll call her back," Poppy shouted. She would not.

"Here she is," Poppy's father said, coming down the steps, placing the phone directly in her hand.

Poppy pushed past him, through the kitchen, into her bedroom. She closed the door. "Hello?"

"Phew! Poppy! I've been so worried. How are you?"

"Yup, all in all—life is just so lovely and fun. Okay, well, speak soon. Bye!"

"Poppy! Come on. *Please*," Jetta said in a breathy plea. "You can't just run out like that and not be in touch. You can't ignore me. I've been so worried about you."

"I can do what I want," Poppy snapped. She sat back on her bed.

"Can I come down and see you? I could get the first train tomorrow."

"No." Poppy needed more time. An amount of time which she couldn't yet determine.

"Have you spoken to Sam?" In the background, Poppy could hear Jetta's daughter wanting something. "Go and ask Daddy," Jetta said in a different voice.

"No," Poppy said again.

At 3:30 a.m. the previous Saturday, Poppy had left Dandelion's flat, left Jake, and got a night bus to Paddington station. Around five, sitting on the pavement outside McDonald's, very cold, she called Sam and left an answerphone message thanking him for the heads-up about the betrayal, and letting him know that she knew what he did. When the trains started again, she bought a ticket and left London. Sam had messaged her the next day. I don't know what you're on about. Sounds like you're confused. Let's talk this through when I'm back, face to face.

"He hasn't admitted anything. I really don't know if he will, frankly." Poppy predicted more lies. "I need to go back to the flat soon, I guess. Pack up all my stuff. So I suppose we'll have to hash it out one final time. Will we? I can't quite see Sam bowing out of this without a fight."

"You don't have to do anything you don't want to, Poppy," Jetta said. "I can pack up your flat for you. Stefan and I can do it."

Poppy had been punishing Jetta by giving her the cold shoulder, but she had missed her, and now she understood that she would forgive her—wanted to forgive her—not solely because of Jetta's evident remorse, or the fact that Poppy's own soul deserved that peace, but because, she knew, Jetta had done what she thought was best for her and least harmful overall.

"So, that's why you and Dandelion fell out last year?" Poppy asked. The question came out in a whisper. "Because of what happened with Sam?"

"Course! God, Poppy, it was awful. It was *so bad*. I told her if she went through with it, our friendship was over. But she was so indignant. We screamed at each other, and at the time, I really believed we'd never speak again. I wish she didn't always tell me everything, you know? And just expect me to be on board."

"I cannot fathom what she was thinking," Poppy said, thinning her eyes and running one hand over her hair, trying to find an iota of rationality in her sister's plan. "It doesn't make sense."

"It doesn't. Course it doesn't. But it did *to her*. She was utterly convinced. So much so she was prepared to hurt you, ruin her relationship with me! God . . ." Jetta sighed, clearly reliving the awfulness of it all. "And that whole summer while me and her weren't speaking, I was waiting for this devastated phone call from you, about her, about Sam. And then when it came—it wasn't about Sam at all." Jetta paused, and then Poppy was remembering that day, that phone call. She knew they both were—they were back in that summer afternoon. "And then, those weeks at the hospital, all of it was forgotten, *of course*, and we all rallied around. But one day, while you weren't there, she told me that she'd gone through with it, that she'd slept with him. Only she hadn't been able to tell you, and it was too late by then. So, she asked me to do it, after she died. She made me promise. On her fucking deathbed." Jetta was crying now, really crying. "And I lied to her, I lied to her and said I would, but I didn't want to, Poppy. Honestly, I thought the truth should die with her."

Poppy was breathing very deeply, in and out. "She thought I was too pathetic a person to ever be able to leave a bad relationship." Poppy laughed a deep kind of hurt. "She had no faith in me. Did she? Did you guys think I was totally weak and—"

"Poppy! No. Of course not. And you broke up with him anyway, didn't you? You knew it wasn't right. So, she was wrong to meddle and do that awful thing. The worst thing. I mean, that girl was a law unto herself, and we could really hate her for it or, frankly, we could be very fucking impressed."

"Please, Jetta. Don't! I'll never forgive her for this." Poppy lifted her left hand, stuck her thumb and index finger into the corner of each eye, either side of her nose, rubbed them softly, picking up specks of sediment. "She made out like she was radical, fighting for a higher good and all that crap, but she was cruel. She was selfish and disturbed. My sister didn't understand love, at all."

"Poppy, that's not how it was, or who she was. Dandelion did understand love!" Jetta's voice was full of anguish, but also certainty. "Just . . . differently. She could endure an enormous amount of pain, and so, too, could she inflict it, because she had to fight. She just had to fight! Since we were kids . . . She was never scared of anything, was she?" Jetta spluttered a laugh through the tears. "Not even death."

Poppy covered her face with her hand. She nodded. In the darkness of her mind she saw her sister dying. Dandelion had lost that fight with life and in the end she had surrendered. But she had not been scared. "Not even death," Poppy agreed.

"Can I come and see you?" Jetta asked. "I want to give you the biggest hug. Shall we get absolutely shit-faced and go swimming naked and cry and scream? And, like, fucking . . . build a bonfire and . . . I don't know . . . sacrifice Sam."

Despite herself, Poppy laughed. To have the truth now, to hear it, no matter how savage it was, in some deep way was steadying. She looked up at the far wall, the long mirror, her reflection. She looked really, really terrible, her skin still pink and shining from her mother's lipstick. "Maybe I can come stay with you when I come back to London? I need to deal with it all. Sort my life out."

"Billion percent. Come soon, please. My little terrors want to give you big cuddles. Very much including Stef. I know you've got hundreds of missed calls from him. He's been all green and quiet since his birthday; he's worried sick about you."

Poppy stood and took the dressing gown off. She had an intense urge to get very clean. She was going to scrub herself in the shower until her skin was raw. She would go back to London and she would pack the flat. Talk to Sam. She would call Betty and apologize, explain, make plans. She would put herself back together. One step at a time. She would. She could. She knew.

"And please let me know if there is anything I can do," Jetta said.

"Actually, Jetta, there is something . . ." Poppy let her head fall back; she looked up at the ceiling. "It's sort of a long story. How much time do you have?"

"All the time in the world."

"Well . . ." The moment had come to tell the truth. The whole truth. Nothing but. "You know that night out we had, the rave, the club? And there was that wasted guy, the one we took to the medical unit . . ."

"Er . . . yes?"

Poppy took a hugely deep breath, walked to the window, looked out at the sea. "There's something you should know about him. Lots of things, in fact."

34

Monday, 7th July

Jake

"A crow, eh?" Karla said as she turned and nudged open the door of the meeting room, Kusama, using her arse.

"More like a crow with one wing," Jake admitted, thinking back to himself on the yoga mat that morning, falling on his face during his class with Yan. Jake was on day five of a rigorous health and fitness regime that Yan had drawn up for him, "The Ninety-Day Yan Plan."

In the meeting room, two people were sitting at the far end of the long white table. Karla closed the door behind Jake firmly, sat on the nearest chair, and introduced them. "Jake, this is Teigan from legal, and Ali from HR."

Jake stepped forward, shook their hands. He felt exceedingly nervous, the type of nervousness that surely must be visible, so huge was it in his body. A mass pushing outward and upward, from his chest into his throat. "Yeah, hi, Ali, we met, didn't we, on Zoom?" Ali had been the one to interview Jake about his account of what had gone down that fateful night.

"Firstly," Ali said, "thank you for your patience, Jake. As you know, we have a speak-up culture, and we're committed to listening to all voices. We take the welfare of our employees extremely seriously, which means that these matters must be investigated fully and looked at from all sides. However, I appreciate it also must have been difficult for you. I hope we've communicated with you fully throughout the process."

"Okay," Jake said, nodding slowly, unable to read the room. He moved his gaze to a monocycle that was leaning against the far wall—had one of them ridden it up the corridor? Which one?

"And personally," Karla said, "I want to apologize. You're one of our favorite directors to collaborate with, Jake. We value you and your work so highly."

"Jesus, Karla. What's happening?" Jake wiped the sweat from his hands down his jeans.

Karla looked at Ali and Ali looked at Teigen and Teigen nodded a consent. "A colleague has come forward and told us that you did ingest drugs that night," Ali said, "but unbeknownst to you. You picked up someone else's drink."

Jake's mouth made an elaborate *NOOOO*, though no sound came out.

"Yes." Ali nodded gravely.

"Whose drink?"

"Colin Dubois has admitted he dosed his own drink," Teigan said. She raised her eyebrows.

"With *what?*"

"Acid."

"ACID! I DROPPED ACID?"

"Unfortunately, yes. It does seem that way."

"Colin does *that* for *fun*? I was locked in hell!"

"We think you had a large amount," Ali said, both hands flat on the table. "Colin thought he might have been rather heavy-handed with the dose and so he'd decided to sip at it, slowly, throughout the course of the evening. He put the drink down on the table you were all sharing, and you, apparently . . . presumably . . ."

"Polished it off," Karla finished the sentence.

Jake flicked his eyes to Karla. "But why didn't he take me to the medical place?" His shoulders were hunched and his neck was craning forward like the stem of a plant that was stretching toward the light. "What if I'd, like . . . lost my mind forever? You know that happens to people!"

"We're all very relieved nothing more serious happened," Teigan said, in an impeccably professional measured tone. "However, we do know it was traumatic for you. And so, we'd like to talk to you today about moving forward. How to progress in a way that is going to be most beneficial for everyone and how we, as a business, can give you all the help that you need."

"I felt clinically insane, Karla," Jake said. He couldn't take his eyes from her face. "I had a cut lip and was really bruised. And I have no idea how that happened."

"I'm really sorry to tell you, Jake, but you fell down the stairs. We have CCTV footage."

"What?" Jake looked from left to right, in disbelief, like he was waiting for someone to jump out at him and scream, *This is all a joke!*

"We have the footage here," Teigan said. "If you'd like to see it."

"Can you just tell me what happened?" Jake asked, really not wanting to see himself in that state.

"It was like five steps," Karla said. "You just crumple and roll down them. It's not that bad. You don't look like a stuntman or anything."

"Oh," Jake said, slightly wishing for something more dramatic. "Fine."

"So we think you fell on Sydney just before. Then the stairs . . . then you go outside and puke and the bouncer comes over, and those people all gather around."

"We'd like for you to have a full physical and psychological assessment," Ali said. "And a course of therapy. Obviously, all medical expenses covered by Yesness. Do you understand what I'm saying?"

"Of course I understand! This all happened a month ago, you don't need to talk to me like I'm still high *now*." Jake swiveled his chair on its wheels around and around. "Fuck," he said. "So, what about Sydney's complaint? What happens with that?"

"Since this information has come to light," Teigan said, "there is no longer any complaint. It's resolved."

"Now she knows what happened, she's very upset with Colin," Karla said. "As we all are."

"If you'd still like to escalate this, we'll support that," Teigan said. "But I do want to be very clear that it wasn't a malicious act. Colin was also inebriated. He didn't realize the full extent of what was happening. It's only after that night, when the story of you and Sydney came out, he put two and two together."

Jake kept spinning around in the chair, trying to work out how he felt. Pleased? Definitely pleased. But also really wronged.

"We had no choice but to terminate Colin's contract with immediate effect on Friday. You're not going to bump into him here. We're so sorry, Jake. But, ideally," Teigan continued, "we don't want anyone finding out. Any of our clients, anyone in the industry. And we can compensate you for loss of earnings. We'd like you to look over this offer." Teigan turned over some papers that were on the table. Pushed them toward Jake.

Jake stood up, walked over to the window. They were all falling over themselves to be nice to him now. Probably worried he was going to get litigious. In the distance, Jake could see the Tate Modern, the Millennium Bridge. He thought of Poppy, the beret, how she'd run after it, kicking up shingles. He thought about how brave she was, always. He wanted nothing more than to walk out of the building and call her immediately. Repeat this entire conversation and hear what she had to say, her advice on what he should do.

Behind him, Karla said she had an amazing project she wanted to talk to him about. "There's tons of work for you here, Jake. Always will be."

Outside the window, the river looked like sky and the sky looked like rock. A chink of pale light in the clouds pooled like icy water. Everything was different and strange, but hopefully getting better. Softly, Jake tapped his fist to his heart and his heart tapped back. He was going to be okay.

Jake turned around to face them. He didn't want to work with Yesness anymore, but he wasn't going to make a scene. He would accept what they were offering: the medical stuff, any compensation. He reached for the papers on the table. "Do I have to read these now?"

"You can take them home," Teigan said. "We can discuss it when you're ready."

Karla walked Jake back to reception, where they seemed to be playing the sound of whale song, or dolphins, high-pitched underwater squeals. "Are you all right?" she asked.

"Honestly, I'm relieved," Jake said. "I've had a lot of time to think about a lot of things, and I'm ready for a fresh start. I've started my fresh start, in fact."

"I can tell. You seem fresh, Jake. You seem good." In front of the lift, Karla gave Jake a hug; she looked up into his face. "What doesn't kill you makes you stronger, isn't it?"

"I don't know about that," Jake admitted. "But what doesn't kill you sure makes you feel alive."

"I hope I handled all of that okay," Karla said. "It was really difficult to navigate. It wasn't fun for anyone. I'm sorry if I was too off with you. Maybe I didn't give you enough support?"

"You handled it all amazingly, Karla. As usual. Don't worry."

"Phew." She smiled at him. "Wanna hang out soon?"

"Would love that," Jake said, "though I'm not coming to any raves, obviously."

"Thank God."

The lift doors opened; Jake stepped in, turned back to Karla, and smiled. Behind her, the receptionist was in leather chaps and a harness. He stood and blew a kiss to Jake, which was surprising, but also very pleasing—Jake caught it in his hand.

35

Tuesday, 8th July

After lunch, Poppy came into the sitting room, where her father was standing in front of the telly, with the remote in his hand. He was still cataloging all the home videos, which Poppy had begun to suspect was mainly a cover story—a means to be able to watch the past, all the time.

He paused the video; black-and-white fuzzy horizontal train tracks held it in place. He glanced over his shoulder. "This is one of your plays."

Poppy rolled her eyes. On the screen, Dandelion looked to be about fourteen. She was standing next to the palm tree by the decking, her mouth open, bare feet. She was wearing cycling shorts and her baggy Hypercolor T-shirt. Their mum had brought those T-shirts back from a trip to Colorado in the nineties, and the sisters had been obsessed with them. Dandelion had worn hers all her life.

"You're the d-director of this one and the camerawoman," her father said. "I think the scriptwriter too." He pressed play and Dandelion sprang into motion.

"And I can't believe she . . ." Dandelion began talking to the tree trunk as if it was another character and they were gossiping. As there were only two of them, the sisters often cast that palm tree for major roles. Jetta wasn't interested in acting at all, or being told what to do.

"No!" a young Poppy squealed from behind the camera. "We don't reveal that yet. That's not the line."

A lot of grass came into the shot, and Dandelion slid to a diagonal. "Oh, sorry," she said. "I thought we did."

"Read the script!" Poppy said, with high-pitched exasperation.

Dandelion bent and picked up some sheets of A4 paper from the grass. The script was stapled together at the top left corner. She flicked over one page, then another. "Can we go again?"

The camera straightened. Dandelion tucked her hair behind her ears and turned back to the tree.

Poppy shouted, "Action!"

"Come and watch this one with me, P-Poppet." Poppy's father pressed pause again. "There's a brilliant twist at the end."

Poppy looked into the corner of the room, at the ceiling, trying to recall that particular day, that particular play. "No thanks, Dad."

"In a minute you lose your t-temper and then you both start wrestling." Her father chuckled. Pressed play.

Poppy shook her head, but she came and stood behind him. The scene continued; Dandelion got the lines wrong again and, just as her dad said, the entire shot pivoted and it was obvious Poppy had put the camera down on the garden table. The red light kept blinking. Then Poppy was in the shot, too, a miniature version of Dandelion, wearing cycling shorts over a green swimming costume and a more childish potbelly. The sisters started to squabble, and Poppy was the first to kick.

"Stop!" Poppy put her hands to her eyes.

"You had such a temper on you, Poppet," Poppy's father said.

Poppy coughed. "Are you kidding me?" From the screen Poppy could hear them both squawking as they fought and then their mother's voice on the video: "Girls! Stop it. Girls!"

Poppy's father picked up the remote, muted the sound. "You were a more timid child in public, but you were just as fierce. Especially with her."

"That's not true, Dad. I was forced to be behind the camera. I was manipulated and . . ." Poppy glanced again at the screen; both she and Dandelion were lying on the grass, side by side, and although there was no volume, it was clear they were laughing. They both stood up and Poppy jumped on Dandelion, her legs around her waist, in a piggyback.

"That's not how it was, Poppy, and you know that. You loved being the one behind the camera, filming. Spent all your pocket money in Snappy Snaps. You were a watchful child and you had the more artistic soul and, yes, maybe she was the leader, but she was older. She was p-p-protective. You were a team."

"She was a bitch, Dad! She was horrid to you too. But now, because she's dead—everyone's totally sugarcoating her personality, and it's really effing me off." The French windows were open, and Poppy stalked through them, over the decking, down the steps, past the palm tree that had grown scraggy, and across the lawn to the coastal path.

"Poppy." Her father was behind her. She stopped to look at him, waited for a few seconds, and then began walking, more slowly. He caught up with her, kept her pace, though he didn't try to talk. At the seafront, he took a seat on one of the benches, and Poppy stopped, looked back at him, put her hands on her hips. Still her world reeled and spun too fast. How was she meant to forgive someone who wasn't there? How was she meant to forgive someone she didn't understand and who would never apologize?

"Poppy?" Her father was panting very slightly. He cleared his throat. "Your mother told me what happened. With Sam." He patted the bench next to him. "And your sister."

Poppy shook her head. When they were teenagers, Poppy, Dandelion, and Jetta used to cluster on that bench. Try to look intimidating. "I actually kind of want to keep walking, Dad," she said loudly. "I need the air. See you back at home."

"Well, let's sit here and get some air together." Poppy's father patted the bench again, and Poppy turned away from him, though she didn't leave. It was a gorgeous day and the beach was full of holidaymakers; striped colored windbreakers flecked the sand. "It was f-funny seeing that video, wasn't it?"

"Not really. She did bully me, just not on that day. I get the point you're trying to make. I get you don't want there to be bad blood."

"She did not b-bully you, Poppy," he said firmly. "She always wanted to defend you, defend other girls. Perhaps her methods were unorthodox . . ."

Poppy felt twitchy, took another step toward the beach. What would happen if she ran down over all those towels, through the picnics, kicking sandcastles, and waded right in, went under? How long would it take for a lifeguard to think, *Oh shit?*

"She wasn't a martyr, Dad," Poppy said, turning back to him. "I'm really not enjoying this new narrative."

"But what if she was?"

"Well, she wasn't." Poppy wanted to start walking again. "Dad, I'm gonna keep going—"

"I'll come with you. I need to tell you something." Her father stood up. "You're our b-baby, aren't you? And we all wanted to p-p-protect you. Particularly your big sister."

"Mm." Poppy turned back to him and wrinkled her nose, trying to bring this interchange to a close with some artificial agreement.

"Did you feel like we didn't tell you things?"

"Are you kidding? Yes! I'm the last to know everything."

"Perhaps we suspected you'd rather not know," Poppy's father said. "I'm like that t-too. I'd always rather no-not know. And then sometimes when people tell me things I'd rather not know so s-s-strongly, I don't even believe them. But one can't go around curating reality like that. Suppressing truth, not listening to certain voices."

Poppy was looking at the tip of the lighthouse, which was just visible from where she was standing. She thinned her eyes, not because of the light, but because she had absolutely no idea what her father was talking about. "Anyway? Shall we?"

"Remember when Dandelion shaved your heads?" Poppy's father asked.

"Yes, obviously." Poppy pulled in a long breath and they began walking, painfully slowly. It didn't even seem long ago that her father had worked as a skipper on the local lifeboats, the RNLI, and now he was doddering.

"Remember why she did that?"

"Ostensibly the male gaze, but realistically it was for attention and sadism."

"Male gaze, exactly," her father said, not acknowledging Poppy's other insults. "And why do you think she had issues with the male gaze?"

"Any number of reasons, Dad. Frankly, it was nearly thirty years ago and I really don't care."

"It started with a male gaze. Singular. Greg McCaid. Mr. McCaid. Remember him?"

"No."

"He taught science at your school and—"

Surprise left Poppy's body in the sound of a laugh. She stopped walking and blinked at her father's face. "The science teacher?"

Not the awful science teacher again—the man that Jetta had randomly mentioned when Poppy asked her about this same head-shaving incident.

"Yes. Well. Him."

Poppy lowered her chin, stared at her father out of the top of her eyes, intently, waiting for him to elaborate. When he didn't, she snapped, "Dad?"

"What do you remember about him, Poppy?"

"Literally nothing! Like . . . hardly anything. He didn't teach me. He didn't teach either of us." Poppy trawled her mind for memories. What was it people had said? "He used to get girls to sit on his knee sometimes in class, right? Took their pulses on their upper thighs, took the boys' pulses on their wrists. Then . . . police found stuff on his computer? He went to prison, or something, I don't know. And . . . I mean . . . why are you bringing him up?"

"Remember how you two would cycle to The Shell Shop?"

"Yes, course!" The Shell Shop had been their favorite store as children, now long since closed down. It sold exotic shells that definitely weren't from Devon: huge tiger cowries and pink queen conches. But it also sold sweets, postcards, fridge magnets, trinkets for tourists.

"One day, in the summer holidays, you cycled out there and you were buying sweets—only then you weren't."

Poppy blinked at him. "Right. What do you mean we weren't buying sweets?"

"*You* weren't in there, Poppy. D-Dandelion said you disappeared, just vanished."

"This is . . . huh? Me?"

"She came outside and found you sitting on Greg's knee and . . . she said . . . he had his hand on your l-l-leg and she screamed at him to get off you. He did, but he swore at her under his breath.

When he stood to leave Dandelion got on her bike and she rode it into him. She hurt him. He was bleeding. D-d-do you remember that?"

"No! I don't remember any of this! I have absolutely no idea what you're talking about." Both Poppy's hands were over her stomach. She didn't remember. But why could she now, so clearly, see a man hopping in pain by the side of the road, calling Dandelion names?

"Your sister came straight home and told me about it, and I didn't understand why she was upset, at first. Then she told me about the r-r-rumors at school and it was clear that she hated Greg. Thought he was a very bad man."

"So . . . the head-shaving thing was about the pedo teacher having me on his knee, is what you're saying?"

"We didn't think he was a criminal, Poppy. No one did. He was a very respected man. Volunteered on the lifeboats with me. I spoke to some other parents about what D-Dandelion said, and no one had heard the rumors at all. And you two girls were such fantasists with all your made-up plays. But I did go to Greg and I asked him, and he said that he'd been t-t-talking to you about school when Dandelion attacked him, out of the blue. She'd damaged his Achilles tendon, quite badly. The man had a limp."

"So, it's like a 'he said, she said' thing? And you believed this creepy man over your daughter?" A cluster of clouds had moved over the sun and the air felt significantly cooler. Poppy shivered, rubbed her arms.

"Ye-ye-yes. And Dandelion got in big trouble for attacking him. I grounded her."

"Right. Well. That's awful and gross and, frankly, devastating and just another thing for me to try and come to terms with. Wonderful!"

313

"That's not actually the end of the story, darling. And, in a way, for D-D-Dandelion that was just the start. She couldn't believe how the adults didn't do anything. So she started taking matters into her own hands, in a way that your mother and I thought was bad b-b-behavior. The head shaving, the rages. But, secretly, she had started talking to Greg on the instant messenger on our computer—"

"Sorry, what, what, what, WHAT? She was talking to the science teacher on MSN?"

"Your sister was determined to catch the predator. And she did," Poppy's father said, with more strength in his voice. "She collected lurid messages from Greg. All you kids were always chatting away to each other in those days and so we just thought that's what she was up to. Talking to school friends. But she was pretending to be a made-up girl and she was talking to G-Greg. She never sent any p-p-pictures of herself. But she collected all his requests and just hours and hours of grooming. She printed it all out. She called Childline and they told her to come to us. And that was just . . . awful. When we saw what he was really like. Your mother and I went with your sister to the p-p-police. And I will never forgive myself for pushing your sister into masterminding a sting operation, at twelve years old. I don't think she fully forgave me either until, until, at the . . . end . . . in hospital."

Poppy's eyes were flicking over the sea as she did her best to digest what was being said. She took one small step and then another. Her father at her side. "And Mum knows about all this?"

"When the truth came out your mother was devastated, but she forgave me, because, well, because your mother is your mother."

Poppy blinked at the beach, at the lifeguard in the tower: his legs up, looking out. "So Mum just continued to bake cookies and apply her lipstick and dance around like everything was fine?"

"Your mum isn't the way she is despite the world b-burning

around her, but because of it, Poppy." Her father's tone moved from deep remorse to something more scolding. "That is how she fights. Life, for her, isn't as easy as she makes it look."

They walked in silence until they reached the lookout point—the place where Poppy had taken those photos of her sister turned toward the golden clouds and sea; the framed portrait in her flat. It made an ugly kind of sense—broken pieces of the past washed up like sea glass years later. "Does Jetta know?"

"Yes. We think Jetta was probably involved in the entire crusade in some way, although Dandelion always denied it."

"What happened to Greg? He went to prison, right?" Poppy asked, shaking her head. Her heart was shaking too.

"He did, for a time. But not long after he came out we heard that he'd died, Poppy. Motorbike accident."

"When?" Poppy spun toward her father. They looked into each other's eyes and they read each other's thoughts.

"Dandelion wasn't behind that, Poppy," her father said, a small flicker of amusement in the corner of his mouth. "It wasn't suspicious."

Poppy looked up at the sky, at the seagulls swiping through it. Despite herself, she smiled, imagining her sister in leathers on a motorbike speeding along a high road on a mission to kill.

"All Dandelion ever wanted to do was protect you." Poppy's father put his arm around her shoulder. "And sometimes she did things that were very rash and precarious. But she did them from a place of, I believe, a higher understanding of what is right. She would never have done anything to hurt you, and if it looks like that now—with this ghastly Sam thing—maybe, in time, it will look different. With distance, the outlines change."

Something inside of Poppy's body was pushing into existence, a feeling, a knowledge. She took a step away from her father. Then she was running. Large strides, shallow breaths. She crossed two fields, over the gates, past the pub. She ran down to the cove with the creek that they used to jump when they were feeling fearless. She ran all the way to the church, all the way to her sister's grave. "I know, I know . . ." she gasped. "I know what you did. And I know that you did it for me."

36

Wednesday, 9th July

Jake

"Hi," a woman's voice said through the intercom, "Poppy asked me to come over. I'm her friend."

"Oh! Hi!" Jake looked at his watch; it was 7:56 a.m. Luckily, the new and improved version of Jake, Jake 4.0, had been up for over an hour and had already written Morning Pages (as laid out in *The Artist's Way*, which he'd finally started reading, twenty years after everyone else). He'd done fifty press-ups (almost, he rounded up from forty-three), and he'd whizzed up a very delicious breakfast smoothie (all about the double chocolate protein powder and almond butter dolloped in).

Jake pressed the buzzer, opened the front door of the flat. He watched as a small person in a long, loose orange dress with plaited straps came toward him up the stairs.

"Hi, I'm Jetta." She walked in, without looking him in the face. She tried Dandelion's bedroom door immediately, agonizingly embarrassingly for Jake, putting on a show of making sure it was locked. She turned back to him. "We met before—when you pissed your pants in the club." She went into the sitting room and sat down on the far sofa, right in the middle of it.

"God. Yeah. Did we? Argh. Well. Yes, so . . . I was spiked, as it turns out. Really badly spiked, so . . . yeah." Jake stopped talking because already it seemed like Jetta wasn't listening to him; she was looking around the room with evident suspicion—the side of her mouth and one eyebrow raised. "Anyway . . ." He tried to sound calm. "How's Poppy?"

"That's why I'm here, actually," Jetta said, "she wanted me to come over, check you're on track to move out this weekend? She's got an appointment here and needs everything sorted."

Jake glanced up at the window behind Jetta, concentrated on the leaves of the chestnut tree across the street as they swayed. "Right. Yes. Course. I'll be out on Saturday, not a problem at all." He hoped he seemed sanguine. He hoped he seemed nice. "Is she okay? I've been worried about her."

Jake had been missing Poppy in a way that physically hurt. He missed her stability and her instability. Her calamity and calm. He missed how her smile so often spilled into a laugh and how her laugh was musical. Her smell, which smelled of almost nothing, which smelled of air, of grass, of space. The exact pitch of her voice. The pattern of her thoughts. All the conversations it seemed they'd never get to have. He had banned himself from looking at any of her social media. He had deleted their WhatsApp messages. Even accidentally catching sight of the emoji of the farmer woman with the sweet corn—which reminded him of her—made him kind of want to cry.

"She'll be fine." Jetta was eyeballing him with intimidating green eyes.

Jake inhaled. "I'd love to speak to her, but I know she wants space."

"What do you want to talk to her about?"

"Um, just say sorry and stuff."

"Sorry and stuff?" Jetta scoffed, unimpressed. "I'll pass it on."

"Can you tell her that I feel terrible about . . . everything?"

"Any specifics?"

"Hm . . ." Jake wondered what it was safe to say. "Well, she came over here in the middle of the night and, well, there was this whole *big scene.*"

"Yeah," Jetta said, "I know." Her own distaste for him was palpable. She'd clearly heard terrible things.

"Right. Well, she, er . . ." Jake took a seat opposite—sat in the exact place that he and Poppy had got it on. He looked down at his hands as he spoke. "She was very upset. And she said this thing about Dandelion and Sam, and I just hope that it was all a big misunderstanding. Because, as I said to her, I can't see her sister ever doing—"

"Sorry, Jake," Jetta interrupted. "Why are you being weird about Dandelion?" She shook her head and looked away from him, as if she was disgusted. "Incredibly inappropriate."

"I'm not weird about her. The *situation* is weird."

"You're not weird about her?" Jetta asked, leveling her gaze back at him.

"No." Jake really wished Jetta didn't know about his sleeping-in-the-bedroom indiscretion.

"Why did you just say that Dandelion wouldn't have got with Sam, as if you knew her then? You never met her, Jake."

"Right, no." Jake deserved Jetta's hostility, but he also wanted her to get that he wasn't totally deluded and there was a deep connection that bound them all together. "My mum died young, too, you see."

Jetta's face was blank, no sympathy yet—at all.

"She struggled," Jake continued. "She was depressed and she died by suicide. So . . ." He swallowed. "I understand how hard it is. And I know that Dandelion, like my mum, was really fucking special. Sweet, inspiring, thoughtful, silly—"

"Oh dear, you've got things very, very wrong, my friend," Jetta said loudly, interrupting. "That's really terrible and sad about your mum, and I'm sorry for you, I am. But you didn't know Dandelion, at all. She wasn't sweet. She was lemony. She was salt. And I highly doubt she was like your mother. And she didn't die by suicide, Jake. She wasn't depressed, if that's what you think. She rinsed each fucking day with joy. So, I'd like to politely suggest," Jetta said in a way that sounded a long way from polite, "that you think about getting some intense professional psychiatric help and nip this whole morose fantasy in the bud. And please pack your little bags."

"I'm getting intense professional psychiatric help, actually, Jetta!" Jake snapped, gravely offended. Though as soon as he heard this sentence out loud, he regretted it. "Specifically for the spiking-drugs thing," he clarified.

The previous day, Jake had his first therapy session as organized by Yesness, and already he suspected he was going to become the type of person who starts sentences with, *My therapist says* . . . He'd found the fifty minutes of psychotherapy to be deeply rewarding. Though the impetus for Yesness paying for it all was to deal with any potential issues of his having been drugged, in actual fact, Jake had spent the entire session talking about his mother's death and the general sense of abandonment he'd experienced from the twenty years of not having a present dad. "And, anyway . . ." Jake said, looking back at Jetta's face, "what do you mean that's not how Dandelion died?"

"That's not how she died. What bit of that sentence do you not understand?"

"I thought she—"

"I heard! Who told you that?"

"Um . . ." Jake leaned back on the sofa, crossed a leg up onto his other thigh, and held his foot. "Ummm . . ." He ran through memories, trying to recall the time Poppy had told him how Dandelion had died. Or was it . . . the condolences? "I didn't make it up, if that's what you think," Jake said, trying to sound as authoritative as possible. Though, actually, he was panicking now that maybe his mind had filled in the blank spaces with the colors he already knew. Had he *projected a suicide*? Had he *wanted a suicide*? He swallowed. He definitely wanted Jetta to go. He stood up, crossed his arms in front of him. "Better get ready for work, so . . ." he lied. He didn't currently have a job.

"Dandelion was very ill, Jake. Okay? And that's why she died. It was unexpected and it was a terrible tragedy." Jetta wasn't standing up. "I want to make sure we're clear, because it sounds to me like you've made up a wonderland as a means of not dealing with your own shit and there's some pretty major Mummy issues going on."

Jake couldn't believe it. He wondered if she was lying to him. He was giddy now, with a defensive type of rage. A shame. A devastation. And a shock. "Look, Jetta, I get that you don't like me . . ." He wasn't mad about her either. "I'm sorry for being a moronic man. But would you mind if we skip the character assassination part? I've got the memo. I've done a million things wrong. I know!" Outside the window, there was the sound of lots of small children in a gaggle, like a whole crocodile of them—two by two—walking past. "I'm really, really sorry for everything. I'm really devastated I hurt Poppy, and I'd do anything for her to forgive me, but I also don't think it's fair you coming in here and talking to me like this. I didn't hunt Poppy down, you know. Or Dandelion. And although, yes, I've done bad things, I would also like to point out that this story starts with Dandelion liking me on Hinge and then Poppy messaging me and pretending to be her dead sister." Jake stepped back into the hallway in a physical attempt to get Jetta to stand up and come toward him so he could usher her out the door, then slam it, then lock it.

"So? What?" Jetta still didn't stand up, but she did lean forward. "You think Dandelion would have fancied you?"

"That's not what I'm saying at all."

"You do think that, though, don't you?"

"We'll never know."

"I *do* know, Jake. And she wouldn't have. Dandelion matched with people for fun on that thing. She matched with people out of boredom. She matched with people ironically. For gags. *We* matched with people for her! My husband played with Dandelion's dating apps more than she did. It's entertainment. It's a computer game. You're not her fucking type, Jake, and I'm not surprised she blanked you."

"That's fine! That's cool!" Jake said. It wasn't cool. It was horrible. "I don't care!"

"So why were you sleeping in her bed and lying to Poppy and telling your family that you had a really serious relationship with Dandelion and something about . . . speaking at her funeral? Why did you do and say all that?"

"Because Poppy lied!" Jake was shouting now. "And I went along with the story!"

"I don't believe you." Jetta used her hand to sweep Jake away like he was nothing, like he was actual dirt. Her small body popped up into a stand. "This creepy fantasyland ends here. Okay? Move out. Move on."

"I'm not saying I fancied Dandelion!" Jake lifted his arms beseechingly, desperate now. "Stop making it sound like that! You're making out like I'm perverted and delusional." He combed his hands through his hair repeatedly, trying to work things out. He had a very disconcerting feeling that he was playing the part of a villain, that he was in some sort of scene. He wanted someone to shout *CUT* and give him notes.

"Look, Jake." Jetta was speaking slowly, her voice no longer raised. "It's really bad that Poppy lied to you, of course I can acknowledge that. I'm shocked. She's shocked. But clearly you understand all too well what grief can do, and when Poppy first messaged you, that was only a few months after her one and only sister died at thirty-nine years old."

"I know, Jetta. I know," Jake protested, but Jetta wasn't stopping; she was maybe even ramping up.

"You know Poppy slept on a camp bed on the floor of the hospital every night." Her voice broke with emotion, but she cleared her throat and continued. "They were holding hands when Dandelion died. Okay? I know because I was there too." She had to stop talking. She raised the back of her hand to her mouth. Blinked hard. Gasped. Cleared her throat again. "So I want you to understand that although Poppy did something absolutely bizarre, she was utterly lost and broken, and she was desperately looking for her sister but, unfortunately for everyone—who she found was you."

Jake's eyes burned so hot that he put his fingers in them, rubbed and rubbed. "Look, I'm sorry, Jetta, I think—"

"Sorry, Jake . . ." Jetta hadn't finished. She was going to leave nothing of him. "Those two sisters were, and are, and will always be the most astonishing beings I've had the privilege and the honor to call my closest friends. And through some fucking weird *whole thing*, you've ended up in Dandelion's home and in Poppy's head, and, as far as I can work out, she's shown you nothing but warmth and hospitality. So you need to get over yourself, Jake, got it? As of right this second, stop projecting your own shit onto Dandelion and pointing any sort of finger at Poppy, because you're far from worthy of her time, let alone her love." Jetta walked past him into the hall and looked over her shoulder. "So you'll be out on Saturday, yes?"

"Jetta?" Jake followed her. She stopped at the front door. "I'm really, seriously, sorry." Jake's voice was quiet. He felt like falling to his knees in front of her. In front of all of them. "I really want to talk to Poppy . . ."

"No. Poppy is going through a lot at the moment, Jake. And let me be clear, if you ever hurt her again, I will kill you—and I'm not joking. Do you understand?"

They stared at each other. "I don't doubt you'd kill me, Jetta." Jake absolutely did not. The woman was an assassin. "But my intention isn't to hurt Poppy. I want to do the opposite of that, and I only want five minutes of her time, her life, to explain, to apologize. Never speaking again would be a huge mistake, I know that now. For both of us."

"I'll pass that on, Jake." Jetta pulled the front door toward her, and Jake ran to it, held it open, watched her jog down the stairs.

"Jetta?"

She stopped. Looked up at him.

"And can you . . . will you . . . tell her . . ." Jake wanted Jetta to tell Poppy that it had always been her. From the very first minute. And it would be until the very last.

"No, Jake," Jetta said. "I fucking won't."

37

Thursday, 10th July

Poppy

"May I add, in the least letchy way possible," Stefan said, nodding at Poppy's red slip dress, "very spicy au revoir outfit, that, pal."

"Total minx," Jetta agreed.

Stefan had made beef shin ragù. He put the bowls down in front of Poppy and his wife.

Poppy batted a hand, very lightly blushed, though she reveled in the compliment. The red dress was one of her new outfits. In Devon, she'd gone on a rogue online shopping spree, bought some pretty left-field looks. Poppy's old wardrobe didn't feel right anymore; neither, for that matter, did Dandelion's.

"So . . ." Jetta said, "what did Sam say?"

Poppy had come up from Devon that morning and had spent the afternoon packing her stuff into boxes at the flat she'd shared with Sam. It was all done by the time he came home from work. "He didn't deny it. Said he'd been seduced and, essentially, took very little responsibility for sleeping with my sister."

"What did you say to that?" Stefan asked, twirling a fork into his pasta.

"I don't disagree with him, I expect he was seduced," Poppy said. "But that doesn't change the fact that it happened, that he did it. It doesn't change the way I feel." She held the base of her wineglass as Jetta refilled it and she moved her eyes from Jetta's face to their daughter's wooden toy kitchen, which was pushed up against the wall. She thought of herself that afternoon with Sam, standing in their sitting room.

"You know that if you walk away from us, you're kissing goodbye to your chance of having children, right?" It had been a very hot day, and Sam's pale gray T-shirt was speckled with dark sweat. "I don't want to sound like the world's biggest dickhead, but we all know what it's like for women once they get to a certain age. It's not fair. I get that. But I'm prepared to work through our problems, if you are. People come back from a lot worse than this, Poppy. You're just giving up."

Poppy had turned her head to the window and, in a flat opposite, she could see a TV screen. Maybe it was *Love Island*; a woman in a gold lamé bikini was reclining on a very large chair. "I cheated on you too," she said, looking back at him, exhausted but unemotional. "In spring, before we got engaged."

"WHAT?" And that had been the end.

After Poppy had loaded the van she rented, she left, and she'd known that she and Sam would never speak to each other again.

In Jetta and Stefan's kitchen, there was a silence that pulled them all together in its arms. Looking back at her friends, Poppy felt as if her sister was in the room, too, and she welcomed the feeling. She hadn't yet spoken to Jetta about what her father had told her, about The Shell Shop, the science teacher, the catfishing, and everything that had gone down afterward, but even so—she suspected Jetta knew about it all. Poppy wasn't cross with Jetta and, in fact, she preferred to think of her sister not always fighting alone.

"Can we please make a promise to not keep things from each

other moving forward?" Poppy asked. "I don't want to be the little girl who gets protected from the truth anymore."

"Okay, so, well, um, in this new vein of full disclosure . . ." Jetta pushed her plate away a little, and Stefan took his fork to her leftovers.

"Oh God . . ." Poppy looked from Stefan to Jetta. "What?"

"Sam already matched with a girl I work with."

"What do you mean he *matched*?" Poppy asked.

"On some new dating app," Jetta said. Through the monitor there was a disgruntled gurgle, and she turned the screen so they could all see the youngest in his cot.

"How did she know you know him?" Poppy asked. "I don't get it?"

"She recognized him from my Instagram. She showed me his profile, Poppy. I've got the screenshots, if you want to see?" Jetta turned her phone over from where it was on the table and lifted it up.

Sam had taken a selfie in their bathroom mirror with a towel around his waist, holding the phone down low so his face and body were visible—as was their bathroom, Poppy's shampoos and conditioner. She scrolled through the rest of his pictures. "That's me! He's put an emoji over my head . . ." It was a photo of them both that Sam had taken while they were hiking in Scotland. He actually had his arm around her, and Poppy's shoulder and hair were visible, only now there was an asinine grinning circle over her face.

Poppy didn't care though. "Whatever. That's fine." She thought of her mother and her unfailing equanimity. "I wish him well!"

"Let's get you a dating profile set up," Stefan suggested. He drummed the table with his fingers.

"Absolutely not." Poppy exchanged glances with Jetta. "Those apps are not for me."

Jetta cleared her throat, lifted her glass, held it in front of her mouth. "Soo, um, you know how you wanted me to go over to Dandelion's and check on the situation with your tenant?"

Poppy's cheeks were hot from wine and life. "Yes? Did you?" She'd been waiting for Jetta to bring this up.

"Yup. And he's definitely moving out first thing tomorrow."

"You met him?" Poppy's heart flipped. Her stomach scrunched.

"We had a little chat. Yeah . . ." Jetta took a sip of her wine. "I can indeed confirm that he's a wrong'n. But . . ." She paused, held Poppy's gaze. "He knows that he's a wrong'n, and he's sorry for being a wrong'n."

"Who's this wrong'n we're talking about?" Stefan asked. He stood and began clearing the plates. "I love wrong'ns."

"I know you do, my love."

"I used to be one," Stefan said.

"I know you did, my love."

Poppy looked at the door and had a vision of Jake walking through it, pulling out a chair, and sitting around the kitchen table with them. She thought about how nice that would feel. She imagined holding hands.

"For pudding we have coconut ice cream," Stefan called over to them, "mushroom chocolate. Or both?"

"Neither," Poppy said. "I'm fine."

"Right, well, all the more for me," Stefan said, opening the freezer.

Jetta twisted in her chair and called to her husband, "Ice cream, please!" Then she turned back to Poppy, leaned forward over the table. "And I got the distinct impression that your wrong'n loves you in a uniquely cuckoo way."

38

Friday, 11th July

Jake

"Hey, B!" Amisha smiled at Jake and Billy. She was wearing flannel pajamas and sheepskin slippers. Half a croissant sat on the plate in front of her, and the newspaper was spread across the table.

"There's some coffee," she said to Jake. "Just made it. So you're moving in today? Is that all your stuff?"

"Amazing, thank you." Jake opened the fridge and found the juice for Billy. "Yeah, I mean I only have two bags, a guitar, and a plant." He nodded at Cindy, who was propped up in the corner, not looking too well. "I put loads of stuff in storage when I moved last month. So, we travel light, don't we, bud?"

Jake and Billy had spent the last night in Dandelion's flat the previous evening. Although, technically, he didn't have to be out until the following morning, he was pleased to leave. Get everything cleaned up and in good shape for Poppy. He had bought Marigold gloves and new cleaning products and had spent the entirety of the previous day giving the place a thorough once-over, including a quick whizz around Dandelion's bedroom, which did mean unlocking it again, but he couldn't *not* change the sheets. He had also bought Poppy a card (nice flowers on the front) and found he had so much to say that, in the end, he'd folded two extra pieces of paper into it. He wanted to write, *Sorry, sorry, sorry,* again and again, five hundred times. But instead, he'd told her exactly how he felt about her, what he'd done, who he was—who he hoped to become. How much he missed his mother, and that he was talking to a therapist about it all now. He said he knew that things had got incredibly inappropriately conflated in his mind with Dandelion, and that he'd regret hurting Poppy for the rest of his life.

And so now Jake was back at his dad's place, before he and Billy, Zoe, and Yan went to Copenhagen for August and the first half of September. Zoe had told Jake, in the future, they were considering moving out there. "Come with us this summer," she'd said. "Have a look. Let's all see how it feels."

Karla had put Jake in touch with a creative agency in Copenhagen who were doing very cool things, and who were interested in talking to him about some opportunities to make a series of short films for Louisiana, the Danish museum of modern art. Which would be incredibly exciting. The thing about endings was, Jake had realized, they almost always meant the start of something else.

"Amisha, I wanted to say . . ." Jake began. "It's really kind of you to let us stay." Jake wouldn't have thought any of his dad's girlfriends would want him and his son cramping their style. Especially not one of his dad's girlfriends whom he'd had liaisons with.

"It's a pleasure," she said, meeting his gaze. For a few seconds they were silent, and if Billy hadn't been there, maybe Jake would have mentioned that, thanks to her, he could now draw a diagram of the ovaries, uterus, cervix, vagina, and the entire clitoris, from memory.

"When are we going to Go Ape?" Billy asked, putting down his empty glass. "I want to go now."

Jake looked at his watch. "Yeah, soon, bud. I just want to talk to Dad. How about a croissant?"

"I guess . . ."

"Want me to watch him?" Amisha asked.

"Is that okay?"

"Yes. No probs." Amisha stood and opened the oven, pulled out a tray. "Does Spleen want a croissant too?"

Somewhere along the way, Billy had accepted Spirulina's rebranding. "But actually, Daddy?"

"Yes?"

"She actually wants to be called Lazy Spleen now."

"Oh, brilliant, yes, I like that," Jake said, smiling, pleased with this nod to Lazy Susan. He looked at Amisha. "One croissant is all good, thanks. What do you say, Billy?"

"Bum cheeks?" Billy already had the croissant in his mouth and, as he spoke, he sprayed golden pastry over the table.

"Billy! What do you say?"

Billy looked at Amisha, more sheepish. He swallowed. Coughed. "Thanks, Granny. Very much."

Jake found his father sitting by the pool with closed eyes. His wet hair slicked back. His chest hair was white. His pecs sagging, but not terrible.

"Sorry, Dad, are you meditating?" Jake asked quietly, when he got over to him.

His father opened his eyes. "Just listening," he said. He stood up. Reached for Jake, gave him a hug.

"Hear anything?"

"That's a song thrush, there," he said, holding up his hand. "Their song repeats."

Jake listened to the day around him, a lot of birds and their different tweets.

"Come sit." Jake's father put his hand on Jake's thigh as he sat next to him.

"Dad, I kind of want to talk about something." Jake didn't want to. Of course he didn't, but he needed to. "Soon, it will be the twentieth anniversary of Mum's death. Can you believe that?"

"God rest her soul," Jake's father said wistfully and patted Jake's leg again, like he was nine years old.

But Jake would not let his father dismiss his mother, not this time. The leg pat felt like a miniature offense. "Why did you leave us, though, Dad?" After this first question, the others were just there, everywhere—there was nothing else. Jake could feel his cheeks heating; he could hear how impassioned his voice sounded. "How could you have left when she was sick? Why have you never apologized, for any of it? You've never said sorry to me about being totally absent. Do you even feel remorse?"

Jake's father opened his mouth to respond but seemed to think better of it. He pulled air in through his nose and closed his eyes as he exhaled. "She didn't want me there, Jake. I made things worse." He opened his eyes. "I made her sicker."

"But, Dad, I was *a child*."

"She needed you. She needed me not to be there."

"But, Dad—"

"I'm sorry, Jake. Life is unpredictable and terribly difficult." His father studied him for a moment. "I loved your mother, very much."

"Um . . ." Jake looked away at the flower bed of tall delphiniums and fat white roses. "I don't think that's good enough, Dad," he said eventually, quietly. "Because it didn't seem like you loved her, and it didn't seem like you loved me. Everything you did was for yourself." Jake looked back at his father. "You didn't even come to her funeral."

"Her family all hated me, Jake. It would have caused a scene. It would have taken away from what the day needed to be. My presence would only have brought drama."

"But you had a son who needed you! And you can't just be a dad when it suits you. When you want to be. You don't get to decide those things—you have to be a parent even on the hard days, especially on the hard days."

"Well, I didn't have a dad," Jake's father said, and in his eyes—Jake was surprised to see the clouding of emotion. "My father was wayward, you know that. He was rotten. And so maybe I never learned how to be a father. And maybe I let you down, because I was let down too."

"I don't accept that excuse anymore. I'm sorry, I don't buy it." Jake had thought a lot of a conversation he'd had with Poppy, back in spring. They'd been standing outside the Tate, and she'd told him he wasn't stuck in a cycle, or at least if he was, it was one that he could break. And Jake had decided he wasn't going to hand Billy any of that ancestral shit; the buck would stop with him, right here—in his father's garden, looking at these abundant flowers. "*You* didn't cheat on your wife because *your dad* cheated on your mum. And you weren't an absent father to me because your own father left, Dad."

"You don't get to tell me what I am, or why I am, my boy." Jake's father's voice was raised. "You do not get to talk to me like that."

"Well, I just did," Jake said. He turned his gaze back to his father. "You don't get to be my dad now, and tell me what I can or can't say to you. You sacrificed that right thirty years ago when you left."

Jake's father stood up and walked away, and Jake laughed to

himself, because it was too predictable that his dad would walk off again, but then he turned around and he held out his hand to Jake like he was scolding. "You're lucky I wasn't there, Jake. To have a father who is a negative influence is a very difficult thing and can ruin a life." He sniffed; he raised his eyebrows, and blinked away the possibility of tears. He cleared his throat. "I found being a husband and a father very hard. I couldn't do it. I'm sorry. It took me a long time to grow up and I know I let you down and I let your mother down. I don't know what else to say."

"You can say you're sorry, Dad," Jake said.

"I am sorry. I'm very sorry. But I also hope to show you my love and remorse through my actions. I know apologies will only take a man so far and these things are difficult to talk about." He cleared his throat again. "At the time, rightly or wrongly, I felt you'd be better off without me and, honestly, so did your mother. And maybe you won't believe this, but I think she was right. Look how well she brought you up. Look at what a cracking job she did. You and her were always as thick as thieves, and I was an inconvenience. I wasn't in your gang."

"Dad, that's not true. We wanted you in the gang!" Jake said, his eyes stinging. "And Mum did a good job, of course she did, but . . ." He thought of his mother making him dinner while she was trembling with anxiety, how she gave him all her life and how much that took from her. "What if my love is poisonous?" Jake thought of Poppy in the doorway of her sister's flat, the hurt and hatred rising from her visibly. He thought of Zoe, too, shaking, his phone in her hand after she'd read his messages to that other girl.

His father came back to the bench, sat and put his arm around Jake, pulled his shoulders into him, and held him with an affection that he never had before. "You were the best thing in your mother's life. She loved you more than she loved herself. Your mother . . . she didn't want to be alive sometimes, and I believe that when she knew that you would be okay, when you were a grown-up man and you'd left home and you were doing so well—she knew that she could leave. She'd struggled since she was young, Jake, you know that. Long before you were born. Ever since I met her on Brighton Beach when she was sixteen and I gave her that backy on my bike. My God, your mother was beautiful, and when she laughed, everyone laughed! But, privately, she suffered, she had her demons—even then. And you must know, Jake, that you're not the reason your mother left this life so young. You're the reason that she stayed so long."

Jake was properly sobbing now. His father took him by the shoulders and sat him up, looked him in the eye. "You are a very good father, Jake. And your little boy is the light of all our lives. We all love him so much. And your mother would be so proud of you. And she is so proud of you because death is not the end of love."

From behind them in the garden, Jake heard his son squeal. He turned to see Billy and Amisha. He watched Billy show her his handstand. Amisha clapped. Jake's father patted him on the leg again. "Are you all right?"

"Yes." Jake nodded, wiping at his eyes.

His father shook Jake's shoulders in a manner that was rousing, more manly, like a coach. "Do you want to talk about anything else?"

"No. Thank you." For the first time in his life, Jake felt he really had a father. A very loving dad.

"Well, thank you for bringing these things up. I know it's not easy." He smiled and Jake smiled back at him. "I love you, Jakey. And I loved your mother. Perhaps, the problem was, as a younger man, I was not able to love myself."

Jake watched his father stand up. He clapped, perhaps as a way to change his mood, or rid himself of emotion. He began walking toward the others. Jake had always felt that his father had rejected him and his mother and instead chosen a life that was more exciting, full of lovers and dinners and money, but now he could see that his father battled with his own shit—there was nothing romantic in that. Still, Jake's father was someone's son, and still he resented his own dad.

Jake moved his gaze to his little boy; Billy seemed to have grown taller, his limbs had thinned and were not as doughy as they once were. "Granddad!" he shouted. "Granddad . . ."

Billy had Jake's eyes and Jake had his mother's eyes, and there was something powerful and reassuring about that, the continuation. Because it wasn't just the eyes; it was the humor and the heart. Jake thought about what his father had said, and he knew then that his mother still lived within him. Within his son. He felt her and he saw her. Was that the truth that Jake was looking for? That love didn't end with life.

"DADA! Daddyyy! It's time to go! It's time to go!" Billy shouted and then began running toward him, his head down, charging, his legs kicking out to the side, clutching Lazy Spleen's hand.

Jake wiped the last of the tears from his eyes. "Coming, Billy!" he called.

39

Saturday, 12th July

Poppy

When Poppy woke with the sunlight at quarter past seven, she got up, slipped her sister's gold snake ring on, and pulled her new red dress over her head. The previous night, Jetta and Stefan had hosted a barbecue, and they'd all sat outside until late, and now, as Poppy padded barefoot down the stairs, it was evident from the empty bottles in the kitchen, not to mention her headache, that perhaps they'd drunk a little too much.

Poppy wrote Jetta and Stefan a thank-you message on the back of an envelope, left it on the kitchen table, and slipped out. She walked down the canal, then cut through the northeast London streets. The walk was refreshing; it was Saturday and, for the most part, people were still sleeping. She sang along to the playlist she'd made in Devon, which she'd titled "Wildest Moments" (after the Jessie Ware song that she and Dandelion thought of as being theirs). At Newington Green, she bought peonies from the florist the moment the man pulled up the blind of his shop.

In the silence of her sister's flat, Poppy hung up her coat on an empty hook in the hallway. In the kitchen, she turned on the lights and saw Jake's key on the table. "Okay, so he's gone," she said, through an exhale. She unwrapped the peonies from the brown paper and reached for a glass vase on the top shelf over the sink and filled it with water from the tap, nudged the stems around until their configuration pleased her. "You're welcome. I thought you'd like them," she said, carrying the jug to Dandelion's bedroom and unlocking it.

The bed was made up. She went over to it, could tell the sheets were washed and ironed, but apart from that, everything looked just the same. She placed the flowers on the dressing table. Through the petals she could see her reflection, slivers of her sister too. "So, what did he get up to in here?" she asked. "Do I want to know?"

She slipped off her trainers and climbed on the bed, lay there with her hands on her stomach looking at the glass orb light that hung from the ceiling, then turned onto her side and closed her eyes and imagined Dandelion lying next to her. It had been an entire year since she'd got sick. Poppy thought of the day that her sister had told her the truth of what was happening—they had been for a walk along the canal, and Dandelion had been wearing a jumpsuit in pastel colors, her hair tied up with a satin bow. They veered off into Springfield Park and had been standing in long grass.

"You know how I've been getting these pains?" Dandelion asked. She lifted her sunglasses, took them off, but she wasn't looking at Poppy. Her head was tilted up to the branches of a very large oak tree, and she put her hand flat on the bark.

"No," Poppy said. "Look, butterfly!" She pointed at a cabbage white that was fluttering in front of her face. It looped. It landed on her shoulder for two seconds.

"Well, I've been getting pains. And I'm tired."

"Everyone gets pains and is tired."

"Yeah. Well. I went to the doctor, Poppy. I had some tests. You'll never guess what?" Dandelion turned around.

That first death moment was scorched onto the surface of Poppy's soul, scarring so deep that it had changed the shape of her mind and the direction of her life. Lying on her sister's bed, it played back to Poppy like a home video, but one where they were grown-up. A close-up of her sister's hand. The yellow grass. The birds singing supernaturally loud. Behind them, someone's fucking dog fucking barking. Dandelion taking Poppy's face in her hands and Poppy feeling all her sister's rings on her skin and seeing all her sister's freckles, her pores, the pale, the dark. And there it was—the illness, the start of death—she could see it. *She could see it.* It wasn't ugly or poison—it was the end of life.

It took hold quickly. Had to be managed. Palliative care. Two weeks after that conversation, Dandelion's body had been ravaged. Four weeks after—and she was gone. Poppy had always thought the time between her sister's diagnosis and death had been around a month. But now she had another theory—now she believed Dandelion had known her fate for longer and had kept it from her, from all of them, and that's why she slept with Sam.

It was the type of unfathomable badness for the sake of goodness that only Poppy's big sister would think of. To protect Poppy from the ruination of loss, she had devised an alternate agony to kneecap her instead. What if seeing Sam off was the bonus? In a barbaric act of sacrifice and mental violence, Dandelion had slept with Sam when she knew she was sick because she knew that when Poppy found out about the betrayal, she would have no choice but to hate her. And maybe, just maybe—Dandelion had hoped—Poppy's anger would scorch through the grief and she would feel a bitterness that would propel her onward and away. Dandelion had not wanted Poppy to miss her, or to miss out on her own life. She had not wanted Poppy to look back and think of her lost and only sister, but to look forward and think of herself. But Dandelion had grown too ill, too quick, to ever tell Poppy about Sam, and Jetta had not been able to.

There were a hundred reasons why Poppy could hate her sister, but there were infinite reasons why she would never. When they were girls and Dandelion led them into trouble, afterward she would always take the blame. She never shirked responsibility. She looked after Poppy and protected her fiercely and, sometimes, Poppy pointed the finger right at her sister, like she had done when she met Jake.

Poppy had believed she'd lied and duped another person because her sister had influenced her, nudged her into it. She had used Dandelion as a shield, a scapegoat, and a license for bad behavior. Dandelion could be the devil, when she herself made out she was a saint. Dandelion was the voice Poppy attributed to not wanting to be with Sam, when really she had known he was wrong for her for years. For Poppy's whole life, anything that was difficult, or unacceptable, she had passed off as her sister's influence— never her own desire or original thought. Dandelion had been the bad one. The brave one. The fun one. The seductress. The one that lit up the room. The beauty. The twisted, evil sister. And, perhaps because there were two of them, Poppy had seen them only for their contrasts, been blind to all their similarities, and to their constant shift and flow.

Poppy sat, nestled her bare feet into the rug, and then stood and went over to the long mirror. She looked at herself. She looked at her sister. These last few months, she had thought all that was alluring about her was Dandelion, all that was angry and fierce and strong and wrong was the shadow her sister cast. But it wasn't. Poppy had her own heat and it came from her own heart. The sisters had looked like the same girl, the same woman, but they were completely different, and more similar than either of them had ever known. They overlapped. Increasingly. Forever. More and more, as they pulled apart.

Poppy turned and went over to the window and looked out at the world. Beyond London there were sea and mountains. There were countries she had never even thought of, faces she had no idea about, flavors, fascinations. Cuddles from little babies. Art she was yet to make, photos she was yet to take. There was love, she knew it; already, she felt it. It was totally shocking how lucky she was— how lucky that she, Poppy, still, very much, got to be dazzled by life. The first year of grief had taught her so much, and Poppy knew herself in a different way. Her life was more vivid precisely because of her sister's death. It was an honor and a fucking fluke that she was the one who was still standing and breathing and dancing, and she would live each day double, in dedication, until they were together again.

The doorbell rang, and Poppy went downstairs to meet the estate agent. She showed him around. It would be snapped up, he could assure her. He was very impressed. "Snapped up, Mrs. Greene. Apologies, Miss." Poppy shook his hand and he said he'd be in touch. She stood in the street and waved him off, and opposite, on the other side of the road, Jake was standing in a pair of shorts and T-shirt and his *I'm a Feminist* cap.

40

Still Saturday, 12th July

Jake

"What are you doing here?" Poppy asked, raising her voice at Jake. She was standing outside her sister's house in a short red dress, looking incredible.

Unpacking his stuff at his dad's house that morning, Jake realized he'd forgotten to leave the letter he wrote Poppy and had been planning to put it through Dandelion's letter box, but when he arrived, he'd seen her through the windows, walking around with another man, and so he'd stayed to watch, but then the door had opened. The man got into an estate agent's car and drove off, revealing Jake—just gawping.

Jake held up the letter to Poppy, though instead of saying anything about it, he shouted, "I'm stalking my catfisher!"

Poppy put her hands on her hips. "That's niche," she called back.

They both stood there, either side of the road, just looking. After a minute, or maybe two, or probably longer, Jake called, "Lovely weather we're having!"

"Bit hot," Poppy said.

"Very hot," Jake agreed.

Poppy crossed her arms in front of her. "What do you want, Jake?"

"Just wondering . . ." A silver car drove through the middle of them, and when it passed, Jake yelled, "What are you up to now?"

Poppy's eyes followed the car. Then she looked back at him. "Nothing," she said. "I'm free."

Jake pointed over his shoulder. "Fancy a Twister?"

Poppy went back into the flat and came out a minute later with a suede bag slung over her shoulder. She crossed over to him, stepped up onto the pavement. They didn't touch. "Hi," she said.

"Hi, Poppy."

She nodded at the letter in his hand. "What's that?"

"It's a letter I wrote you. Just delivering it." He held it out to her. She didn't take it. "What does it say?"

"It says sorry five hundred times, and some other things."

"That doesn't sound like enough times," Poppy said. She started walking up the street.

They headed toward Clissold Park in silence. Just before they turned onto Church Street, Jake realized Poppy had stopped walking. He looked back at her. She was standing by a parked silver Mercedes, maybe even the same one that had passed them outside Dandelion's flat, though now there was no one in it. Poppy bent down and looked in and Jake came and stood next to her, bent, and followed her gaze. A teddy bear was hanging from the rearview mirror.

"Bit creepy," Jake said. There was something about the bear that made him feel uneasy—it had a horrible sticking-out tongue and was holding a pale pink heart with almost illegible stitched words that spelled out *HUGE!* No. *HUGE ME!* No, *HUG ME!*

Poppy straightened and looked around at the houses on the street. "No way," she said under her breath, remarking to herself. She opened her bag and pulled out a set of keys.

"Whaaaa . . . ?" Jake started a question, potentially a protest, as he watched Poppy key the car, scraping off the silver paint: over the bonnet, the driver's door, the boot, and then around the other side. She took a photo of the registration, kicked the front tire, and said, "I'm coming for you, Dick Man." Then she looked at Jake and began running. Jake followed her, not at all sure what was happening, but he was on her side wholeheartedly; it felt like they were kids.

They couldn't find an ice cream van in the park, but they found a patch of grass they liked by some yellow star-shaped azaleas that smelled strong and madly sweet. "So," Jake said, "Poppy, should I read you this letter? I really want you to hear this stuff."

"I know how to read," Poppy said. She took the letter from him and pushed it in her bag. "So," she said, "Jetta told me you were spiked?"

"Yeah," Jake said. "She was probably pleased about that, right? She really hates me."

"She doesn't hate you," Poppy said. "She loves me, that's all."

"Errr, pretty sure she detests my guts." Jake thought back to their altercation. "I found her to be a very terrifying person."

Poppy laughed. "Well, she'll be pleased to hear that." She lay down on her stomach, her head resting on an outstretched arm.

Jake looked at her ankles. "So, Poppy . . ."

Poppy turned over and put her hands behind her head. Her eyes were almost closed.

Jake lay next to her and stared at her profile, though his heart started beating so hard that he had to sit back up. He cleared his throat. "So . . . how's your work stuff? Feeling any better about all that?"

"When we were kids, me and my sister, we used to make films all the time . . . and I keep thinking about that . . . how much I loved it. Guess I'm thinking, now, about doing something more creative? Maybe I'll bring Betty on full-time as a partner, and we'll still specialize in events, only she'll lead that and I'll set up a different arm of the business."

"Very cool. Well, if you want to bounce around ideas . . ."

Poppy squinted at him and nodded. "Will bear that in mind."

A bee buzzed up to Jake's head and then away. Right, the work chat was done. Jake cleared his throat. "So, Poppy?"

"I don't really like your cap," Poppy said.

Jake took his cap off, threw it, and it landed about ten feet away, next to some teenagers sitting on the grass. "I'm a feminist!" Jake shouted at them. "Be one too!"

One of the boys reached for the cap, looked at it, gave a thumbs-up, and put it on backward.

Jake turned to Poppy, opened his eyes wide, waiting for congratulations. "Just me—spreading feminism." He held up his hands like he was receiving applause. "No problem. Thank me later. Or don't, obviously, because no thanks will be necessary. Just doing my job. It's not work, though, it's a pleasure . . . an honor!" Poppy was watching Jake talk with a vague look of bemusement on her face. "Anyway, Poppy," Jake said, "about this apology . . ."

"Go on then." She rolled away from him so she was facing the azaleas.

Jake looked at the shape her waist and her hip made: a valley, a hill, a wave. He touched her shoulder and she rolled back to him. "I would like to take this opportunity to tell you that I'm sorry. The most sorry. Which is saying something because I've let a lot of people down before and—"

"Jake, I am quite hungover. I'm not sure I have the capacity right now, I might cry. I will read your letter later, I promise. Okay?"

"Poppy, I have to say this to you, I can't just sit next to you, pretending we're best friends—"

"Obviously we're not best friends, Jake."

"No," Jake said. "I didn't mean that, what I meant was . . ." He couldn't let this be the last time he ever saw her. "I don't want to push anything down anymore, Poppy. I don't want to hide from myself. From you. From life. The truth. I . . . so . . . I'm trying hard to be open and honest and I would actually *really like* to be best friends, maybe? Or, ideally, um, a lot more than that, because I find you to be an astoundingly attractive and deeply lovable person, and, like, sometimes just looking at your face makes me laugh . . . not because your face is funny! But because you're funny and because, I guess, it's funny that I like you so much, um . . ." *FUCK.* Jake was in love with her. He was totally in love with her, and his heart was trying to climb out of his chest; it was bulging in his throat like a big beating toad. He swallowed. Swallowed again. "Obviously, I would like to say . . ." He coughed, tried to sound normal. He was looking down at his knees and legs, at the two daisies by his big toe, but now he turned his head to Poppy's face again, very purposefully. "I know I was weird about your sister, but it actually wasn't about her at all. I bet she was amazing and cool, but I didn't know her." Jake studied Poppy's eyelashes; they were bulrushes fringing the perimeter of an icy pool. He was afraid of her. He was afraid of himself. He was afraid she'd never forgive him. He was afraid she would forgive him and then there'd be a catastrophe. He was afraid he wouldn't make her happy. That one of them would die. He lay down so he could be on her level, look in her eyes. "You're the one, Poppy. From the very first second I met you, I felt so struck by the connection. When I'm around you I feel like myself, and in the short time I've known you, you've made me a better person. And I'd like to be around you lots more, if you'd like that, and I think of you all the time, Poppy. All of the time."

Poppy closed her eyes, and Jake sat up to give her space. He looked back over his shoulder at her. "I'm sorry I hurt you. I've been selfish. I am selfish. I know that. I've never properly thought about my own grief and acknowledged how warping it's been. But I will, I want to, I am. And I'm ready to let it all go and stop sort of . . . wallowing and feeling sorry for myself and my lot. Because my lot is pretty good. My lot is bloody great. And, I hope, in time, you can forgive me for being such a total navel-gazing disappointment. Because really the only thing I'm missing in my life, Poppy, is being able to spend time with you."

It was the weekend and there were lots of people in the park. A woman walked past them with a cat on a long thin lead. Jake looked back at the teenagers. Two boys, two girls. The girls were looking at the boy who was talking and wearing Jake's cap; all three of them were smiling. The other boy seemed more solemn and uncomfortable in his own skin. He held on to his knees. As the woman with the cat walked by them, the awkward boy said, "Cats are dope." The others kept talking to each other; they ignored him.

Jake wanted to turn to the boy and acknowledge this comment to make it less crushing. He'd say, *Totally! Cats are dope. Interesting point.* Or maybe he'd say, *Look, I know even speaking can be really embarrassing and you feel totally pointless sometimes. But, trust me, things will get better,* or he'd say . . .

"Jake?" Poppy said.

Jake lay back down next to her, on his stomach. "Yes, Poppy?"

"I forgive you," she said quietly.

Jake closed his eyes. He'd never heard anyone say they forgave him before.

"I don't understand all of what's happened," Poppy continued. "Some things I've done, some things you've done. But I forgive you, totally. Can you forgive me?"

Jake felt around on the grass until he found Poppy's hand, and then he held it. "Of course. I can, I have." He couldn't say anything else because it felt as if not only his body was shaking, but the grass beneath him, and the sky above. Everything swayed, and Jake scrunched his eyes tighter and squeezed Poppy's hand and put his other hand to his face—gathering himself, gathering himself—until he felt Poppy move.

Through his eyelashes, he watched her get to her knees and climb on top of him. She lay face down, her whole body on his body. Her legs on his legs. Her tummy on his back. Her arms on his arms. She hooked her chin over his shoulder. Jake couldn't see her anymore because her head was behind his head, but every bit of his body could feel every bit of her body pushing down. It was as if she had fallen from the heavens. He imagined it happening: Poppy in her red dress, arms waving, legs flailing through the clouds, and then, *SPLAT*, here she was—in the center of his life.

"Is it weird me lying on you like this?" Poppy whispered in his ear.

"No. It's normal. Stay there forever."

Poppy stroked hair behind Jake's ear. "I just had an urge to climb on top of you."

"I hear that a lot," Jake said.

"Liar."

"Takes one to know one, Poppy Greene."

Next to them, the teenagers laughed. Jake laughed, too, then fell silent—and they lay like that in the park, by the shockingly sweet azaleas, in the middle of a hot summer day, in the middle of their lives. They inhaled in sync, and Jake felt as if they were one strange monster, double breathing and so strong. Eventually, Poppy slid back onto the grass, and Jake put his arm around her and pulled her right into him. He looked hard at her face. The face he loved. When she kissed him—he was found. He was lost.

Epilogue

ONE MONTH LATER
Sunday, 17th August, 2025

On the first anniversary of Dandelion's death, Poppy went alone to the graveyard. She turned and looked at all the graves around her. The layers and layers of loss.

"How are you, anyway?" she asked. She lay down on her side, rested her head on a bent elbow, and admired the tiny wildflower meadow of her sister's grave.

Her mother had already told her how both dandelions and poppies were growing there now, although she hadn't planted them. "I knew they'd come," her mother had said, "those two always find a way."

Poppy told Dandelion that her home was under offer. She told Dandelion that their father's voice was improving, almost better. That he was going to salsa lessons with their mum. She told Dandelion that Jetta was pregnant again. She told Dandelion that she was looking into freezing her eggs and that, the other night, she had dreamed, again, of a baby girl, who, for some reason, was called Little Weed. She told Dandelion about Copenhagen, about how she was going out there with Jake for a month and how she would help him on a project for the Danish museum of modern art.

And then Poppy let the quietness fill her mind with her sister's voice, her thoughts.

The rain wasn't heavy, Poppy couldn't even see the droplets; the wetness came in a shimmering mist. She sniffed at Dandelion's headstone and the rose that crawled right over it, like wild hair. "Right, well. I'll be off then." Poppy paused. "Yes, I love you too."

She veered off the coastal path and walked back along the beach. There was one stubborn family having a barbecue out of an aluminum tray in the mizzle, two small children digging a large hole in the sand. As Poppy walked past them, the bigger one asked if she wanted to get in with them. He must have been five or six. Long black hair and a face that could break a heart.

"No, thank you." Poppy shook her head.

"Bye-bye!"

"Bye-bye!"

Poppy turned to the sea; a sunbeam was falling down from the sky in a long diagonal slant, as if light was escaping through an opening door in a heaven that existed. On the surface of the water beneath was a small patch of gold. Poppy slipped her sandals off, left them on the sand, and climbed up onto the red rocks. She was sad. She was happy. Forever muddled with her sister. She was brave. She was scared. It was dusk and she was in love. At the peak, it was windy. Poppy wobbled and started laughing. This was life. It was shocking, and in the end it would kill her, but before that—it would blaze.

Acknowledgments

I could write a whole book of acknowledgments solely for my mother. Mum, thank you for never making me feel like writing a secret manuscript in various darkened rooms was an extraordinary way to spend my thirties. You have been my greatest support in writing, and in life. Thank you forever. You really are the very best.

It's sad that Dad died before anyone knew my book would evolve from a Google Doc to a hardback. Although, let's face it, this would not have been his thing, so at least he is spared from having to read this and feel, I expect, perplexed. Perhaps this seems like an arbitrary thing to acknowledge, but I am grateful for my parents' sense of humor and that of my mother's parents—I treasure my childhood memories in Devon and the rude words and songs my grandparents taught me. I hope their sense of mischief lives on in all that I write.

After a long time writing alone it's wild to feel part of a team. Jemima, thank you for your editorial prowess and good humor, and for being there on the less wonderful days. Clare, Giulia, Sam, and all at DHA, you've done incredible things. To Josie, my editor pre-editors. And to the publishing teams—it's difficult to put my gratitude into words. Jen and the stars at Berkley. Jo and the brilliant Borough Press. To both Julia at DTV and Sabine at Neri Pozza, thank you for taking Dandelion on holiday—I hope she behaves. (She won't.) Maria at See-Saw Films, what a thrill.

To friends, old and new, who have shown love in a myriad of ways, whether it be sharing their thoughts on my writing, giving me a place to stay, or treating me like a success when I was feeling like a terrible failure. Including, but not exclusively: Jemma, Em, ffrenchie, Liz L, Jay, Nicky, Hannah, Jess, Cal, Liz B. Thank you to my lawyer big sister for questioning the small print. And all those who talked to me about so many topics in the book, including photography (special mention to Louise and Jonny), weddings, directing, ecstatic dance, HR policies, hard drugs, and small children.

At the heart of this book is love, but there is also death. I would like to acknowledge those people in my life who have suffered terrible losses—I am saying your names silently. I am thinking, too, more widely, of all the sisters, husbands, brothers, mothers, sons, and friends who have gone up ahead; this book is written in their honor and with the total acknowledgment of how cataclysmically unfair it is that they're not here anymore.

This book is dedicated to my radiant friend. I can't begin to imagine all the dazzling things she would have done if she were still here. She was an inspiration, a shooting star, and I will always feel her heat. Love doesn't end with life.

I miss you. Meet you at the after-party.